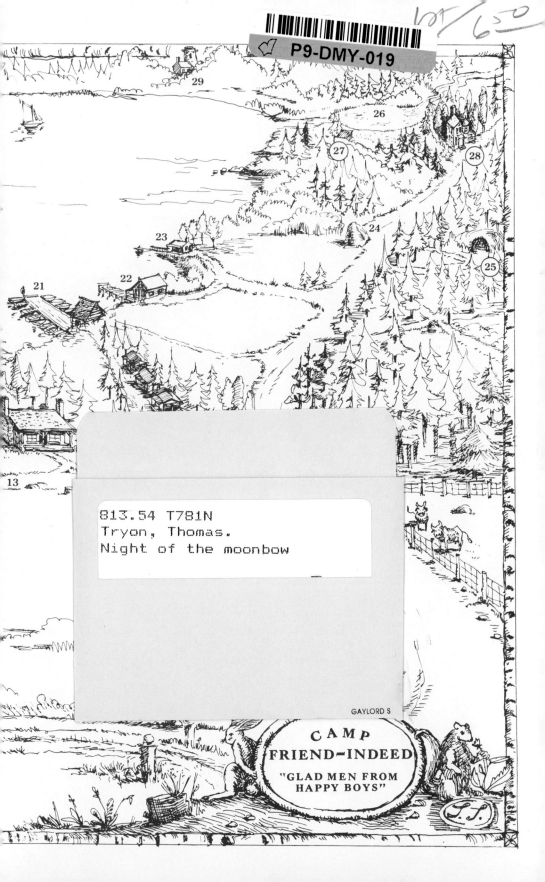

CAMP
FRIEND-INDEED
"GLAD MEN FROM
HAPPY BOYS"

ALSO BY THOMAS TRYON

THE NIGHT
OF THE MOONBOW

THE NIGHT
OF THE
MOONBOW

THOMAS TRYON

Alfred A. Knopf   New York   1989

THIS IS A BORZOI BOOK
PUBLISHED BY ALFRED A. KNOPF, INC.

Grateful acknowledgment is made to the following for permission to reprint
previously published material: *Columbia Pictures Publications/Belwin, Inc.:*
Excerpt from "That Old Feeling" by Lou Brown and Sammy Fain. Copyright
1937 (Renewed 1965) by Leo Feist, Inc. All rights assigned to SBK
Catalogue Partnership. All rights controlled and administered by SBK Feist
Catalog. International copyright secured. Made in U.S.A. All rights reserved.
Warner/Chappell Music, Inc.: Excerpts from "The Music Goes 'Round and
Around" by Ed Farley, Michael Riley, and Red Hodgson. Copyright 1935
Chappell & Co. (renewed). Excerpts from "Poor Butterfly" by Raymond
Hubbell and John Golden. Copyright 1916 by Warner Bros. Inc. (renewed).
Excerpts from "You Go to My Head" by J. Fred Coots and Haven Gillespie.
Copyright 1938 by Warner Bros. Inc. All rights reserved. Used by
permission.

Library of Congress Cataloging-in-Publication Data

Tryon, Thomas.
Night of the moonbow.

I. Title.
PS3570.R9N54   1988   813'.54   87-46109
ISBN 0-394-56006-X

Manufactured in the United States of America

FIRST EDITION

For Scott Tryon

1957 – 1982

It has always seemed to me that the two loveliest words
in the English language are "summer afternoon."

HENRY JAMES, *in a letter to Edith Wharton*

Contents

PART ONE   *The New Boy*   1

PART TWO   *The Forest Primeval*   51

PART THREE   *Dreams in the Midsummer Dark*   127

PART FOUR   *The Night of the Moonbow*   209

PART ONE

The New Boy

Prologue

ho, having heard it firsthand from the lips of Pa Starbuck, could ever forget the famous tale of the moonbow? Who could account for its fatal charm, or explain of what singular enchantment the story was concocted? An aura it had, certainly; a unique kind of sorcery—but of what was it made? What caused it to happen? Why did it cast such a spell over everyone, this magical moonbow that no one at Moonbow Lake had ever seen?

In truth, until that fateful night when the last council fire was held in the pine grove, no one in that northeastern corner of Connecticut could recall ever having seen the spectacle, a silver rainbow of the night arched across the shimmering waters of the lake, a span of friendliness and Christian fellow-ship, as Pa described it, pointing up the moral of the Moonbow Tale.

Why, then, did the campers keep telling one another that one day, someday, the moonbow would appear? Perhaps they wished for it to be real because it gave them something to hope for; the moonbow was dreams come true, the impossible made possible, the infinite finite, a boy's reward for being a boy. This *summer it would come*, they said, or this—or next, surely; wouldn't it?

And when, in that final camp season of 1938, it did come, how was it possible that there, at Camp Friend-Indeed, where the summer sang among the trees, where no Moonbow boy had ever raised his hand against another, hatred, rank and profound, should have shown its face? Someone with a bucket of paint and a brush should have daubed an X on the door of Cabin

7, the cabin called Jeremiah, for it was there that the red-speckled death had first appeared, to pass among the boys, spreading contagion, until one by one it claimed them all, poor luckless boys of lucky Cabin 7.

What had it been? Some momentary moonbow madness? A bad dream? So Pa Starbuck often thought in those dolorous after-years when, having been relieved of his long tenure as founder-director of the camp, he had come to eke out what time the Almighty had allotted to him in a squalid, sun-parched suburb of Miami, where whichever neon moons that rose above the withered palm trees behind his stucco bungalow were merely the bitter reminders of his sorrows.

Perhaps it was only a dream, thought the Reverend wistfully, bathed in the silver glow of his Philco television screen, the kind of dream that is born of moonbow magic, gossamer and gone. He sighed again and told himself the Lord knew he had tried—He did, didn't He?—he had, hadn't he?

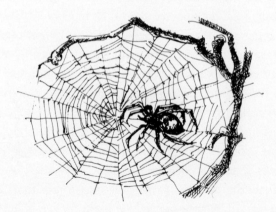

1

he afternoon the new boy arrived, a scorcher for that early in July, the Red Sox were playing the Braves. Tiger Abernathy, captain and star catcher for the Sox, shouldered his Louisville Slugger and stepped to the plate, tapped his bat, waited as the pitcher wound up and let fly, then took a mighty swing at the ball. Dusty Rhoades, the Braves' first baseman, missed it altogether, and Oggie Ogden, the outfielder, leaning sideways with outstretched glove, also came up empty-handed, and there went the ball smack through the back window of Ma Starbuck's office. A shattering of glass was briefly heard, then the victory cheer as Tiger beat it to home plate for his third run that afternoon.

Hap Holliday, the camp athletic director, marched up and congratulated the boy. "But did you have to break Ma's window?" His laugh was bluff and hearty as he clapped Tiger on the back.

Slewing the bill of his cap from back to front and shading his eyes, Tiger grinned up at the coach. "I guess I didn't have to, but it sure helped, didn't it?"

Hap nodded. "Now maybe we'll get some action around here." His beefy red face covered with sweat, he wiped his brow as he scanned the baseball diamond, which lay close between the dining hall and the old farmhouse whose rear quarters served as the camp office. For years the coach had been lobbying to have the ball field moved farther away from both buildings, but nothing had come of the idea. A few more broken windows and maybe Rolfe Hartsig, the camp's benefactor, would see that the new field should be the next object of his largesse.

As players and spectators alike abandoned the field for the hike down to the lower camp, Tiger blew out his cheeks emphatically and rubbed his scalp under his cap. "Well, I guess if we want our ball back I better go get it from Ma. Dump, I'll see you back in Jeremiah," he called to his cabinmate Dump Dillworth, busy storing their team's equipment in the shed.

"Let me talk to Ma," Hap suggested. "I can get around her if she's going to be mad."

"I can get around Ma good as anyone." Tiger knew his onions when it came to Ma Starbuck. He started off, then stopped. "Can I have my knife back?" The hunting knife was one of Tiger's most treasured possessions; he had won it two years before in the competition for best all-round athlete; Rolfe Hartsig had provided the prize, a Bowie knife purchased at Abercrombie & Fitch in New York.

Hap handed over the knife in its leather sheath, then collected his golf bag and favorite driver and headed off to whack some balls on the lower playing field, while Tiger dutifully trotted toward the farmhouse, a ramshackle structure whose sides seemed to slant toward each other as much for comfort as for support. Approaching it, he circled a clump of lilac shrubs, then mounted the red sandstone block that served as the office stoop, on both sides of which grew ragged clusters of sunflowers.

He opened the screen door to find Ma with broom and dustpan, sweeping up the broken glass. Jezebel, Ma's prized Persian, reclined the length of the windowsill, where a fatigued sanseveria held up its mottled blades in the arid soil of a majolica planter. Under a monochrome of *The Angelus,* hanging askew on the wall, Harpo, a limp-haired canine of dubious pedigree, opened an eye to glance at Tiger when his name was spoken, then, eagerly banging his tail on the floor, scrambled noisily to his feet, made his way to the boy, and began licking his bare legs.

"Hey, Harp, hey, boy, good fellah," Tiger said, burying his face in the dog's neck.

"Oh, honey, don't kiss Heinz-y, he hasn't been washed this week. He gets so dirty, too." Though the dog was called "Harpo," Ma sometimes referred to him as "Heinz-y" because, she said, he was fifty-seven varieties. "And then some," she always added.

"This your ball, Tiger Abernathy?" she demanded, hands on hips and

6

trying to look fierce. "I don't think you know your own stren'th, Mr. Charles
Atlas."

"I'm really sorry, Ma. Here, let me do that." He took the broom from
her.

Grateful for his assistance, Ma lowered her considerable bulk into the
swivel chair behind the large rolltop desk that was her pride and joy. The
ancient chair, its high back upholstered in cracked leather and studded
round with brass nailheads kept eternally polished by the friction of her
plump thighs against them, protested loudly as she took possession. She
leaned her face, plain and hardworked but serene as a full moon, on a worn
hand, and peered through the thick lenses of her glasses at Tiger as he
swept up. What was a windowpane? she asked herself—it wasn't the broken glass that worried her, not with 120 campers pulling the tricks that 120
campers could pull; what worried her were the broken arms and legs and
cracked heads.

"You sure play a swell ball game, Tiger," she said admiringly.

He looked up at her, eyebrows raised in silent question. Ma had to
restrain her amusement. "Sure, me and Jezzy ben watchin' you most of the
afternoon. Say, what d'you suppose that smoke is over yonder?" she wondered, swiveling to peer past the window shade.

"Maybe it's Injun smoke," Tiger said with a straight face, down on his
hands and knees now, meticulously pinching up the last bits of glass the
broom had overlooked.

"Tiger Abernathy, you're a caution! Why, you couldn't find a Injun
within a hundred miles of Moonbow Lake. Looks like it's comin' from the
old Steelyard place. I just hope nobody's lightin' fires over there."

She watched as Tiger, the smallest boy in the intermediate unit, but a
winner for all that, clambered onto a chair to have a closer look. It wasn't
likely anybody'd be stupid enough to build a fire at the Haunted House in
broad daylight, but, then, you never knew what those crazy Rinkydinks
might get up to. Though the existence of the Rinkydink Club, a motley
collection of the camp's older boys, was kept hidden from Pa Starbuck, Ma
was not fooled; she knew they held secret meetings down in the cellar of
the house, where they smoked Lucky Strikes and talked about "doing it,"
in defiance of camp rules, not to mention the ghost that roamed the premises and was reputed, from time to time, to have been "seen." If Tiger
gauged matters correctly, however, the smoke was coming not from the

Haunted House but from Indian Woods, where a work detail of "firebuild-ers" was policing the Seneca campfire area for that evening's initiation rites. Tonight, being the end of the first two-week camp period, would see the first all-camper council fire and torchlight parade, when the newest members of the Seneca Lodge would be initiated. Yesterday, at a special meet-ing, seven inductees had been chosen for the honor.

Reassured, Ma returned to the papers she had been perusing before Tiger's line drive interrupted her, while Tiger finished his task. Presently, he shook the dustpan into the tin wastebasket beside her chair, then asked for his money envelope.

"Coop's not open, honey. You can't have your money envelope less'n store's open, you know that."

"I want it so I can pay for the glass."

"So's he can pay for the glass," Ma repeated to no one in particular. "Tiger Abernathy, there's not another boy in camp would come in here of his own accord and offer to pay for a smashed windowpane. You aim to break that record as well?"

He waited while she riffled with plump fingers through the alphabetized money envelopes standing in the Thom McAn shoebox she used for filing purposes. Her eyes, always troublesome, were bothered by the afternoon sun streaming through the back window, and she reached for her green celluloid eyeshade, the sort that gamblers and railway baggage-masters favor. Ma had her own homey style. With her broad, maternal bosom, made for comforting boys, her graying hair that hardly knew which way to grow, her round, puffy cheeks, untouched by the artifice of makeup, her firm little chin, and the slip straps that always showed through the tops of her dresses, she was every camper's "ma."

Still waiting as she searched, Tiger added helpfully, "I'm the first one, Ma. *Ab,* remember?"

"Shucks, and don't I know it. Abernathy, Brewster—here you are."

Tiger winced at the name; nobody, except at his peril, ever called Tiger "Brewster," not even the teachers in school. The last guy who tried had had the wind butted out of him by Tiger's granite-hard head and been sent sprawling.

Ma flicked the envelope out of the box and handed it over. With tanned, grubby fingers, Tiger pinched the clasp, lifted the flap, blew, and peered inside.

"How much do you figure the damage'll be, Ma?" he asked.

"Well, lessee, glass ought to be 'bout a quarter, don't you think?"

"How about the putty and the glazier's points?"

"Hell's bells, what do I know about putty or them other doodads? You slap a quarter there on the desk and we'll call it square."

Her chair swiveled with a screech as she turned to face her desk again. The cubbyholes of the old rolltop were stuffed with an array of envelopes and papers, and more of the same littered the oaken surface, along with ledgers, open and shut, and a cast-iron spindle piercing a sheaf of pink laundry slips. A blocked-out campers' chart, showing the allocation of bunks in the cabins of the various units, stood out amid the jumble. Ma's desk was, so to speak, the central switchboard and nerve center of Friend-Indeed; from it were disbursed all payments, all orders and announcements, practically all the comings and goings of the entire camp.

"Before you go, Tige, I need a word with you."

Glancing past the pale, balding spot on the top of her head, Tiger saw she was staring intently at the chart.

"Something wrong?" he asked.

Ma shook her head. "There's this new boy coming tomorrow, is all"— she rummaged through the papers on her desk—"the one replacing Stanley Wagner, you know."

Tiger knew. This summer Howie Bochman, one of their regular cabinmates, had been lost to the Jeremians as a result of having contracted a case of infantile paralysis, a blow that had been compounded by Howie's replacement, the unfortunate Stanley Wagner. Unfortunate because Stanley's presence in Cabin 7 had not worked out. He had been, in a word, a spud, and the entire camp still smarted from the embarrassing and shameful episode that had ended his brief stay at Friend-Indeed.

"Not good camper fodder," had been the judgment of Reece Hartsig, Jeremiah's counselor, and no one had disagreed. A bedwetter (at fourteen!), a crybaby, and incurably homesick, Stanley had proved the wimpiest camper anyone could recall ever having come to the lake. Demerits had rained like hailstones upon Cabin 7 for Stanley's sundry errors and malfeasances, and the camel's back had been broken when, after a visit by a select group of campers to the Castle, a crystal paperweight had been discovered missing, in consequence of which Ma's friend, Dagmar Kronborg, had declared her home and its "trophy room" off limits for the remainder of the season.

The paperweight had eventually turned up hidden at the bottom of Stanley's suitcase, and after an official meeting of the Sachems' Council, the camp's governing board, the culprit had been "sent to Scarsdale," which meant nobody in camp was allowed to talk to him for three whole days; then, having survived this trial, the next day Stanley had simply gone up in smoke, his parents spiriting him away with neither farewells nor apologies, and leaving behind only the yellow-stained length of canvas in his bunk. Now that bunk would get a new canvas, and a new boy in it, and all the Jeremians were looking forward to his coming.

Ma found what she was looking for, an already opened letter. Tiger, who knew better than to read over a person's shoulder, waited until she looked up; her face was suddenly dyed emerald as a sunbeam pierced her eyeshade.

"Name's Leo," she said. She adjusted her spectacles—"Leo—Joakum? I guess that's how you'd say it."

"Where's he from?" Tiger asked.

"Saggetts Notch." She gave him a glance. "Fact is, he comes from Pitt."

"The Institute?" Tiger was surprised. "An orphan?"

Ma nodded. "Dr. Dunbar and the Joshua Society folks arranged it."

Tiger mulled over this unexpected news; he didn't know any orphans that he could recall. Ma held up the three pages of script and explained. The letter had been written by one Elsie Meekum, an assistant to Edwin Poe, supervisor of the Institute, and that gentleman's liaison with Dr. Dunbar, the president of the Friends of Joshua.

"It's a sad case," Ma said, her face expressing sympathy for the plight of this Leo Joakum. "We must be sure he has a good time. Try to see he fits in, so he doesn't end up like—" Though she left her sentence unfinished, Tiger knew she was thinking of Stanley.

He put the question uppermost in his mind. "Does he play baseball?"

Ma was vague on this point. "I don't really know. I should think so, though—most boys play baseball, don't they? He plays on the violin, anyways—the lady says he's a real—real what?" She consulted Miss Meekum's lines. "Yes—'prodigy,' she writes. Mercy, we could be getting our own Bobby Breen." She laid down the page with the others. "I expect he'll find it a bit strange at first, so I'm counting on you to show him the ropes, you and Bomber, in particular. Maybe you can hang him some netting so he don't get eaten by mosquitoes." She fixed him with her eyes, large and round as a raccoon's behind the magnifying lenses. "I'm depending on you to be good pals to him. See that the other boys treat him right. They'll follow along if you lead 'em."

"Yes, ma'am. But—"

Further comment was cut off by a slice of Ma's hands. "Buts are for goats, dear. You just do as your old Ma asks, hm? It's important for Pa that this boy gets a nice stay. And for Doctor Dunbar, too."

"Yes, ma'am." But Tiger was having private doubts. What the Jeremians needed was a boy who would add to their cabin's luster—a boy who could take over as shortstop for the Red Sox and swim a good Australian crawl, and do all the things a good camper could do—not some orphan who played the violin and needed a nursemaid.

Ma's chair screeched again as she turned in it and heaved herself up. "Wisht somebody would oil this darn old thing." Walking gingerly, for her feet troubled her greatly, she went into the next room where someone had turned the radio on full blast.

"Now, now, honeybunch," she said, "that ain't no way to play the raddio. Turn it down before we wake the dead."

Through the open doorway Tiger glimpsed Ma's daughter, Wilhelmina-Sue, settling herself and her doll into Pa's Morris chair. Tiger smiled at her, but she just sat with her chin resting possessively on the top of the doll's head, staring glumly at nothing. It wasn't easy getting Willa-Sue's attention, ever. Halting of speech, she was a "late" child, and the butt of many a camper joke. Thirteen now, she was still in fourth grade and couldn't do simple sums; but, although mentally feeble, she was remarkably precocious in her physical development, her greatest attraction for any camper being the size of the newly developed lumps under her dress.

Tiger wiggled his fingers at her but received no more response than he had before, and, giving up trying to amuse the girl, he turned away; his eye happened to fall on the paperwork scattered across Ma's desktop. The letter about the new boy lay open before him, and he was unable to resist the opportunity of glancing at what it contained.

. . . Mr. Poe and I both felt it was important that you and Reverend Starbuck be fully apprised of the circumstances, he read, *upsetting as they may seem—but what is so upsetting in life that we cannot seek God's succor in time of need? You will quickly comprehend what a tragic story is Leo Joaquim's. We naturally trust these transcripts of the notorious case will be*

11

for your knowledge only, and that you will safeguard the enclosed information from prying eyes. We would not see the boy further wounded through the cruelties of unthinking—

He read no further, for the groaning floorboards gave warning that Ma was coming back in.

"S'long, Ma," he said, tugging his cap down and opening the screen door. The moment he stepped outside Harpo was whining and scratching at the screen. The dog nosed the door open and licked Tiger's hand, begging to accompany him down to the lower campus.

"Can he come with me?" Tiger asked.

"Why not? I suppose he's more your beast than mine. But you best send him back up for his supper," Ma said. "And if anybody says anything, you just tell 'em Harpo followed along on his own."

"Ma, you're a peach."

"That's me, dear, fat and ripe and lots of fuzz."

When Tiger and the dog had gone, Ma sank back into her chair. No sooner was she settled than the cat roused itself, arched its back, and noiselessly slipped into her lap, where it began kneading her bosom with its paws and purring like a motor. "Yes, pussy, yes, Jezzy," Ma crooned, stroking its fur.

Setting the cat against her thigh, she retrieved the letter and scanned its last lines again. *We pray,* Miss Meekum had written, *Leo will find a safe berth there, and make the sort of friends the Friends of Joshua boys are famous for.*

With a smile Ma picked up the quarter Tiger had deposited on the desk and returned it to his envelope, which she replaced in its proper order at the head of the box. When this minor task was seen to, and after adjusting her eyeshade against the light, she poked around until she found a fresh file folder, then wrote out a label: "Joaquim, Leopold," and slipped the boy's medical reports and other documents into it. It was only as she folded the letter to include it in the file that she noticed something written on the back of the last page—a postscript from Elsie Meekum:

So awfully sorry—have just checked bus times and find there's no bus for Junction City on Sunday. Will have to send Leo Saturday afternoon.

Now, there was a fly in the ointment. Ma pondered matters. If the boy was coming today, that meant he was bound to arrive on the five o'clock bus from Hartford. She must get cracking so she could arrange with Henry

Ives to meet him at Four Corners with the jitney. Henry could deliver him straight to Cabin 7, where Tiger would be on hand to look after him.

She returned the letter to its envelope, and placed it in the folder, which she set aside. From the back of the shoe box she took a fresh "spending" envelope like Tiger's and across the top she began the name. She wrote:

LEO

then stopped; what was that last name? She had reference to Miss Meekum's letter, then added:

JOAQUIM

"Joakum," she murmured to herself as she wrote, "Leo Joakum." She slipped the envelope back in the box, then laughed to herself. The envelope was empty, and likely to stay that way. In such times as these, who had spending money for a poor orphan boy? She opened her pocketbook and extracted three quarters—all the change she had. She had intended it for some new hair ribbons for Willa-Sue, but there were better uses for money than fripperies. She closed up the envelope and reinserted it in its place among the others, then took the file folder and, pulling open the yellow varnished cabinet drawer, filed it between "Jackson, Jerome," and "Jones, Bertram."

The clock chimed the quarter-hour and Ma's chair squeaked again as she started; Jezzy hit the floor on four light feet. It was nearly powwow time. She must see to Willa-Sue's supper. She hung her eyeshade on its hook, and was about to shut the drawer when, her fingernail flicking along the row of tabs, she recalled Miss Meekum's admonition. Taking the new boy's folder, she opened the door of the old pie safe she used for "important personals." The safe had a lock against snoopers. She placed the folder among the documents, shut and locked the door, then fed the key under her ink-stained blotter with its advertisements from Bloom's Stationery Emporium in Junction City, *Est. 1926.*

2

The string of six cabins making up "Harmony," the intermediate or junior unit of Camp Friend-Indeed that stretched between "High Endeavor" (seniors) and "Virtue" (cadets), were spread out along the linepath leading to the council ring in the pine grove at the lakefront and the Teddy Roosevelt Memorial Nature Lodge, heart of the lower camp. Modest nine-bunk dwellings of brown-creosoted, tongue-and-groove siding set on blocks, identical in shape and size, each with its porch in front and clothesline beside or behind, the cabins had been built twenty years before to replace the original canvas tents, and had instead of solid walls sets of hinged side flaps that opened the entire structure up, bringing the outdoors inside. Each cabin had its name and number carved on a varnished pine plaque over the door: "Ezekiel—6," "Jeremiah—7," "Hosea—8," "Isaiah—9," and "Obadiah—10," and from the porch of each, through the red and brown tree trunks, could be seen the gleaming lake and waterfront, its boat dock and swim dock, the canoe racks, the diving float with its thirty-foot tower and board, and, out on the point, the cluster of High Endeavor cabins.

A dozen feet in back of Jeremiah, between the chrome-pipe faucet and wash rack that the cabin shared with Hosea and Ezekiel, stood "Old Faithful," the geyserlike drinking fountain that was the social center of the Harmony unit, and farther along the path was the "Dewdrop Inn," as the six-hole privy was called—another social hub.

Among the cabins, the late-afternoon sunshine filtered through the dark pine branches that formed a shady canopy overhead. Languorous, desultory talk and low, easy laughter emanated from the bunk racks in which campers reposed, at the lazy end of another summer's day. The heat had died, the locusts had stilled their noise, the air was cool, with just a bit of breeze. Yet, the tranquil harmonies of the late afternoon were all but lost on the boys of Jeremiah, who were come together in a moment of ferocious ecclesiastical endeavor.

"GenesisExodusLeviticusNumbersDeuteronomyJoshuaJudgesRuthFirst SamuelSecondSamuelFirstKingsSecondKings—um—Ezra . . ."

"Chronicles, you forgot First Chronicles, Second Chronicles, *then* Ezra—" Monkey corrected.

"Shit, *Chron*icles," Eddie said, socking his forehead in frustration.

"Yeah, shit," echoed Peewee Oliphant.

"Aw, can it, twerp," ordered Monkey. "Who said you were allowed to swear? You want your mouth washed out with soap?"

"Heh heh." Young Peewee eyed Monkey warily from under the tan felt brim of the Tom Mix ten-gallon hat that was his preferred headgear. As the youngest boy at Friend-Indeed, Peewee Oliphant, age seven, was tolerated in Jeremiah cabin only by virtue of the fact that he was camp mascot. His father, in addition to being Friend-Indeed's doctor, kept a summer cottage adjacent to the infirmary in Three Corner Cove, and since his romper days Peewee had been doggedly attempting to follow in the footsteps of the older boys.

Furrowing his brow in concentration, Eddie took it from the top again. Come Monday, he would have to stand up in Bible-studies class and recite the books of the Old Testament without a mistake, so for the past quarter of an hour Monkey Twitchell had been coaching him.

"GenesisExodusLeviticusNumbersDeuteronomyJoshuaJudgesRuthFirst SamuelSecondSamuelFirstKingsSecondKingsFirstChroniclesSecond—"

"Ohhh mi-iiii *Gaawd!"*

This time it was the Bomber who interrupted the recitation, staring in lubricious disbelief at the copy of the King James Version of the Good Book open on his broad lap. "Listen to this, you guys, willya? This'll whack you out! Sex—*sex* in the Bible!"

"Sex in the Bible?" Monkey repeated blankly. Such things were not possible, not even in this modern world of marvels.

To prove the truth of his dubious statement, the Bomber read for them the verses he had just stumbled across: *Thy two breasts are like two young roes that are twins—*

Wow! they exclaimed. Tits in the Bible!

"Wait, wait, that ain't all!" He read more: *This thy stature is like to a palm tree, and thy breasts to clusters of grapes. I said, I will go up to the palm tree, I will take hold of the boughs thereof; now also thy breasts shall be as clusters of the vine—!*

"See what I'm tellin' ya? This here's the Bible and this guy's woggin' on this dame's tits!"

Eddie, who had been lounging on his bunk, sat up, his eyes bugging with astonishment. "Boy, have we been missing somethin'! Who *is* this guy, anyways?"

"I think it's Solomon."

"Solomon?" Dump's voice, changing this summer, climbed an octave. "For cripes' sakes, if he's supposed to be so wise why can't he tell the difference between dates and grapes?" Baptized Donald Dixon Dillworth, Jr., Dump, who had the glasses and perpetually concerned expression of a serious scholar, bore his name heroically. His studious side, however, did not keep him from regularly lining out home runs for the Red Sox.

"Aw jeez, willya listen to the guy?" The Bomber chortled. "Grapes or dates—if it's tits, what's the diff? *Tits,* man, big friggin' tits—and they're in the *Bible!*"

This much was true, although Pa Starbuck would have perceived the Bomber's interpretation of holy writ to be distressingly literal. Bomber Jackson had chanced upon the verses while leafing through the New Testament in search of Romans 5 (on mortal sin and atonement)—his assignment for the same Bible-studies class. If either he or Eddie should fail in his recitation on Monday morning he would earn demerits for Jeremiah, a fact helping to account for the boys' zealousness in their pursuit of ecclesiastical knowledge.

The talk now turned to a consideration of sex closer to home, however; to wit, the sundry eroticisms of Gus Klaus, occupant of Hosea cabin, next door.

"Gus was doin' it again last night," the Bomber observed with relish. He put aside his Bible, brought out his torch and began whittling on it, making ready for tonight's council fire.

16

Of the five campers, only Peewee did not know what "it" was, but, anticipating ridicule, he forbore to ask, hoping to deduce the answer from the general discussion.

"How couldja tell?" inquired Eddie Fiske, dangling his legs over the edge of his bunk. Red-haired and freckled, with a mouth as wide as a slice of pie, Eddie had the sort of pale, liverish-looking skin that would peel all summer.

"I seen him. Seen his sillarett." The Bomber pantomimed furious onanistic activity, to the hilarity of Monkey and Eddie. Dump, who was inclined toward prudishness, and didn't care for the endless stream of sex-talk that flowed in and around every cabin in the camp, didn't think it funny.

"Gus has sex on the brain," declared Monkey. All bony ribs and hyperkinetic, Monkey Twitchell was well nicknamed: there was a simian quality to his small narrow face, large ears, and bright, swiveling eyes. And Monkey was right about Gus Klaus, who this year had arrived at camp with a sheaf of typewritten pages—the letterhead bore the legend "For Better Plumbing Kall Klaus"—containing the racier portions of James T. Farrell's *Studs Lonigan,* assiduously copied out for Moonbow reading fare. "If he doesn't watch out," Monkey added, "he's gonna get warts."

"Or grow hair on the palm of his hand," Eddie stated.

"Or go blind," put in the Bomber authoritatively.

The older campers were repeating the Reverend Starbuck's oft-stated predictions of the consequences of this particular pastime.

"Hey Bomber," Peewee said. "How's about givin' us a look at Tits O'Shay?"

"Oh, come on, Peewee," said Dump. "You're too young for that stuff."

"No, I ain't."

"Then ask your father, don't go looking at dirty pictures."

"Hell, Tits O'Shay ain't dirty," declared the Bomber. "She's cute."

Dump groaned a protest as the Bomber heaved himself up to retrieve the battered cardboard box he kept stored in his assigned space on the overhead shelf, and from it produced a small piece of polychromed cardboard, the end flap of a pound carton of Land O'Lakes butter showing the picture of a smiling Indian female kneeling and holding up before her chest a carton of Land O'Lakes butter on which was the picture of the identical smiling girl holding up another pound of butter, and so on, presumably, into infinity. In this instance, however, the portion above her hands where the carton rested had been cut out and the maiden's bare knees were folded up into the excised rectangle, presenting the alluring picture of a smiling Indian maid holding in her hands two eye-filling breasts—the luscious Tits O'Shay. Monkey and Eddie were practically drooling, while Peewee stood bug-eyed on the bed behind them.

"Okay, you guys, that's enough for one day." As the Bomber slipped the card into the box and stretched to return it to its hiding place, he emitted a volley of rude noises.

"Pee-yoo, you farted!" Holding his nose and screwing up his face, Peewee pointed out the obvious.

"Bombs away!" Eddie shouted, and began chanting, "Beans, beans the musical fruit, the more you eat the more you toot." Then they all took up the refrain, "The more you toot the better you feel, so eat your beans at every meal."

"Aw, come on, you guys—"

Despite his brashness, the Bomber was easily embarrassed, but it was because of this singular talent that he had been nicknamed "Bomber" in the first place; or sometimes the Brown Bomber, a cognomen stemming from a certain resemblance to boxer Joe Louis, who only the year before had knocked out Jim Braddock to become heavyweight champion of the world. Joe, of course, was a darker shade, but the swarthiness of the Bomber's complexion, as well as his chunky features, furrowed brow, and poll of kinky black hair, marked a distinct likeness.

Monkey and Eddie and Dump stopped their razzing, but Peewee, never knowing when to quit, continued to pinch his nose and repeat his pee-yoo's. When at last he subsided, they all seemed to run out of talk. Dump frowned at his watch; what was keeping the others? he wondered. All Boats In had rung, the lake lay deserted, the waterfront too. Just about everybody, campers and counselors, was already indoors, engaged in the before-dinner routine known as "powwow," the final one for the first group of two-weekers.

Fourteen days of camp had already passed, and tomorrow, Sunday, July 3, they would be going home, to be replaced with a new incoming group, among them, the longed-for replacement for the infamous Stanley Wagner, and the talk in Cabin 7 now turned to speculation on this interesting subject. Whatever he turned out to be like, all the regular Jeremians hoped he would be the kind of boy who would help get them back in the habit of winning. For, until this summer, "Hartsig's boys," as they were called, had been prime stuff at Friend-Indeed. Thanks to the leadership of Reece, who had a peculiar knack of urging his campers to feats of prowess that outdid those of the other cabins (although even Reece had been stymied by Stanley), they had garnered more "happy points" and fewer "blackies" two years running, and (until Stanley had been inflicted on them) had fully expected to do the same again this season. If the new boy lived up to expectations, if he could "show some good old moxie," and "bring home the bacon" (to use two of Reece's favorite expressions), and, well, just "fit in," they might still pull it off; they might still see the names of the Jeremians and their counselor formally inscribed on the plaque at the base of the Hartsig Trophy, the handsome silver cup donated by Reece's dad, Big Rolfe Hartsig.

Voices were heard out on the linepath, and in a moment two more Jeremians entered the cabin.

"What's going on?" demanded Phil Dodge, the taller and huskier of the two. "Jesus, Peewee, are you completely nuts!" he exclaimed, spotting the boy lolling grandly on Reece's cot.

"No. Why?"

"You're messin' around on Big Chief's bed, that's why." The counselor's cot stood in the center of the back wall, between the sets of double-decker bunks (four to a side), and was made up in the military style, with a footlocker at the foot (monogrammed "R.A.H."—"rah-rah Reece!"—for "Reece Adam Hartsig").

Phil shagged Peewee off the cot and went about neatening the blankets and pillow.

Meanwhile, Peewee had turned his attention to the frog dangling by its hind legs from the second boy's fist.

"Boy, that's a whopper. Where'd you get it?"

"I caught it," said Wally Pfeiffer, his tongue bright pink from the Necco wafer he was sucking. "I stunned him with a rock."

Phil gave Wally an exasperated look. "So what? Who waded in and grabbed him? Don't think you're so hot. And listen, kiddo," he added, "didn't I tell you that candy'll make you break out? You know how Big Chief feels about pimples."

Wally gave his pal a grim, tooth-clenched look and spat out his half-melted wafer. Phil Dodge, a square-headed boy with a hard-packed body, a spiky pineapple haircut, and eyes that never told you anything, was cabin monitor and Reece's second-in-command, enforcing the counselor's dictums as he could (which meant mostly in matters concerning the unassertive Wally) and even aping his mannerisms. "All right, camper, let's hop to it," Phil would say, and "Listen, kiddo, I don't want to have to tell you again"—and when *Reece* said "Listen, kiddo," Phil really did "hop to it."

Now he couldn't mask a certain satisfaction in having bent Wally to his will, which made Wally burn silently. Wally could never hope to measure up to Phil; he was a skinny, dour-looking lad with limp, flaxen hair and the pale, puffy-lidded eyes that resulted from an overactive thyroid—a condition that probably accounted for his perpetually drowsy expression and morose disposition.

"We both caught him," Phil asserted, willing now to be generous. He took the frog from Wally and gave the creature a shake. It emitted a croak of protest.

"Boy, he sure is fat," Peewee said admiringly. "Can I have him?"

"What for?"

"I bet Oats'd let me keep him in the lodge," Peewee said. Oats Gurley was the camp nature director. "In a box. I could have him for a pet. Or we could blow him up."

"What're you talking about, runt?" Phil demanded.

"You know, like a balloon," Peewee said, refusing to be cowed by Phil's contemptuous glare. "I seen Reece do it once. He took a soda straw and shoved it up this frog's ass and blew it up. It floated in the water but it couldn't swim."

"Oh, come on, Peewee, that's disgusting!" Dump exclaimed.

"*I* didn't do it! Reece did!" Peewee protested.

A frog-balloon was a good gag, after all. Didn't campers chloroform frogs for dissection in nature study? Not that Reece Hartsig would bother with anything so pedestrian as that. In fact, he would never do anything ordinary, even when it came to frogs. And when you got right down to it, there wasn't anything much Reece *couldn't* do and do with style. Who else did the boys know whose sleek, tanned features had turned up in the Sunday rotogravure, grinning among a group of important-looking individuals? Who else had surfed at Waikiki Beach, and sailed to Europe with his parents to see the Berlin Olympics? Who else had climbed Mount Monadnock and paddled-and-portaged the Quinnebaug clear down to New London; who else wore a tux and went to country-club dances, and carried a silver flask on his hip? Who else had been courting the matchless Nancy Rider, subdeb daughter of the lieutenant-governor of the Commonwealth of Pennsylvania; had even, it was rumored, danced with Dixie Dunbar at the Rainbow Room in Radio City? Who else had left a trail of broken hearts (which was why the Jeremians sometimes liked to call him "Heartless") up and down the whole of the Eastern Seaboard? Who else, after this, his last Moonbow summer, was going off to be a flier in the Army Air Corps, and get a pair of silver wings? At Friend-Indeed, Reece was the "Big Chief," former ace camper—a bunkee in Jeremiah, as his father had been before him—and current top-rated counselor, and it was a rare Moonbow boy who didn't look forward to the day when, like his hero, he too would have been made one of Pa's "Glad Men from Happy Boys" (Pa had dreamed up the camp motto and had decreed that it be painted on the sign at the highway turnoff), who could take up smoking a pipe in public—the same kind of briar Reece's father had given him, in a smart gold-stamped leather case with a green satin interior, the kind you saw in an *Esquire* ad.

Phil dumped the frog into the fire bucket and partially covered it with a box until Reece should decide its fate. No sooner had he and Wally hit their bunks than the missing Jeremian came in over the back sill.

"Tiger!" Peewee crowed happily.

"Hi, sprout, what are you doing here? It's powwow time."

"I'm powwowing with you guys."

"Jay say it was all right?" Jay St. John was the counselor of Habakkuk, Peewee's cabin.

"Yes-s."

"I bet he didn't," Phil put in.

"Nerts to you," Peewee said with a scowl. He tried chinning himself on Tiger's bunk rail, then gave it up.

"Where's Reece?" Tiger asked, looking around.

"He's havin' his picture taken with his dad," Eddie reported.

"How come?"

Phil explained: On Big Rolfe's order, Reece had donned his military school uniform and gone to have a newspaper picture taken at the Blue Ribbon Rathskeller over on the highway.

"It's for the Bund," the Bomber added.

Tiger knew about the weekly meetings of the German-American Bund, a popular local group to which Reece's father paid allegiance. "Mail come?" he asked, looking around.

Phil produced the afternoon's allotment: only two letters for Cabin 7, one for Reece, another for Wally. When Tiger tossed Reece's letter onto his pillow, Peewee snatched it up and proceeded to inspect it closely.

"Y'know something, you guys? This thing really stinks!" he said, greedily sniffing the blue envelope, noting the return address penned in a light, feminine script with circles for the dots over the i's, and a puckered lipstick print on the flap. "It's from Nancy Rider," he added, glancing at the tinted snapshot of a shapely girl in the bathing suit tucked into the mirror frame over Reece's cot.

"Listen, small fry, you better not go screwing around with that letter," Tiger advised as Peewee sprang into a bunk. "Reece won't like it."

"Aw, Heartless don't care," Peewee protested, giving the letter another sniff and leaving a greasy thumb mark on the envelope as he returned it to Reece's pillow.

Tiger wasn't so sure of that; nor was anyone else. While the fact that, in the absence of Nancy Rider, their counselor was this summer newly smitten with Peewee's sister, Honey, gave the kid points, it didn't necessarily follow that he could get away with messing around in Heartless's private mail.

"Gosh, look at that." This from Eddie, who spoke in a confidential tone, his eye fixed on the linepath. The others looked too.

"Who d'you suppose it is?" Wally wondered, staring at the odd sight that had suddenly presented itself: twenty feet away someone was standing on the path—a strange-looking guy, with ears that stuck out and a comical hat on his head. A skinny, gawky type, who'd appeared out of nowhere. They couldn't see his face because he was positioned with his back to the cabin.

"What's he doin' here, anyways?" said the Bomber.

"Betcha it's your new boy," Peewee said, revealing hitherto unrealized psychic powers.

"Cripes, you gotta be kidding," the Bomber said in dismay.

"He's not supposed to be here till tomorrow," Phil added.

"Maybe he came early," Tiger suggested. He jumped down from his bunk and signaled to Phil, and together they stepped out onto the porch. "Phil, you're monitor. Go and bring him in."

"Are you kiddin'? Not me. You really think it's the new guy?"

Though he couldn't be absolutely sure, something told Tiger that the boy on the path was indeed Leo Joaquim. If ever there was an orphan, this spud filled the bill.

"Holy maloley, take a gander at the luggage, will ya?" the Bomber muttered from inside the cabin.

The boy's "luggage" was a worn cardboard suitcase, its clasps reinforced by a length of frayed rope. Beside it rested a blanket roll and a stack of small wooden boxes, both tied with twine, and a limp-looking pillow, and leaning against these was a black violin case, battered and scarred.

"Knock it off, Bomber," Tiger said. "The rest of you stay here. And don't act like a bunch of tools."

Leaving Phil on the porch, Tiger went down the steps and made his way along the path. The newcomer stood amid his sorry paraphernalia, looking lost and tired.

"Hi," Tiger said in a friendly voice. "Who're you looking for?"

"Cabin 7. Jeremiah."

"You found it. You must be Leo Joakum."

"Joaquim," the boy said, pronouncing it *Wack-eem*. "And you must be Tiger Abernathy."

"What makes you think so?"

"Mr. Ives described you." His voice had a rusty quality, a weary inflection.

"How come you got here today?"

"No bus Sunday."

Tiger measured himself against the new boy: Leo was a good six inches taller, taller than any of the Jeremians. And he was thin—too thin, Tiger judged—sort of scarecrowish, all arms and legs, joints and angles. His clothes were a haphazard job: shorts of some heavy, rough material that looked as if it must itch, and far too tight. Black buttons were sewn with white thread onto the waist, and to these were attached suspenders of scalloped elastic that hung loosely over his narrow shoulders. Instead of sneakers he had on a pair of brown leather shoes, badly scuffed and worn, with thick, rigid soles, and maroon socks that drooped around his ankles. And then there was the hat—an old felt "crown," its narrow brim cut in a sawtooth and embellished with an array of brightly colored soda bottle caps and political buttons. All in all Leo Joaquim was as unlikely looking a specimen as could be imagined at Friend-Indeed. And what, Tiger wondered, would Reece say when he saw the new Jeremian? Yet—he was here. Tiger remembered Ma's admonition.

"How old are you?" He was making conversation.

"I was fourteen last February. And you?"

23

"Fourteen too. Last month."

"Congratulations."

"Gotta pee?" Tiger asked, noticing that the boy was practically hopping from one foot to the other. "Help yourself. Take any bush."

"It was a long bus ride," Leo explained sheepishly as he stepped behind a shrub and relieved himself.

He was, Tiger thought as he waited on the path, decidedly weird. Still, there was something appealing in his shy, awkward manner, in the dusty, raspy voice. "Well," he said as Leo rejoined him, "I guess we don't want to stand around here all day, do we? Let me help you with something." He took the cardboard suitcase. It felt heavy. "What you got in here, anyway?" he asked as they moved toward the cabin.

"The family jewels," Leo replied.

Tiger laughed, and between them they got the stuff to the porch where Phil and, now, the others were waiting. There was a good deal of shuffling around while everyone said Hiya and shook hands and scratched elbows and the Bomber dropped the torch he was holding and picked it up again, and they all tried to act natural and naturally failed. Tiger performed the solemn introduction, getting the new boy's name right, and one by one each of the Jeremians offered his hand and received in return an awkward handjerk.

Phil looked the newcomer up and down. "My name's Dodge," he announced, a bit over hearty.

"Mine's Jackson," the Bomber offered, and then the rest told their names, and Dump's full title of Donald Dixon "Dump" Dillworth, Jr., was proclaimed amid much laughter and hoots of derision.

"And my name's Peewee Oliphant," crowed Peewee, whipping off his ten-gallon hat and sticking his mug out.

"And where is your trunk, Mr. Pee Wee Elephant?" came the new boy's quick reply.

This made them all laugh and the new boy laughed with them, then blinked his eyes once or twice as though they hurt, and said in his dry, sandpapery voice, "Glad to know you all." His face was just a face, nothing extraordinary there except perhaps for the large, dark eyes—they peered out with a kind of faraway expression that went past you, or even through you.

The formalities seen to, the group filtered into the cabin, the Jeremians sending out silent signals to each other saying, What the heck? and Beats me. As yet, Tiger had given no indication of how far they ought to extend their hospitality, and this was odd, because Tiger usually provided them with guidelines regarding any new or unexpected situation. He now stood by the infamous yellow-stained bunk as if to say This is yours.

"Who slept here?" Leo asked. He looked from the bunk to Tiger.

"Belonged to a fellow named Wagner," Tiger said.

"You're his replacement," the Bomber added.

"What happened to him?"

"He went home with his tail between his legs," Phil said.

"I see he left his yellow badge of cowardice."

Tiger shot the new boy a look. That was a good one, especially for a guy from Pitt Institute.

Leo was regarding the cot in the middle of the room, a scant yard away. "Who sleeps there?" he asked.

"Reece."

"Reece?"

"He's our counselor."

"Where is he?"

"Havin' his picture took," the Bomber explained.

"For the newspaper," Wally chimed in.

"The *Sunday* paper," Monkey added with emphasis.

Watching Leo trying to unknot the twine around his blanket roll, Tiger slid his knife from its sheath and handed it over. When the twine was cut, releasing the bedroll, Leo returned the knife.

As he carefully moved his violin case aside and started to undo the dented clasps of his suitcase, the others by ones and twos crept into their bunks, watching, eyes filled with curiosity. The suitcase was unstrapped and the lid folded back on its wobbly hinges; it produced nothing remarkable, however, among its contents. Then Leo began to undo the twine holding together the stack of small wooden boxes.

"Whatcha gonna do with those?" the Bomber inquired, trying not to sound overly curious.

"I'm going to collect things in them."

"What kinda things?"

"Ohh . . . flora and fauna."

"Flora who?"

"Floradora."

25

Ha ha. The Bomber made a goony face to the others. Someone snickered. Leo, still having trouble with the knot, asked Tiger for the loan of his knife again. After he had cut the twine and unwound it from the boxes, he sat holding them, still stacked, between his knees. And though every camper in the cabin was bursting to know their real purpose, the new boy did nothing further to relieve them of their curiosity.

"What do you play in baseball?" the Bomber asked, hanging his head over the end of his bunk.

"In b-a-ase-ba-all?" Leo drawled the word, as though its meaning eluded him. Then, "I don't play anything."

The Bomber sat up in surprise. "You don't?"

"I'm afraid not."

Tiger's look went to Dump, in the opposite quarter of the cabin. "Well, there goes the ball game," it said; Stanley Wagner's bunk must be jinxed.

Just then the bell rang for dinner, breaking the tension, and all along the linepath campers exploded from their cabins and streamed across the playing field, heading for the dining hall in the upper camp. Not inclined to hurry, the new boy sat on Stanley's bunk rail and emptied a pebble out of one of his shoes.

"I see you brought your own pillow," Tiger remarked, waiting with the Bomber at the door. "That was smart."

"Was it? Good. I never go anywhere without Albert."

"Who's Albert?" Peewee wanted to know.

"My pillow."

Oh.

When he had put his shoe back on and laced it up, Leo went to join Tiger and the Bomber. As the second bell for dinner sounded, the three broke into a run.

"Hey Wacko, you forgot your hat!" cried Peewee, short legs churning as he tried gamely to catch up, in his hand the bottle-cap cap.

Peewee didn't realize it then, but he had bestowed a new nickname on Stanley Wagner's replacement: Wacko Wackeem, who played the violin and kept a pillow named Albert, who wore a funny-looking hat—and who didn't like baseball!

3

ll together, the Jeremians could never just walk down the road from the dining hall to the lower camp, but, as they did this evening, they would form loose, lollygagging knots, dragging dust, kicking fannies, elbowing ribs, clipping shoulders, tripping feet, now seeing which of them could throw a stone the farthest or hold his breath the longest or strike the deepest tone, now knitting together, now spreading to both sides of the road, now joining up again to make cracks about Willa-Sue's busted brain, coming closer to delve into the mysteries of all womanhood, with the Bomber telling—the Bomber was forever telling—about how he'd seen a naked female in the window of the tenement next to his tenement and what *that* looked like, and always, always, Peewee Oliphant's plaintive cry behind, "Hey, you guys, wait up!"

Tonight, though, there was a difference: tonight they came down with Leo, the new boy in Cabin 7. There was no doubt but that he'd made a splash at dinner; campers couldn't take their eyes off him, and he was the subject of numerous jokes. "Hey, get a load of Mortimer Snerd." "Where'd the yokel come from?" Jokes about his Adam's apple and his ears and his bottle-cap hat. Things had quieted down some during the meal, but no one could ignore the fact that it seemed Cabin 7 might have drawn another Stanley Wagner. But, Tiger thought, twisting the bill of his baseball cap, this boy really was nothing like Stanley. For one thing, he was smart—his odd-shaped skull looked like it housed a full quota of brains. They must eat a lot of fish at the Institute. Still, he *was* odd, with his pathetic suitcase and mysterious codfish boxes, his beat-up violin case and weird hat, and his pillow named Albert. There were other strange things about him, too. His gawky kind of walk, the jug ears that stuck out, the habit he had of ducking his head before he spoke, the surprising way he had of phrasing things, the kind of things he said. Like when the Bomber asked him the question everybody else had been wanting to ask but refrained from.

"How come you came by bus? Couldn't your mother and father bring you?"

"I'm afraid they couldn't."

That might have been the end of that, but the Bomber was like a dog worrying a bone. "Father have to work?" he pressed.

"No."

"You don't have a car?"

"That's correct. No car." He walked one or two more steps before adding, "No mother and father, either."

"Oh." That one was a shocker to all but Tiger.

Peewee piped up. "Yikes! You an *or*phan? You live in a orphanage? Do they feed you gruel—?"

"Peewee, for cripes' sakes, give the guy a break, will you?" Tiger said.

"I was only askin'. Gruel's what they gave Oliver Twist in a orphanage."

"Oliver Twist wasn't in any orphanage," Dump corrected. "He was in a workhouse."

"What's the diff?" Peewee wanted to know.

"Not much, to be truthful," Leo answered.

"But don'tcha know who your mother and father *are?*" Peewee persisted.

"Yes," Leo returned deadpan. " 'My mother was an Indian princess and my father was the Emperor of China.' "

The guys wanted to laugh outright; yet—there was something in the way he spoke the words that made them hold back. Peewee, however, had to titter. What a twerp, his laugh said. Not being absolutely sure, he looked to Tiger for a guiding sign, but was offered none. Then he looked to the Bomber, who shrugged, then behind him to Eddie; still, nothing doing.

"What did he do, your father?" Phil inquired.

"About what?"

"No, I mean—well, what did he do for a living? What was his job?"

"Butcher."

"Huh?"

"He was a butcher. You know—loin of pork, lamb chops, rib roasts. . . ." Clearly these words were meant humorously, but they served to bring a frown to Phil's brow. The Bomber, however, was getting a kick out of the new boy.

"Hey, your ma must've liked that. She was real lucky."

"Yes. *Real* lucky," Leo said, but there was something odd in his tone that made the Bomber wonder; Tiger, too.

"What did you think of Ma Starbuck?" he asked, having just introduced Leo to Ma outside the dining hall.

"I guess she runs the place, huh?"

"How'd you guess," said the Bomber.

"Does everybody call her Ma?"

"Everybody around here does."

"Ma." The boy repeated the word. "Everybody's ma. Well, every boy should have a ma, shouldn't he? A boy's best friend is his m-mother, isn't that what they say?"

By now they had come onto the playing field, but instead of going over to watch the evening one o' cat game, they split up, most of the Jeremians heading for the Dewdrop Inn, while Tiger took the new boy on toward the pine grove and council ring to introduce him to the setting for tonight's campfire.

Though Tiger had known the pine grove for seven summers, knew it as well as the palm of his own baseball mitt, this evening the place seemed to have taken on a tinge of mystery, of unnatural quietude. Occasionally a bird chirped, a brief, fleeting melody of evensong, and now and then a call came from one of the canoes out on the lake, bright gold in the last of the sun. Beside him, Leo stood gazing at the giant flat-topped chunk of granite—Tabernacle Rock, they called it—that lay altarlike at the foot of the tallest pine in the grove.

"What an extraordinary tree," he remarked, sighting up to the topmost branches.

"They call it the Methuselah Tree," Tiger explained. "Because of its age."

"It's awesome. Hercules would have trouble felling it. How old is it?"

"Oats Gurley thinks it must be over two hundred. Oats is our nature director."

Head thrown back, Leo continued to stare up at the tip of the tree.

" 'This is the forest primeval. The murmuring pines and the hemlocks . . .' " he quoted. "Do you like Longfellow?"

" 'Hiawatha?' " Tiger ventured.

" 'Evangeline.' Sorry." There was a pause, presumably so Tiger could digest this nugget, then the silence was broken by the sound of backfiring over on the road. Leo laughed. "Mr. Ives's jitney leaves a lot to be desired. I suggested he call it Bellerophon." Clearly he was out to impress Tiger. "You know who Bellerophon was, don't you?"

"No."

"He was one of Alexander the Great's horses. He had another: Bucephalus. It appears you have an owl in your tree," Leo added; the sequence of his thoughts seemed slightly disordered.

Tiger allowed as how it was indeed a horned owl, a common enough species in that locale. "You can hear him sometimes," he said. He cupped his hands and hooted softly, but the bird remained aloof and silent.

Out of the blue, Leo pronounced a name: "Icarus."

Tiger looked at him. "Icarus?"

"That might be a good name for the owl," Leo said. "What do you think?"

Tiger bit his lip, then grinned, amused that the new boy, not two hours in camp, was loftily bestowing names on a broken-down jitney and a bird that had been part of the Moonbow scene longer than Tiger himself.

"I hope you don't mind me being under you," Leo went on. "My bunk, I mean."

"It's fine. It's real close to Reece, I know, but don't let that bother you."

"When do I meet him, anyway?"

"He'll be back for the council fire."

"Do you think we'll be friends?"

"You and Reece?"

"No. You and me."

"Sure, we'll get on—don't worry. The Bomber, too," he added.

They left the ring and headed for the cabin, where they found the others lying around in their bunks. Tiger and the Bomber set about showing Leo how to double-fold his blankets, half on top, half under; to accomplish this they had to empty the bunk of its interesting paraphernalia.

"Whatcha really got in them boxes?" Peewee demanded as Leo picked up the stack—six white-pine Gorton's Codfish boxes, all identical.

Leo looked down at them and blinked. "Nothing," he said. "They're empty. All but this one." He held it up. "There's a ferocious creature in here." He held it out. "Want to see it?"

Peewee drew back in alarm. "No."

"Shaddap, squirt. Show us," the Bomber said.

Leo was agreeable, but first he instructed them to shut their eyes, and when he said to open them again they saw that the top panel of the box had been slid back. Inside was a large black spider, fixed in place with pins.

"Yikes!" cried Peewee, jumping backward. Tiger also shied from the sight of the hairy and fearsome-looking thing.

"Holy maloley!" exclaimed the Bomber, and no comment was made when he broke wind, clambering down from his bunk for a better view. "Is it a black widow?" he asked.

"Nope," said Dump, who knew about such things. "I bet it's a tarantula."

Leo nodded confirmation. "It's from New Mexico and it's called *Lycosa tarentula.* A wolf spider."

Eddie was impressed. "Boy, I'll bet it could kill you if it was alive."

Leo shook his head. "Not true. Tarantulas can bite, but it's not fatal."

The boys exchanged looks; evidently the new boy was something of an authority on spiders. In fact, he seemed to know a lot about a lot of things.

Then everyone began talking at once, not directly to Leo, but speaking for his benefit all the same, expanding bit by bit, describing boat tests and canoe tests, and discussing next week's Snipe Hunt and the Water Carnival later in the month. Leo, who had been privately surveying the immaculate cot positioned a scant three feet from his own, the shiny footlocker with its brass studs and stenciled monogram, the row of neatly pressed garments hanging from an over-pole, the Indian clubs against the wall, the tinted snapshot of a bathing beauty tucked into the frame of a mirror hung on a nail, ventured a question about their owner.

"What's he like, anyway?"

"He's Big Chief," Phil said proudly.

"He's Heartless," the Bomber said.

"Heartless Hartsig." Leo tried it out.

"Better not let him hear you call him that," Wally said. "He doesn't like it."

Phil spoke up again. "He's the best counselor at Friend-Indeed. And we're the best campers. You'll never go wrong if you do what Reece says."

"True?" Leo asked, looking around the circle of faces.

True, they chorused. There were Reece stories galore: about his father, Big Rolfe, and his mother, Joy, "den mother" to the Jeremians; about Reece's car, the famous green Chevy coupe dubbed The Green Hornet, and about the governor's daughter and the waitress at the Blue Ribbon he had dated last year and dropped in favor of Honey Oliphant.

As this discussion went forward, Peewee had been busying himself with an impromptu change of attire and was now standing with his feet on Reece's cot admiring himself in the mirror.

"Jesus, Peewee, are you completely nuts!" Dump exclaimed, watching him cavort.

"No, why?"

"If Heartless catches you like that you're really going to get it." Peewee had substituted for his cowboy hat Reece's garrison cap, bright with gold insignia, which he was trying on at various rakish angles, and, to add to the startling effect, he had taken the athletic supporter from the counselor's rack and pulled it on over his shorts.

The Bomber wagged his head glumly, predicting dire consequences. "I'm tellin' you, Peewee, you're really askin' for it, y'know that? If Heartless catches you, your ass won't be in a jock, it'll be in a sling."

A silence uncommon to the cabin ensued; but not for long. The next subject of conversation was, inevitably, the Haunted House, which Leo had passed in Hank's jitney, and the Bomber launched into the history of the place and how one careless camper had fallen—or been pushed by "unseen hands"—through a trapdoor and broken his leg.

"Is there really a ghost?" Leo asked.

"Darn tootin'," said the Bomber fervently.

"You betcher boots," Monkey agreed.

"Me, I *seen* it!" Peewee declared.

The Bomber made a scoffing sound. "Aw, you did not, you little spud. Shut your hole before I sit on you and squash you flat."

"Did too! Did too!" Peewee persisted. "A great big hairy monster with pop eyes and horns and tusks like a elephant. Honest I did, honest!"

As always, nobody heeded the boy's clamor, with the exception of Leo, who listened attentively to the farfetched description of the ghost, darting glances from one Jeremian to the next, as if trying to put names and faces together. "I believe you," he said finally when Peewee's protestations died down.

Outside, it was turning to twilight; soon the torchlight parade would begin. The boys lit the lantern, then went about getting their equipment together for the council fire—sweaters, torches, flashlights, and little chamois bags that each camper hung around his neck on a rawhide thong.

"What are those?" Leo asked.

"Seneca medicine bags," said Tiger, and went on to explain about the Seneca Honor Society and how, at tonight's council fire, each new inductee would be presented with a red feather and a medicine bag, marking him as a "brave-to-be," and then escorted to the Wolf's Cave in Indian Woods to be formally initiated. All the regular Jeremians were already Senecas. When Leo asked what the medicine bags contained, however, he got short shrift from Phil for an answer: The contents of the bags was secret, only a Seneca brave could know.

Leo shrugged and studied the dusty toes of his shoes, then looked up suddenly. "Want to see a trick?" he asked Peewee.

Peewee gave him a suspicious look. "What kinda trick?" he asked warily.

"Like this. Watch closely."

Peewee observed with wonder as Leo's ears began performing weird and amazing feats, wiggling and wagging up and down. In a moment the younger boy was giggling at the comical sight, then laughing, and his childish crowing was soon joined by the deeper laughter of the others.

"Now play something!" Peewee shouted, shoving the violin case at Leo. "Go on, play!"

Leo shook his head, his expression clearly stating he had no wish to go on entertaining them.

"Yeah, play somethin'," urged the Bomber; then they were all yelling for him, pressing and cajoling until he had no choice. With a glance toward Tiger, who'd said hardly anything since they'd come in, Leo unsnapped the catches and laid back the top of the case. With the fingernails of one hand he plucked a tiny flurry of notes from the instrument. They were all waiting. He picked up the violin and began tuning it, making rapid, professional forays on the strings until he seemed satisfied, then tucked it under his chin and began to play. Seated on the edge of Reece's footlocker, his thin arm bent, the hand and fingers curled upon the butt of the horsehair bow, he played with a faint smile on his mouth, his eyes now flashing, now remote, his head moving with a rhythmic grace all its own as he drew forth a soft, intense melody that held his listeners in thrall.

But the roof of Jeremiah could not contain the sound of his music, nor the walls—how was this possible with all four flaps open to the evening?—and before long, all up and down the linepath they gathered, campers and counselors, on the porches of Hosea and Isaiah and Obadiah and Ezekiel, and of all the cabins of Virtue and High Endeavor, to listen as the music floated out from Jeremiah.

Zipper Tallon heard it in the Dewdrop Inn and, buttoning up, was lured across the field by its sound. Henry Ives, his duties completed, stopped and listened. In Hosea, Gus Klaus put away his *Studs Lonigan* excerpts to lend an ear, finally abandoning his bunk altogether to take a gander at the music maker in Jeremiah. Ezekielites Dusty Rhoades, Emerson Bean, and Junior Leffingwell did likewise, while over in Three Corner Cove, in the gathering twilight, Honey Oliphant, giving herself a beer shampoo, heard it and wondered.

Then the music became louder and merrier as the fiddler changed his tune. Jumping onto the footlocker, he began playing an antic ditty, and as he played, beating out the time with his foot, he sang the words:

> I push the first valve down.
> The music goes down and around,
> Whoa—ho—ho—ho—ho—ho,
> And it comes up here.

Fiddling, all angles and long fingers, with a bright gleam in his eye, he seemed to Tiger like some mad musician at a crossroads fair in a storybook, whose spellbinding music would so enchant the village folk that they must jump up and leap about until they dropped of exhaustion. And, indeed, as the song gained momentum all the campers crowded into Jeremiah were suddenly on their feet, knocking one another about, leaping from bunk to bunk as they sang, faces red and perspiring in the lamplight, the excitement building to a fever pitch with pillows flying through the air and Eddie, who could walk on his hands, proving it.

Then to the scent of pine and citronella that pervaded the cabin was added another odor: the sweet, sickish pungency of tobacco smoke—Rum and Maple, though in the wild confusion no one noticed until the Bomber, dizzy, spun backward toward the porch and collided with Reece Hartsig.

Everything stopped at once, the music, the laughter, the movement, all stopped and every head turned to face the tall figure in the doorway, nattily attired in his military school uniform, the shiny visor of his cap casting a dark lunette across his eyes.

"What's going on here?" demanded the soft, emphatic voice.

Pandemonium. The visitors to Jeremiah scattered out the back, out the sides of the cabin, seven of the occupants retreated in considerable alarm and confusion to their bunks, while the violinist, still on the footlocker, lowered his instrument slowly, then stepped down and crossed to his bunk. Only Peewee made no move, but stood in the middle of Reece's rumpled cot, turned to stone.

Either failing to notice or choosing to ignore the newcomer's presence in the cabin, the counselor directed stern attention to the quivering Peewee. Making fists of his hands, Reece jammed them on his hips, widening an already broad set of shoulders.

"Get . . . off . . . my . . . bed," he commanded, still speaking softly. Peewee seemed to shrink visibly before getting down, presenting a sheepish and pathetic figure by anybody's standard.

"All right, Kemo Sabe," Reece said, now snapping out the words, "suppose you tell me what you think you're up to."

"I wasn't doin' nuthin', Big Chief, honest," came the plaintive response.

"The cap. Take it off."

Peewee did so.

"Now put it back where you got it from."

Again the boy obeyed.

"Now the jock." Again Peewee did as ordered.

"Now come here." Digging into his uniform pocket, Reece produced a shiny quarter and handed it to the boy. Peewee, who had no idea why he should be so rewarded, merely blinked.

"Toss it on the bed." Reece indicated his cot.

Peewee again did as he was told; the coin dropped softly amid the slackened bedclothes.

"Fix it, spud. Stretch it till that quarter bounces."

The Jeremians watched while Peewee hustled around the corners of the bed, jumping over the footlocker as he tugged and pulled the blanket so the quarter bounced. When this was seen to, Reece reached out with a long arm, turned the offender over his knee and gave him a sound whack on his bottom.

"Get the idea?" he said, setting Peewee upright.

"What idea?" the boy asked in an outraged tone, his eyes sparkling with telltale tears.

"No more jumping on the counselor's cot. You don't belong here anyway. Get back up the line where you do belong." He marched Peewee to the door. "Okay?" he said, holding out the quarter.

Peewee ignored the peace offering and sprang out onto the linepath. When he had put sufficient distance between himself and his tormentor he pulled up short and from the depths of his wounded pride shouted defiantly, "I'm gonna tell my sister! I'm gonna tell Honey you got a lousy letter from Nancy Rider and it stinks of perfume and it's got a big fat lipstick mark on the back!"

He ran away among the trees. No one laughed. Turning back into the cabin Reece noted the envelope on his pillow. He picked it up and was about to pull the flap when his eye came to rest on the new boy. He slipped the letter under the pillow for later, then, straightening, said, "And who might this be?"

Leo opened his mouth to say something, but no words came out, and he swallowed with a noisy gulp.

Tiger was quick with the explanation that this was Stanley Wagner's replacement. Reece said nothing at first, merely looked the new arrival up and down with a bland expression. He removed his cap and tucked it away on his shelf, then glanced in the mirror, running his palms over his hair, which gleamed with blond highlights. Satisfied, he turned back to the new boy, withholding his greeting for a moment longer. Leo gulped again, his face turned red, and he dropped his look to the floor, still unable to think of anything to say.

"How is it he's here tonight instead of tomorrow?" Though Reece looked at Phil for an explanation, again it was Tiger who replied, mentioning bus schedules and giving the new boy's name. A faint frown appeared between Reece's sun-whitened brows.

"Wackeem," he repeated, thoughtfully, while Leo stared wordlessly back at him. No one presumed to speak; the moment drew out. Finally, Reece broke the spell, by putting out his hand; when Leo took it he felt his own engulfed.

"Welcome to Jeremiah, camper," said the counselor crisply, and gave Leo a curt nod.

This salutation ventured, Reece engaged in a series of neatly executed moves, changing out of his uniform to his regular camp outfit. Wary and silent, unsure of what might happen next, the boys all watched as the ritual was performed. "You weren't due till tomorrow," Reece commented as he stripped off his neatly pressed shirt and shrugged on a sweatshirt. "We're not ready for you."

It was getting chilly, and Leo felt himself start to shiver. He glanced around, saw the Bomber's confident grin, Dump's owlish look, and Tiger—what was Tiger thinking?

"I guess he's going to have to bunk in Stanley's pee tonight," Reece remarked to Phil. "You'd better get Hank over after church tomorrow with some new canvas." Then, noting Leo's shivers, he added, "You'll need a sweater. Have you got one?"

"Yes."

"Put it on, then. I don't want any of my boys catching cold." He half turned away, then turned back as Leo pulled on a moth-eaten wool sweater and replaced the cap on his head. "Are those the duds they sent you off with?"

Leo colored and stared at the floor again.

"Yes," he replied.

"They don't look very camperlike to me. If you're to be a Jeremian, we'll have to get you outfitted properly. Phil, all of you, see what you can dig up. And for gosh sakes find him some sneakers. Those shoes . . ."

Avoiding further comment, he completed his transformation from military man to camp counselor. Accoutred now with Friend-Indeed insignia and a host of impressive-looking merit badges, he made a splendid sight. He favored the faded khaki shorts that were the traditional Moonbow uniform, each leg meticulously rolled in a double turn on the thighs. Instead of the beat-up sneakers commonly worn around camp, however, his feet were shod in well saddle-soaped moccasins and immaculate white-ribbed wool socks, turned down precisely one turn over the ankles. On his finger he wore a ring carved from a soup bone, and on one wrist a gold watch gleamed. The other wrist sported an elaborate braided band of leather, and at his neck, over a colorful bandana kerchief, was a dark thong of weathered rawhide from which hung a small heart carved of cedar, varnished and polished to a high gloss. He was like an illustration out of *American Boy.*

After combing his hair and checking the part from two different angles, he added his personal Seneca medicine bag to his outfit, then used the mirror again; when at last he looked around, his eye fell on Leo's violin case.

He stared at it for a few moments, as if asking himself a question. "You play that thing a lot?" he asked finally.

"No. Just sometimes."

Reece's expression offered no hint of what thoughts he entertained.

"Didn't ya hear him, Big Chief?" The Bomber was enthusiastic. "He's a regular Pagliacci."

"Try Paganini, Jerome," Reece said. He swung his look back to Leo. "Just so long as you don't play it again in here. We don't want a guy sawing away on a squawk-box when campers have important matters to concentrate on—like winning the Rolfe Hartsig Memorial Trophy. Right guys?"

Right, they chorused.

"I see you brought your own pillow," Reece went on.

"Yes."

"He calls it Albert." This from Phil.

Reece's eyebrows shifted fractionally. "He has a pillow named . . . Albert?" He frowned. "And the hat? Does it have a name, too?"

"No. It's just a cap."

"My boys generally say No, *sir.*"

"No, sir."

"And try standing straight. Jeremians don't slouch like that."

Leo did as he was told.

Reece nodded satisfaction. "As for the chapeau, maybe you can lose it for the council fire. We don't want to give Ezekiel cause for jealousy." This sally got its anticipated laugh.

With no more words, Reece sauntered out onto the porch, where he consulted with his two lieutenants, Phil and Tiger. Leo heard his name being spoken, then Phil said the word "orphan" and Tiger once more put forth an explanation; Ma Starbuck was mentioned, then something about a letter from the orphanage, then Phil said something Leo missed.

"What's that?" Reece said, his deep voice skating upward in surprise. *"He doesn't like baseball?"*

The rims of Leo's ears burned; in another moment the porch conference broke up. Reece issued a couple of reminders about proper deportment at the campfire and keeping the noise down after taps; then, saying he'd see everybody later, he loped off toward the Nature Lodge.

Leo was left wondering. "Isn't he coming with us?" he asked, as the boys shuffled outside to greet Hank Ives, ambling down the linepath with his can of kerosene for their torches.

"Reece? Don't worry, you'll see him," Tiger assured Leo, escorting him onto the porch. By now full dusk had crept across the playing field; up and down the linepath, campers were waiting for the runners to arrive with the Flame of Friendship.

"Okay, fellows," Phil said, "it's time. Let's hop to it. Wacko, duck the hat," he added, going down the steps.

Leo lobbed the cap back over his shoulder; it landed squarely on his bunk, where it rolled and came to rest beside "Albert." Tiger supposed he had never heard the superstition about hats on beds being bad luck.

4

t began like the Attic games of ancient Greece, with a single flame. At eight-thirty sharp at the head of the linepath by the mailbox rack, in the manner dictated by custom, Pa Starbuck ignited the Great Torch, and from this four-footer in turn ignited the torches of the three honorary runners, one from each unit, who passed their torches over Pa's fire, then struck out Prometheus-like, moving from cabin to cabin, presenting their flames to light the torch of each counselor, who in turn lit those of his campers, roundly 120 of them, and when the last torch had received its kiss of fire the campers, bearing aloft the dipping wavering quivering lights, slipped from their porches and began wending their way toward the council ring, the Virtue campers falling in behind the Harmonyites, they behind the older boys of High Endeavor, all linking up in single file with the solemn, ceremonial air of a procession of monks belonging to some devout sacerdotal order, the irregular line of flickering flames growing longer still, a bobbing stream of lights snaking in and out among the trees, to spread out across the semicircular tiers of the council ring, back and forth along the rows, until each camper stood in his allotted place.

Here they waited until Pa Starbuck appeared beside the Tabernacle Rock, which bore a handsomely wrought teepee of twigs and branches. This pyramid Pa ignited with his torch, then, his ruddy features painted by the orange light, his blue eyes under white shaggy brows sparkling with eager anticipation, he offered in mellifluous tones the invocation to the Friendship Fire, enjoining "his boys" to loyalty and devotion everlasting, reflecting earnestly on the true meaning of good fellowship, lauding the rewarding principles of Camp Friend-Indeed, and offering thanks unto the Joshua Society, whose generosity had made it all possible.

As decreed by Moonbow tradition, and having extinguished and laid aside their torches, the campers now forged among their ranks a chain of hands in token of their truest feelings, of the good fellowship to be found in a host of such evenings by the lake, and of those qualities that, properly instilled, shall create "Glad Men from Happy Boys." The air was pungent with wood smoke and snapping sparks that eddied upward into darkness like whirlwinds of fiery dust, gusting beyond the fir boughs to the stars, whose bright gleamings tried to make up for the lack of a moon, the pale ghost of which had faded long before sunset. And in unison their voices rose up as well, lifted in the familiar camp anthem (music based on an Old Welsh air; words by G. Garland Starbuck):

> Camping in the pines of Moonbow,
> Down by the lake,
> Here our loving hearts are off'r'd,
> Our gift we take.

When the anthem was ended, everyone sat, the campers on the logs, Pa in a rustic, thronelike chair constructed from the anatomical parts of trees—limbs, crotches, elbows, and knees; then, making himself comfortable as he was accustomed to doing, he presented Coach Holliday, who, as Pa's second-in-command, acted as master of ceremonies at all council fires, and who now offered the assemblage a preview of the many pleasures that lay ahead for Moonbow campers.

Tucked away to the side among the nest of Jeremians, Leo sat enthralled as the coach rose to spill out a cornucopia of exciting events like so many gold coins from a troll's pot, a kaleidoscope of Fun Nights and Movie Nights, a Watermelon Crush, a Major Bowes Amateur Night, a Friendship Lottery, a Water Carnival, and the "piece of least resistance"—Hap chortled at his own joke—this year only, the awarding of the Hartsig Trophy, celebrating a full twenty-five years of camping in the Moonbow wildwood, to that cabin whose campers earned the highest number of happy points (after demerits

41

were deducted), and thus exemplified in highest degree the qualities of Good Christian Campers. There was more: as an added incentive, next spring the winners of the cup would attend an All-State Civic Jamboree at the New York World's Fair, all expenses paid by Rolfe Hartsig and the German-American Bund.

At this welcome news three cheers were given for Big Rolfe Hartsig, the benefactor of Friend-Indeed. But what, Leo wondered, glancing around again, had become of the benefactor's son, who was nowhere to be seen? Hadn't Tiger said that the Jeremiah counselor would be at the council fire? What was keeping him? Leo had no time to dwell on such mysteries, however, because of what the coach next had to say: as of the end of the first two-week period not Jeremiah (the favorite) but Malachi, in the High Endeavor unit, was the front-runner in the trophy competition—all owing to the hapless Stanley Wagner, whose name Phil Dodge now muttered *sotto voce,* with accompanying descriptive epithets.

Next up were the other members of Pa's staff: Rex Kenniston, water-front director, to announce the trial heats for the swimming competition in the Annual Water Carnival; Oats Gurley, nature director and overseer of the dining hall, to solicit contributions to *The Pine Cone,* the camp newspaper, of which he was the editor; and Fritz Auerbach, the new crafts supervisor, a wiry, dark-haired, intense-looking young man, who rose to offer some general remarks about how much he had enjoyed his first two weeks at Moonbow Lake; a refugee from the Nazis, who in March had overrun his homeland, Austria, Fritz was grateful for the place he had found among the Friend-Indeeders. His warmly expressed feelings brought an enthusiastic round of applause, which lasted until, from far off, there came the melodious sounds of singing, signaling that something special was about to occur. All eyes were on the lake, even Pa's, as out of the darkness they glided, the Singing Canoes, a flotilla of craft, each bearing a paddler and members of the camp glee club, the leaping flames of torches lighting up the darkness as they glided shoreward, the singers' voices floating across the water. Applause swept the ring as the boys on land clapped for the singers, and for another Moonbow tradition, a blend of sound and sentiment, drama and glamour, that never failed to produce a sense of awe among the campers, and an awareness, no matter how dim, of belonging to a greater whole. Leo thought he'd never heard or seen anything so beautiful.

When the canoes were beached and the singers had joined their fellows in the council ring, the usual sing-along followed, starting with the camp pledge (as sung to "Maryland, My Maryland"):

> O Friend-Indeed,
> My Friend-Indeed,
> When I am
> A Friend-in-need . . .

As they sang, Leo—utterly unfamiliar with the words of the songs, yet gamely joining in—had intimations of a powerful bond being forged between him and the other campers, a warming comradeship that said he too was part of it all. From what did it spring, this sudden sense of belonging? From feeling the pressure of Tiger's knee signifying the importance of a moment here or there? Or the mute, mirthful heave of the Bomber's girth? From the fire's friendly glow, the fresh, outdoorsy fragrance of the pines? Leo couldn't tell. All he knew was that the good fellowship that suffused the gathering, knitting it together in mood and purpose, was enveloping him as well, filling him with eagerness and resolution.

The sing-along finally ended and then, with his audience settled back, waiting for what was to come next, Pa began speaking (as he could always be relied on to do) about his old friend William F. Cody, otherwise known as Buffalo Bill, and about how, when Pa was a young man and working for the Friends of Joshua, he had had occasion to meet the famed Indian scout and showman, and to receive from his own hands the revered Buffalo Bill War Bonnet.

Pa's remarks were but the prelude to what was now to come. He paused, a moment stretching into several. Atop the slab-sided rock the crackling of the fire grew louder, and Leo felt a tingling of anticipation. Then, without warning, there was an explosion of colors, a whirling shower of sparks, and through a sudden, further blossoming of smoke a tall, dark, savage-looking figure appeared, his sharply chiseled features painted in vivid streaks of red, green, yellow, and white—the Moonbow Warrior! What magnificence! There he stood before the gathering, looking for all the world like a real Indian, with his chamois breechclout, a breastplate of bones and beads, hammered bracelets ornamenting his biceps, and beaded moccasins on his feet. More impressive than anything was the splendid headdress he wore, the Buffalo Bill War Bonnet Pa had just spoken of, with its glorious fan of multicolored feathers, its pendant train behind, and the gewgaws that hung down either side of the Warrior's face.

For a moment longer, he remained immobile, then, folding his arms across his chest and stretching his neck muscles, he surveyed the semicircle of campers, his eyes glinting as they searched out those who had been chosen for induction into the Seneca Lodge. When he had spotted each of them, he gestured, and from the shadows beyond Tabernacle Rock a tom-tom started beating out a slow, syncopated rhythm. The Warrior dropped into a crouch and began a sinuous, prowling dance around the fire: heel-toe-heel-toe, stamping the toe, then snapping the heel down smartly, heel-toe-heel-toe, moving back and forth behind the campfire and chanting as he moved.

> Ah wah ta na hay
> Ah wah ta no ho
> Ho *tah!* Ho tah *ha!*
> Na wah ha na toe!

When he had made several circles around the fire, he proceeded along the first row of campers, bending to peer closely into each face. In one hand he held a cluster of red feathers, in the other empty medicine bags, like the ones the Jeremians wore. Pausing before a camper, he bestowed one each of these items on him, to warm applause from everyone; then, winding up among the tiers, he graced another boy and another. As he drew nearer to the Jeremians, his painted features sharply etched by the vermilion light, Leo became aware of the overpowering presence of the half-naked figure, and he strained forward as the same tokens were offered to a fourth camper two rows ahead of them.

"Attaboy, Bosey," someone whispered.

Pivoting on his moccasin-shod feet, the Indian straightened for a moment, tensing his muscles, then crouched again and moved to the end of the next row, where the boys of Cabin 7 sat. But every Jeremian had already become a Seneca, so there would be no feathers or bags handed out to them, and yet—Leo saw how the Indian was moving along the row, passing the Jeremians one after the other, coming toward the new boy. Suddenly Leo felt a surge of excitement. Was such a thing possible, a new camper being made a Seneca, achieving Brave status on his first night at camp? The

44

crouching figure came nearer. Nearer he came; nearer, until he stood poised directly in front of Leo. Suddenly the features disguised by the dark makeup made sense to Leo, and he realized that under the war paint the Warrior was Reece Hartsig!

He wanted to lower his eyes, but found he could not. Hardly daring to return Reece's penetrating look, he waited—hoping—not daring to hope— the moment stretching out until, like a rubber band, it snapped and he blinked. And as the Indian passed on, Leo was filled with an incomprehensible sense of wrongdoing, as if his capricious thoughts might have been read. He sat glued to his log as the Warrior retreated down the aisle and at the foot of the ring, having presented the last feather and medicine bag to another camper, stood erect, and, in a few panther strides, emerged into the light again. Bringing his feet together and taking a deep breath that expanded his chest, he raised his two brown arms in a majestic salute, then lowered them as he bowed before Pa Starbuck. A single step backward, out of the circle of firelight, and as magically as he had appeared he disappeared again, swallowed up in the velvety dark.

No sooner was he gone than, at a nod from Pa, the inductees rose and were ushered from the ring, to be instructed by the Moonbow Warrior in what was to come later, when all the members of the Seneca Lodge would gather for the secret campfire at the Wolf's Cave. Applause followed their exit, and when the clapping had died away a silence gradually fell along the tiers. From his chair beside Tabernacle Rock, Pa Starbuck coughed and hemmed a bit, then suggested that everyone have a stretch before the rest of the program began.

After this general stirring about, they all sat again, gradually settling themselves into a renewed state of anticipation as the moment approached—the telling of the tale that by tradition crowned each council fire. Fresh logs were chucked onto the burning ones, sending sparks popping like Chinese firecrackers into the blackness, and the flames cast their amber glow along the sets of tanned legs picketing the front row, where rested pair upon pair of rubber-soled U.S. Keds, lined up as on the shelf of some outsized shoestore.

☽

Now is the time. The moment all the boys have been waiting for, time for the ancient tale, that mixture of old-time native lore and birchbark legend that is the warp and woof of the camp, woven from stories far older than anyone present. Such moments as these are what make Camp Friend-Indeed the place it is. The spirit of Moonbow Lake lies among the words the boys know they will soon hear, words that newcomers like Leo Joaquim have been told to pay attention to. A born teller of such tales, Pa addresses his listeners with adroit turns of phrase, conjuring the Moonbow Princess who once lived in this same place, here within this very grove of pines, and the Moonbow Warrior, her secret lover, whose lodge stood on the opposite shore, among her foes—their rival tribes for decades warring with each other over some long-forgotten quarrel.

"Alone and lorn of love," Pa says, "the maiden waits, while deep night draws on apace, and the old Star Maker takes out his tools to cut the shape and pattern of the stars, which he pins onto the dark cloak of night. He cuts the moon as well, full and round and silvery, to shed its light over all, while still the beauteous princess waits for her warrior to come to her, across the shining water, secretly so no one will know. On her soft cheek a tear glistens, bright as the Pole Star itself, for she is resolved to rebel against the tribe and all her people, to be united in love with the man that Sagittai, the Ancient Seer, has foretold shall be hers. . . ."

All along the rows the boys harken, some leaning forward, some back, some gazing up at the star-strewn sky, some staring into the fire, all hanging on Pa's every word. How they relish the telling; how silky and intricate the design as the threads of the familiar story are drawn out: whimsy and enchantment, shot through with moonlight; for to have the moonbow without a moon is impossible.

Pa goes on: "Alas," he declares, "the princess waits in vain, for her warrior is by fate forestalled—each time he embarks, a fearful tempest, the work of Misswiss, the Evildoer, arises and forces him to return to shore. He cannot succeed until the fateful Night of the Moonbow, when, the seer proclaims, a bridge of moonlight will be magically created for him to cross upon."

Aahh, the boys murmur, the moonbow, and Leo strains forward to catch each word.

Many nights pass, and days, and the moon wanes and waxes again, and still the moonbow does not appear. The princess weeps, the warrior chafes. Then, one night when the moon is full, the impatient maiden commandeers a canoe and paddles toward the opposite shore where her lover waits; but before she can reach it, her flight is discovered. She is overtaken and for her treachery is condemned to death; nothing, no one, can help her now, her fate is sealed.

"There the doomed princess lies," Pa goes on with a lift to his voice, "there, upon the giant rock—this same rock where our council fire burns tonight. Misswiss holds aloft his knife. The sharp blade glints in the moonlight; see how he clutches it, ready to plunge it into her heart. Ah, hear her piteous moans—but who shall hear her pleas, who shall succor her?"

A ripple of sound traverses the rows, for the boys know that this is the best part of the story. By now Pa has risen to his full powers of description, and tonight's moonless night seems moonless no longer, but clear and bright as can be, a night transfigured, filled with the wonder and magic of the tale.

Now, see it, boys, picture it in your minds: As the vengeful braves look on, silent and breathless, and Misswiss stays his hand yet a moment longer, little by little the miracle takes place. Yes! Look there, up in the sky! Forming itself from the tiniest, most infinitesimal particles of incandescence, attracting one another as though magnetized, gathering more and more substance, only faintly visible at first, a trembling shape of something not quite real, then, growing brighter and fuller, a filmy skein, and now, taking clearer shape, it becomes a visible band—yes, see it, boys, see it—a horizontal band that, ever so slowly, begins to bend at either end, to arch above the lake that mirrors it, its gleaming terminals linking one shore with the other, until, at last, behold the completed wonder, a luminous bow, a glorious rainbow of the night!

And so, taking heart as he prepares to meet his beloved, the Moonbow Warrior makes haste to cross the bridge of light—only to meet horror on the farther shore. Taken prisoner, bound with thongs to a sapling tree, he must witness the execution of his beloved. Again Misswiss raises his knife and prepares to strike; the warrior cries out as the mortal blow is struck, and while the blood gushes from the maiden's heart, red as poppies, he bursts his bonds and throws himself upon her lifeless corpse. Seizing the knife that has killed her, he rises up and faces his foes, lunging toward them, desperate, until finally he falls, mortally wounded, upon the breast of the murdered princess.

Pa pauses, milking every last drop of juice the drama holds. A single pin could be heard if it fell among the pine needles. Then, once more, he goes on, telling how the Old Chief, father of the fallen warrior, vowing vengeance, rouses his braves to man the canoes, commands them to sally forth and destroy the murderers of his only son, to smite them, Pa says, even as Samson smote the Philistines. But wait! A vision has appeared before him. It is the spirits of the two lovers, united in death, who now with tender words and looks entreat the chief to be merciful, to turn the cheek that has suffered the blow, to find it in his heart to return evil with good, vengeance with forgiveness, and in so doing shatter forever the cruel chains of hate that have for so long shackled the rival tribes.

And so there comes a happy ending, of sorts. Instead of seeking retribution, the Old Chief paddles the moonlit path across the glittering waters to the camp of his enemy, there to smoke the pipe of peace and exchange ceremonial gifts. Thus, the two tribes bury the tomahawk in the earth and pledge to live together in that same spirit of friendship and amity exemplified by Camp Friend-Indeed and all its boys.

The story draws to its end; Pa Starbuck sits back to reap the harvest of thought his words have planted. By custom, no applause ever follows the telling of the tale; in silent accord the boys rise from their places and by the beams of their flashlights leave the council ring, some to make their way to the Seneca honor ceremony in Indian Woods, the remainder to return silently to their respective cabins.

There is one camper, however, who does not leave, but remains seated upon the log, lost in some private reverie. Tiger, who has started off, returns, and is shocked by the sight of the stricken new boy, who sits huddled and shivering, his brow furrowed, his mouth agape, staring at the rock at the foot of the Methuselah Tree, as if the bloody death of the Moonbow Princess were still being enacted before him. He clasps and unclasps his hands, pressing them between his bare knees. It is a painful sight, and troubling to Tiger. With a comforting word, he brings Leo to his feet and leads him from the ring in the beam of his flashlight, and up through the pine grove toward the cabin called Jeremiah. But Leo, mortified by his behavior, refuses to go inside, where he will be left alone.

Tiger sits him down on the porch step, where they talk together. Whatever feelings had upset Leo seem to be forgotten; he offers no clue as to their source. He is knowledgeable about star-gazing and points out some constellations in the glittering sky—Cassiopeia's Chair, Ursa Major, the North Star. Soon he begins to yawn. It has been a long day. Tiger sees him into his bunk and settles him down for the night. When Leo closes his eyes, Tiger slips away to join the Senecas at the Wolf's Cave in the heart of Indian Woods.

Later.

Taps has sounded. The night breeze hums among the pine needles; overhead the stars pale and wink out one by one; among the sentinel trees the camp slumbers, as if the invisible hand of Morpheus had passed across lake and cabins, sprinkling moon dust, urging happy dreams. Yet there is one whose repose does not go untroubled, who shifts restlessly under his blanket, whose lips move, articulating distressful but unintelligible sounds. And while he mutters aloud against his pallid phantoms, beyond the cabin sides a tiny murder is enacted: high in the Methuselah Tree, the owl inquires of the night—"Whoo? Who?"—then sails from his branch like a gray whisper. On silent pinions he floats downward among the dark pine boughs, soft as shadows, soundless as falling snow, talons splayed, topaz eyes round as saucers, wizard-wise, seeking his prey, and with feathered finesse plucks from a patch of spear grass one hapless form whose feeble squeak of protest is choked off in midair as, soaring once more, the bird reaches his treetop and gives himself up to his midnight feast.

The new boy awakens with a cry.

PART TWO

The Forest Primeval

1

roud son of a clever man, Icarus had watched his father, Daedalus, make for them both pairs of wings from feathers, wood, wax, and at his father's side he had mounted the air upon those makeshift wings, flinging himself into space from the highest promontory, to soar upward and scale the banks of romping clouds, to look from on high upon the earth made small—its rivers and hills, towns and cities, its populace of insect-folk. What jubilation, what wonder, what glorious pride he felt, free as a bird, faring forth as no man before him had ever done. Icarus the darer, Icarus the bold. And yet, he must beware, for with flight comes error; a single miscalculation and the force of gravity takes over, and disaster, death.

Balanced at the edge of the large rock, Leo feels himself unfettered, free to spread his wings and fly, to flash across the sun's broad shining face. Slowly he raises his arms, extending them outward from his sides like wings; marvel of marvels, they start to quiver, lift lightly, gently, upward, palms cupped as though to touch the supportive, not-quite-touchable element of air. Oh yes—let him try. Now. With a deep breath he launches himself into space. Ah—yes—like this, like this. He is the bird-god, feather-winged, hawk-eyed, sharp-taloned monarch of the air. He soars, leveling out across the vast blue-white garden of clouds, his heart bursting with rapture.

Too late he remembers: Even gods may not fly too high; too close to the sun their wings may be singed, the wax melt, the feathers loosen, upsetting the delicate aerodynamic balance. He will be dashed to pieces for his folly. Below him the starless void, spiral of darkness, never-ending night. And he is falling, down and down and down and—!

"Leo!"

Appearing as if by magic, Tiger Abernathy came dashing across the meadow to give him a hand up. "Did you hurt yourself?"

Leo wasn't sure; he felt gingerly of an ankle, an elbow, his neck. "I— slipped." He laughed sheepishly. What must Tiger think of such crazy behavior? For the life of him he couldn't remember how he had got to the top of the rock, or how he had slipped from it. He pressed a fist over his heart to calm its wild beat, while Harpo, who had come bounding along behind Tiger, wagged his shaggy tail to a fare-thee-well and with a wet pink tongue passionately washed Leo's face.

"Harpo! Hey, boy—hey, boy!" He wrestled the dog and hugged him to his chest. "Good dog, good dog!"

Tiger flopped down beside Leo and regarded him quizzically. "What were you doing, flapping your arms like that?"

Leo reddened. "I wanted to fly." He said it like "I wanted some rice pudding; a new union suit." How foolish it sounded, put into words. Yet, something told him it was okay, he could express such ideas to Tiger. Flights of fancy served Tiger's mind, too.

"How did you find me?" Leo asked. "Did Harpo sniff me out?"

"This is where you usually are mornings," Tiger explained, adding that he himself was on his way to Orcutt's store at Four Corners; Harpo had trailed along. "Great spot, isn't it?" he added, looking around.

Leo agreed; Kelsoe's Pond was indeed a fine spot. That Tiger also considered it such gave him considerable satisfaction. He had discovered the place several days ago, while on a spider hunt. Spurred on by Oats Gurley, who had promised to put Leo's accumulated arachnids on permanent display in the Nature Lodge (and to award him and Jeremiah a generous number of happy points for every new addition), he had visited here several mornings since, slipping away on a solitary "nature walk," his violin and music case in tow, along with a couple of empty codfish boxes in his canvas knapsack (a loan from Tiger), while the majority of the campers were hard at work in the crafts barn, banging away at copper ashtrays to take home to their Uncle Louies.

"What d'you think of my latest prize?" he asked tentatively, gesturing toward his most recent find, a black-and-gold specimen whose web glittered in the sun like a diamond necklace suspended between twin stalks of milkweed, gossamer filaments spun out of the abdominal workings of a creature the size of a quarter. For the past half-hour the spider had been industriously engaged in this miraculous act of manufacture, tossing out the silken threads to create the delicate design characteristic of her species.

Tiger conceded that the spider was worth Leo's time and patience, and Leo lay back, fingers laced behind his ears, well pleased. Though Tiger did not share his fascination for spiders—indeed, he had shown a decided aversion to them—this morning, sprawling companionably beside Leo on the turf, he, too, watched closely to see what wonders the little creature would perform next.

A moment more, and her preliminary work was done; she scurried to the upper quadrant of the newly fashioned web, where, camouflaged by the flickering light and shade, she sat waiting for her prey. Before long an errant, pale-winged bug came flitting by, a poor, innocent bug up to no bad, but not a careful bug at all. It bumped into the web head-on, and in a flash the spider abandoned her corner, scrambling down the ladder of her web to pounce on the trapped insect. In his notebook, Leo detailed what happened next: the quick injection of paralyzing fluids, the last flutter of hapless wings, the wrapping of the victim in more filament until it resembled a miniature mummy. At last the spider dragged her dinner to the heart of the web, where she deposited it for safekeeping; then, having resumed her corner, she settled down again to wait.

Having rounded out his notes with a quick sketch of the spider's web, Leo capped his pen and lay back, reaching his hands over his head and stretching his body like a cat. He really was tall for his age, Tiger thought, secretly envying him his height; he wished his own arms and legs were longer; his physical size, or its lack, had always been to him a disadvantage, and something told him he'd never see six feet, never be tall like Reece Hartsig. But then, as his dad always said, Napoleon had been forced to deal with the same problem, and look how far he got. You just couldn't give up on things. "Never Say Die," that was Tiger's motto. He had got it from the famous Count Von Luckner, the crafty German naval officer whose ship, the *Sea Devil,* had wreaked havoc with Allied shipping during the war. When the Count came to Pequot Landing to lecture, Tiger had even got an autograph on a picture of the famous vessel: "Never Say Die, Tiger Aberna-thy." Tiger was determined he would not.

"I kept a diary once," he remarked.

This revelation interested Leo. "Why did you quit?" he asked.

Tiger chuckled. "I was doing so many things every day I never could find the time to write them all down."

Leo could see how this might be so: a fellow like Tiger Abernathy was always busy, with a dozen irons in the fire. Was there anything he wasn't interested in? A patrol leader in the Boy Scouts, he was also active in Christian Youth Fellowship and the Junior Grange and the Civic Guard. He had, moreover, a number of time-consuming interests and hobbies—stamp-collecting, model-airplane- and boat-building—while the complicated layout of his electric train set was known to fill half the attic. All in all, he was a real powerhouse, with his bright, quick, lighting-up smile, and the gleeful laugh that he made such generous use of. What he lacked in physical size he made up for in character, and compared with him, all the boys Leo had known at the orphanage—even his pal Arnie Kretchmer ("Kretch the Wretch")—seemed commonplace and lackluster.

Leo congratulated himself on his good fortune. On that first evening in camp he hadn't been at all sure how he would fare at Tiger's hands. Tiger had been helpful enough, but he'd said so little, seemingly weighing "the new boy" in his mind, pondering whether they would be friends or not. And now they *were* friends, sort of. Leo felt it was so. Sometimes when he came here to the pond, Tiger would show up—like this morning. Leo frequently asked himself why the most popular boy in camp would bother with the likes of him, an orphan from Pitt Institute. Maybe he just felt sorry for him (Tiger was the kind of guy who always stuck up for the underdog); still, to be singled out for his attention was deeply gratifying, and in the end Leo decided it was probably his music that had won Tiger over (he *had* laughed a lot at Leo's rendition of "The Music Goes 'Round and Around").

Now, grinning his crooked, saw-toothed grin, Tiger said, "So tell me. How come you were trying to fly?"

Leo's response was simple. "It's the thing I want most in the world—except for two other things."

"Like what?"

"First, to own a dog."

"Yeah? What kind?"

"Name it."

"Didn't you ever have one?"

"Sure. Once." Leo blew out his cheeks; his eyelids fluttered and closed.

"What happened to him?"

"Got killed."

"How?"

"Curiosity."

Tiger thought that was the cat, but before he could comment Leo went on.

"Actually he got run over by a truck."

"Gee, that's tough. Hit and run?"

"No. It was my f-father's truck."

"Gee, I bet he felt bad."

"Not so's you'd notice. If you asked me, I'd say he enjoyed it."

"What?"

"You had to know him. He never liked Butch. He didn't like him in the house. Butch knew . . ."

"Knew what?"

"Butch knew Rudy. That was his name, Rudy. His black heart. Rudy was the only person Butch didn't like. Rudy knew it. He was just looking for a chance to do him a bad turn."

"So he deliberately . . . ?"

Leo nodded somberly. "Butch was lying in the driveway. He liked the warm concrete. Rudy backed the truck out and just ran over him as nice as you please."

"But—maybe he didn't see him."

"He saw him all right. Butch was asleep. Rudy gunned his motor and hit him before he could get out of the way."

Tiger's eyelids lowered, his lips stretched in a grim line. He remained that way, wondering why Leo had made so personal a confession on such short acquaintance. It was, he decided, one way to cement a friendship.

Leo spoke again. "That night I brushed all the dog hair off of Albert—"

Tiger's lids lifted again. "You mean—Albert was Butch's pillow?"

Leo nodded. "I cut the hairs up real fine and whenever I carried the plates in from the kitchen I sprinkled some of them on Rudy's food."

"Did it make him sick?"

"Not so's you'd notice; but it made me feel better."

Tiger smiled, then grew thoughtful. "How'd he die?" he asked.

"I just told you—oh, you mean Rudy. He had a bad accident. In that same truck he ran Butch over with. The funny thing was," Leo went on, "I always thought for sure I'd die before Butch did. Then, when I was dead, he would come and lie by me on my funeral pyre. You know—like a Viking's funeral."

Tiger nodded; he had read *Beau Geste*. A Viking always took his farewell of life with a dog at his feet.

"And your mother? How'd she die?"

"Sh-she—" Leo gulped, and his jaws worked as he tried to articulate the words, but no sound materialized. His face flushed.

"That's okay," Tiger said, "let's skip it." Raising his wrist, he checked his Ingersoll. "Jeez, I better be getting to the store so I'm back in time for Swim." He reflected for a moment, then framed a tactful question: "Aren't you scheduled for ball practice with Coach this morning?"

"Mmmm . . ." Leo nodded, closed his eyes, and lay back. The last thing he wanted to do right now was practice baseball, especially with Hap Holliday. Among the montage of images jumping about under his eyelids was a picture of the coach—"the all-American jockstrap," as Leo had dubbed him in his journal—glove in hand, waiting for Wacko Wackeem to field a few flies. But Wacko was not Coach's "kind of guy." Nor, for that matter, was Coach Leo's. That red, jolly face seemed to corrugate with consternation and dismay the moment Leo came upon the scene, and what point was there in trying to "measure up" when, where Hap was concerned, the percentages were so low?

All in all, Leo decided, he preferred staying where and as he was. Presently, he heard Tiger steal off, and through slitted lids watched him and Harpo cross the meadow and head for the Old Lake Road, a hundred or so yards away. Leo closed his eyes again, basking in the warm sun. How glorious to lie in a sweet-smelling meadow with nothing to do but make notes on a spider replenishing its pantry. He told himself he should collect the specimen and get back to camp (he *was* due at baseball practice before Morning Swim), but it was hard giving up such a spot as this; it was so *quiet* here; that's what he noticed more than anything. At Pitt the stone hallways forever echoed with the frantic clamor of discontent, dissatisfaction, and despair, 150 boys in their leather-soles clattering up and down, the incessant racket of scores of voices, admonishing, correcting, quarreling, wheedling, whining, complaining, crying, cursing. Seventy-five double-decker wire-spring cots, each with a boy top and bottom, lined up in a brick-walled dormitory with barred windows and a coal stove at the far end, a long low-ceilinged room once used for the drying of hops for beer, a place where the nights resounded with coughing and moans, with whispers and mutterings and outcries, and dreams that flew about on dark wings, like bats.

This was a sweet corner of the world all right, the valley that cradled Moonbow Lake, with its red-siloed barns tucked like so many play-farms amid the softly rolling countryside that unfolded among the Jurassic outcroppings of schist and shale, and its thickly shaded forest glades, the tall, dark fir trees whose tips pointed like village church steeples toward the heavens. Until now, for Leo "the country" had meant only the hot, insect-teeming tobacco fields of upper Connecticut, arid, dusty acreage enclosed by endless miles of suffocating mosquito netting that was worse than a winding sheet for those unlucky fellows destined to spend their years sweating breathlessly beneath it, while so-called fresh air was the stuff you got in the cement-floored, rusty-fenced playground at the Institute, with its jail-like steel-pipe jungle gym and oil barrels to play on.

But this—this was Longfellow land, the forest primeval and its murmuring pines and the hemlocks, and the sweet green meadow where Leo lay was as close to utopia as he was likely to get—his own private domain, as he'd begun to think of it. It was almost as if he had been *drawn* to it, he decided, because getting here wasn't easy. This is how you did it: You left Jeremiah and walked up the linepath to the cow-crossing, where the sagging rack of mailboxes defied the force of gravity, then turned left down the Old Lake Road, passing along the northern flank of Indian Woods, laced with a confusing network of paths, a maze that—if you knew its secrets— eventually brought you out at the Wolf's Cave, where the Senecas held their sacred campfires (and where the uninitiated didn't dare venture). But if instead of entering the woods you walked on a little farther up the road, past Pissing Rock, you came upon a pair of decrepit posts and, bisecting them, the beginnings of an old trace, a grassy track that ran between two rows of tall pines to form a wide, shaded lane covered with fallen needles, a soft, luxurious carpet under your feet. At the other end of the lane lay the meadow, contained on one side by the pond, and on the others by a palisade of dark fir trees, their apexes piercing the bright-blue sky, seeming now to impale the fleecy clouds, shepherded east to west by a light breeze.

The blue-green grass, dotted with buttercups and daisies, grew tall, so that, on his first foray to the meadow, he had almost missed the pond altogether—a body of water no more than five hundred feet in length, half that across, still as glass at the near end, at the far stirring itself and falling into rapid motion where its outlet crossed a weir to fret its way in a noisy babble some fifty yards to the ruins of Kelsoe's icehouse and the small cove called the China Garden, filled with lotus-like water lilies.

There was another feature of this place that made it special, however, that in an odd way made it seem to belong to him, to be his personal property. Off to his right, on the far side of the meadow, partly hidden by the stand of sentinel pines, he could make out the bay window in the "tower" of the old Steelyard place, the Haunted House. The house had struck a profound chord in him that first evening when Hank Ives had driven him past it in the jitney. And afterward—there had been something to do with the house in his dream, something connected with Pa Starbuck's story of the Moonbow Princess, only Leo hadn't been able to figure out what it was.

What he did know was that there had been just such a turret window in the house over Rudy Matuchek's butcher shop on Gallop Street. Leo had hated that house—*his* house—but the window was different. The window had belonged to *her,* to Emily, his mother—and as he looked over to the Steelyard property now, it was almost as if he expected to see her sitting up there, just as she used to when he was a child, waiting for him to come home from school, with Butch beside her, waiting too.

Now Butch was buried under a tree behind the garage, and Emily, she was buried—well, Leo didn't know where, because he'd never seen her grave, or Rudy's, for that matter; though he knew they were buried somewhere together, somewhere at Saggetts Notch—Mrs. Kranze had told him so—hadn't she? Funny about Mrs. Kranze, whose face he'd known so well, but could no longer remember—along with all the other things he had trouble recalling.

He turned from the house and his eye fell on his violin case. The sight of it prodded him: he had promised Miss Meekum that he would practice every day. Carefully he opened the case and lifted out the violin; then, seated there beside the pond, he began to play, softly, for no other ears, his bow moving and angling as it coaxed sweet notes from the hollow heart of the instrument.

He had played for half an hour or so when, suddenly, he stopped, his concentration broken by the rapturous trilling of a bird somewhere above his head. Was it a mockingbird? Certainly it possessed an extraordinary repertoire. Leo craned to find it: yes, there it was, feathered gray and white, perched above him, its throat throbbing with song. How was it that such a plain, unlikely-looking creature could produce such a glorious melody?

"No rhapsodies in this house!"

He heard the detestable voice saying the hated words.

"Shut up!" he shouted, sitting up and addressing the air. "Go away! Leave me alone!"

The cry sprang from his lips before he realized it; he glanced around in embarrassment. Then he threw himself back on the ground and covered his head with his arms, lids squeezed tight, while the same voice rang inside his head.

It grew momentarily chilly and, opening his eyes, Leo shivered as an errant cloud swept across the face of the sun, casting an unwelcome shadow. He peered upward, half-expecting to see a large-winged roc, Sinbad's roc; but there was no such creature, and he forced himself to relax as the curtain of shadow was raised and he was laved again with gratifying warmth. Easy, pal, he told himself impatiently. There's no one to hear, no one to make fun of you. But they'd heard him that first night in camp all right, when he'd had the bad dream and waked up hollering his head off. Even now he still hadn't erased the memory of Pa's gory tale, of the knife of Misswiss glinting in the moonlight and the scream of the dying maiden, which had become his own scream as he fell . . . fell, down into darkness.

He had come to blinking in the yellow beam of Reece's flashlight. While the other Jeremians stirred groggily, trying to dope out what was going on, Reece had accompanied him out to the fountain, where he urged him to drink, then he'd walked him around the baseball diamond, talking quietly, the sound of his voice both soothing Leo and distracting him from his disturbing anxiety.

When he was yawning widely, they had returned to the cabin, where, shamed to silence, Leo wriggled in over the sill and flattened himself under his blankets, while several of his rudely awakened cabinmates gathered out at Old Faithful. Lying in his bunk, Leo heard his name on Phil's lips.

"What was Wacko making such a ruckus for, anyways? Only sissies and twerps have nightmares. Cripes."

"Cripes yourself," came Tiger's retort. "You don't know what you're talking about. Everybody has dreams."

In the morning Leo had faced queer looks, especially from Phil and his shadow Wally, as well as from some of the Ezekielites and the Hoseans on either side of Jeremiah, whose rest had likewise been disturbed. But Reece behaved as if nothing had happened and evidently he cautioned the boys to do likewise, for by the time they formed for the march to Sunday chapel the incident seemed to have been forgotten. And by the time services were over even Phil had quit grumbling.

Was it the magic of Pa's oratory that did the trick? Leo had heard from Hank Ives that when it came to preaching a sermon the Reverend Garland Starbuck was possessed of the golden throat and silver tongue of a William Jennings Bryan, that his words, of honey or of fire, "could turn a Moonbow camper to stone" at the first hearing. And Leo had been impressed by Pa, decked out in his Sunday best (a full-sleeved, blousy shirt of snowiest broadcloth, touched up with a small black clip-on bow tie, a pair of gallused black trousers, seat shiny as a dime, and still shinier high-laced boots whose knoblike toes curled right off the ground), greeting his campers and staffers from his place beside Tabernacle Rock, thereafter speaking out boldly in the name of the Lord God Jehovah, entreating, cajoling, coaxing, and commanding these, his sons (and a single daughter) to bow down and make obeisance to the Maker of us all. (The camp schedule, as Leo had discovered in a few short days, left no doubt that Friend-Indeed was a "Bible camp": morning chapel worship in the council ring was commonly followed by more prayers in the dining hall, more hymn singing, more Scripture reading, more ecclesiastical homilies bandied about, the saying of Grace at noon, too, vespers observed thrice weekly, as well as impromptu sing-alongs, with eager voices raised in praise of both "The Old Rugged Cross" and "The Old Oaken Bucket.")

Though the memory of the morning's embarrassments still caused him to blush, that night Leo had taken heart from the friendly bull session before Lights Out, conducted by Reece himself. The counselor had stretched out on his cot and led the discussion, about what it meant to be a Jeremian—a true-blue member of the team, as he put it—and how they were all looking forward to seeing the Hartsig Trophy emblazoned with their names under the heading "Best Campers of 1938." And Leo, who had envied his cabin-mates their camaraderie and lighthearted give-and-take, the way Reece kidded around with them (especially Phil and Tiger), and the bonds they had formed through years of close association and shared experience, had felt—actually, physically felt, he thought—those bonds now being extended to include him.

Luckily there had been no bad dreams that night, no disturbances whatever, and next morning he had got up before reveille, ready to attack his first real camping day. He was off to a flying start—well, no, not quite. As a greenhorn at Moonbow he was bound to make a few mistakes, that would have been okay; unfortunately for him he had come a cropper three times in a row, which hadn't upped his stock with either the Jeremians or their counselor.

First, the camp inspection committee, made up of a revolving panel culled from the Sachems' Council, showed up in Jeremiah on its twice-weekly rounds, to find that Leo's cap had been left on his pillow—one demerit—and the contents of his suitcase were not up to standard neatness—a second demerit, making Leo the only Jeremian to receive blackies that day.

Next came his introduction to the traditional soap bath. Monday was "wash day," when first thing in the morning everyone fell out for the weekly soap bath in the lake, and Leo was tugging on his swim suit when he noticed he was getting funny looks from his cabinmates.

"What are you doing, kiddo?" Phil demanded, wrapping his husky waist in a towel.

Leo gave him a look back; he was putting on his trunks, what else?

"Nobody wears a bathing suit to soap bath."

"They don't?"

"No. They go buck-assed naked."

"Oh." Leo crimsoned, and, pulling off his trunks, wrapped a towel around his waist. Though he was used to the casualness of dormitory life, the idea of standing around naked in the open air offended his sense of propriety, and when, within minutes, he found himself dockside amid a sea of robust male forms, legs, arms, and pale behinds, a forest of limp penises, of corrugated scrotums drawn up tight as walnut shells in the nippy morning air—all of Pa's campers gathered to worship Hygeia, goddess of "cleansiness," with their pious offerings of pink Lifebuoy or green Palmolive soap cakes—he clung desperately to his towel. The result had been a spate of scornful taunts.

"Come on, lily-white, dive in!" "Hey, Wacko, drop the laundry!" "Yeah, screwball, let the world see your dong!"

This last from an older, thick-necked camper with a round, pimply, pug-ugly face and a nasty swagger, who wore a tattoo on his forearm, like Popeye. His name, Leo had already learned, was Claude Moriarity—more often known as "Bullnuts," Leo now perceived, for obvious reasons. The sight of the new boy, covered with goose pimples, knees knocking from the morning chill, seemed to goad him, and he advanced menacingly.

"Okay, you guys!" he boomed. "Let's get 'im!" And five or six campers had sprung on Leo and stripped away his towel, leaving him trying to cover his nakedness with both hands. This show of modesty further provoked Bullnuts and his pals, who, before Leo realized their full intent, had picked him up and chucked him off the dock into the swim crib, where he landed on his back and got water up his nose. Not knowing what else to do, he paddled helplessly around until the Bomber came to the rescue and loaned him his block of Ivory soap ("It floats"), then dived for Leo's cake of Lifebuoy (which didn't).

The third incident of note occurred after dinner that evening, and marked the beginning of Leo's troubles with Hap Holliday. He had been heading for the Dewdrop Inn, giving a wide berth to the playing field, where late baseball practice was in progress, hoping to go unnoticed by the coach, who Leo was afraid might try to trap him into playing. Swinging madly, Junior Leffingwell had hit a pop fly that sailed across the field and (having been missed by Oggie Ogden, in the outfield) bounced within ten feet of Leo and continued rolling toward him. Leo had stood transfixed, unable to do anything but stare at it, as if to touch it would do him injury.

"Come on, Wackeem, for cripes' sake, throw the ball!"

This command, from Dump Dillworth, had finally roused him to dazed action. He had picked up the ball and awkwardly launched it toward the plate, but the throw had gone wild, and as Junior rounded third and sprinted for home, the entire field, players and spectators alike, had erupted in scornful hoots and catcalls ("Woo-woo!" "Chicken wing!" "Hey, Wackoff, where'd you learn to throw, at dancing school?").

Hap had made no secret of his scorn and mandated this morning's private practice session, and later Leo had overheard Phil muttering that it looked like the new boy might turn out to be every bit as twerpy as Stanley Wagner. Wally agreed: Leo was twerpy. Tiger, however, had gone to bat for him: just because every Jeremian excelled at some sport or other, even if it was only Ping-Pong, didn't mean Leo had to. He'd rack up plenty of happy points for Jeremiah other ways, they'd see.

Leo had been grateful—but worried, too. Because the truth was that every true-blue Jeremian made a good showing at athletics; his cabinmates were not an assortment of wimpy oddballs—not, as Reece pointed out to Leo at that night's bull session, the kind of boy who had a pillow called Albert and wore a hat that looked like something out of the funny papers. There followed a lecture on the nature of teamwork and about winning. The Jeremians, Reece reminded them, were winners because they operated as a team (led by a leader like himself), and if you played the game properly you came out a winner, too, while, if you didn't . . . well, look at Stanley Wagner.

"Yeah, look at him," said Phil, scowling. Then, tossing his cap by its bill, he led the Jeremians out to Old Faithful to brush their teeth.

"So how do you like it so far, kiddo?" he asked, fetching up beside Leo at the fountain.

Leo replied that he liked it fine so far.

"Well, don't screw up," said Phil. "We don't want any more spuds in Jeremiah."

"Aw, can it," the Bomber growled. "He's going to get us plenty points. And wait till he plays his fiddle at Major Bowes."

Fifteen minutes later, when taps sounded, Phil's remark still rankled, but as Leo lay on his bunk, staring up at the molded impression of Tiger's backside pressed into the canvas overhead, he felt reassured. Stanley Wagner *had* been a spud, no doubt about that, and Jeremiah had paid the price. As cabin monitor, and second-in-command to Reece, Phil felt responsible, that was all.

Unfortunately, however, that night had been a repetition of the first, with another bad dream that had again disturbed the cabin and left Leo wrung out with imagined horror, as well as the butt of more jokes, especially from Phil, who now let it be known that in his view, the new boy was fast proving that he had inherited not only the bunk of Stanley Wagner but his shoes as well.

Deeply shamed, Leo made feeble apologies, but how could he explain? Whom could he confide in, tell about the dreams that haunted his sleep and woke him up screaming? It was the same old story all over again, only in a new setting.

At the Institute, Superintendent Poe had repeatedly cautioned him:

"These dreams of yours are affecting your daily work, my boy. We must do something about them. It doesn't do to be made prey to foolish fancies. I shall arrange for you to talk to our Doctor Percival, he'll get you over this childish business quick enough. . . ."

So Leo had seen Dr. Percival, who asked him to talk about his dreams.

Leo tried: dark, fearful, frightening, something large and hideous waiting in the dark to seize and devour him.

"What sort of thing?" pursued the doctor. He might as well have asked, Animal, Vegetable, or Mineral? Leo tried to describe it but failed; it was nameless, springing from who knew what hidden corner of his mind. He tried to picture it; couldn't do that either, just . . . big and dark and terrifying.

"You must just make up your mind to stop dreaming," Dr. Percival had concluded. "Or simply try to dream nice, pleasant dreams, hm? It's as easy to dream happy dreams as unhappy ones. Just make up your mind." He wagged his head sadly. "Until you do, I am afraid you will never grow up. You will always be a boy, with a boy's thoughts and a boy's fears. Therefore you must govern your thoughts, discipline yourself, put on blinders and reins."

But the doctor had no answer when Leo asked him how he was to accomplish this, when every day he could hear the laughter of the boys echoing along those green grim corridors, and the mocking jingle they loved to sing:

Oh my oh me oh, a crazy boy is Leo
Oh me oh my oh, his nightmares make him cry-o . . .

He would have given anything to be able to get away from that chant, to find someplace where no one knew anything about him, someplace where he could forget. And, miraculously, now he had his chance: Moonbow Lake was waiting.

"Hey, Nutbread, those two old farts want you in the administration office pronto." This from Measles, the head proctor and Pitt tattler, who poked his ugly puss in at the dormitory door, his loud voice echoing in the long, Spartanly furnished room.

Leo had been pasted with the name Nutbread for so long that he answered to it readily enough, and he had leaped from his cot to make tracks to the administration office, where he found thin, prim, dry-as-dust Supervi-

66

sor Poe seated behind his desk; with him, thinner, primmer, dustier Miss Meekum. Mr. Poe eyed him across his glasses rims and inquired starchily how Leo thought he might enjoy spending a few weeks in the country, then without waiting for a reply began explaining how, through the merciful intercession of the Society of the Friends of Joshua, who maintained an affiliation with the Pitt Institute for Boys, a place had been made available at a summer camp on Moonbow Lake.

The matter was settled inside fifteen minutes. Miss Meekum helped him to assemble his paltry possessions and put them into the cardboard suitcase he'd been loaned, with its broken corners and its fake-alligator-paper hide. In addition, two army blankets, stiff with age, had been made up into a bundle along with Albert, without whom he hadn't slept a night since Butch got killed.

"Regrettably, there is no time to sew nametapes in your things," she said. "You must take care and not lose them, clothes are hard to replace these days." And, as though to apologize for the lack of printed identification in his underwear, she pressed on him a fresh cake of Lifebuoy soap, and a celluloid soap "keeper." "If you are frugal with your soap it should last all summer. It's really a wonderful opportunity," she went on, drawing her hanky through her ringless fingers. "Just imagine—a lovely lake and green trees and meadows and . . ." She paused in her recitation of the charms to be found in the Connecticut wildwood, her wrinkled face sobering while behind her pinched-on steel glasses her eyes, like the eyes of a doe, swam liquidly at the thought of his journeying all of fifty miles away for eight weeks of camping. "You'll be able to get a fresh start, Leo, in a new place, where you can look forward, not back. And, please, no talk about . . ." She trailed off, her lids fluttering. He regarded her solemnly, waiting for her to finish her sentence. ". . . about the bridge and all of that. You must erase life's blackboard and put the past behind you. Will you do that?"

"Yes," he had said, thinking how silly she was, Elsie Meekum. Foolish words just seemed to come bubbling out of her like Nehi rootbeer when you shook up the bottle.

But there *was* a bridge, wasn't there? And carbonated though she might be at times, Miss Meekum was also often wise and prudent. He must remember.

"And be truthful at all times," she went on. "You know your penchant for—exaggeration."

"Yes," he said.

"And don't forget to practice your music, practice every day. You'll be rewarded and the boys will like you for it. Play that pretty Paganini piece you've worked so hard on. Promise, now."

Yes, he promised again. He was always promising her.

Following these cautionary words there was further bounty as she presented him with, first, a fake tortoiseshell toothbrush holder, then a blue-covered spiral notebook with lined pages, a fountain pen, and a bottle of Parker blue-black Quink.

"Take these, my dear, and keep a record of the happy time that lies ahead of you," she said. "A few jottings every day, and long afterward, when you are older, you will be glad to have such a memento." She thrust out her face to kiss him.

He had shivered at the touch of her withered lips, unused as he was to such intimate contact, and his eye caught the flecks of her pink face powder as they sifted from her cheeks. Poor, shriveled, woebegone Miss Meekum—yet he honored her gentle claim on him, for who else was there for him to love?

Besides, he owed her; he knew that. Owed her plenty. Foolish, flat-chested spinster though she was, she'd proved a mother to him when he'd had no other, when his own mother was gone . . . gone across the L Street Bridge.

2

Suddenly he was sobbing, his body racked by painful spasms. *Stop,* he told himself, don't be such a jerk. She's dead and gone— dead and gone, and where's the help for that? Who had the magic to bring her back? He lifted his tearstained face and pulled away bits of straw and grass. This wouldn't do, wouldn't do at all. If there was one thing he couldn't stand, it was a crybaby.

Once more, high in the sycamore tree, the mockingbird offered its lighthearted song, its practiced notes interrupting his thoughts. He stiffened his spine, staring at the violin in his hand. If he wasn't going to practice baseball he had better practice some more music—not just because he'd promised Miss Meekum he would but because he had been entered as a solo performer in the Major Bowes Amateur Night contest. He was a cinch to take a prize, Tiger had declared, and if he did he'd win extra points for Jeremiah. Extra points meant Reece would be pleased, and if Reece was pleased, everybody would be pleased.

Taking up his violin again, he fiddled an impromptu accompaniment to the mockingbird's song, and when the singing stopped, Leo went on, segueing into an old favorite: "Poor Butterfly." Of all the tunes from his earlier years, the ones his mother used to sing to him, this was the song he knew best. It had been her favorite; she'd heard it in a Broadway musical show she'd seen back during the World War. Such a wistful song, too; she always said it made her want to cry. Now, though she was gone, he remembered the song and played it often.

> Poor Butterfly!
> 'Neath the blossoms waiting

the words went,

> Poor Butterfly!
> For she loved him so.

Leo had loved that song from the first moment. He loved watching his mother as she played it, her pale lids fluttering, a little blue vein beating in her temple, her eyes shining—until there would come the brutal knocking from downstairs in the butcher shop; *he* would be pounding the broom handle on the ceiling, telling Emily to shut up, the noise was driving him crazy.

He rolled over and fingered his wallet out of his back pocket, then wiped his thumb and finger on the roll of his shorts and carefully extracted her photograph from one of the glassine windows. He held it with the utmost delicacy, for one corner was badly dog-eared, and the paper was in danger of cracking. The photo had been taken behind the pleated curtain of the little automatic picture booth by the entrance to Kresge's 5 & 10—four shots for a quarter, ten cents more for "artistic hand tinting." "Smile, Mom," he had told her, but she wouldn't, she didn't like showing her uneven teeth. What the camera had therefore captured was this other, gentler, and more tender smile, filled with caring and a pensive yearning—a trifle fearful too, the least tinge of anxiety in the eyes, those large, deep-set eyes.

He could see her still, her face framed in that high curved window that looked down on Gallop Street, watching for him as he came up the street from school, when she would smile and wave behind the glass. She would hurry down the hall stairs, finger to her lips to tell him that he shouldn't make noise and tip off Rudy, who, if he knew Leo was home, would make him fetch the broom and sweep the butcher shop. "Come upstairs," she would whisper, and there she'd have a treat waiting, hot chocolate and cinnamon toast on cold days, lemonade and cookies on warm ones.

On rainy days they would sneak up into the attic together, where they would go through boxes and old trunks, or she would read to him, fanciful stories, from Palfrey's *Golden Treasury* or Hawthorne's *Tanglewood Tales,* while he sat by her side and poured over the colored plates tipped in among the pages and protected by opaque sheets of paper, illustrations of Aladdin with his magic lamp; of Ali Baba in the Cave of the Forty Thieves; of Robert the Bruce, whose kingdom hung on the gossamer thread of a single spider; of Daedalus and Icarus, and Theseus killing the Minotaur.

She was always thinking of things to amuse him, like taking him to the double bill at the matinee (despite Rudy's objections), to *The Big Trail* and *Min and Bill,* maybe the latest *Gold Diggers,* or to *Cimarron.* Sometimes they'd visit the merry-go-round in the park, where a couple of times they'd accidentally happened across a friend of Emily's, Mr. Burroughs, a nice gentleman who bought Leo a balloon and a box of saltwater taffy and suggested that Leo not mention their fun to Rudy. But Leo didn't need any prompting, because he never told Rudy anything. He hated Rudy. Always, after school, while picking up scraps of fat from the floor, he would watch him, surly and frowning under his trademark straw hat, his strong, hairy hands wielding the sharp-edged cleaver, a cigar butt plugging the corner of his lips like a cork in a jug. The sight of him in his long butcher's apron, blotched with the blood of dead animals, made Leo sick at his stomach.

Rudy didn't like Leo either; didn't want him around, and he resented the time Emily spent with him, accusing her of making a sissy out of the boy. One night, when he went up to bed and failed to find his wife waiting for him, he went to look for her. Hearing voices from Leo's room, he came rushing in and, yanking her out of the chair, flung her against the wall in a jealous rage, shouting that the boy was a mollycoddle and would grow up worthless. Leaving Emily, he rushed at Leo and dragged him to the window, where he threw up the sash, and turning Leo upside down, dangled him over the windowsill by his heels.

Below Leo, the world was spinning around; he was sure his end had come. The ground seemed to swirl up to meet him, making him sick, and Emily was struggling with Rudy, trying to drag Leo inside. Finally Rudy let go, and Leo felt himself falling! Falling down and down—a moment later he was safe in Emily's arms. She soothed him and said it would be all right, while Rudy went around kicking the furniture. But when Leo was put to bed again and left alone, the panic rose in him and he lay there sweating, afraid to shut his eyes, for as soon as he did he saw himself looking down from a great height, and then he would start to fall, over and over, endlessly falling, falling . . . falling . . . down into the darkness. . . .

That had been the start of his bad dreams, the dreams that sometimes roused him to screaming wakefulness and brought Emily to his side, calling him, while the awakened Rudy ranted and raged.

71

Rudy wasn't Leo's father; his real father had died when Leo was very young, and Emily had remarried. Why Rudy Matuchek? This was the subject of much speculation among the neighbors, why a sweet, attractive young woman would ever marry "a man like that!" Leo had no answer. All he knew was that he had loved Emily more than anything in the whole world, and now she was dead. He blamed Rudy, and why not, since it was all his fault, making her cross the bridge with him when he knew it wasn't safe, leaving Leo with nothing but a cold bed in an old hops-drying room.

No, that wasn't true, not quite. For Emily had left him something beyond price: the music, and her violin.

One day, when Emily had gone upstreet and Rudy was taking care of customers, Leo had sneaked into the front room and lifted down the black case from the shelf. He set it on the floor, unsnapped the catches. The instrument lay in its bed of shiny-worn purple plush, and as he took it out his thumb struck the strings and it made an interesting sound. Turning, he saw his mother in the doorway. He was afraid she would be angry at him for touching her violin, but she had come toward him, smiling, with outstretched arms and tears in her eyes. She wasn't angry, she was pleased. She told him about his famous ancestor, the composer and concert violinist Joseph Joachim (the name had since received a minor alteration in spelling), who had played for the Emperor of Austria, and she showed him just how to tuck the instrument in the crook of his neck, moving his hand with her own so the bow slid across the strings, pressing his fingers on the fingerboard—there and there. That had been the start of Leo the violinist, and Emily put all her hopes and dreams of life in him: one day, she said, he would be a famous concert artist like Jascha Heifetz or Yehudi Menuhin.

Every afternoon, she gave him a lesson the same way her father had taught her, until he became technically proficient. She was patient and dogged, Leo was clever and persistent. He learned quickly. She called him her "prodigy," her "little Paganini," and she took him next door to Mrs. Kranze, where he offered up "Poor Butterfly" for the old woman who lived in the back room, whose husband had played the viola with the Boston Symphony. The old woman kissed Leo's cheek and said, *"Ja, gute, gute, sehr gute."*

But when he was old enough to help out in the shop, the lessons stopped. "We need a butcher here," Rudy barked, "not a music man. No rhapsodies in this house! Hear me?" That was when Leo learned just how determined a person his mother was. Before sending him off to school next morning she told him everything would be all right, and Leo divined that she intended he should continue with his lessons. But not here, not in the house. He must now begin with a professional teacher.

There was only one teacher of the violin in the whole of Saggetts Notch, a Mr. Schneidermann, who occupied the quarters over the law offices in the Wooster Block at the end of L Street, on the other side of the river. Three days a week, after school, Leo would get on the trolley car and ride the length of L Street to the corner stop, where he would get off for his lesson. Emily told Rudy that Leo had gone to the YMCA branch for a swim lesson, and to put him further off the scent Leo would leave the empty case on the shelf and sneak the violin out under his jacket. Mr. Schneidermann was a kind man and would never give Leo away, while—this was a happy coincidence—the lawyer on the street floor proved to be the same Mr. Burroughs who'd bought Leo the saltwater taffy at the park, and he was happy to let Leo sneak up the back way, safe from prying eyes.

Soon the trip on the green trolley to Mr. Schneidermann's became a regular part of Leo's routine. As he passed over the bridge he would gaze from the streetcar window down into the river thirty feet below, where Mr. Kranze and his crew (Mr. Kranze was a foreman on the state bridge-and-highway commission) were working to replace some badly rusted beams in the old king span. The view both exhilarated and repelled Leo. He knew he was safe on the streetcar—the gong went ding-ding, the wheels went rattle-and-clank, and on the overhead wire the little wheel that ran along gave off bright sparks—yet what if the bridge were to give way? Two years before, the thaw-swollen Cataraugus River had overflowed its banks and risen to street level, carrying away entire houses. And though the bridge itself had held, a woman and her child had been drowned in the flood, and Leo imagined that the woman was Emily, he the child, and that the bridge actually *did* give way and they both drowned in the foaming torrent.

Sometimes, when Rudy was too busy in the shop to miss her, Emily would go upstreet on the trolley car with Leo, to listen to him play. And sometimes, while Leo went upstairs for his lesson, Emily would wait downstairs in Mr. Burroughs's office—she could hear perfectly well, she assured Leo—and when the lesson was over, Mr. Burroughs, who said to call him John, would offer Leo taffy treats wrapped in colored waxed paper.

For a time Leo—and Emily—had been content in the belief that they were getting away with their subterfuge. Rudy seemingly paid no attention to their comings and goings (he was giving them enough rope to hang themselves, Leo later decided), all he cared about was his butcher shop. Then Leo had exciting news: John Burroughs arranged for Leo to travel by bus to Hartford to play an audition at the music school in that city, and Leo played so well that he was offered a special scholarship to continue his music education.

Emily was ecstatic. Her dream, she said over and over, was to have Leo play for the great conductor, Toscanini, and someday to be accepted into his radio orchestra, so she could tune in the program and hear Leo play. There was no doubt in her mind that she was raising a true musical prodigy, like Mozart or Chopin, and she craved the same sort of fame for her son.

But it was not to be. One day Rudy discovered the box of saltwater taffy John had given Leo, and he forced from him the truth about where the candy had come from. He cursed the name of Burroughs and swore he'd kill the man. He dragged Emily by the hair into the bedroom and berated her. Then he beat her mercilessly, until the terrified Leo ran down the stairs, out through the door, and over to Mrs. Kranze. She called the police, who came and took Rudy away in the wagon, and Emily had a mouse in her eye for nearly a week, and an ankle she'd fallen on that had to be taped for her to walk.

When they let Rudy out of jail he came home sullen and unchastened, and snicked his belt out of his loops and bent Leo over his knee. And if the punishment failed to fit the crime, what did Rudy care? Leo was sent to bed without his supper and Emily wasn't allowed near him. He cried himself to sleep and awoke to cloudy skies: that day the rains came and the river began to swell—the river that would free him from Rudy's tyranny, but lose Leo his beloved mother as well.

He returned the photograph to his wallet, then rolled over on his stomach, feet crossed in the air, chin propped in his palms, as he regarded what he could see of the Haunted House: its yellow-painted clapboards and mermaid's scales aged to an unappealing mustard shade, its tall, narrow windows bare of shutters, the glass broken out long ago, so that the empty oblongs stared out with a grim sort of blindness. Not surprising, Leo thought, when they had only a weed lot and a heap of coke cinders to gaze upon. Strange, the feeling the house gave him. What was it? Terrible things had taken place in those empty rooms that reminded him of—what? *What* did it remind him of?

He shut his eyes tight, trying to squeeze out the dark thought that was like a slippery fish, an eel, maybe; it came swimming out of the black ooze, to dart past his eyes in a bright flash, then, before he could catch it, to be swallowed up again in the inky blackness. It was like fishing at the bottom of the sea, where stinging, paralyzing creatures lurked, anemones that bloomed like flowers and then shocked you to death.

A piece of the puzzle was missing, something he needed to put it all together, but like the little fish it eluded him. Perhaps it was better this way; sometimes it didn't do to pry into these matters too much. Lift up a rock and you never knew what might crawl out. Maybe that was why people got amnesia, so they wouldn't remember what they wanted so badly to forget. Leo knew a thing or two about amnesia. He remembered the doctor's face, not Dr. Percival at the Institute, but the other doctor—Epstein was his name—who wore the white coat with the row of pens and pencils picketing the edge of his starched pocket. Eagle pencils they were, funny how Leo could remember a minor detail like that when he couldn't remember—again that little fish of thought swam into his ken, but though he baited a hook he had no luck.

Resettling himself in a more comfortable position, he took his pen and notebook and began writing. Miss Meekum had been right: the notebook would give him a record of his Moonbow summer, one he'd cherish at a later time, and he'd been not only jotting down accounts of his day-to-day activities, and making notes on spiders, but trying his hand at stories, and character sketches of some of the campers he'd met so far—the ones he didn't care for, bullies like Bullnuts Moriarity, and some of his cronies from High Endeavor, and the ones he did, like the other Jeremians, especially Tiger and the Bomber, and, next door in Ezekiel, Junior Leffingwell and Emerson Bean and Dusty Rhoades, who had all been friendly toward him.

His concentration was broken as he heard a Tarzan yell, and, looking up he saw Tiger and Harpo charging across the meadow; with them came Eddie Fiske and the Bomber, venting the throaty cry of the born Berserker, charging at Leo head down, arms spread like airplane wings, palms flattening the tops of the Queen Anne's lace. He threw himself down beside Leo, narrowly missing the violin case, which Tiger yanked from destruction only at the last moment.

"Cripes, spud, watch where you're dumping that big can of yours, will ya?"

The Bomber looked around him. "I didn't do nothin'. Jeez . . ."

"You would've crushed it if you'd sat on it."

"But I *din't* sit on it!"

"Yeah, but you *almost* did."

"Nerts."

The Bomber made himself comfortable, then pulled an Oh Henry! bar from his pocket and began peeling off the wrapper. The three boys had met up at Orcutt's and made their purchases together. Tiger spilled out between his bare knees the contents of a small paper sack: flat squares of brightly wrapped bubble-gum packets, each one containing a card bearing a portrait of either a befeathered Indian chief or a famous baseball player. He offered Leo his choice of the packets to start his own gum-card collection: Leo got Lefty Gomez.

"Hey, Leo, aren't you supposed to be at Sandbag College?" the Bomber asked, munching on the Oh Henry! bar.

Tiger darted Leo a look that said he agreed with the Bomber. It wouldn't do to rile Coach, who was already down on Leo because of his chicken-wing.

"That's okay," Leo said, more unwilling than ever to tear himself away from the meadow now that his friends had come. "I'd rather stay here. Besides, there's time. I can practice with Coach during swim."

Tiger still looked doubtful—Coach didn't like changes in his plans, and Leo needed swim practice, too—but the Bomber, having consumed the remains of his candy bar at a bite and licked his sticky fingers, chose that moment to insert them into Harpo's mouth to finish the job.

"Come on," said Tiger, disgusted. "He's not a napkin, you know, he's a dog."

The Bomber looked properly chagrined, while the dog went on licking his chops. For a moment they were quiet. The stream bubbled over the weir, the birds sang in the trees, the scene was properly bucolic. In the distance they could hear the sound of the *Moonbow Maid,* Doc Oliphant's new Chris-Craft.

"I bet that's Heartless and Honey," Eddie said, and they all jumped up for a better look. Out on the water they saw the bright flash of chrome, and the glossy red mahogany hull of the gorgeous speedboat creating a feathery wake as it spanked across the water. And even at a distance they could make out the bare-chested figure of their counselor, a jaunty white yachting cap on his head and his pipe clenched in his mouth. He was lounging on the back of the seat, piloting the boat with his bare toes, and, beside him, her golden hair flying, looking curvy and kissy in a yellow bathing suit, was Honey Oliphant.

For a while it looked as if the boat might be headed for the China Garden—the icehouse was reputed to be a Heartless rendezvous—and the boys prepared to make themselves scarce. But Reece evidently had other things in mind: the boat went speeding off toward the opposite shore.

As the sound of the motor faded, Eddie ventured a question. "Do you think he and Honey—I mean—you know what the guys are saying—about going all the way?" he asked, his eyes rounding with the possibilities. The Bomber also probed them. Honey Oliphant was a walking, breathing, ugly-duckling story. For years here was this scrawny kid, flat as a bed slat, with her chopped-off hair sticking out all over her head, and *wowie!* This summer the whole camp had been astonished by the incredible transformation, duckling into swan.

"She's sure got a build on her," the Bomber said fondly. Leo agreed. In his brief stay at camp he had already suffered through several manifestations of that ineffable vision, whose name, it seemed, was upon the lips and in the heart of every camper over the age of six. Honey, to use Reece's phrase, was a four-point-oh girl.

Despite his occasional proximity to the luscious creature, however, Honey remained a mystery to Leo (he had yet to address a syllable to her, or she to him). Still, as he imagined the scent of the traces of perfume that she must surely leave trailing behind her, he also imagined what it would be like to hold her in his arms and kiss her and hear her say, "I love you, Leo Joaquim." But who was he kidding? And at this point his feelings about Reece became more complicated—for, along with the classy Nancy Rider, whose snapshot graced Reece's mirror, Honey Oliphant was the sole and exclusive property of the counselor of Cabin 7.

Now the others began kidding about Reece, about how he was a real Don Juan, a sailor with a girl in every port, who always kept a couple of prophylactics (he favored Trojans, the red-and-black pack) in the glove compartment of the Green Hornet "just in case." Leo enjoyed the notion of his counselor being a wolf—certain romantic exploits just made a man that much more to be admired and envied—but when it came to Honey Oliphant, he wasn't so sure.

The talk dwindled away and for a few minutes the four boys again fell silent. Then, "You all set for the big hunt, Leo?" Eddie asked, referring to the annual Snipe Hunt, which was to take place that evening.

"I still don't get what it's all about," Leo said. "I mean, what exactly do we do?"

"You'll find out," Eddie replied mysteriously.

Leo felt a creeping suspicion. "Just where do we hunt these famous snipe?" he asked.

"Over in Indian Woods," said Tiger, sitting up.

"They build their nests there," the Bomber added.

Leo looked from one to the other, assaying their expressions. "If you ask me, I think there's something screwy about this whole deal," he said. "These birds must be awfully stupid. Why don't they just fly away?"

Tiger shook his head. "They can't. They're like penguins, their wings aren't big enough."

Leo was not impressed. "I still think there's a catch to it," he insisted.

"Sure there's a catch," the Bomber said. "A catch of snipe." He rolled over and presented his amiable features to Leo. "Whyn'tcha play somethin' for us?" he urged, changing the subject.

Obligingly, Leo again opened his case, and took out the violin.

"What's that s'posed to mean?" the Bomber asked, looking into the open lid, which showed a label of frayed gold silk printed with the words "Heindorp Brüder. Leipzig."

"That's the name of the people who made the violin," Leo replied, adding that the Heindorp brothers were famous in Leipzig.

"What about them initials?" The Bomber indicated the almost worn-off gilt letters stamped on the forward rim of the case.

"My mother's," Leo said. "This was her violin. What would you like to hear?"

Before the Bomber could respond, Tiger put in his request.

"How's about 'The Music Goes 'Round and Around'?"

Fair enough. Taking up the violin, Leo began fiddling up the corny melody in a mock heroic style with lots of exaggerated swoops and arpeggios, making the ditty sound comical, yet performing in the most straight-faced manner possible, with no trace of humor or mischief in his face. As he sawed off the "Whoa-ho-ho-ho" part his listeners laughed, then joined in on the bridge.

I push the middle valve down.
The music goes down around below, below,

> Dee-dle-dee ho-ho-ho,
> Listen to the ja-azz come out.

Then, without finishing the piece, Leo segued into the Mendelssohn "Spring Song," for a fillip adding a clever bird-whistle. The boys were impressed; this was what music-making was all about. But it was getting on toward Morning Swim—time to head back to camp—and at the conclusion of the piece Leo laid his violin again in its case, shut the lid, and snapped the catches. When he looked up, he saw the Bomber trotting off, not in the direction of the road, but heading for the Haunted House, Harpo sniffing in his footsteps.

"Here, boy," Tiger called, but the dog paid no attention as he tracked the Bomber's spoor. When Tiger started off toward the Old Lake Road, Leo got up, tapped the spider from its web into the codfish box, slid the panel shut, then gathered up the remainder of his gear.

"Hey, you guys, you comin'?" the Bomber called impatiently as he made his way around a clump of pricker bushes and marched across a patch of weeds to the line of trees separating the house from the meadow.

Leo shot a querying glance at Tiger, who shook his head. The fact of Leo's failure to attend baseball practice ought not to be compounded by any illegal activity, and the Steelyard house and property were strictly off limits. "Skip it," Tiger said, "let's hop it," and went on toward the road, while an irresolute Leo lagged behind with Eddie, both of them darting looks to where the Bomber was just disappearing among the trees.

Eddie winked at Leo. "Want to . . . ?"

Leo was staring at the house now, at the window in the tower. "It's against the rules . . ." he said halfheartedly; part of him would go, part stay.

"Oh, sure, but that doesn't stop anybody," Eddie replied blithely. "Come on, one look won't hurt. You've never seen anything like it."

"I better get going." Leo was feeling guilty: Tiger had reached the road and Leo should be with him.

"There's time," Eddie coaxed as he started away. For another moment Leo stood undecided; then, knowing he should go back to camp, he left his knapsack and violin in a hollow at the foot of the sycamore tree and followed Eddie toward the house.

As they threaded their way through the screen of trees to the backyard, Leo's eye fell on the sealed-up well.

"Did somebody really put a dead body down there?" he asked.

"That's the story," Eddie replied.

"What's the rest of it?"

"You're gonna have to wait and hear it from Hank Ives on ghost-story night. It's a wowzer. Come on," he added, leading the way past the well to the front of the house. The Bomber was on the porch, peeking through a window.

"Hey, you guys—get a load of this—" he called over his shoulder.

"Whatcha got?" asked Eddie.

"Wait'll you see," said the Bomber, his tone inviting their participation.

Leo hung back, his heart suddenly pounding, but Eddie sprang nimbly onto the porch. "Screw off, Jerome, I bet it isn't anything."

"That's what you think. Have a look." He pointed to the window. "There's a dead body in there."

"Aw, come *on*, Fat Stuff. Can it, willya?"

"If you don't believe me, see for yourself. There's a stiff in that room: it's lyin' right there on the floor, a real live dead body. If you don't see no corpse in that room I'll let you have my desserts for a whole week."

Eddie, whose great weakness was desserts, was snared. He crossed the porch, leaned on the windowsill, and looked inside. What he saw provoked a scornful exclamation, and as he yanked his head back he banged his crown against the sash.

"So, wasn't I right?" the Bomber crowed. "Didn't you see a dead body?"

"It's only a bird," Eddie said.

The Bomber gloated. "So what? Dead's dead, ain't it? I win."

"The heck you do," Eddie declared. "That's not a fair bet."

Eddie's indignation fell on deaf ears as the Bomber dropped to the ground and gave Leo an elbow and a wink, then made his way along the side of the house. Harpo, ever curious, went bounding after him. By the time Eddie and Leo came around the corner, the Bomber was waiting on the top step of the cellar hatchway. Were they actually going down there?

Eddie tossed Leo an encouraging nod and disappeared after the Bomber and Harpo, leaving Leo staring at the gaping hatch. Once again his heart was pounding. Over the low doorway was a crudely crayoned legend:

RINKYDINKS
MEMBERS ONLY

ALL OTHERS KEEP OUT
AT PERIL OF LIFE!

and under this warning, a skull and crossbones. A moment more Leo stood at the top, trying but failing to hear the voice of conscience, knowing the others would think he was merely scared if he turned back now. Then he ducked his head and, imperiling the only life he'd ever get, entered the dim, musty room.

In the dim light, he could just make out the other two, busy doing something in a corner. As his eyes grew accustomed to the gloom, he saw that the Bomber was bending over a long bench, lighting a candle stub. Soon a wavering glow was making the shadows dance in the corners and along the ceiling.

"So what d'you think?" the Bomber asked as if he were welcoming a guest to his new house.

Leo shrugged; what could he say? The cellar was large and—well—spooky. It had a strange, earthy smell, but, then, what else could you expect from the cellar of a haunted house? Of ample proportions, it formed a spacious, below-ground room with stone walls, a hard-packed dirt floor, and a low-beamed ceiling supported by squared-off posts, into which a hinged trapdoor had been cut and from which a broken stair-ladder hung at an angle. There was an old furnace and an empty coal bin, and a cobweb-covered fuse box was attached to one wall. The mixture of odors—of dampness, soil, must, dust, and rust, of stagnant rain pools in the corners—gave the place a special character that both attracted and repelled, a place for sinister doings.

"What does the sign mean?" Leo asked. "What are Rinkydinks?"

While Eddie described the illegal organization, the Bomber marched over to a wall and paced out a distance along the footing, then knelt and dislodged a stone, from behind which he extracted a coffee can. Bringing it back to the bench, he removed the lid and pulled out a half-empty pack of Old Gold cigarettes, along with a finger-soiled envelope.

"Smoke?" He fished a squashed cigarette from the crumpled pack and lit up.

"Sure, give us a drag," Eddie said. The Bomber handed over his butt, then watched Eddie draw and choke, expelling the smoke in three gusts through both mouth and nostrils. The Bomber was contemptuous.

"Cripes, Ed, you know somethin'—you smoke just like an old lady. Why don'tcha learn to inhale like I showed you?"

"It hurts my throat."

"You got to get it way down into your lungs and then blow it out. See? Like this." The Bomber offered an eloquent demonstration of this procedure, puffing voluminously, then proceeded to blow three uniform smoke rings that waffled gracefully through the air.

"You want a drag, Leo?" The Bomber held out the fuming butt. "These have 'latakeeah' in 'em," he pointed out.

"Latakeeah's only a kind of Turkish tobacco, that's all," Leo said knowledgeably. He took a drag, inhaled it, then coughed it out in a thick cloud.

"Must be the latakeeah," the Bomber said with a smirk.

Leo took another puff; the pungent tobacco was at once heady and dizzying. " 'Kaf kaf,' said Major Hoople," he said; Eddie and the Bomber both chuckled. The blowhard major with the Shriner's fez was a comic-strip favorite.

The three continued puffing on the cigarette, passing it back and forth; while they smoked, the Bomber made Leo privy to the contents of the envelope: half a dozen dog-eared photographs, which he ceremoniously tendered to Leo for perusal.

Leo blushed; he had never gazed upon their like before—though he'd heard of such phenomena often enough at Pitt, the large-buttocked women clad only in black stockings, the gentlemen self-conscious in funny-looking underwear, gartered socks; one of the men wore a derby hat, which rendered him ridiculous, given his activity.

"They're French," the Bomber explained, about the cards. "From Gay Paree."

Leo nodded, hoping he appeared sophisticated. He wondered what Kretch would have to say about all this. The Bomber made a sudden move, holding out his hand for silence.

"Cripes!"

"What is it?"

"Sssh. Button up. Somebody's up there. Hear?"

Leo cocked an ear and, indeed, the Bomber was right. From overhead came the sound of stealthy footsteps. Someone was tiptoeing around up there! *Cripes.* The Bomber snatched the pictures from Leo's hand and stuffed them back in the coffee can, then hastily returned it to its hiding place. Leo listened hard, wondering whether to bolt or stay put. Yes, definitely—someone was moving around up there. Now he was wishing they hadn't visited the cellar—it was a mistake—they should have obeyed the signs and avoided the place like a pesthouse.

Suddenly the silence in the cellar was broken. Bounding toward the hatchway steps, Harpo began to bark. *Harpo!* His noise was bound to give them away.

"C'mon, let's scram outta here," the Bomber said and started toward the hatchway. But before they could gain the stairs, Bullnuts Moriarity came thundering down at them bellowing like a Blue Briton, followed by what seemed to Leo like a horde of savages, all yelling and waving their arms. Among the foe he glimpsed the moonlike features of Moon Mullens; Billy Bosey was there too, and Barty Tugwell, all bent on punishing the boys who had intruded into their sanctum. Leo felt himself slammed from side to side until he became dizzy. Someone gave him a jab in the ribs, while another had got his fingers into Leo's hair and was trying to yank it out. Then, using brute force, the Bomber muscled his way through, dragging Leo along with him, Eddie in their wake. Before he knew it Leo was out the lower door and scrambling up the hatchway steps to freedom.

At the top he barked his shin on the edge of the stone step. The pain was excruciating and, biting back his moans, he hopped around on one foot, then hobbled off to hide in a clump of sumac bushes. By this time Eddie and the Bomber had reached the road and were nearly around the bend. From the cellar came angry voices, disputing whether or not to give chase. Evidently the decision was against pursuit, for no Rinkydink reappeared. Finally, feeling himself safe, Leo made his way back to the pond to collect his knapsack and violin; then, brushing the leaves from his knees, he headed down the lane to the road where he turned toward camp. When he reached the bend, he glanced back over his shoulder, as if checking to make sure that the house was still there; as he looked, he saw, or had the impression of, a shadowy figure seated in the upstairs window, gazing out—at him or at the view? He could not tell.

3

ut on the lower playing field the hour was on the cusp, gently poised between the setting of the sun and the rising of the moon, as the campers at Friend-Indeed gathered for the Snipe Hunt. Odd currents of barely stifled excitement whiffled among the knots of spectators and would-be nimrods who stood about conversing, not in giddy boisterousness, but soberly—an indication of the sport's importance as a Traditional Camp Activity. Observing somberly from the sidelines, Leo wondered what they were saying, the old campers who were exchanging knowing winks and glances. Something was up, definitely.

Leo had no spirit for the evening's activity, this hunt that the others expressed such a rousing passion for. Frankly, he'd just as soon skip it. As anticipated, his reception upon his return to camp had been on the heated side. Hap Holliday, fuming over the missed practice session, declared that Wacko could go on throwing a ball like Clara Bow for all he cared—he was washing his hands of the chicken-wing. Reece was even more put out and inclined toward stern measures. Having got wind of the illegal visit to the Haunted House, he docked all three malefactors three days' worth of desserts. Since the Bomber and Eddie were old-timers and knew better than to go near such off-limits places, they were also deprived of their free-swim privileges, while Leo got a private dressing-down from his counselor, who let him know in no uncertain terms that if he wanted to fit into camp life he was going to have to play by the rules; alienating Coach by standing him up—and earning himself five blackies—was no way to get on at Friend-Indeed.

Leo would willingly have borne all without a twitch, if his misadventure hadn't affected his friendship with Tiger Abernathy. Though Tiger had little to say about the morning's matters, his very silence spoke volumes, and after dinner he broke a date with Leo to go canoeing; instead, while everyone was getting ready for the Snipe Hunt, he lay in bed reading a book and studiously ignoring Leo.

In the end, however, having decided that the real fault lay with the Bomber for coaxing Leo (and Eddie) into the cellar in the first place, he took pity, and when the other Jeremians left the cabin to join the group on the field, he detained Leo for a personal word. Slipping from his pocket something resembling a watch, he tucked it surreptitiously into Leo's hand.

"Take this along," he urged. "In case you need it."

"What is it?"

"A compass. See?" He unsnapped the case of crocodile leatherette.

"Am I going to get lost?"

"No, but if by any chance you do—" He gave Leo a quick briefing on how to use the instrument. "And here's a Hershey Bar—you might get hungry." He slapped the candy bar into Leo's palm, along with a packet of matches, also "in case," and gave him a friendly poke. "C'mon, let's hop it."

Brrrt—brrrt—brrrt—! Chest out, whistle shrilling, Hap Holliday came strutting across the field in his billed baseball cap and jacket with a white felt B sewn on the chest (Harold Hampton Holliday was a three-letter man from Bowdoin). " 'Ray, Coach, 'ray!" the boys cheered, and Hap clutched his mitts overhead boxer-style, then called for quiet and began counting heads. "Hey hey, guys, who's missing here?" He consulted his clipboard. "Wackeem. Where's Wackeem? Let's get Slugger Wackeem over here."

Finally, when Leo and the rest of the new boys had been obliged to come forward and suffer the mirthful scrutiny of the others, Hap proceeded to the matter at hand, explaining how the hunt worked. Campers experienced in the art of hunting snipe would be teamed up in pairs with a tyro, forming a hunting threesome, two to beat, one to catch. The "old" boys on each team would use tin pans and batons to flush the snipe through the woods and roust them in the direction of the catchers—the new campers, who would handle the sacks and do the actual catching. Each team would report back to the lodge with its catch; the team that trapped the most birds would win.

Then it was time to pick the teams. One after the other the pairs of old boys stepped up, one by one the new boys were assigned. Tiger and the Bomber drew Leffingwell; Tallon and Klaus got Dusty Rhoades. Hunnicutt of Malachi, one of the new boys in the High Endeavor unit, went with his cabinmates Bosey and Mullens, while Emerson Bean fell to Dump and Eddie Fiske. Finally, of the new boys, only Leo was left; of the leaders, Phil Dodge and Wally Pfeiffer.

"Okay, Wacko," Phil called, rubbing his palms briskly together, "I guess that makes us a team." Leo moved reluctantly to join his assigned partners.

"All right, now, fellows," Hap was shouting, "step up and collect your gear. One sack to each new boy. Beaters, grab your pans, let's get going here." He shoved a burlap sack smelling of fertilizer at Leo. "Take it, Wackeem," he ordered. "If you can't pitch a ball, maybe you can catch a bird," he added, drawing a laugh.

Leo accepted the sack, feeling his cheeks heat up. Before he started off, Tiger swung by for a final pointer.

"Remember, when you're in Indian Woods, the Old Lake Road is always to the north," he said, then hurried away to catch up with the Bomber and Leffingwell, who were already halfway across the field, leaving Leo to Phil and Wally. Soon the boys had crossed the road and entered Indian Woods; in another few moments each team was out of sight and sound of the others, and on its own.

"This way, not far now," Phil said encouragingly. They tramped along a while longer, until Phil stopped and cupped a hand to his ear.

"There! That's them all right—snipe! We're really in luck."

"Sure are," Wally seconded quickly.

Leo darted him a look, but Wally's bland, noncommittal expression told him nothing, and Phil began issuing crisp instructions: Leo was to remain here, *in this spot*, with his sack, and wait. As beaters, Phil and Wally would make their way circuitously to the "other side," where they knew the snipe were gathered. Beating their pans, they would flush the covey in Leo's direction; all he had to do was shine his flashlight in their eyes to blind them, nab them, and carry them off.

"Where will you guys be?" Leo asked.

"We'll meet you back at the lodge," Phil said. "Here, better have my flashlight," he added, exchanging it for Leo's. "It's got fresh batteries—you don't want to be caught in the dark out here." He jerked his head at Wally and they moved off together, calling ever more remote encouragement until they had disappeared into the encroaching darkness.

Leo waited, one, two, five minutes. Presently he heard the noisy clatter and bang of sticks against pans, a terrible racket doubtless designed to flush the snipe from their hiding places, but one (Leo noted) that instead of coming nearer was fading. The beaters were moving not closer, but farther away. In a few more minutes the noises had stopped altogether.

"Okay, you guys, that's it, how do we get out of here?" he called after his erstwhile teammates. There was no answer. He called again; again no answer. Not a sound, not a peep, nothing. Just Leo Joaquim and the forest primeval. Letting the useless burlap sack slip to the ground, he squinted into the fading light, asking himself where the heck he'd been left.

The silence was eerie—a different silence from the quiet of Kelsoe's meadow with its birdsong and butterflies in the sunshine—a brooding, ominous silence filled with menace; and in it, Leo realized, there was a message: like every last new boy in camp, he'd been had. There were no snipe. The Snipe Hunt was one of those Moonbow traditions that left dumb spuds like Wacko Joaquim holding the bag. Hello, sucker, ha ha. Some joke. Standing there like a dope in the middle of Indian Woods, he didn't think it so funny. How was he to find his way out of the woods when every path looked just like every other? He could call out again, of course, hoping for an answer, but even if he and Bean or Hunnicutt found each other—unlikely in the dark, and it was getting darker by the minute—they would still be just as lost. Meanwhile the old-timers would be back at the lodge, gorging on watermelon and laughing their heads off.

Now he understood why Tiger had insisted that he take the compass, and, wondering if he could figure out how to use the thing, he sat down on a stump and opened it, then switched the button on Phil's flashlight. Nuts; the flashlight didn't work. When he unscrewed the barrel his probing fingers told him it was missing a battery. He swore and tossed it into the bushes, then brought the compass up close to his eyes, squinting. No dice: he couldn't see the markings on its face, much less take any kind of bearing.

A chill breeze had arisen to rustle the leaves overhead, and he shrugged on his sweater. Finally he decided to take the same path Phil and Wally had taken—they would not, after all, have followed a route that led anywhere but straight back to camp—and, sticking his arms out in front of him to grope for bushes or tree trunks, he started off, blindly footing his way along the path, stumbling and blundering into things as if he had been set not to hunt the mythical snipe, but to run an obstacle course.

He soldiered on for a while, until, having twice barked his shins and once twisted his knee, he made out a fallen tree trunk and plunked himself down again. He strove to think, cudgeling his brain to come up with a way out of his predicament. It occurred to him that he could wander along these paths for hours and get nowhere. And no one would find him. He shivered, slapping at the mosquitoes that swarmed around his bare legs—they seemed to thrive on the citronella he had doused himself with—then roused himself, telling himself he must do something; he couldn't sit here forever like a bump on a log. He arched his back and was about to get up when— what was that? A shaft of alarm nailed him in the chest. Out there—in the dark—something . . . Yes, squinting hard, he could just make it out, a dark shape, over there, he could hear it moving around. Something . . . something was there! This was no joke. This wasn't his imagination working overtime. He peered along the path. If only he could see better! His teeth began to chatter. He would get up and run, but his legs were too weak, his knees were wax. What *was* it? Hardly daring to breathe, he stretched his eyes wide in an attempt to pierce the shadows.

From the sounds in the underbrush he supposed the thing to be large and clumsy, heedlessly shattering twigs and branches as it came lurching nearer . . . nearer. . . . Oh God, there it was—he could almost feel its breath, hot and panting on his neck. A moan of fear escaped his lips and, raising his arm to ward off the attack, he struggled to his feet and began to run. Unable to see where he was going, he managed to move only a few yards before he tripped and went sprawling to the ground. The beast was upon him—!

"*Moooooooo . . .*"

The panic-stricken cow came crashing through the underbrush, apparently eager to make contact with a fellow creature, be it only a dumb camper as lost as she was.

The disconsolate sound mocked Leo, marking him a greater fool than he already felt. What if someone had been watching? He'd never live it down. The cow looked so ridiculous and out of place. He shooed it off, then considered his situation, rubbing his chilled arms; even under the wool sweater his goose bumps wouldn't go down. Overhead the pine boughs whispered softly in the breeze. He was panting with nerves and fatigue. He had no choice; he must move on. But further probings into the dark now failed to locate any trees to guide him along the path. There was no longer a path, none at all. In trying to get away from the cow, he must have stumbled into a clearing. Utterly discouraged and despondent, he kicked a stump and jammed his fists deep into his pockets—but wait! He had forgotten the packet of matches Tiger had given him. He could read the compass in the light of a match. He fumbled them out and lit one; the flame blew out before he could get even a quick look at the compass face. He lit another, and another, with similar results. There were only a few matches left. To conserve them he would build a little fire to see by.

He scrabbled up some tinder of needles and twigs, and struck another match. The tinder caught quickly; when he had it going he added some bigger twigs and pieces of branches so the blaze lighted up the clearing sufficiently for him to get his bearings. What he found himself looking at caused him to blink in surprise and wonder. In the center of the open space was a circle of round rocks marking off a campfire site—there were charred bits of wood scattered about—and, a little way off, the dark mouth of a cave. The trunks of the nearby pine trees were blazed with ax markings and knife carvings, Indian signs like the ones on the old campers' torches, with initials and dates.

As he peered around in wonder, it dawned on him that he had stumbled onto the site of the Senecas' council fire. It also occurred to him that he had no business here, that he was trespassing: in this sacred spot were performed those secret rites that were taboo for nonentities like Wacko Wackeem. He could picture the scene, the Seneca braves and warriors with their painted faces, turkey feathers in their hair, gathered around the fire, making Big Medicine in the night.

Eager to investigate further, he stifled his misgivings and, using a pine branch that when lighted proved a satisfactory torch, he made his way into the cave. The space was much larger than it appeared from the outside. Its roof, formed by a solid slab of rock, slanted upward from the aperture, so that upon entering the cavern you had to crouch, yet once inside you were able to stand again. Raising his torch higher, he proceeded farther into the room, following a trail of symbols and pictographs. Here was a deer, here a beaver, here a raccoon, here a snake, and here—he brought his light closer—this was the picture the others pointed to, an Indian brave armed with a bow and a fistful of arrows, standing over the body of a buffalo. What did it all mean? The answer, like the contents of the little chamois bag each Seneca wore around his neck, was known only to a few, and to none who did not belong.

His torch began to gutter and he hurried outside again—to see, to his horror, that his little blaze had ignited the pine needles at the edge of the clearing he had made and was spreading out of control. A wave of panic surged up from the depths of his belly as he pictured the whole of Indian Woods going up in smoke, and, cursing his stupidity, he ran from one spot to another, stamping out the flames. But as fast as he stifled them in one place they sprang up in another. Water—he needed water! Desperately he unbuttoned his fly and peed as hard as he could. When he had quenched the last of the flames he discovered that he had also put out his original fire, a mistake that had again left him in the dark. A fine Seneca he'd make. Except—

He wasn't in the dark after all. It was true—the moon was up! Finally a bit of luck! Now, if he could just figure out how to use Tiger's compass. He dug it out again, holding it up so that the light fell across its face. He picked out a tree trunk in a beam of moonlight to the north and moved toward it. From there he sighted another tree and, referring to his compass, another, until—a light! Yes, certainly; he could make out a winking light through the trees. Civilization was over there somewhere.

He pushed on, feeling a creeping excitement as he thought of winning his way out of the forest and getting back to camp. He couldn't wait to tell Phil and Wally he hadn't been fooled, that he'd known all the time there were no stupid snipes. Then, almost without his being aware of it, he found himself clear of the trees and standing on the sloping shoulder of the Old Lake Road. Car lights! That was what he'd seen, the headlights of a moving car! He laughed with joy and relief. He was saved! Now to get back to camp.

Wondering how far he had to go, he turned left and started walking—and stopped as he rounded the bend. The hulking silhouette of the old Steelyard place loomed before him. Chance had dumped him out upon the road almost in front of the Haunted House! For an instant he was actually glad to see it; he knew now that he wasn't far from camp. But then, as he stared up at the tower window, at the peaked gable, the bent lightning rods and the gimcrack bits of gingerbread, the house seemed to transform itself, to become that other house, on Gallop Street, the way it had been before . . . before . . . when he was the butcher's boy; and Emily, she was the butcher's wife; and *he,* Rudy Matuchek, was the butcher, damn him to hell, and . . .

"No rhapsodies in this house!"

Out of the inky darkness filling his head, that same bright, slippery fish of thought swam by, recalling—what? Still, it wouldn't come to him, but eluded him as always. What *was* it he was trying so desperately to remember?

"No rhapsodies in this house!" Again the angry voice sounded in his ears. "How many times I got to tell you, *no rhapsodies in this house!* Damn that kid. Where is he anyway? He's never here when I want him! I get the strap now!"

"No! Don't you touch him! Not again!"

"You shut your face! He's no good, that boy! He needs discipline. I give him!"

"You so much as touch him, you'll be sorry!"

"What you say?"

"You heard me. Don't you lay a finger on him!"

"You shut up!"

The sound of his hand striking Emily's face made Leo jerk back. Her sobs filled his ears. He let out an audible groan of pain. No! Don't let it happen! No—please. Don't hurt her! Overcome with fright, he tried to master the involuntary spasm that now gripped him. Then, the great storm broke from a great height, smashing down on him just as it had that night; an ominous thunderclap, a deep, tumultuous peal, and suddenly he is—yes—up there, in the window, watching for her—mother—*mother*—MO-THER—where are you?

He can hear the heavy downpour beating against the windowpane, drumming on the roof slates. The river is rising, rising fast to flood the dikes that laborers have spent two years throwing up, sweeping them away in a torrent, and the same tide is now loosening the footings of the L Street Bridge, and Emily—Emily is coming on the trolley car—the L Street car—*Mother!*—and Rudy is shouting and then the world begins to spin, a maelstrom sweeping everything away from him—*Mother!*—he hears her cry—

"Leo, oh Leo . . ." that dread sound of agony, her white hand fluttering, and—oh, *Mother!*

Suddenly he was running toward the house, up the crazy paving, up the steps, onto the porch to the open doorway gaping before him and—

He stopped; he could go no farther. Whatever it was, he could do nothing about it. It was too late. She was gone. He was alone. . . .

Terrible sobs were wrenched from him, his eyes blurred with tears, tremors ran through him like electric shocks—for a while he stood there on the threshold, trapped like a bug in a spider's newly spun web; felt himself cocooned in silken gauze that spun around his body, tighter and tighter, until he was made a small neat package of. Then, suddenly, a cold wind drifted across his back, chilling his neck, and the spell was broken. He turned away from the house and broke into a trot, down the walk to the road, pelting hard along its shoulder, never stopping for breath until he reached the rack of mailboxes at the top of the linepath, and beyond that, camp.

He forced his disturbing thoughts from his mind, determined to have the last laugh on his erstwhile snipe-hunting partners. As he came down the linepath he heard from the lodge sounds of merriment and lusty singing—no doubt the old boys enjoying their watermelon and making fun of all the dumb suckers still wandering around in Indian Woods. Shunning the lights, he made his way toward Jeremiah. He had an idea he wanted to execute. The cabin was dark and deserted when he reached it. He borrowed the Bomber's extra flashlight, then hurried away to the toolshed behind the cottage where Fritz Auerbach stayed, and located a trowel and two small clay pots. From there he proceeded into the woods behind the cottage and dug up two pine seedlings, which he quickly transplanted into the pots; then, having returned the trowel to the shed, he hurried back to the cabin. He set one of the pots in the center of Phil's bunk, the other on Wally's, then stretched out on his own bunk to wait. . . .

He must have dozed off; he was suddenly aware of subdued laughter, and he glimpsed figures coming down the linepath.

". . . I bet he'll never find his way out of there." He recognized Phil's voice, and there was a nasal chortle that sounded like Dump. "We'll probably have to go out and wet-nurse him home," Phil went on sourly, and in they came, five of the Lucky Seven—Tiger and the Bomber had yet to show. In the dim light no one noticed Leo at first, and he lay still, watching through slitted eyes as Phil, slurping the remains of a slice of watermelon, went to his bunk.

"What's this junk doing here?" he demanded, turning with the potted tree that had been set out on his pillow.

"Evening, all," Leo said, sitting up and grinning. "It's a present. Wally has one too. Like them?"

Phil ordered the lantern lighted, then strode over to Leo and stared down at him.

"What the heck do you think you're doing? You got dirt all over my pillow."

"Sorry for that," Leo replied, with no spark of humility.

"How'd you get back so quick?"

"Yeah, how?" echoed Wally.

"It didn't take long, did it?" Leo was relishing the baffled looks on their faces.

"You cheated," Phil said. "You followed us out."

"I never. You thought you'd gotten me good and lost, but you didn't. I knew where I was all the time."

"The heck you say!"

"And before I forget, thanks a lot for the loan of your flashlight. It was really kind of you guys. It didn't work, though, so I threw it away." He dipped into his pocket and produced the compass. "The reason I didn't get lost was because I had this."

Phil's brows shot up. "That's Abernathy's. Where'd you get it?" As he reached for it, Leo put it behind his back.

"Tiger gave it to me."

"Liar! He never! Hand it over."

Leo defied him. "No, why should I?"

As he stuck the compass back in his pocket, Phil threw himself on him and shoved him back to the bunk rail.

"Ow!" Leo cried, nursing an elbow. "That hurt!"

"What's going on?" Tiger was standing in the doorway with the Bomber.

"He's got your compass, Tige," Phil said. "He stole it from your box."

"No, he didn't. I gave it to him."

Phil was stunned. "You got to be kidding! You won that compass—it's a prize."

"That's okay. I gave it to him."

"Well, if that's not—well, damn it anyway!"

"So how'd it go?" Tiger asked, turning to Leo.

"It—" Leo swept the circle of faces with bright eyes. "It was grand," he said with profound satisfaction.

Phil glowered and turned away; he grabbed up his seedling and chucked it with the pot through the door; its fellow followed in short order.

"What was that all about?" Tiger asked.

Leo chuckled. "Those are the snipe I was supposed to bag."

Tiger and the Bomber looked puzzled.

"He's just being a weisenheimer," Phil said. "They're little pine trees!"

"I don't get it," Tiger said.

"It's an anagram," Leo explained. "Pines. P-i-n-e-s. S-n-i-p-e."

Tiger darted a look of covert amusement to the Bomber. It wasn't easy getting a leg up on Phil Dodge.

" 'Samatter, can'tcha take a joke?" the Bomber said, laughing. His bunk squeaked as he heaved himself up and hauled out his pajamas.

A moment later an angry expletive was heard from the porch.

"What the damn hell—!" Reece boomed out as he tripped over a pot. When he appeared in the doorway, he clutched a pine sapling in each hand, the roots exposed, pots gone.

"What's this crap lying around out there for?" he demanded, looking around for the guilty party.

"It's nothin', Big Chief," said the Bomber, hopping down to intercept him and forestall trouble. "Just a little gag is all."

Reece wasn't to be put off. "I don't get it. What gag?" He turned to Phil for explanation.

"Ask Wacko," came the sullen reply.

"All right, Wackeem, is this some of your doing?"

Leo shrugged and feebly echoed the Bomber's comment. "Just a joke."

"I don't like jokes. Not this kind anyway," Reece fumed. "What do you think this place is, a shit-house? This is no Dewdrop Inn, it's *Jeremiah!*"

"He's got Tiger's compass, too," Phil was compelled to say.

"Is that true?" Reece demanded of Leo.

"I used it, sure."

"Give Tiger back his property."

"That's okay, he can keep it," Tiger said.

Reece scowled. "My dad awarded you that compass. It's a good one. You take it back."

To avoid further argument, Tiger pocketed the compass.

"And you can have two mornings extra K.P. in exchange," Reece said to Leo. "Post yourself for duty in the morning. And if anybody asks you why, tell them it's because you're a wiseguy."

"Aw, c'mon," the Bomber protested. "Have a heart."

"Yeah," Leo said, "have a heart . . . Heartless."

There was an awkward silence in the cabin; what Leo had intended as a joke hadn't come off that way. Reece slowly turned his eyes on him. "What did you say?" he asked softly.

Leo blanched. "I just said . . . have a . . . h-heart."

"You called me Heartless. Nobody calls me Heartless, got that?"

"Yes . . ."

"Yes, *sir!*"

"Yes, *sir!*"

"Now, you take the broom and clean up that mess out there." Reece gestured toward the door.

"Yes, sir." Leo took the broom and went out. He was disposing of the debris in the trash can when he saw Tiger waiting for him at the fountain.

"I guess I screwed up," he said sheepishly.

"We told you he doesn't like that name. The Bomber gets away with it sometimes—*you* forget you ever heard it. But ya done good, camper. Real smart." He gave Leo a clap on the shoulder.

Leo warmed to the compliment; praise from Caesar. Still, he wished it had come not from Tiger, but from Reece himself.

Later, as he climbed into his bunk to settle down to sleep, he looked over at Reece in his cot a scant three feet away. His eyes were slitted open, staring at him it seemed; Charlie Chan eyes that made Leo nervous.

"Shape up, Wacko," they were saying. "Remember Stanley Wagner."

Resolved to heed the silent warning, Leo shut his own eyes and tried to get some sleep. But sleep would not come that night, and he lay long awake, thinking about the luckless Stanley, who might have had bad dreams too, and about his sudden, mysterious departure. Leo decided he didn't want to know too much about Stanley.

4

a Starbuck, seated with her ear as close to Pa's static-riddled Atwater-Kent radio speaker as her bulk would allow, nodded emphatically. As usual, "Ma Perkins" was right. If Lauralee, a "modern" housewife, really wanted to hold on to her mate, Buzz Morgan—a "real good" garage mechanic who tuned up engines over at Zeke's Service Station—she was just going to have to quit flirting with every Tom, Dick, and Harry who happened by.

"Ma Perkins" was a latter-day oracle in the Starbuck household, and no matter how busy she was, Ma stopped what she was doing to catch the quarter-hour broadcast, which just now vied with the whirr and clatter of the antiquated Gestetner machine grinding out *The Pine Cone.* Ma was used to doing several things at once (there was a brace of apple pies cooling on the shelf outside her kitchen window), but "Ma Perkins" was too good to miss, and not until Lauralee had agreed to watch her step (though she sure would like to "get outta this burg and see some city lights") did Ma return to her typewriter, set up by the window so she could keep an eye on the compound formed by the three façades—barn, store, and office—that was the hub of the upper camp.

Across the way in the barn, morning crafts session was in full swing. One of the oldest in the district, the barn was well suited to its current purpose, its old stalls, tackrooms, and lofts having been readily transformed into workrooms—the Marconi Radio Shop (in the hayloft), the Swoboda

Wood-Carving Shop, the Rembrandt Paint Shop, the Silas Marner Weaving Shop, the Paul Revere Metalworking Shop—and on any morning except Sunday the place rang to the din of ball-peen hammers on sheet copper and saws eating wood, to the ceaseless hum of voices as young craftsmen went about the business of creating a work of art, this summer under the gentle guidance of Fritz Auerbach.

From time to time one of the boys would lay down his tools and come out to the pump for a cooling drink or to make a purchase at the Coop (stopping by the office first to get the money from his spending envelope). The Coop had once been exactly what its name implied, a chicken coop housing a flock of Rhode Island Reds, from which, in the camp's earlier years, Ma had extracted her mickle of "egg money." Nowadays, for two hours every morning and another in the evening, from behind its full-length oilcloth-covered counter, the counselors took turns vending materials for leather craft, beadwork, woodburning, and other handicraft projects, as well as candy bars and soda pop kept chilled in an old cold box upon which the legend MOXIE had all but worn away.

Now, through the window of the barn that marked the Swoboda Wood-Carving Shop, Ma glimpsed the feathered Tyrolean cap belonging to Fritz Auerbach. He was hard at work on his pet project, a scale model of a village in Austria called Durenstein, which, when completed, was intended as a special gift for Camp Friend-Indeed.

"Hi, Fritz," she called. "How's it going with all the little folk?"

Fritz put his head out the window and laughed. "No little folk today, Mrs. Starbuck, only little houses."

"I thought you was gonna call me Ma, like everybody else at camp."

"Okay, Ma, you're the boss." He tipped his hat brim over his eye and withdrew, catching his feather in a knothole. Ma beamed approvingly. She liked Fritz; everyone did.

Though he supervised all arts-and-crafts activities, the Swoboda Wood-Carving Shop was Fritz's personal duchy. Here he had set himself up with a sturdy workbench, a vise, chisels, knives, scroll saws, and other wood-working tools, and the adjacent walls were hung with tiny figures, human and animal, cleverly carved from chunks of wood and destined for the village: bushy-tailed squirrels, a tortoise, a deer, a man in lederhosen and a feathered cap. For Fritz was a master woodworker, and the Swoboda corner had become extremely popular with many of the campers, from the older boys in High Endeavor, eager to learn his carving secrets, to the cadets from Virtue like Peewee Oliphant, who crowded around him as he perched on his stool amid the aromatic sawdust and wood shavings.

Durenstein, the village on the outskirts of Vienna, was a place Fritz knew well—a little corner of his childhood that held many happy memories, unclouded by the misfortunes that had befallen him since. Sometimes, as he worked, he would tell the campers stories about how on Sundays in springtime he and his family would drive out of the city in their big touring car to take lunch under the arbor at a little café where the hasenpfeffer was tasty and they would drink May wine with strawberries in each glass and afterward sing the old German songs.

But no more. Fritz did not care to hear those songs any longer. It saddened Ma, for it didn't seem likely he would ever see his family again—at Durenstein, or anywhere else. The Auerbachs had been one of the oldest and most respected banking families in Vienna; since the Austrian Nazis began their bid for power they had coveted the fortune of the family of Jews, and one night—this was some months before the Anschluss, when Hitler's panzer units had rolled across the border into Austria—the Brownshirts had descended on the Auerbach house, breaking in at the front while the family escaped through the alley with only the clothes on their backs and a few bits of jewelry. Fritz, who had been away at school in Geneva, was sure his father would try to reach New York, and had himself made his way to America to wait, boarding with a family in Middletown and earning his tuition at Wesleyan by private tutoring in the German language. Among those he had taught had been Rex Kenniston's younger brother, and it had been on Rex's recommendation that Fritz, though a Jew, had been offered the post at Camp Friend-Indeed.

The results, Ma decided, had been gratifying. For Fritz, who had the most reason for complaint of all the young men on Pa's staff, gave the impression of being the most content, and was the most easygoing and pleasant to be around, doing his utmost to hide the anguish that had already touched his dark, curly hair with silver. He was also—as Ma's friend Dagmar Kronborg had pointed out with satisfaction—responsible for bringing to Friend-Indeed something of the "culture" the boys had encountered heretofore only on occasional visits to the Castle. Indeed, he had turned the so-called White House, the small cottage of which he was sole tenant, into the acknowledged cultural hub of the entire camp.

Ma smiled to herself. Being a "cultural hub" suited the little house, she thought, picturing it set in the grove of slender birches: the low, narrow doorway elegantly fronted by a sliver of porch, with its decorative bits of curlicue and filigree, and boasting a pair of Doric columns that had once framed the doorway of a building in Junction City. The tiny one-room "playhouse" Pa had contrived with Henry Ives in order to keep Ma close to him in that long-ago time when love was fresh had in recent years been the residence of Hap Holliday, who had been far from pleased at being relegated for the season to a bunk at Bachelors' Haven, the staff dorm. But Ma had made up her mind as soon as she heard Fritz's tragic story from Dr. Dunbar. "That boy'll need a *home,*" she had told Pa, "a place where he can be alone." And when Fritz had moved into the cottage with his meager possessions—the few treasures he'd brought with him from Switzerland (an antique chess set, an album of stamps, and a pewter-lidded stein reputed to have come from "King Ludwig's castle at Neuschwanstein"), a small shelf of books, and a collection of classical and jazz recordings that he played on an old Victrola he'd picked up in a Junction City secondhand shop—she knew she'd done the right thing. Besides, lately Fritz was proving an agreeable companion for Leo Joaquim, giving him a game of checkers and lending him books. A well-educated, cultured person like Fritz was bound to have an effect on the poor orphan, might even influence his entire future, help to mold him into the sort of person Ma believed him capable of becoming. "Glad Men from Happy Boys," wasn't that the Moonbow motto, Pa's favorite slogan?

The sun having crept into her eyes, she adjusted her celluloid eyeshade to cut the glare as she checked on Willa-Sue, who was sitting on the slatted bench under the grape arbor, among the ragged clumps of snapdragons and hollyhocks, cradling her doll, and watching Jezebel, who was on the hunt for mice among the arbor's sagging posts.

Ma sighed. Pa himself had carpentered the arbor some twenty-five years before, and in those happier days he and she would sit side by side on that same bench, holding hands and planning the future, in anticipation of which Pa had also constructed a cradle. But it wasn't until the thirteenth year of their marriage that their union had been blessed by the precious gift of a child, a baby girl born just before Christmas, and when two whole summers had passed and they had yet to hear her first words it had dawned on Ma that there must be something wrong. Medical science and Doc

Thomason had confirmed her suspicions. Pa had been brokenhearted, taking it as a personal insult—Starbuck males didn't breed mental defectives—and a new chapter had opened in the life story of Mary and Garland Starbuck.

Pa took to sleeping in the spare room in the narrow bed and turned away from his daughter and his wife; even the camp that he had founded, and its "boys," seemed to lose their place in his heart. As for Ma, being by nature optimistic and resourceful, she had taken the disappointment in her stride. If Willa-Sue was a bit slow, that was all right; at least she wasn't sickly or peaked, the way some children were, and Ma could help her along with her lessons. The trouble was, the boys enjoyed making fun of her. One camper in particular, and that had been most upsetting because of who he was; though it had happened so many years ago now, Ma had never forgotten it. She had been sitting right here in this very chair in this same office; the boys were hiking past the window to the dining hall. A few had stopped to play with Willa-Sue; another—Reece Hartsig, then a camper in Harmony—had impatiently urged them to hurry up.

"Come on, you spuds, leave the dummy alone and let's hop it!"

The dummy.

"Dum-dum dummy," the boys shouted and ran away. Ma had grabbed the child from her playpen and carried her inside as if she'd been burned by fire. Pa, connected up to his radio set by earphones, had missed it all. She never told him what had happened. It would have done no good, no good at all.

It was then Ma finally realized that the man she lived with was no longer the man she had married. And nowadays—nowadays, out for a walk among the Moonbow byways, he had his eyes forever on the treetops and the little birds that hopped about among their branches, and on the clouds floating above the trees, and on the sky beyond the clouds, and saw almost nothing of the doings of "his boys." And this was too bad, because there were some problems Ma couldn't solve—in particular those concerning that same Reece Hartsig and the new boy in Jeremiah, Leo Joaquim. The morning after the Snipe Hunt Reece had come storming into the office, griping about the dumb trick Leo had played on Phil and Wally and demanding that Ma switch him with Talbot in Isaiah; the new boy, he said, would never make a Jeremian, and would cost the cabin the Trophy. Ma wouldn't budge. To Jeremiah had Leo come, in Jeremiah would he stay. Frankly, she thought him real clever, resourceful too (not many new campers so much as suspected the truth behind the Snipe Hunt), but even if she had been so inclined she would not have acceded to Reece's request, which would have meant separating Leo from Tiger Abernathy. She had reminded the counselor of the happy points his new camper was already earning for Jeremiah with his spider collection, and Reece had seemed mollified. Still Ma couldn't be sure; if only Pa would have a word with him—but she knew the likelihood of that was small, the summer would be gone before he did.

She forced herself out of her morose reverie and returned to the task at hand. As she completed the last page of *The Pine Cone* and peeled it from the machine, Leo himself appeared in the barn doorway and headed for the pump. For some reason Willa-Sue had fixed her interest on the new boy from the first day—probably because he was one of the few campers who paid her a degree of attention—and now, slumped on the bench, she ogled him across the compound, idly fingering the ribbon Ma had put in her hair.

"Willa-Sue, pull your dress down," Leo told her as he passed. "People can see up it."

Ma shook her head at the child. "Willa-Sue, honey," she called through the window, "you heard what Leo said. And leave off tugging your ribbon, it looks so pretty. The way you look today, you could be a movie star if you wanted. What would my lambie-pie like for lunch? How's about a nice cold plate?"

Willa-Sue's dour features set like plaster and she eyed her parent with a sulky expression.

"Horsecock," she blurted.

"Now, hush you, Willa-Sue, I told you, nice girls don't talk like that, that's boy talk. If you don't want a cold plate, how's about a nice sammich?"

Willa-Sue jammed a thumb in her mouth and stared.

"What kind of sammich would my honeybunch like?" Ma prompted.

"Penis butter and jelly."

That old joke; Ma shook her head despairingly, and called through the window for Leo to keep an eye on Willa-Sue while she went into the kitchen to make lunch; obligingly he carried his copper mug full of water over to the arbor and sat down beside her.

"Wacko Wacko, chews tobacco. . . ." Willa-Sue stared at Leo, her bug-eyes slightly crossed, a giddy expression on her sallow face.

"Wacko, Wacko, chews tobacco," she said again.

101

Leo spoke sternly. "I asked you not to call me that. My name's Leo: L-e-o. Leo. For 'Leopold.' It's the name of a king. Leopold, King of the Belgians."

"Lee-pole."

"Pold. With a d. Lee-*oh*-pol-*duh.* Can you say it?"

"Leo-pol-*duh.*"

"Well, it's better than Wacko," he muttered.

"Wacko, Wacko." She rolled her eyes and burred her lips at him.

He blew out his cheeks in exasperation. "What do you want, Willa-Sue?" It turned out she wanted him to do the Three Stooges imitation the Bomber had been coaching him in, so he obliged, making his stupid Curly face, doing "Nyuck nyuck nyuck," and slapping his cheeks, squeaking, and rolling his eyes idiotically, while the girl clapped her hands in excitement.

"Moe, Moe!" she cried. "Now do Moe!"

He did Moe for her, combing his hair forward and slapping his face some more. Willa-Sue became more excited and began to laugh shrilly. She held out her doll to him.

"Wacko hold dolly," she commanded, and Leo took the doll and held it on his lap.

Just then the jitney pulled into the drive; Hank Ives debarked, and began to ring the bell for Morning Swim. Almost before the first peal died away, craftsmen by the dozen erupted from the barn.

"Woo-woo, look at Wacko," one of them called.

"Playing with your dolly, Wacko?" said another.

Burning with embarrassment, Leo grabbed Willa-Sue's hand and marched her across the lawn toward the office, where he delivered her up to Ma and the penis-butter sandwich. Then, before he could be detained further, he headed down the meadow path at a fast clip. He didn't want to be late for Morning Swim.

As he came trotting along the linepath the rest of the Jeremians (except for Tiger and Dump, who were getting in some practice with Hatton, the new Red Sox first baseman) exploded through every cabin aperture and raced off toward the waterfront. By the time Leo had jumped into his trunks and joined them and scores of others on the swimming dock, everyone was already lined up according to cabins, and Rex Kenniston sat up on the lifeguard stand. His silver whistle blew, calling the large, boisterous group to order; he reminded them of the waterfront rules (threatening to expel anyone who disobeyed). Again the whistle sounded and at once the place erupted in watery riot, but no sooner was the crib full than Rex sounded his whistle a third time, calling for buddy check, waiting until all campers' hands were paired in the air (Leo had drawn Monkey as this week's swim buddy). A fourth whistle—double this time—was the signal for activity to continue, and the boys were off, the Bomber cannonballing through the water with Eddie (*his* buddy), and Monkey following with Leo, who was not a strong swimmer. When they reached the raft, instead of boarding it, the Bomber sucked in a breath and sank from sight; Eddie and Monkey, then Leo, followed suit, and when they surfaced they were in the hollow chamber beneath the raft, surrounded by eight metal drums harnessed together. A golden web of reflected sunlight darted about them, transforming the space into a glorious underwater cave, and their voices in medley reverberated crazily under the wooden floor.

Suddenly there was a loud clamor overhead. Dozens of feet were stamping and pounding on the floorboards, cries became shouts, focusing attention on those sequestered underneath. Then the raft began rocking back and forth, the metal drums sounding a hollow roll as the agitated water splashed against their sides.

"We better scram out of here," Monkey said, seeking to avoid having Rex blow his whistle on them, and they all gulped a breath and flipped down into the watery depths.

By the time Leo came up outside the raft, Monkey was aboard her, and Leo clambered up after him. Eddie and the Bomber were going in, Monkey said—the Bomber wanted to get in some rowing practice. The Bomber was the intermediate unit's star oarsman, and was expected to win the boat race—and ten happy points for Jeremiah—at the upcoming Water Carnival. Leo nodded. He watched as Bullnuts Moriarity, wearing a rubber bathing cap strapped under his double chin, his beefy body sausaged into trunks, clambered onto the raft, followed by his fellow Endeavorites Bud Talbot, the biggest boy in camp, and Jack "Blackjack" Ratner, whose name suited him, since he was of a thin, dark, and distinctly rodentlike character with a mole-spangled face. Presently they were joined by Phil and Wally, who exchanged a few words with them, after which they all sidled over to arrange themselves around Leo.

"Hey, Wacko," Ratner began, affecting casualness, "us guys are all goin' up the tower. Whyn't you come on up too?"

So that was it. "No, thanks," he said.

"Aw, heck, be a sport, Wacko," said Talbot, dancing around on the balls of his feet.

Leo shook his head. "I'm heading in. Coming, Monkey?" he called, but his swim buddy remained where he was, stationed beside Phil and Wally. No help there, then. Suddenly Moriarity loomed in front of him.

"Come on, Wacko, don't be a sis. It's not as high as it looks." He used his belly, nudging Leo along toward the ladder. "You never know if you like it till you've tried it, ain't that right, boys?"

Leo glanced helplessly about. The water surrounding the raft was crowded with the curious faces of boys waiting to see what would happen next.

"You comin' or not?" demanded Moriarity.

"I said no." Leo scowled. He mustn't let them see he was scared of them.

"*Ooh,* he said *noooo,*" Bullnuts squealed, and gave a lewd shimmy of his midsection. "Then I guess we'll just have to . . ."

Their intention clearer now, the group pressed closer and, using his belly as a ram, Bullnuts forced Leo to the foot of the ladder, where they held him perpendicular and fixed his feet on the first rung.

"Go ahead, Wacko, climb," Moriarity commanded, goosing him upward. Leo jerked, then climbed a rung or two higher.

"*Higher!*" Moriarity goosed him again. Leo looked around frantically, praying for a miracle. The top of the ladder seemed so far away; he would never make it. And if he did he would fall, he knew it. He was sick with fear and panic. *Help, someone, help me;* but there was no one to help. All across the waterfront, every eye was on him. Even the tadpoles in the swimming crib flailed their arms and passionately screamed; and the perfidious Peewee Oliphant—there he was, hanging on the crib rope and hollering, "Wacko! Wacko!" and " 'Ray, 'ray, all the way!"

Looking across the water to the dock, Leo sought the help of Rex—surely Rex would do something, wouldn't he? Only it wasn't Rex on the lifeguard stand any longer, it was Reece, and he was calmly shading his eyes to observe more clearly the action on the float; so much for any help from that quarter—it would never occur to the counselor that a Jeremian would refuse to climb the tower; even Stanley Wagner had managed that.

In an attempt to escape his tormentors Leo climbed three or four more rungs: Moriarity pushed in right behind him, forcing him on. Up he went until his eyes were level with the diving platform, and there was nothing for it but to step onto it. Breathless and fearful, he watched as Moriarity, followed by Phil, then Wally, then Ratner and Talbot, then six or eight others with smirks and grins came off the ladder behind him. He inched his way closer to the edge of the platform, summoning his courage, telling himself he could do it. He *must* do it! But when he dared to look down he blinked and froze, then backed away along the railing. A resounding *boo!* greeted this feckless action and again the air rang with taunts.

"Whatcha waitin' for, Wacko?" Moriarity jeered. "Ya gonna take the jump or do we make ya walk the plank?" Worse, much worse, were Phil's contemptuous words: "Come on, Wackeem, don't make any more of a fool of yourself than you have to. Get it over." Leo looked from Phil's red, aggressive face to Wally's pale, pimply one and hated them both. And Monkey, where was he? Down below, twiddling his thumbs. "Watch out you don't crack your skull on the cable," Phil added. "Go ahead, I dare you."

Leo could see the thick steel rope receding at an angle to the bottom of the lake and the heavy cement block that held both the float and its tower fast, and it seemed to him that if he were to jump he would hit it. Yet the watery abyss pulled at him like a magnet. He must go over . . . must fall. . . .

Feeling Moriarity's hand pressing the small of his back, he gasped, then clutched the railing tighter. Go on, coward, the piggy eyes seemed to say, go ahead and jump. Ashamed, Leo lowered his head; he could feel the sickish heave of his insides. His stomach gurgled and turned over, and then, losing all control, he threw up his breakfast. Moriarity, the recipient of this unexpected eruption, let out a roar of indignation, and with a bellow flung himself from the platform and plummeted into the water below.

On the platform, still shaking with fright and mortification, Leo turned to face the rest of his tormentors. It was clear to them all—to Leo himself—that he had no intention of jumping, and so must take his punishment. They stepped aside as he moved toward the ladder and began his slow descent into shame. At the bottom, he dived from the raft and stroked for the dock, where he could see Reece hopping down from his perch, while excited campers, shouting and capering with gleeful anticipation, came skittering from everywhere: Wacko was going to get the paddle!

There was no rhyme and little reason to the business, organized as it was according to long-standing custom. The paddle, broad and thick as a breadboard, was borne aloft from the hook where it was hung, and Leo was bent over the paddling barrel and held in place. Then Moriarity—first in line by virtue of the indignity he had suffered—stepped up, spit on his palms, drew the board back, and swung.

As the blow fell, hard, Leo jerked forward on the barrel and a cheer went up. Then Reece took the paddle and handed it to the next boy, itching to have a go. Before long what had begun as a sporting affair, the traditional camp chastisement for lack of nerve, had turned into an ugly demonstration of camper brutality. Pain, humiliation, and shame: Leo suffered all without a whimper. How could he whimper? He had passed out.

"Hey, you guys—he's out cold!" cried Ratner, looking down at the limp form drooped over the barrel. As the clamor slowly died and a guilt-laden silence ensued, Fritz Auerbach pushed his way through the gathering to emerge at the head of the line. "All right, that's enough!" he said, grabbing the paddle from Bosey.

"Hey, what's the big idea?" Reece demanded, stepping up. "What d'you think you're doing?"

"Putting a stop to this sadistic business, what does it look like?" He shoved Reece aside, then leaned over and lifted Leo up in his arms. "This boy is hurt. I will take him to the infirmary. Get out of my way, please."

Reece wasn't about to let him pass. "That kid's not really hurt. Why don't you just stay out of this, Fritzy? I'm in charge here."

Fritz stared. "What kind of man are you, to allow such a thing to be done to a boy? What kind of place is Friend-Indeed that it would permit this to happen?"

Reece was at his most condescending. "Look, Fritzy, you're new around here. This happens to be a camp tradition, it's been going on for years— right, boys?" He glanced around, from Phil to Moriarity to Ratner to Bosey, all of whom exchanged sheepish looks but had nothing to say.

"Then it is time it stopped," Fritz replied forcefully. "Such childishness. Now, step aside, please; otherwise I shall be obliged to knock you down."

Everybody stood silently by while Reece reconsidered matters, and when he finally gave way Fritz pushed past him, carrying Leo's limp form from the dock, passing along the waterfront in the direction of Three Corner Cove.

y siesta time, after lunch, the waterfront lay tranquil and serene, the lake lapping the shore with its meekest touch, boats docked, canoes beached in squads, the punishment paddle hung on its hook. It was as if the camp could stand only so much of violent activity, of clamorous voices and hypertense confusion, before it must retreat again into order and serenity, to catch its breath before the next upheaval should occur.

Whatever Fritz Auerbach (a foreigner, after all, and not privy to Moonbow traditions) might have to say about it, the paddling of a camper who had failed to go off the tower after having climbed it was a tradition, and even though everyone had witnessed the way Moriarity had boldly goosed Leo up the ladder, that fact was already being overlooked. Notice had been served that this kind of "differentness" would not be tolerated at Camp Friend-Indeed, and Wacko Wackeem had better shape up or else. Nor did the fact that Fritz had opposed Reece in the matter do Fritz's own case much good. Taking public issue with the counselor universally regarded as the best Friend-Indeed ever had, had only served to place him together with Leo in the same camp, so to speak.

Fritz did have two allies in the matter, however. At the infirmary, to which he had conveyed the sufferer, Wanda Koslowski, the camp nurse, had been outraged. Leo's "baganza," she declared, looked like "an Italian sunset," and in short order she had popped him into a fresh, clean-smelling white bed, applied soothing lotions, given him a pill to relieve the pain, and positioned a pillow to jack up his hips and an ice pack to cradle his backside. Indeed, so tenderly did she treat his wounded posterior (without further injury to his dignity) that the grateful beneficiary of her ministrations decided he was considerably better off than Emerson Bean, who had acquired a case of poison ivy during the Snipe Hunt and lay four feet away in the adjoining bed, looking wretched and uncomfortable under a chalky pink coating of calamine lotion.

Fritz's other ally was Doc Oliphant, whose arrival at the infirmary just as Leo was getting settled required that the ice pack be removed. "Good God, man," he muttered to Fritz, "what have they done to this boy?"

"Paddled him," came Fritz's flat response.

"I should say they did! Blast those savages!" snapped the doctor. "Why didn't Rex stop it?"

"Rex wasn't there, I'm afraid. He had to take a phone call."

"Then who had charge of the waterfront?"

"Reece Hartsig was on the bench. He said it was the tradition."

"So it is." The doctor sighed. "But they went too far this time. You'd better keep the lad here overnight, give him a good shoring up, then send him back. Slip him a little mickey, so he'll rest. Here's Honey; she'll cheer him up." He smiled at his daughter, who had just appeared in the doorway. She kissed him, then came into the room, looking down at Leo, who turned red to his ears at being viewed (by Honey Oliphant!) in such an ignominious position.

"Goodness," she said, "that looks awfully sore. And Emerson—you poor thing—"

She clucked sympathetically and made the sort of mothering sounds that went straight to Leo's heart. Having Honey Oliphant in the same room with him was almost worth getting paddled for. Of course he couldn't really talk to her; he wasn't given to conversing with goddesses, or maybe not a goddess, maybe just an angel with a halo—all that bright-yellow hair that reminded him of Emily's. But, then, he didn't have to talk, because she did, chattering gaily in a way that made him forget his stinging backside, joking about "Tillie," the skeleton that stood on a metal stand in the corner—a former camper, she said, who hadn't got enough to eat during his stay at Friend-Indeed, which reminded Leo that he had missed lunch. Honey smiled. She and her mother were going to make strawberry ice cream for supper and she'd bring over some for the patients. Meanwhile—here was Wanda with the trays.

After Honey left the room, it seemed to dim, and nothing happened to brighten things much, since next to arrive was Heartless himself. He came striding through the door accompanied by Fritz and Wanda, who had had their heads together in the dispensary, to "check on his camper." Having lifted the ice pack and tugged down Leo's shorts, Reece humorously voiced the opinion that the Italian sunset didn't look so bad to him. "If you knew you weren't going to jump," he said to Leo, "why did you go up the tower in the first place?"

"He didn't go up of his own accord," Fritz put in quickly. "He was forced. You were there—surely you must have seen."

Reece's teeth clenched and the muscles in his jaws pulsed as he half-turned to reply. "This is *my* camper, Fritz. I'm sure he's perfectly capable of speaking for himself."

"You talk about him as if he were a possession, something you own."

Reece gave an angry snort. "He's a Jeremian, isn't he? He may not be the best one, but he's still a Jeremian. Which makes him *my* camper."

"Not now it doesn't. Since he's in this infirmary, if he's anybody's camper he's Wanda's. Besides, if you'd been looking after him properly, he wouldn't be here." He frowned. Reece was staring at him from under a cocked eyebrow. "Excuse me, please," Fritz said stiffly, "but is there something about me that offends you?"

Reece's eye was on Fritz's chest: the Star of David he always wore on a chain around his neck was hanging outside his shirt.

"What do you wear that thing for, anyway?"

Fritz glanced down. "Why should I not?"

Reece scowled. "Maybe you didn't know it, Fritzy, but we don't wear stuff like that around here."

"You do."

"What are you talking about?"

"I mean the cedar heart you wear—and your Seneca knot as well."

Reece's hand went to his throat. "That's different. The Seneca knot's a badge of honor. Members of the Lodge have always worn it. It's something we believe in."

"As I believe in this," Fritz replied calmly. "Really, I don't see that there's a great deal of difference. Is there?"

Reece gave him an exasperated look. "Okay, Katzenjammer, don't make a big thing out of it."

Fritz's eyes flashed. "Please don't call me that."

"Why not?"

"I don't like it. It is the name of a pack of low German comics in the funny papers, and, to tell the truth, I don't happen to think Germans are very funny folk these days." He turned to Wanda. "Now, if you will all excuse me, I have things to do. I'm sure Leo is in good hands with you."

With a nod to Leo and Emerson, he left the room.

"Gee," Reece said to Wanda, "I didn't know your boyfriend was such a prima donna." He gave Leo's elastic waistband a brisk snap, then dropped the ice pack on the table with a bang. "Okay, kiddo, hop out of there, we've got things to do."

Wanda was outraged. "He'll do nothing of the sort! He's staying right where he is—in bed!"

Reece showed surprise. "You don't mean to say you intend to keep him lolling around just because he got a couple of bruises on his fanny?"

"It's not just a couple of bruises. He can barely move. Besides, he's under doctor's orders. He's to stay here overnight at least."

Reece looked genuinely puzzled. "Gee, Goldilocks, I just don't get it. A guy gets a little paddling and you want to treat him like he's the Dying Gladiator or something. That stuff doesn't go in Jeremiah. I won't stand for any of my boys malingering."

"He's not malingering," Wanda retorted. "He has quite a painful hematoma. A boy can't take a beating like that and then be expected to go hopping around on both feet. Tomorrow will be soon enough. Why don't you just scram on out of here—"

"Now don't get yourself in an uproar, nursie," Reece began playfully, but nursie wasn't in a playful mood.

"Oh, get out," she growled, and, pushing him from the sickroom, she went to fetch some more cubes for Leo's ice pack.

Wanda Koslowski was, Leo and Emerson decided, just what a camp nurse ought to be, with her cap with the two blue stripes on it identifying her as a graduate of Saint Francis Hospital in Hartford, and the crisp crackle of her starched uniform, the slippery slide of her white stockings, the puckery tread of her rubber-soled oxfords on the green linoleum floor. They liked the brisk, efficient way she went about looking after them, and especially the way, when she leaned over to administer the thermometer, the feminine swell of her bosom (embellished with a nurse's pin of red-blue-and-gold enamel) pressed against them.

The afternoon wore on, bringing no more visitors, but enlivened by the sight of Honey Oliphant over at Three Corner Cove: she had taken her drum majorette's baton down to the dock to practice, and was tossing the flashing rod into the air and catching it in a series of deft moves, never missing once. Togged out in her white shorts and halter, with her lissome figure and her golden hair and dimpled smile, Honey was (the boys decided) like a Petty Girl out of *Esquire* magazine.

At powwow time Fritz came back with Rex Kenniston, who expressed sympathy and blamed himself for having left his post.

"I'm okay," Leo said.

"Are you kidding?" said Fritz. "I'd like to be in a nice clean bed, such as yours, waited on hand and foot by this Valkyrie."

He grinned at Wanda, who gave his hand a push.

"I brought you this," Fritz went on, holding up a book he had under his arm. "We'll speak of it when you're feeling better. In the meantime, you must get well if you're going to play for us in the Major Bowes Amateur Night contest."

Fritz said he'd stop by again in the morning, Rex said goodnight, and they left. Leo glanced through the book Fritz had left him, a collection of stories, tales in verse, old classics, some of which Emily had once read to Leo, and which he was now free to enjoy again.

But right now he did not feel like reading. Where were the Jeremians? he wondered. Why hadn't they dropped by to say hello? Were they mad at him? Finally, not long before bedtime, they appeared, Tiger, Bomber, Dump, Monkey, and Eddie—all but Phil and Wally. Still, five visitors was plenty; the room was small and their talk and laughter reverberated off the tongue-and-groove walls. No direct references were made to Leo's injuries, and they all seemed bent on speaking of other things: there'd been a baseball game and then powwow, and after supper an archery contest, which Reece naturally expected all Jeremians to attend.

Then two more visitors arrived: Honey, accompanied by her mother, Maryann, bringing the ice cream, dishes, and spoons. Honey had thoughtfully brought along her radio, which she left with the boys so they could listen to "Lights Out." At nine o'clock, except for the invalids, they all prepared to head back to camp, but Leo asked that Tiger and the Bomber be allowed to stay a little longer—there was something he wanted to tell them. Wanda okayed the request and, when she had dispatched Emerson to the Dewdrop, Leo called the Bomber to come away from the windowsill where he was perched. He wanted to explain, he said, why he'd been unable to jump off the tower.

"Aw, that's okay, you don't have to explain," the Bomber said. "You'll get over it anyways. By the end of summer you'll be doing swan dives off the tower."

Leo shook his head. He would never go up that ladder again, would never jump off the platform. The mere thought sickened him. "Acrophobia—that's what Dr. Epstein called it."

"Who's Dr. Epstein?" the Bomber asked.

"The doctor at the as-as—" He tried to get the word out but couldn't.

"Never mind," Tiger said. "You don't have to talk about it if you don't want to. . . ."

"But I do. I wa-want to, only it's—it's hard. I n-never told anyone. Dr. Epstein was—at the as-asylum."

"You mean"—the Bomber showed surprise— "the loony bin?"

Leo nodded.

"Why? What happened to you?"

Leo giggled. "I guess they must have thought I was loony."

There was a bit of a laugh over that. Leo was feeling better.

"Yeah, but, really, why were you there?" the Bomber insisted.

Leo shrugged. "I couldn't remember anything. My mind just went blooey. You know—" He imitated the "cuckoo" in a cuckoo clock. "That's when they told me my mother was dead."

"Jeez," said a sympathetic Bomber. "How'd that happen, anyways?"

There was a pause; Tiger watched and listened, saying nothing. Leo interlaced his fingers and rotated his palms together, thinking it out.

"There was this bridge," he said at last. "The L Street Bridge. It was old and rusty. They'd been working on it, trying to repair it. The river overflowed, it—it just carried the bridge away."

The Bomber leaned on the foot of the bed. "And your folks were on it?"

"Yes. On it." Leo was staring out the window. All he had to do was close his eyes and he would see them, Emily and Rudy in the delivery truck, driving onto the bridge—and below, the deep and rushy river swirling and foaming, that boiling witch's pot—and hear her cries—*"Help! Help!"*—the words ringing in his ears. "Mother! *Mother!* MOTHER! I'll save you"—but he cannot save her. No one can. The bridge begins to sway, it humps up like a camel's back and buckles, and all at once goes crashing down into the river, taking with it all the stars in the sky, all of them falling and drowning in the Cat River and—

Leo had a siege of coughing that he relieved with a full tumbler of water. When he had drained the glass the Bomber took it, and Leo lay back against the pillow. His backside was hurting again; maybe Wanda would give him another one of those little pills.

Nobody said anything more until Emerson came back from taking his pee and climbed stiffly into bed, pulling up the sheet until only his itchy, swollen, bunny-pink face was visible.

"Jeez, Emmy," the Bomber boomed, "you shoulda heard what we just heard."

"Yeah? What was it?" Emerson asked.

"Forget it, Emmy," Tiger said. "You didn't miss anything." He slipped Leo a wink and leaned closer to the bed, his gray eyes shining in the lamplight. "It's getting late," he said. "We'd better break it up."

A look to the Bomber forced him reluctantly to his feet just as Wanda reappeared to send the two visitors on their way and get her patients ready for bed. Deftly she touched up Emerson's calamine lotion, then gave Leo a refreshing witch-hazel sponging, afterward folding down his coverlet a precise eight inches and smoothing it with deft, professional strokes. It was like being put to bed by Emily, a little.

"Do I get another pill?" Leo asked in a small voice, looking as pathetic as he knew how.

"Is your baganza hurtin' again?" She brushed his hair back. "I'll go get one for you," she said, and went out; her pharmacopoeia was in Doc Oliphant's keeping at Three Corner Cove.

No sooner had she gone than Tiger's crewcut head reappeared at the windowsill. He leaned over and tossed a pillow onto Leo's bed, following it with a small cardboard box that rattled. The pillow was Albert, the box contained Black Crows.

"In case you get hungry," Tiger explained. "Don't say anything to Wanda."

"Thanks," Leo said.

113

"Anytime. Listen. . . ." Tiger's voice sank to a whisper. "I'm really sorry—about what happened, I mean. It wasn't fair of Reece to let it go on that way. You shouldn't have been paddled. Sometimes things just go too far, that's all. It won't happen again. Friend-Indeeders don't act that way."

He said it with such assurance that Leo got the feeling Tiger was making himself personally responsible for seeing to it.

" 'Never say die,' " Tiger added, then was gone.

Emerson took a drink and gave Leo a curious look. "What was that about?"

"Nothing, Emmy, something between us Jeremians, that's all. Have a Black Crow," he added. "Just don't get licorice on your sheets."

Hearing a footstep, he tucked the candy under his pillow and swallowed as Wanda returned to dole out his pill, give the boys another drink of water, and turn out the light. When she'd gone again Emerson corked right off; he was a good sleeper. Ten minutes later, however, Leo was still awake, and, lying there, he turned his head and stared out the window into the velvety summer dark, where gleaming fireflies hung in luminous clusters, and the thick air hummed with the persistent twang of night peepers.

It was such sights and sounds that reminded him of earlier, childhood days, when Emily was still alive, when he and she would sit sipping lemonade on the back porch, watching the nightpeepers at the bottom of the yard. Before . . . well, just "before."

His last living memory of her was on the evening of the big storm, when he was alone with Rudy in the Gallop Street house, anxiously waiting for her to come home. He would never forget the storm raging outside, the wind that banged the shutters against the clapboards and threatened to loosen the chimney bricks—and the river rising hourly, the Cat River that threatened to carry the whole bridge away. The L Street Bridge that would bring her home on the trolley—the bridge everyone feared would wash out.

It had rained so hard all day that Rudy hadn't opened the shop—few customers would have come—and the streets ran with water. At the south end of town the river flooded the dike, and the torrent rushed under the L Street Bridge. Schools were closed; Leo stayed in his room, praying that Emily would come home: there had been a telephone call and she had hurried away right after lunch, telling Leo only that she had to go see somebody. As the hours passed he became panicky. Where had she disappeared to in all this awful weather? If she was going upstreet she would have to cross the L Street Bridge; it was the only way. What if—No, he wouldn't think it, he mustn't! Suddenly he wanted to go and shout at Rudy, tell him to do something to save her.

Rudy was downstairs in the front room, drinking whisky from a glass, his ear glued to the radio for the latest bulletins, and from time to time Leo would go lean over the stair railing and listen to the announcer giving further details: roads were being washed out; more volunteers were manning what remained of the levees, and a special crew had stayed all afternoon sandbagging the supports of the bridge.

Around four Leo lay down on his bed and dozed; the storm seemed far away; the rattle of the rain in the tin drains lulled him. He was awakened by the sound of another trolley car coming down the street; he tiptoed to the front window. Yes! There she was! He watched with relief as a man helped her down. He recognized John Burroughs. John was coming to their house! Something wonderful was going to happen, Leo felt sure of it. Something that would change his life. He was going to the music school after all! He was sure of it! He ran into the hallway and leaned over the banister, saw them coming into the vestibule. Glimpsing him from below, Emily motioned for him to stay upstairs and wait. The doors to the front room closed behind them.

To calm himself, Leo found his violin and began to play. The song was "Poor Butterfly." But then had come Rudy's footsteps on the stairs. The door was flung open. *"No rhapsodies in this house,"* he shouted, and Leo put the violin away. When he heard the parlor doors slam shut again, he crept to the head of the stairs and listened. He heard their voices, Emily's, Rudy's, John's.

"Didn't I say? *No rhapsodies in this house?!"* came the angry roar from below.

When John spoke in a reasonable tone Rudy only shouted more angrily. Then Emily was crying out, and John was saying he would take Emily away, Leo too. "You don't love her, Matuchek," John went on. "You use her badly. She is a good woman and doesn't deserve such treatment."

"You call her a *good woman?* When you have her in your bed? What kind of man are you?" Rudy ranted. "To run off with another man's wife!"

From that moment Leo's memories remained a blur; he recalled a series of images, yet all occurring at the same time, frozen, as in a tableau, and illuminated by blinding flashes of lightning, while the storm raged outside:

"You can't take her!" Rudy is shouting. "She'll never go with you. If you want the kid so much, go ahead—take him."

"I'm taking him with me—" That is Emily's voice.

"Shut your mouth, you whore!"

Rudy must have struck her then, for she cries out in pain; Leo can bear it no longer; he starts down the stairs, then stops, cowering against the wall as the doors slide open and Emily comes hurrying through, John behind her, then Rudy. Rudy grabs John by the shoulder and swings him around, and the two men struggle.

Catching sight of Leo on the staircase, Emily reaches out to him. He wants to rush down, to fly to her and throw his arms around her, hide his eyes so he can't see. But at that moment the combatants break apart. John stands disheveled, breathing heavily, while Rudy pulls away and with another curse runs into the shop. Emily entreats John to leave quickly, before there is more trouble. "He'll do something terrible, I know it." But John refuses. "Not without you. Come with me, now. Leo too. We'll all go."

Leo starts down the stairs. Quickly—quickly—Mother, let's go before—before the bridge—we must get across the river. . . . All around, the thunder crashes. A livid streak of lightning turns everything silver. He trips on the stair, stumbles, sees, in another flash of lightning, Emily's white face twisted in an agony of pain and despair—"Mother!"—he reaches out to her—*Mother!* MOTHER!"—and then he is falling . . . falling . . . falling. . . .

He awakes. Where is he? In a white world, pristine in its brightness. A white room, in a white bed with white sheets and coverlet; white, everything is white. In the corner someone sits, a nurse: she wears a white uniform and cap. Is he in a hospital, then? Shortly afterward a doctor comes in; Leo is sure he's a doctor because of the stethoscope around his neck. He talks in a coaxing sort of voice, asking lots of questions. Later the nurse talks to him. Her name is Miss Holmes. He doesn't like her much. She is determined to amuse him. She lays out cards for a game: Authors. Right off Leo draws four Longfellows and a pair of Hawthornes; it's not hard to beat someone as dumb as Miss Holmes. She has a mustache like the bearded lady in Barnum & Bailey's.

Later, he has a visitor. A woman calling herself Mrs. Kranze, who says she knows him. Is she crazy? Leo has never seen her before. A friend, she tells him; she is a friend of his mother's.

"I want my mother," he says, as if the saying would produce Emily's corporeal form. Mrs. Kranze's face is all screwed up, tears are squeezed from her puffy eyes.

"Gone. She's gone." She sobs into his hair. "Poor child, poor, poor boy. What is to become of you now?"

Mother? M-mother? Where is she? The pain in his head is bad; the darkness is coming back, the white room is turning to black, and out of the blackness, the terrible jolt of memory. Something about the bridge? Yes, that's it—the bridge—the L Street Bridge—his mother—the bridge. "Did she go over the bridge?" he asks. "Did she go across?" Mrs. Kranze stares at him, biting her lips, the tears running down beside her large nose. "Yes," she says, at last, "across the bridge."

☽

Over at Three Corner Cove the darkness was suddenly cleaved as the Oliphants' porch light came on. In a moment the phonograph began playing:

> You go to my head
> Like a sip of sparkling Burgundy brew
> And I find the very mention of you
> Like the kicker in a julep or two.

Honey appeared and sat down on the top step, eating from a dish propped on her knees: Ice cream? Leo wondered. Her hair burnished by the lamplight, she seemed to go with the music; she was sparkling burgundy, and he wished he were sitting next to her. But then, as he watched, someone else materialized from the shadows. Reece sat beside her until she finished her ice cream and set the dish down. Then he got up and pulled her to him, and they began dancing to the music.

> The thrill of the thought
> That you might give a thought
> To my plea casts a spell over me.

> Still I say to myself,
> "Get a hold of yourself,
> Can't you see that it never can be."

Leo's heart was doing flip-flops. If he required any schooling in the way of a man with a maid, there it was, chapter and verse, the music, the starlight, the sweet nothings whispered in the ear. That was how grown-ups behaved, he guessed; Reece wasn't a boy, but a man, a combination of brains, muscles, glamour, and good looks, the flickering flame around which pretty moths like Honey Oliphant were bound to flit. And even after he had fallen asleep he continued to see the pair, turning and turning together, whirling like love phantoms in the dream dark, round and round in each other's arms while the music played and the moonlight danced on the water of Moonbow Lake and there were kisses in the shadows.

6

he luscious lipsticked damsel with tresses of gleaming gold leaned languidly upon the casement while down below her lovesick troubadour strummed his *mandolina* and crooned "Come into the Garden, Maude." The more passionate his song, the more languidly the beauteous creature leaned across the sill, her hand like some pale and fragile blossom as it gestured for her lover to ascend, à la Rapunzel, by making a ladder of her long lustrous locks. The song ended, the troubador flung away his instrument (it was a ukulele) and climbed—or tried to—in order to receive a kiss from his lady's rosy lips. Success, however, was not in the cards. It was a difficult moment; the weight of the amorous swain loosened the poor damsel's hair, which when it pulled free revealed Gus Klaus in female disguise, while the troubadour (Zipper Tallon) tumbled to the floor amid shouts and laughter, and the stage curtains (campers' blankets strung on a wire) swung to.

Cheers and jeers and thunderous stamping of feet greeted the conclusion of the skit, the noise rising to the roof beam from which the famous Camp Friend-Indeed horn chandelier shed upon the scene the glow of some two dozen kerosene lanterns. In the camp's earliest days Pa and Hank Ives had put the structure together out of the antlers of countless deer, elk, and moose, along with a pair from an African antelope contributed by Dagmar Kronborg and taken from the trophy walls of the Castle itself. More than six feet in diameter, three times that in circumference, suspended on a thick hawser through a block and tackle screwed into the rooftree, the fixture now actually shook, so great was the din.

Until a few years before, the Major Bowes Amateur Night theatricals had been held in the dining hall, but, thanks as usual to the generosity of Big Rolfe Hartsig, who had sent one of his construction crews over to put up the Teddy Roosevelt Memorial Nature Lodge, all such camp activities were now presented in the building on the lower campus, which this evening was filled almost to overflowing; every seat was taken, with the younger fry seated crosslegged on the floor in front of the stage, each camp unit with its respective group of counselors, each counselor doing his best to quell the high-spirited rowdiness that always enlivened such gatherings. Up front the center section had been reserved for staffers and their guests, among whom tonight was Ma's old friend Dagmar, making her first visit to Friend-Indeed since Stanley Wagner's malfeasance had led her to bar the Castle to campers. When she walked in, there had been a buzz among the boys—did this mean all was forgiven?—and embarrassed looks, but now, after the third skit of the evening, she seemed one of them again, obviously enjoying herself, her laughter ringing out above that of the loudest camper in the room.

Next to appear, a solo effort, was Mr. Jerome Jackson, the Brown Bomber, performing one of his *spécialités,* his famous impression of Fats Waller ("I'se a-muggin's, boom-dee-ah-dah"). Leo, sitting rather gingerly among his other cabinmates, glanced around, checking the rows for some sign of Reece, who hadn't shown up for the entertainment. His nose was out of joint because, having assigned "his boys" his own choice of a skit— "The Kindergarten," one of his favorites and an old chestnut—he had discovered at the last minute that a switch had been made. Without consulting him, Tiger and the Bomber had persuaded the others to veto the classroom comedy in favor of an idea Leo had gotten while in the infirmary. Learning of the change, Reece had branded the whole business a conspiracy ("A Jeremian is loyal to his counselor and sticks by a bargain"), and a violation of the team spirit that had always heretofore characterized Cabin 7 (Phil and Wally, out of deference to their leader, had refused to take part), and after dinner he had driven off with Honey Oliphant in the Green Hornet to take in a drive-in movie.

The curtains had closed on the Bomber (to loud whistles and applause), and the succeeding presentation was about to get under way. Once again the rafters shook to hand-clapping, foot-stamping, catcalls, and cheers as Pa made another introduction, venturing the announcement that the Ezekiel cabin's contribution to Major Bowes Night would be nothing less than the famed entertainment known as "The Old Lady and the Cow"—groans around the hall—or "An Udder Laff Riot"—laughs and applause—the role of the Old Lady to be essayed by that sterling thespian Emerson Bean (now recovered from his poison ivy), the cow jointly by those sterling look-alikes the Smith twins, otherwise known as the Coughdrops.

Watching this corny routine, the Bomber whispered to Tiger that Ezekiel was attempting either to empty the hall in a hurry or to put the audience to sleep. Having played the rear end of the cow often enough himself, he knew you couldn't help getting a boffola laugh when the front end, feet crossed, sat down on the rear end, and then both ends sat on the Old Lady, whereupon all three wound up on the floor; but the Smith brothers were woefully inept and in need of rehearsal, while the old, moth-eaten costume, which kept stretching perilously, then sagging, had nothing whatever about it that might be considered bovine. Then Smith-behind got tangled up with Smith-before, Old Lady Bean's long skirt was heavily trodden upon, and when the fabric tore away altogether, revealing undershorts printed in sloops and maritime pennants, the unlucky accident produced the single genuine laugh the skit afforded.

" 'All right, all right,' " Pa said when the hilarity subsided, imitating the familiar nasal monotone of radio's famous Major Bowes as he gave the "Wheel of Fortune" a good spin. " 'Round and round she goes, and where she stops, nobody knows,' " and the sock and buskin were passed along at last to the Jeremians. After a positive bouquet of an introduction, which wilted from its very floweriness, Pa announced the title: "The Doctor Is Definitely In," or "Oh, Doc, You Struck a Nerve," and no sooner had the performance begun than everyone in the audience knew that here was surely the hit of the evening.

The stage curtains parted to reveal a large bedsheet stretched taut across a wooden frame. A spotlight from behind illuminated this makeshift screen, and there appeared upon it the silhouette of a figure who pantomimed being afflicted with a bad stomach ache. Next, the audience was treated to the sight of a buxom nurse featuring an oversized *poitrine* and *derrière*, who assisted the patient in ridding himself of his coat, then proceeded to take his temperature with a three-foot-long outdoor thermometer. The nurse (the Bomber) grew considerably agitated, while the patient (Monkey Twitchell) became sicker by the moment. Presently an offstage bell rang and a voice announced "Dr. Mackinschleisser—call sur-ger-ee."

Now onto the sheet were tossed the capering shadows of three assistants (Fiske and Dillworth, and one shorter than the rest—Abernathy, of course), and the nurse proceeded with a remarkable amount of ado to scrub up, using a jumbo sponge and a basin the size of a potato tub. Ablutions completed, the three assistants heaved the protesting patient onto the operating table, then stumbled over one another getting out of the way as the gangly silhouette of the doctor was catapulted onto the screen as though shot from a cannon. Tall, thin, and of an antic disposition, Dr. Mackinschleisser, hero of the piece, was rendered the more hilarious by his very two-dimensionality. Alternately tipping his derby like a boulevardier and furiously twirling his furled umbrella, which he spun between his fingers like a drum major's baton, he brought down the house as soon as he appeared onstage. By the time he had executed the complex business of removing his gloves—starting each fingertip with a neat clip of his choppers, and finally rolling the gloves into a ball, popping them into his mouth, and devouring them—tears of laughter could be observed. Now, opening his Gladstone bag, the doctor pulled out a stethoscope, whose rubber cords he first snapped at the nurse's behind, then got stuck in his eye as he attempted to fit the instrument into his ears. Keenly listening to the patient's heartbeat, he wagged a disconsolate head: the prognosis was bad. Not so bad, however, that the patient might not once or twice lift his head from the table, for which trouble he received a whack with the doctor's oversized mallet.

At last, after some tricky mathematical calculations with a jumbo set of calipers upon the patient's chest, presumably to determine the location of the heart, the incision was made (by means of the vigorous employment of a lumberman's cross-cut saw), the body cavity was exposed (held open by a pair of carpenter's clamps), and the doctor proceeded to remove the sundry causes of the patient's discomfort: a pair of hip boots, a baseball bat, a hot-water bottle, a tennis racket with three balls, a pocketbook, some ladies' hosiery, a string of breakfast sausages, a toilet plunger, assorted crockery, cutlery, and cookware, a head of cabbage, a waiter's tray, plus yards of stuffing which even in silhouette looked suspiciously like excelsior. Finally, after further intensive probing, there followed a baby by the heels, crying, for which pains it received a stiff whack with the mallet.

"My dolly! Don't hurt her!" came an anxious cry from the audience.

"Hush, Willa-Sue," Ma was heard to say, "he's only doing make-believe."

The child's outburst earned another laugh, serving to remind the audience that the performer, the comical Dr. Mackinschleisser, was none other than Wacko Wackeem, actor extraordinaire, who now invited his patient to take a bow (thanks to the surgeon's wide medical experience, he had made a "full recovery"). As the cast reassembled and took its bows in front of the curtain, there was no question: Jeremiah had no rival in the skit department.

But there was still more to come: after a brief intermission, during which the actors shed their costumes and resumed their seats in the audience, Henry Ives sheepishly shuffled on and read from his copy of Chic Sale's book of backhouse humor, then played his one-man band. This entertainment was followed by Pa on his jazz whistle with "Yes, We Have No Bananas," and "Don't Bring Lulu," and Wiggy Pugh's rendition of "I Can't Get Started" on the same cornet he used for sounding taps. Next on was Charlie Penny, Job's counselor, in a cowboy hat and neckerchief, twirling a lariat and telling Will Rogers jokes, after which Ezekiel's counselor, Peter Melrose, led the camp chorus in "Darktown Strutters' Ball" and "Sleepytime Down South," inviting the audience to sing along.

Knowing that his solo violin performance was to follow this act, Leo circled around to the back of the room, where he had left his violin case. His bow had been rosined, the violin tuned, so he had only to wait to be introduced. When he heard Pa announce his name, with an awkward shift of limbs, he circled behind the audience to the stage. There was a murmur of anticipation as Pa announced the first selection, "In a Monastery Garden" by Ketelby, a piece Leo knew well, and the audience stirred in their seats, falling silent when, hunching his shoulders, Leo raised his violin, tucked it under his chin, lifted his bow, and began to play.

For the first few moments he had to fight the attack of nerves that always besieged him when he played on stage, but, presently, he experienced a familiar lift of spirits, that welcome sense of authority that seemed to carry him out of himself. He had only to give himself up to his deepest instincts and play the best he knew how. As his bow drew forth the deep, rich melody, his eyes roamed the faces of his audience, then the section reserved for the Harmony unit, where Tiger and the Bomber sat among the other Jeremians. Across the tip of the moving bow, he saw the look of rapt anticipation on their faces, as if they were just waiting for Leo to show what he could do. But at that moment Leo was most aware of Dagmar Kronborg, who sat calmly in her place, her eyes alive with interest, a bit quizzical, but appreciative. He could tell from her frequent nods that she approved, and this heartened him, spurring him to play his absolute best. Well, he thought, as he approached the final bars of the piece, it's all going well—as well as he'd hoped it would. First the skit, now his own recital.

When the number ended, the applause was generous, the audience eager for more. Leo made a brief adjustment to his strings, tested them once or twice, and prepared himself for his encore. The room fell quickly silent. He had started to raise his instrument and slide it in under his chin again when a loud sound was heard at the entrance; the double screen doors had opened, then slammed with a clatter. Heads turned at the disturbance, and a murmur of recognition swept through the crowd. The newcomer was Reece Hartsig. With him was Honey, her waist encircled by his arm. Appearing to enjoy the stir their entrance had caused, Reece tipped his cap in greeting to Ma and winked at Dagmar. He made no attempt to sit down but rather, keeping Honey close beside him, remained standing in full view of all, lounging against a post as he looked toward the stage.

Leo swallowed; felt a rush of panic. Suddenly, inexplicably, his fingers began to tremble, and his Adam's apple bobbed nervously in his throat. Then, mustering his courage, he took a deep breath, shut his eyes for a moment, and began.

Almost from the instant he first drew his bow across the strings, the audience was aware that something had happened. The performer was no longer exhibiting the ease and assurance he had demonstrated before. His eyes had taken on a harried expression, never lighting anywhere, but always returning, as if drawn by a magnet, to the back of the room, where Reece still leaned against the post, his arm around Honey's waist.

A jarring off-note set teeth on edge, an unexpected sharpness, then, quickly, a second mistake. The bow faltered, slurring clumsily across the strings, producing a shocking series of dissonances. Ma glanced at Dagmar, who stiffened in her chair. Tiger's brow was creased with bewilderment.

Then the final humiliation: Leo broke off midway through the bridge, halting with dismaying finality, and just stood there, awkward and embarrassed, blinking into the light. For a moment it seemed he might take up his melody again, but instead the violin slid away from the notch of his shoulder. He made a short, oblique movement backward, paused for a moment, then, clutching the violin in one hand, the bow in the other, he swerved abruptly and headed for the nearest exit. Eyes still lowered, shoulders hiked up, he reached the door, fumbled with the screen, trying to pull it toward him when it wanted pushing, then, outside, fled into the engulfing dark, while, in the excitement that greeted his precipitate departure, Pa rose from his seat and, hands clasped, announced the final presentation. Above the sound of the audience, clearly audible, came the voice of Claude Moriarity: "Wacko forgot his machine-gun case."

His joke produced a wave of jeers and laughter that spread throughout the hall until Pa had to call "All right, now—all right, now," so the closing act might begin. Only Dagmar Kronborg, silent and rigid in her place, and Tiger Abernathy, flushed with embarrassment at the humiliation of his friend, refused to join in the merriment as onstage Joey Ripley of Malachi and his ocarina had a go at "Dardanella."

PART THREE

Dreams in the
Midsummer Dark

1

uly 17, the date of the annual Water Carnival, had a big red circle drawn around it on Ma Starbuck's calendar, for not only was the event another long-standing Friend-Indeed tradition, attracting families and friends of campers from as far away as Hartford, but it was also customarily attended by the Elders of the Joshua Society and their spouses. Some had arrived in time for morning chapel in order to hear Pa's sermon, and afterward to attend Sunday dinner in the dining hall, an occasion that proved somewhat embarrassing to Leo, who was called to the staff table in order to shake hands with Dr. Dunbar and his wife. Blushing and stammering, he obeyed Pa's promptings in matters of appreciation, thanking the four-eyed pair for his Moonbow summer, and they in turn beamed and called him "our little orphan boy," after which he stumbled away, relieved to have got through it all.

As it did every Sunday noontime, even before the dinner hour ended, the lower playing field had begun filling up with honking automobiles disgorging visitors in a holiday mood—uncles and aunts and cousins swelling the ranks of parents, smoothing the wrinkles out of their sticky garments after the drive from the city, and wide-eyed little sisters trying to pick out big brothers from among the throng of campers. Some of the moms (as they had on previous Sundays) displayed to other, lesser cooks the fresh baked goods they'd brought along, while their spouses, in straw skimmers, two-tone shoes, and jackets with swing-backs, gladhanded one another and said things like:

"Swell day for the race, huh?"

"Which race?"

"The human race!" Oh boy!

Soon the line of vehicles bordered the entire length of the field, clear to the end of the Harmony unit, and by the time the boys got down to the lower camp the whole place had a festive air. Among the last to leave the dining hall was Leo, who along with Eddie Fiske had pulled waiter's duty, and who had to pass inspection, not only with Oats Gurley, but with Bullnuts Moriarity, dining hall "captain" for the week.

"Hey, Wacko," he bawled, as Leo headed for the door. "Whyn'tcha play us another tune on your ukulele!"

Leo ignored the crack, but as he hiked down the road with Eddie, who chattered away in his eager fashion, Leo scarcely heard him, still feeling the sting of Moriarity's remark and lost in thoughts of his own. Whatever foolish hopes he had entertained that his contribution to Major Bowes Night would redeem his reputation at Friend-Indeed after his failure to go off the diving tower had come to naught, the success of the skit (sixty points for Jeremiah) having been vitiated by his embarrassing performance afterward, which had made him a laughingstock. How, he asked himself, how could something that had begun with such promise have gone so awry? Why had the sudden appearance of Reece and Honey caused his fingers to become as wax, the notes to blur in his mind, turning what should have been a rousing success into the single most humiliating experience of his life?

After stumbling out of the lodge in shame and mortification, he had hidden out at the infirmary dock, where he was sure no one would bother looking for him. But he was wrong; Tiger and the Bomber had tracked him down. When he tried to thank them for their support Tiger had merely winked. " 'All for one, one for all,' " he had said. "Isn't that right, Bomber?" And that had made Leo feel special—more than a Jeremian, one of the Three Musketeers.

They had coaxed him back to the cabin, where he was forced to face his cabinmates. No one had said much while they were getting ready for bed, but after taps there had been fits of giggles sputtering in the dark. Mercifully, Reece had not been present; Phil announced that he'd gone off somewhere in his roadster—with Honey or without, who could say? Lying awake, Leo imagined them together laughing about him, heads close, Reece touching, holding her, nuzzling her neck, smelling her cologne, whispering in her ear, she making jokes about Wacko Wackeem; pin-the-tail-on-the-donkey Leo.

Strangely, however, breakfast the next morning had come and gone with no mention by Reece of Major Bowes. It was almost as if, having revenged himself for Leo's violation of Jeremiah's hard-and-fast principle of teamwork by showing up in that disquieting way at the lodge, the counselor had made his point—whatever point that might be. And no one else had said anything more on the subject either (except Ma, who asked why she hadn't heard Leo practicing; he needed to replace a broken string, he told her) until last night's powwow, before the torches were lit for the second biweekly council fire. Then Reece had given his boys one of his pep talks, announcing that "all things considered" they'd "done good" in the last week, though, unfortunately, the results of the Major Bowes Amateur Night had been less than expected: Jeremiah had certainly taken top honors in the skit department, but had lost the hoped-for points from Leo's recital (Hatton's "Insidious Ice Cream Cone" had scored first). Still, he thought he could "say without fear of contradiction" that, though they were going to have to "sweat their underpants" to "bring home the bacon" in the next day's competitions, if they all "pulled together" they would doubtless pick up enough points to "erase the most recent blot from the family escutcheon." He didn't have to remind them—did he?—that, as would be announced officially tonight, Jeremiah still stood behind Malachi in points.

And that, Leo thought now, was the rub. Since he was the only Jeremian who wasn't entered in any swim events, he couldn't do much there to better the overall score, or erase the humiliation of Major Bowes.

Eddie had made a stop at the Dewdrop Inn before going off to find his folks, and Leo was alone, crossing the lower playing field, when he overheard two campers making snide remarks about a couple of visitors.

"Jeez, who d'you suppose those two old goofers are?" Zipper Tallon was muttering to Klaus.

"Look like a couple of real hicks to me," Gus replied.

Leo followed their looks across the field to a man and woman who stood by themselves beside a rattletrap car, blinking in the sun as if trying to get their bearings. He had a sudden sinking feeling as he recognized them: Miss Meekum and Supervisor Poe. He couldn't believe it! What were they doing, turning up here like this? And with no warning? He grew suspicious. Was he being sent back to Pitt for not measuring up? Was his Moonbow summer to be over so soon? For an instant he wanted to turn and run as far away as he could, but it was too late; they had spotted him. With a stone for a heart he dragged his feet toward them: bedraggled Miss Meekum, in her brown dress of home-knit boucle, wearing a brave little hat; Supervisor Poe, looking like an old black crow in his shiny suit and celluloid collar, glasses pinched on the bridge of his red nose.

"Surprise, surprise," caroled Miss Meekum, beckoning with her hanky as Leo approached.

"Leo, my boy, here you are," Mr. Poe declared in his pale, papery voice, giving Leo's hand a single, formal jerk. Too stunned by their unexpected advent to say anything, Leo darted him a glance.

Porcelain-pale under her coating of white vanity powder, Miss Meekum was already fussing at him, tugging his collar and brushing off his shoulder, inquiring how he was getting on. "Are you having a good time?"

Leo ducked his head. "It's okay, I guess."

"*Okay*—you *guess!*" Miss Meekum's fa-so-la laugh climbed its way up the scale. "Why, I should hope it's *nice!*" The steel rims of her glasses sparkled in the sun when she gazed at Leo, as if to assure herself of his well-being. "My goodness, will you look at him," she went on. "He's put on weight—hasn't he put on weight, Mr. Poe? And see how tan he is. I can't get over it. You seem so—so *different!*" She gave his arm a squeeze. Quickly Leo withdrew it. Several campers were hanging around now watching.

"Did you drive all that way just to see me?" he asked.

"Of *course* we did," Miss Meekum replied. "We were simply panting to get out of the city—so hot. *And* we wanted to meet Reverend and Mrs. Starbuck and the Society people."

Leo breathed a sigh of relief. So they hadn't come to take him back after all. But cripes, he thought; the fact that this was just a social call meant he'd have to introduce them around to everybody. He looked from Miss Meekum to the supervisor, who was eyeing him narrowly.

"Which of these cabins is yours, Leo?" he inquired.

Leo pointed out Cabin 7. "It's called Jeremiah."

Miss Meekum craned her neck to look. "Jeremiah," she repeated. "How quaint. May we have a peek?"

Left no choice, Leo reluctantly escorted them across the field, self-conscious because the only family he could put up against all the others was no relation of his, only these two gray birds, looking so out of place in their badly wrinkled, ill-fitting city clothes. Why hadn't they at least given him warning so he could have cooked up some kind of story about them?

Mercifully, Jeremiah was vacant when they got there, so Leo, in his chagrin, was not required to deal immediately with making introductions. But as Miss Meekum exclaimed over his ceremonial torch (the carving of a ceremonial torch was one of the most important traditions at camp, and each incoming camper must perform the ritual of cutting a branch in Indian Woods and decorating it with occult Indian symbols), and Dr. Poe noted approvingly the military neatness of the cabin, he spotted Tiger and the Bomber (thank goodness it was them!) coming along the linepath with a man and woman who turned out to be the Abernathys, pleasant-looking people with kind, sympathetic faces, who had driven up for the big event from their cottage on Long Island Sound. (The Bomber's folks never came on Sundays—or any other day, either. "My ole lady's glad to get rid of me," he bragged; his father, a school janitor with a yen for booze, never seemed to know what his son was up to—or care.) They all walked right inside, and in his easygoing, cheerful way Tiger presented himself, his parents, and "our friend Jerome" to the older couple. Leo was ready to jump out of his skin. What would Supervisor Poe and Miss Meekum talk to the Abernathys about? He quailed at the thought of some inadvertent disclosure, about the goings-on at Pitt, or the unhappy events that had seen him brought to the Institute in the first place. And though the skies were blue, with no sign of rain, in the echo chamber of his mind he heard the alarming crash of thunder and the familiar sound of rain rattling in the downspout, heard the chink of Rudy's bottle against the glass and his angry voice—

Tell him, you bitch—no rhapsodies—

"I hope you'll play your violin for us, Leo," Miss Meekum was saying, as if reading his mind. "I hope you've been practicing. Have you?"

"Yes'm."

A bold-faced lie, but what Miss Meekum didn't know wouldn't hurt her.

Then the others began to appear—first, Eddie with his folks, then Monkey with his—and Leo began to relax. What was there to worry about? Everyone seemed to be getting along just fine. Why, Mr. Poe and Miss Meekum were talking away with the Abernathys as if they were old friends, nodding and smiling, fitting right in, just like regular folks! Maybe things were going to turn out okay after all. Maybe they *had* just driven out for a little holiday, to see how he was getting on.

Before long the Dodges, the Pfeiffers, and the Dillworths had joined the

group, and as the crowd spilled out onto the porch, Reece Hartsig, counselor supreme, moved among the parents of "his boys," speaking with each
in turn; discussing with Dump's father the chances of St. Louis winning the
pennant this year (now that Dizzy Dean had been traded to the Cubs);
confiding a new joke to Wally's dad; raising his stock with Phil's parents by
remarking on the fine job of work their son was doing on his radio transmitter project; even complimenting Miss Meekum on her hat.

Then across the field a disconcerting one-bar melody was heard—an
automobile horn blaring the four zany notes of "How Dry I Am"—and a
shiny new car—the latest model Lincoln Zephyr—rolled over the rise and
came to a stop in front of Cabin 7. The Hartsigs senior had arrived: Big
Rolfe, a large, florid-faced man in a wrinkled seersucker suit, with a Zeiss
camera hung around his neck, and, shoved back from his warm brow, a
straw hat with a band of striped silk; and his wife, Joy, a petite woman with
a shingled bob of bright blondined hair, lots of lipstick and rouge, and a gay
laugh, who was attired (in honor of the day's nautical theme) in a sailor
outfit, with a striped collar and gob's cap emblazoned with an anchor and
cord and little gold stars.

"How do you like her, fellows?" Rolfe bawled heartily, flourishing his
skimmer at the car, which was now surrounded by campers admiring their
reflections in the glossy black finish and the liberally applied chromium trim.
Then, with his wife on his arm, he made his way up the porch steps to greet
the parents of the Jeremians, most of whom were old friends, and regale
them with the tale of how he'd come by his new two-hundred-dollar Swiss
watch—"got it for cash off this little sheeny on a street corner. Hot goods,"
he joshed, and they all laughed immoderately—while inside the cabin Joy
sat herself down on Reece's cot (she was the *only* person ever permitted
such a trespass) and smiled brightly at Miss Meekum and Supervisor Poe,
saying wasn't Leo *lucky* to get into Jeremiah, where all the really tiptop
campers were.

By this time the crush inside the cabin had become considerable, and
Leo, seeing that Miss Meekum and Mr. Poe were in safe hands, ducked
outside, where he found the Bomber leaning on the porch rail and observing
the arrival of yet another vehicle, a Pierce-Arrow with black lacquered
fenders and a dark-green cab taller than that of any of the other autos on
the field. "It's Dagmar," the Bomber informed him as the chauffeur, a
colored man wearing a straw hat and no jacket ("His name's Augie," said

the Bomber), got out and opened the rear door, and Leo recognized Ma's friend from Major Bowes Night—witness to his humiliation. He had decided when he first saw her that in no way could Dagmar Kronborg be called conventional, and now, in close proximity, he found her both compelling and intimidating. Her blue eyes sparkled with such a bright blueness—keen eyes that missed nothing. He suspected she might be older than she looked: sixty-five? seventy, maybe? She had salt-and-pepper hair and leathery skin, tanned and wrinkled, and beyond a careless use of lipstick on her puckered lips she wore no makeup. He was intrigued by the husky timbre of her voice and the forceful energy behind it. Her English bore only traces of her Swedish origins, and when she laughed the sound was a rich, robust explosion of mirth.

"Hello—hello, all," she called, nodding to the lineup of boys and adults who now crowded the porch of Jeremiah for the express purpose, it seemed, of greeting her arrival.

"Well, Dag, how are you?" Big Rolfe pushed his way through and enfolded her in a bearlike embrace, loudly kissing her.

"I'm fine—but don't call me Dag. I don't like it." She gave him a sock on his shoulder and put her cheek out for Joy to kiss. "And here's Mr. Jack-in-the-Box himself," she added, as Reece sprang out the side of the cabin to land in front of her.

"Hello, Auntie—how are you?" He threw his arms around her and, lifting her off her feet, bussed her roundly on both cheeks. "Come on up to the porch and take a load off. It's time to catch Dad's Sunday broadcast."

Nearly every Sunday afternoon around this time, Reece's father tuned in to the weekly preachments of Father Coughlin, the "Radio Priest," whose multitude of admirers were convinced he was America's savior and would keep its people from falling victim to the Red Menace. Since this host of advocates included Pa Starbuck as well as Big Rolfe, not many at Friend-Indeed disparaged the prelate openly, though Fritz Auerbach had declared that the man was a rabble-rouser and demagogue, and should be silenced.

Dagmar, evidently, was not a Coughlin admirer either. While the priest held forth on how Franklin Delano "Rosenfeld" was "selling America short"—Rolfe had thrown open every door of his car "so all could hear"— she excused herself and marched over to the fountain for a drink. Leo stepped up beside her and gallantly pushed the button, and as she straightened and blotted her lips, accepting his courtesy as a matter of course, she found his eyes studying her.

"Eh? What's this?" she demanded. "Do you think I'm funny-looking, then? You'll see a lot funnier sights before you grow up, young man—and learn some manners!"

Leo was speechless in the face of this outburst. He felt his face blazing scarlet, and mumbled an apology.

"Gode Gud," Dagmar exclaimed in Swedish, lifting her glass to her eye. "It's the violinist. Now, why didn't I recognize you? What a stupid old thing I am!" Leo was mortified—she *had* noticed him, then, at Major Bowes, and now recalled his shame—but she cocked her head at him and in a quicksilver change of course, she said, "You were very amusing in the skit the other evening, too—very funny. He *was,*" she assured the cluster of visitors who had been watching the exchange. "And he thought the whole thing up himself," she added. "How do I know that? Because Ma told me."

Before any more could be said, the voice of Hap Holliday—its stentorian tones enhanced by a megaphone—was heard from the waterfront, inviting guests to come and be seated in the council ring. The afternoon's events were about to begin. As Peewee Oliphant came pelting down the linepath, waving his arms to a fare-thee-well and hollering for all campers to get a wiggle on—Coach wanted all boat-parade participants at the lodge in five minutes to get into costume—a couple of shrill blasts from Reece's whistle galvanized the Jeremians to heed the summons. Then Reece himself headed for the dock to confer with Rex and Hap on matters pertaining to the swim competition, while Dagmar rejoined the Hartsigs and the entire adult contingent connected with Jeremiah headed toward the council ring. Even Father Coughlin could offer no competition to the prospect ahead of them. The Abernathys, Leo observed, had Mr. Poe and Miss Meekum in tow, and when the cabin was empty of visitors, he scrambled about, snatching up items of gear, and ran off to join the others, forgetting his humiliation, for the moment at least, in anticipation of things to come.

All around the council ring, campers, counselors, and guests alike were dispersed among the tiers, the overflow scattered along the waterfront, the ladies, wafting improvised fans (pleated programs), ensconced in folding chairs, the gentlemen seated on cushions on the ground beside them. And here was Pa Starbuck making his official progress through the assemblage of parents and guests, nodding and smiling and generally behaving as if all this—every glint of sunlight, every lap of the waves, every glittering splash and dive, every foot of cloudless sky, every joyful camper and approving parent—was the work of his own hand and no other's—until, exhibiting enviable spryness for a man his age, he climbed onto the flat top of Tabernacle Rock to offer a welcoming address whose floweriness embraced "the piney fragrance of the grove," how happy he was "to gaze upon so many happy faces," the "salubriousness of the day God hath wrought" for the proceedings, and the "one or two special guests of note": Dr. and Mrs. Justiss Dunbar, the doctor being the "First Chairman of the Committee for the Endowment of Young Males by the Friends of Joshua Bible Society" (as he and his organization were formally known). Then, with a gracious wave of the hand, Pa brought on Fritz Auerbach ("our visitor from foreign lands, to whom Dr. Dunbar and the Friends of Joshua have seen fit to offer sanctuary"), who, as arts-and-crafts director, was the guiding spirit behind the famous "Parade of Ships" that led off the afternoon's program—the event that annually gave the broadest scope to the campers' wit and ingenuity, requiring as it did the transformation of humble rowboats and scows into representations of the triremes and galleons of yore.

Fritz, equally gracious, expressed his gratitude for the opportunity the Society had given him, and, his gently modulated voice amplified through the megaphone, proceeded to introduce the various entries as they traversed the five hundred yards from the boat dock to the swimming dock, where they were rated by a panel of judges (Pa, Doc Oliphant, and Henry Ives) on originality, execution, and presentation: Columbus's famed *Niña, Pinta,* and *Santa María* (three for the price of one)—the Job entry; a Mississippi River paddle wheeler, with its smokestack puffing—Malachi; even the *Titanic,* Hosea's entry, which, in full view of all, "struck" an "iceberg" and "went to the bottom"; and finally—this was ultimately awarded the first prize (twenty happy points and an extra helping of dessert all round)—Jeremiah's entry, the old camp whale boat converted into a "Cleopatra's barge" of remarkable configuration, her gunwales festooned with flowered swags and wreaths. A stern-visaged Marc Antony (Phil Dodge), complete with an approximation of a helmet and a scarlet cape, posed dramatically, sword in hand, on the foredeck, while a stalwart Roman centurion with a trumpet (Tiger Abernathy) and the queen's own brother-husband, young Ptolemy (Leo Joaquim), exchanged murderous scowls just behind him. Astern, the plump and gaudy Egyptian queen lounged amid a bower of wild flowers, one hand trailing languidly in the water as its mate dangled a bunch of gilded grapes over a pair of bright-red lips: Mr. Jerome Jackson, ludicrously lipsticked and rouged, bedecked in an outrageous wig and a tin brassiere cleverly wrought from a pair of kitchen funnels. An outsized "diamond" was ingeniously attached to his navel, and his husky physique was swathed in folds of gauzy fabric (dyed cheesecloth), yards of which drapery trailed prodigally in the barge's wake.

While everyone awaited the judges' decision, and those entered in the swim competitions went off to change into trunks, Leo, having performed his part in the proceedings, headed toward the council ring, making his way through the boisterous throng now jamming the docks—campers of all sizes clad in swimming trunks, skinny young boys with bat ears and xylophone ribs, older boys exhibiting burgeoning musculature. As they pranced around, snapping towels and giving Indian rubs, waiting for the first event of the meet to start, their collective eye was fixed on Hap Holliday, who, as master of ceremonies, was huddled with Rex Kenniston over the list of contestants on his clipboard.

"Where's your bathing suit, Leo?" Miss Meekum asked as he joined her and Mr. Poe and the rest of the Jeremiah "family." "Why aren't you with the other boys?" Leo flushed and ducked his head; the moment he had feared must come, had come. Unable to think up a good story, he was stuck with the truth, and he explained to them how he had come in a loser in the preliminary heats.

"Well, that's all right," Miss Meekum said, patting his knee. "It means we'll have you here with us, all to ourselves." She leaned her spare form toward her neighbor, Mrs. Abernathy, who smiled and nodded as if to affirm that to have Leo among them was to enjoy a special treat.

Leo was relieved when Hap, taking up the megaphone again, announced the start of the first race, the "Tadpole Relay," in which Peewee Oliphant was a top contender. As everyone sat up attentively, Rex's whistle shredded the air, and a dozen small, brown, leggy bodies sprang like so many frogs into the water inside the crib rope.

The first lap of the race was swum amid great thrashings and splashings, and cheered enthusiastically by the whole crowd. Peewee, who was his team's anchorman, would be among the last to swim, and he stood, chewing on a thumb and hopping impatiently from one foot to the other, waiting his turn to enter the water. When it came he seized the baton and plunged headlong into his lane; he was in the lead as the last batch of boys surfaced, the baton clamped between his teeth and swimming hell-for-leather.

" 'Ray, Peewee! Come on, Peewee!"

The Oliphants, seated down front with the Starbucks and their invited guests, rose cheering to their feet, and a burst of enthusiasm washed across the waterfront.

"Come on, Peewee—kick it! Swim!"

As first Peewee, then the others touched the canoe dock, flipped over, and headed down the home stretch, most of the crowd was on its feet. Peewee was flagging now, with Bouncer Williams, an older, bigger cadet, gaining on him. But at the finish it was Peewee who touched home first, and Reece Hartsig was there to lift him from the water and sling him onto his shoulders, parading him around to accept the acclaim of the crowd, then swing him down and turn him over to his own counselor.

"Isn't it exciting!" Miss Meekum gasped, pressing a palm to her breast. "And he's such a little sprout, isn't he?" Leo agreed that Peewee was indeed a "sprout." He was feeling better about Miss Meekum and Supervisor Poe being there. Mr. Poe was obviously enjoying himself, and Miss Meekum was acting gay as spring.

One after another, the tadpole races were run, each succeeding heat exciting the audience's collective blood and bringing them to their feet with louder, more encouraging shouts. Leo could hear Big Rolfe's booming voice avowing that this was what Camp Friend-Indeed was all about, striving and winning, and as he looked down upon the array of campers on the dock, popping the bubbles from their ears and bulling around with each other while they awaited the next event, he racked his brain, trying to think of something he could do to shine: something that, after Major Bowes, might redeem him in the eyes of the camp (standing on the Cleopatra's barge pretending to be Ptolemy certainly hadn't done it). But nothing came to mind, and so he sat there like a bump on a log, a face in the crowd, while the tadpole events came to an end and the Harmonyites marched out onto the dock.

As the fans of Jeremiah (Leo included) rose up to cheer, the Bomber did a Joe Louis handclasp over his head, jumped into Number 12, flung himself upon his oars, and proceeded to win the rowboat race hands down. Monkey Twitchell, who more aptly might have been nicknamed Fish, for that was how he swam, copped the 220-freestyle medley, while Tiger took the crawl. Watkins of Obadiah and the Smith brothers all won firsts in other events, but Phil Dodge won top honors in the breaststroke—husky arms and shoulders and a strong frog-kick made him a winner here. Eddie Fiske came in second in the hundred-meter, losing by a hair to Dusty Rhoades of Ezekial, and the Bomber took a first in the underwater race. Like some subaqueous leviathan, he remained submerged for two minutes and fifty seconds, traversing the crib four times, a new camp record. Wally, poor fellow, came in third in each of his events; still, Leo thought, it was better than nothing, and he watched enviously as Reece strode about the dock, beaming, congratulating his winners.

"Isn't this fun?" Miss Meekum said to him, hugging her knees and smiling. She leaned over to speak to Mrs. Abernathy. "We were so happy that Leo was able to come to camp—and to be in Cabin Seven."

Mrs. Abernathy agreed loyally that Jeremiah was the best cabin to be in.

"Leo tells us your son is his friend," Miss Meekum went on. "Everyone seems to think very highly of Tiger."

Mrs. Abernathy was both modest and friendly. "Pat and I are glad Leo likes Tiger. We're very proud of our Brewster, but of course we're prejudiced. And don't tell him I called him Brewster, he'll kill me." She turned to include Leo and Mr. Poe in her next remark. "Perhaps when camp is over Leo might like to come and spend the weekend with us. We've plenty of room, haven't we, Pat?"

Pat Abernathy nodded amiably. "Yes, indeed, Tiger's got the whole attic for a room, bunks and all. Leo would be most welcome."

The conversation was interrupted as, down at the lifeguard stand, Rex reached for his megaphone and addressed the crowd with mock solemnity.

"Ladies and gentlemen, your attention, please. My colleague—I refer to the estimable Hap Holliday—has instructed me to announce that the scheduled proceedings will be delayed some fifteen minutes to allow the presentation of an extra added attraction to mark the final year of Friend-Indeed camping on the part of Reece Hartsig.

"Yes, folks," Rex went on, "the counselor of Jeremiah cabin has agreed to provide us with an exhibition of authentic athletic prowess by executing several spectacular dives from the high springboard."

Ardent sounds of approval rippled through the crowd; cheers, whistles, and applause rang out, as, with an unaccustomed display of modesty, Reece emerged from the crowd and doffed his cap, then proffered it with exaggerated formality to Rex and dived off the dock. When he reached the float he once more saluted his enthusiastic fans, then mounted the ladder and trotted to the tip of the diving board, testing it with a controlled spring that flexed his heavy thigh muscles. Moving back, he meticulously aligned his feet, palms flat at his sides, rolled his shoulders, and then took a neat three-step approach and jump-struck the board, which catapulted him into the air. His sharp jackknife seemed to be over before it had begun as legs and feet slipped into the circle of water that his head, hands, and shoulders had already made.

" 'Ray, Big Chief!" the Bomber shouted, his voice carrying above the applause. "Yay—Heartless!" Other boys took up the cry, while their elders laughed indulgently at the epithet.

More applause greeted the counselor as he surfaced, cleaved a neat, economic path through the water, and ran nimbly up the ladder for a second demonstration, this time an elegant swan dive, which was succeeded by a one-and-a-half-gainer, the dive he was best known for, then the more difficult double-gainer with a half-twist. When he came out of the water the last time, his tanned body glistening in the sun as if dripping with diamonds, it was on the dock, and the cheers of the crowd, which thought the display must be over, rose mightily. But Reece made no bow. Instead, he bounced on each foot to pop his ears, then marched over to Rex and spoke to him. The pair were subsequently joined by Hap, who attended with a grave expression. Was something wrong? As a murmur compounded of curiosity and excitement swept the crowd, the talk among the staffers went back and forth for a few moments more; then, while Hap went off in one direction and Reece dived once more into the water and headed toward the raft, Rex again resorted to his megaphone.

"Ladies and gentlemen, your attention, please! Will Tiger Abernathy please come forward!"

At this, the Bomber, who had been leaning against the lifeguard tower, dove into a knot of boys, from which he emerged in a moment, shoving Tiger into full view.

" 'Ray, Tiger! 'Ray, Tiger!" The eager shout was taken up all across the waterfront as Tiger trotted out onto the dock for a quick conference with Rex, which was followed by a second announcement.

"Ladies and gentlemen, Mr. Brewster Abernathy—'scuse me, folks,

Mr. *Tiger* Abernathy—has consented to perform for us today, in tandem with Mr. Hartsig, a piggyback swan dive."

Yet another rumble of excitement sounded among the spectators, and the enthusiastic cheers and applause of his pals sent Tiger pelting off the dock into the water for a quick sprint out to the raft. On the high platform Reece hoisted him onto his shoulders, then, supporting him by his hands, with perfect ease and coordination he stepped onto the board and moved to the end where he paused, adjusted his hands to clasp Tiger's ankles, and, breaking his knees slightly, straightening them with a snap, he sent a forceful jolt into the board, whose limber spring propelled the pair into space. The two melded forms soared forward, each with arms outflung; they remained in tandem for another beat, then gracefully parted, the single figure dividing as their heads went down and they dropped headfirst into the water, four feet apart, with hardly a splash. The crowd went wild.

Returning to the tower, the two divers encored with a half-gainer, followed by a standing back dive; then, graciously abstaining, Reece dispatched Tiger up the ladder for a trio of beautifully executed solo dives before joining him in the swim to shore.

From the edge of his seat atop the council ring, Leo observed it all, awed by Tiger's performance, admiring his agile, compact body and envying his natural athleticism, his grace of movement; envying, too, the adulation from the crowd, and the modest way Tiger accepted it. He caught the glow of pleasure in Mrs. Abernathy's eyes, the quiet pride in her husband's, and he itched to jump up and show himself off to advantage as well, to make people look that way because of some feat he had performed. But how? What could he do? How could he ever hope to rival Tiger's stellar performance?

He sat back as the two divers came dripping onto the swim dock and disappeared among the huddle of contestants. The applause died down, but the scheduled proceedings were further delayed when, instead of the Endeavorites, the white-clad figure of Pa Starbuck appeared suddenly upon the dock. Waving his hands about his head, he gestured for Rex's megaphone.

"I wish to pause a moment more in this afternoon's program," he declared through the varnished mouthpiece, "to say before this gathering how privileged we of Camp Friend-Indeed have been to have known Reece Hartsig, a young man of rare qualities, who began here at Moonbow Lake at an age not much more advanced than our Peewee Oliphant is today"—appreciative laughter and applause greeted this sally—"and I know my own good wife and helpmeet, my Mary"—he pronounced it "May-ree"—"concurs in these sentiments, for she has been 'Ma' to Reece as she has been to all the other boys. I say to you that no camper, staffer, or counselor who has passed up the linepath has brought more honor to our blessed camp. This is his last summer of Moonbowing, and I say that when he departs our shores, a Glad Man made from a Happy Boy, he shall be sorely missed."

"Don't worry, he'll be back," Big Rolfe called out through cupped hands. "You haven't seen the last of our boy, Gar. He'll plunk that plane of his down on the playing field, he'll give the fellows a spin."

"Hear! Hear!" Louder cheers and more enthusiastic shouts among the adults greeted these sentiments, while the boys went crazy.

" 'Ray, Big Chief!" they shouted, after which Pa gave Reece a warm handshake and returned to his chair. Left alone, Reece spoke a few words of thanks, then, modest to a fault, retired into the crowd of congratulating admirers as the senior events got under way.

Watching his counselor, who stood beside Tiger now, taking in the senior freestyle race, Leo brooded on the image of the pair flying off the tower, hearing again the tumultuous applause and cheering, his heart pounding with excitement at the memory. No matter how many races Jeremiah won, or how many happy points they earned today, in Leo's mind nothing would match the sight of those glorious dives. And over and over again the burning thought: What could *he* do to shine? Then, suddenly, he knew! He jumped up and pushed his way along the row to race up the aisle, leaving a perplexed Miss Meekum staring at his sudden departure.

He was still absent when the contests among the High Endeavorites came to an end, with Malachi the leader in unit points. Since Jeremiah had come out ahead in Harmony's swim events, as well as taken first prize in the Parade of Ships, the two cabins were running neck and neck in overall camp point score as the popular and dramatic canoe-tilting contest began, and the excitement was intense when, after several elimination rounds, the two finalists paddled to "center stage"—Tiger and the Bomber up for Jeremiah, Blackjack Ratner and Moon Mullens for Malachi: the winning team stood to put its cabin in the lead for the Hartsig Trophy. Given that Tiger was an expert canoer, while the Bomber was noted for his balance and deadly aim, the contest was expected to be an easy win for Jeremiah. Still, the audience was tense as they watched the Jeremian, spraddle-legged and precariously balanced in the bow of the canoe, the tip of his long bamboo lance inserted into the neck of a rubber toilet plunger, face his challengers, Ratner in the bow, Mullens paddling. Like two knights in a medieval tourney, the rivals began jousting with each other, each warrior trying to knock the other into the water.

Wearing the Joe Louis frown of concentration that had earned him his nickname, the Bomber skillfully parried and thrust, and the outcome seemed assured when an unexpected distraction from onshore caught his attention, enabling Blackjack to catch him off balance and smack him alongside the head, toppling him into the lake; over went the canoe as well, tossing Tiger into the water too, while the Bomber, surfacing, hollered, "We wuz robbed!"

But no one was attending; something of livelier interest was taking place at the top of the council ring, where a fantastic figure had appeared, with a grotesquely made-up clown's face and, slung about his shoulders, a red cape, which, as he tore down the path to the lakefront, rippled out behind him like Superman's. Then, as the spectators laughed and began to applaud his antics, he pranced to the end of the dock, where, shedding the cape, he executed a burlesque dive into the water and stroked energetically toward the raft.

Reaching it, he hauled himself aboard, ran for the tower ladder, and clambered upward. At the top, he threw his head back and beat on his chest while uttering a savage Tarzan yell, then, without missing a beat, rushed to the platform edge, launched his body into space, and went plummeting downward; his victorious cry seemed to hang in the air for a moment after he had struck the water and sunk from sight.

The crowd sat now in a hush, waiting for the diver to surface. Where was he? Who was he? they whispered. Having righted his canoe, Tiger paddled toward shore, peering into the water; but there was no sign of the daredevil until, moments later, came the cry "There he is!" and a pale, froglike form appeared at the foot of the dock, where it slowly surfaced, and a rousing cheer went up as Wacko Wackeem climbed onto the dock and stood in full view, bowing to his audience, flexing his "muscles" and tipping an imaginary hat.

As all good things must, the Water Carnival reached its end, and the overall winners were formally announced, with Malachi beating out Jeremiah at the last. When the individual campers had been awarded their ribbons—each one stamped "Honorary Presentation of the Bible Society of the Friends of Joshua"—little by little the waterfront quieted, while in the grove the guests stood about, getting the good of the breeze coming off the water and asking one another if it wasn't time to think about leaving. Those consulting timepieces discovered to their surprise that it was nearly four o'clock; Sunday traffic would be heavy. Already automobiles were being loaded up with families and belongings, while some of the second allotment of two-week campers were bidding reluctant goodbyes to new friends before going back to city sidewalks.

Equally sad to be leaving camp were Leo's guests, and in a strange way he was now sorry to see them go. With traces of his clown makeup still visible around his ears, he lingered as Miss Meekum and Supervisor Poe prepared to be on their way.

"What an extraordinary afternoon!" Miss Meekum exclaimed in a tremulous voice, her eyes dewy behind her spectacles, as she smiled her sweet, sad smile all around. "We're certainly proud of you, Leo. Aren't we, Mr. Poe?"

"Yes. I believe we may say that. Most proud."

Leo felt a vivifying sense of relief. He'd got through the day with flying colors. He was nuts to have thought Miss Meekum and Supervisor Poe had come there to cause him trouble. Everything was jake again.

"Take care of Leo, won't you, young man?" Miss Meekum entreated Reece. "And when he comes back to you next summer, maybe *you* won't recognize him. Oh, but you won't be here, will you? You'll be off piloting your aeroplane." Again the supervisor reminded her that the hour was late. Reece insisted on escorting them to the car, offering Miss Meekum his arm and again complimenting her on her hat. "Just remember," she said to Leo as she got into Mr. Poe's tin lizzy, "if you need me, I'm only a penny postcard away," and her wafting hanky could be seen waving wistfully out the window long after her face disappeared from view.

"I wouldn't count on that." Leo was surprised to find Reece still standing nearby, watching the departing car.

"On what?"

"On what your lady friend just said—about coming back next year. That doesn't seem a very likely thing to me under the circumstances. Suppose you tell me what you thought you were doing. Showing off, grandstanding

145

in front of the whole place, losing us the canoe tilt. Bad enough people laughing at you, you had them laughing at me, too, tipping your cap like that."

Leo was speechless. Reece had it all wrong. Tipping your cap was just something you did after a performance. It was only a joke. But even as he stammered a feeble explanation he realized the futility—if it *was* a joke, as far as Reece was concerned the joke was on him, and he didn't like it.

"And what was the idea of that nutty outfit?" he demanded. "Where'd you get it, anyway?"

Leo faltered. How could he explain that he couldn't just get up in front of all those people and do his stunt as, well, as just Leo Joaquim; that he had to pretend he was someone else, like Dr. Mackinschleisser, or Donald Duck, or Superman, otherwise he could never have done what he had? So he'd borrowed Phil's Marc Antony cape from the boat parade, and used some of Fritz's stage paint.

"I just wanted to prove I could do it," he managed weakly.

"You wanted to show off, you mean. But we don't like show-offs here. Now hop to it, camper. It's time for powwow." And, hiking his shoulders, he marched across the playing field to where Hap was once again driving a bucket of golf balls into the baseball backstop.

In the cabin, the Jeremians were all in their bunks, and Leo had the impression they'd been waiting for him: as soon as he stepped across the threshold Wally gave him the fisheye, Phil an angry scowl; Dump's stare was indifferent, while Monkey averted his gaze altogether, and Eddie offered an unoffensive little shrug, marking his desire to remain neutral. Only the Bomber's and Tiger's expressions said they were still in Leo's corner.

"Well, well," Phil began. "Our hero, home from the wars. I hope you're satisfied, Wacko."

Leo was about to make a retort, but, catching Tiger's look, he turned away and went to his bunk, where he sat on the rail and retied the laces of his sneakers.

Furiously Phil sprang to the floor, his weight causing Reece's footlocker to leap. "Don't you sit down like that when I'm talking to you, kiddo. Stand up! Stand at attention!"

"Easy there," Tiger cautioned him. "Nobody's robbed a bank or committed murder."

"He may as well have." Phil turned back to Leo. "I guess you know what your smart-alecking cost us this afternoon. We would have come out first except for your screwing around. I guess you're really proud of yourself. Well, speak up! Are you *proud* of yourself?"

"No . . ." He looked from face to face. "I guess I just didn't think—"

"Yes, we know, you *never* think. Jeez, don't you get it, Wacko? We want to win around here—that's what it's all about. Reece wants that cup. It's his last year at Moonbow, we have to get it for him. If we *don't*—well, whoever screws up, that's his lookout. And if you don't stop acting like a weisenheimer, you know what's going to happen to you?"

Leo remained silent. Wally, leaning over the edge of his upper bunk, smiled grimly. "If you want to know, just try asking Stanley Wagner," he said.

"Okay, fellows, let's cut it out, huh?" Tiger jumped down and stood eyeing Phil sternly. "That's enough. Leo doesn't have to ask anybody anything. He didn't mean to make us lose, it was an accident. It could happen to anyone."

"Yeah? He didn't *have* to do it. He was just showing off, being a wiseguy. Aren't I right, fellows?"

Phil looked around for support. Wally was the first to respond. "Yes, you're right," he said; Dump and Monkey nodded agreement.

"We didn't ask for him to be in here," Phil went on. "We could get along fine without him."

"Well, he *is* here," Tiger declared, "so quit your bellyaching for cripes' sake."

Phil's scowl deepened. "Say, Abernathy, whose side are you on, anyway?"

"I'm not on anybody's side. We're all friends here. If Jeremiah lost a couple of points, it's not the first time. You're making a mountain out of a molehill. Forget it."

"Yeah, let's can it," said the Bomber. "I'm hungry."

"I won't forget it. If you ask me, it's about time somebody did something." With that Phil turned and marched out the door. "Wally—you coming?" he called from the linepath. Ever quick to respond to Phil's orders, Wally hopped to, and Leo watched the pair cross the playing field, walking side by side. In his mind the two campers had fused into a single entity, like the partners in a law office or a haberdashery, Phil & Wally, Inc. After a moment, Dump ducked out the side and went chasing after Phil, and seconds later, without a word or look, Monkey sidled away; he too caught up with the group, which left Eddie reluctant to make a move.

"Looks like it's four against four," the Bomber said dourly, watching the others disappear beyond the rise. Leo's shoulders rose and fell in a silent sigh. He felt bad that he'd let them down, made them lose top score. But how could he have known his great feat would backfire this way? All he'd wanted to do was prove he wasn't afraid; and shine a bit. Looking around at the empty bunks, so recently filled with his accusers, he suddenly felt an alien in Jeremiah, as if he'd dropped in from outer space, a little green man with goggle eyes.

But then, "Nobody's against anybody," Tiger said, putting on his cap. "Come on, guys, let's shag it."

The Bomber gave Leo a friendly punch. "Ya done good, kiddo," he said. "Didn't he, Tige?"

And together, the three, plus Eddie, trudged off across the playing field and joined the trekkers heading up-camp to the dining hall.

2

n a gray, windy morning several days after the Water Carnival, Leo found himself part of the detail assigned to police the Nature Lodge—such clean-up details were standard operating procedure at camp, a rotation duty, like waiting on table or KP—in preparation for the "ghost-story telling" that, the weather being coolish, would take place in the room tonight, instead of in the council ring. In the midst of an uncommon amount of industry, the great horn chandelier had been lowered to the floor to have its two dozen chimneys washed and its wicks trimmed, while sweepers manned the brooms and dust rags flew, and a couple of Endeavorites raked ashes in the two fireplaces and restocked the fuel supply. Leo, with a rag, a sponge, and a bucket of vinegar-water, was washing windows, as well as the glass in the various exhibition cases; it was a job he liked, and he went at it with a will.

Second only to the council ring in the life of the camp, the main room of the Theodore Roosevelt Nature Lodge was the site not only of theatrical events like Major Bowes Amateur Night but of an uncommon variety of activities, from Ping-Pong and checkers tournaments to nature talks and (during periods of inclement weather) the biweekly council fire. Centered at each end were large fireplaces built of local fieldstone, one graced by "George," a stuffed eagle named after the Father of the Country, the opposing one by the framed portrait of Buffalo Bill (the Great Plainsman wore fringed buckskins and carried a silver-chased rifle). In addition to the nature exhibits arrayed along the walls between multiple windows—a horned owl, a gray fox with a still-bushy tail, a collection of snakeskins, the deadly-looking rattles of a diamondback, Leo's growing collection of spiders, and, in its own cage, the bullfrog that had become Peewee Oliphant's special pet—and the Indian exhibits—assorted masks and headdresses, even a beaded buckskin dress, all "on loan" from Dagmar—the room contained the two objects of primary importance at Friend-Indeed: the Hartsig Memorial Trophy Cup, which rested in a position of prominence in the center of the eight-by-eight beam built into the stonework of the north fireplace, where its silver shape gleamed lustrously, even on the dullest days, and the Buffalo Bill War Bonnet which, when not being worn by the camp's designated Moonbow Warrior, was displayed on a stand of pinewood in a tall glass case nearby.

Now, as the dust and talk both flew, Oats Gurley, in whose loose and liberal charge the clean-up detail went about its business, was himself dusting the shelves of books that were his personal library, a collection of well-thumbed volumes on various natural phenomena, including the local flora and fauna, volumes (especially one on spiders) with which Leo was by now familiar.

Ah-choo! Ah-choo! Ah-choo!

Sweeping the floor with commendable zeal, Emerson Bean had raised a cloud of dust whose particles floated in the air. Tactful as always, Oats quietly suggested to the camper that he lower his energy level by half and damp down the dust with a good sprinkling of water.

Leo, giving one last swipe to the spider case, moved along to the Hartsig Trophy, noting his distorted reflection in its silvery, orotund curves, huffing his breath to shine up the plaque on which at summer's end the names of the lucky winners would be engraved.

More than ever Leo was determined to prove that he could be a true-blue Jeremian, not just another Stanley Wagner. He wanted his name on the cup as much as any of the others, and, despite his screw-ups, wasn't he doing his best to make that happen? His spider exhibit alone had already assured Jeremiah of a full one hundred points—more than Dump's arrowhead display, which was merely an addition to a collection started by others—and his article on tarantulas in *The Pine Cone* had brought in several points more.

Unfortunately he had garnered his share of blackies as well—one for a wet bathing suit accidentally left on the line before inspection, another for having a sheaf of Katzenjammer comics hidden under his pillow, two for rolling his shorts more than the permissible double turn—so that with Jeremiah's unexpected defeat in the canoe tilt (undeniably his fault), he was now responsible for more minuses than any other Jeremian.

He was going to have to try even harder, that was all, as Reece had gone to the trouble of pointing out to Tiger. The fact was that since Sunday Reece had not only been unwilling to let bygones be bygones, he had chosen deliberately to misunderstand Leo's innocent intention, and to misrepresent it to others, which had put Leo in a bad light, and not just among the Jeremians; cadets and seniors alike were saying Wacko had been acting wacko. Almost nobody would believe he hadn't been burlesquing Reece.

In his bunk with a book yesterday evening during the after-supper free period, Leo had caught snatches of a conversation coming from the vicinity of Old Faithful.

"I just don't get it," Reece was saying while Tiger dropped his lips to the water spout. "Why do you bother with him, anyway?"

"No bother. I like him. I know he goofs up sometimes, but he knows lots of things, he's smart, and he's funny, too."

"I don't think he's funny. And he's breaking up the team! Don't you get it, fellah? He's just not our kind. He's different. You can see that, can't you?"

"Maybe we'll rub off on him," Tiger said, tongue-in-cheek. "Or maybe *he'll* rub off on *us.*"

"Yeah—that's what I'm afraid of. Remember Stanley?"

"Come on, Big Chief, let's skip the bad news," Tiger said. "Leo's going to be okay—look at the points he's won us. And what does it matter if he *is* different? Everybody can't be the same—"

"He'll damn well measure up to Jeremiah or I'll know the reason why. He's turning into a real troublemaker around here. Maybe a taste of—"

Tiger had been bailed out when Hap's whistle started off the scheduled game of Kick the Can, and Leo had heaved himself up from his bunk to join the fray. Kick the Can was a favorite game of his, he was good at it; his thin frame seemed suited to skulking around in the dusky shadows, suddenly to come rushing out of nowhere to kick the can and free the prisoners, then escape himself, and rack up a score. Unfortunately, there were not many points to be won in so haphazard a sport, especially since Coach Holliday inevitably assigned Leo to teams that were bound to lose.

151

Speak of the devil. Through the lodge doors Leo could see the coach emerging from the path at Five Points; Reece was with him, and Leo watched as the two, carrying several sheets of paper, marched up to the bulletin board at the foot of the lodge steps and posted them—removing several outdated ones to do so. The current demerit list, no doubt, along with the happy-point totals by camper (Tiger was number one) and cabin (still Malachi, alas). They made an ill-assorted pair, the stocky, thick-necked Hap, and Reece, much the taller and leaner of the two, his skin so darkly tanned by now that Leo thought he resembled a cigar-store Indian.

Leo returned to his polishing, and when he glanced out again he saw Reece dressing down one of the new campers whom he'd evidently caught in some infraction. The boy seemed to wilt visibly, and as he slunk away Reece broke into a flashing grin and scribbled a quick note on the piece of paper he'd just tacked up, then he and Hap went off together laughing.

Hearing a cough, Leo looked around to find Fritz Auerbach standing by the next window, likewise observing the little scene. "Your counselor is quite a stickler, isn't he?" He smiled and came over. After Leo's paddling, there had sprung up a warm alliance between the refugee and the orphan, two whose lives had been very different, yet whose present situations were not dissimilar. Fritz asked how Leo was coming with the book Fritz had loaned him, and Leo asked to hold on to it a while longer.

"Reece keeps us so busy, I haven't had much time."

Fritz nodded sympathetically. "How are you and Big Chief doing these days? Is he still angry over what happened on Sunday?"

Leo shrugged. "Now he's mad at Tiger, too," he said.

"Why?"

"Because Tiger sticks up for me."

Fritz drew at his lip. "It's because Reece feels threatened."

"By what?"

"By you, my friend. I know it doesn't seem you've done anything to threaten him, but think about it. That little joke of yours with the pine trees after the Snipe Hunt, then changing the skit on him, then the affair of Sunday—he thinks his authority is being undermined. Don't ever forget he's cock of the walk here." Fritz winked and Leo nodded. He liked being around Fritz, whose eyes were so warm and friendly and who always had time for a little talk and a bit of savvy instruction. The sad situation of his family seldom showed in his manner—though he spoke of his loved ones

152

often enough—and he never felt sorry for himself. Leo had come to admire him more with every passing day, as had many of the other campers, including Tiger.

"By the way," Fritz went on. "I was talking with Dagmar about you." Since coming to Moonbow he and Dagmar Kronborg had struck up a warm friendship: two Europeans roosting in a nest of Yankees, who could speak French to each other (Fritz disliked speaking German). "She'd enjoy hearing you play again sometime."

Leo was surprised, after the way he'd made a fool of himself in front of the woman. "Did she say that?"

"Indeed she did. She's sincere, believe me. You wouldn't mind, would you?"

Leo didn't know how he felt about playing in public after his folly.

"But of course," Fritz said. "That is understandable. Still, Dagmar says it will help if you adopt a more serious approach to your studies. You could do your mother proud, you know. You have said how much she wished you to become a good musician."

"Yes."

"Well, then, perhaps you might think of her and do so. But not by the lazy door, eh? Give it plenty of get-up-and-go." He rolled a fist and gave Leo the lightest sock on the chin. Leo said he was resolved to try.

After Fritz had gone, with the trophy now giving off an unimpeachable luster, Leo looked around to discover that the rest of the work squad was making for the doors, having been dismissed by Oats, who gave Leo permission to leave too, asking him first to put away his gear and take along the broom Emerson had left behind the stuffed fox. When he returned from the utility closet, Oats had disappeared into the staff room. Leo glanced around to see what might have been missed. The place was spick and span and would pass inspection with no trouble—except for a smudge where one of the departing clean-up squad had rested his hand against the door of the war bonnet's case. Using a clean corner of his rag, he blew on the glass and gave it a good buffing until the mark disappeared; then he stood back, looking up at the headdress, thinking of the history behind it, how the Great Plainsman had presented it to Pa, a scene so often described by Pa himself that there was hardly a camper who didn't feel he'd been an actual witness to the event.

A noble gift, Leo thought, and, backing off another step or two, he studied the plaque inscribed with the words "Personal gift of Wm. F. Cody to Garland Starbuck," and the date of the presentation (August 1914), and beneath that the list of names of those who had been given the honor of wearing the headdress through the years: the Moonbow Warriors of Friend-Indeed. First on the list, for the years 1914–1916, was Rolfe Hartsig; and last—at number 5—was his son, Reece, and the year 1934, followed by a dash.

As Leo stared at this last name on the list he mentally appended the year 1938 and under Reece's name his own:

6. Leo Joaquim 1938–

Even though he knew it was a foregone conclusion that, despite his lack of physical stature, the Sachems would pick Tiger Abernathy to inherit the mantle of the Moonbow Warrior, Leo couldn't suppress the fantasy. That's all it was, of course, make-believe; for how could Leo ever hope to be tapped as the exalted Warrior when he wasn't even a member of the Senecas? But *if* by some wild chance he should be presented the red feather and the medicine bag, if he too could join the Lodge—

There was an undeniable power in belonging to that group of honor campers, and the source of that power lay not only in the membership but in those little chamois bags each brave wore around his neck, those "medicine bags" whose secret contents were so potent. What was it, the Senecas' magic? What amulet or talisman did the bags contain and how was it used? Leo longed to know. He had never told anyone, not even Tiger, about his inadvertent visit to the Seneca campfire grounds that night of the Snipe Hunt, but he had thought about it often and wondered and imagined. What did they do there, those chosen warriors, and in such secrecy that no outsider was allowed to witness their sacred rituals? Whatever these were, they bound the Senecas together in lifelong friendship. Tiger and the Bomber had told him about the big holiday reunion held every Christmas vacation, when all current and former members still alive would meet at a Hartford hotel for a happy get-together of handshaking and speeches after dinner. And how, as a grown-up, out in the big world, a Seneca could always turn for help in time of need to one of the brotherhood, and sometimes, like Reece, get his picture in the newspaper as a result of his achievements.

Again Leo let his gaze rest on the war bonnet, imagining what it would be like to be not only a Seneca but the Moonbow Warrior himself—the most elite of that elite corps, whose fierce but noble appearance was meant to instill in every Friend-Indeed camper the desire to be strong and valiant and noble himself, to practice in his daily life all those qualities that made "Glad Men from Happy Boys."

As he stared into the glass case it seemed to Leo that he might actually become the wearer of the feathered bonnet, clad in beaded moccasins and a breechclout—he, Leo Joaquim, crouching low and toe-stepping to the accompaniment of a dozen tom-toms, as behind him rose the silver moon and out of the mist and magic of the night the fabled moonbow formed itself overhead—and, glancing around to make sure he was unobserved by spying eyes, he opened the case, then reached inside, removed the war bonnet from its stand, and placed it on his head. The sensation was indescribable. The instant its weight crowned him he felt transformed, no longer merely Leo Joaquim. A palpable warmth seemed to emanate from the interior of the headdress, permeating his skull and brain, imbuing him with all manner of strange capabilities, as if every warrior before him who had ever worn the bonnet had left a share of his own power inside it, to be passed on to anyone who would put it on—those *worthy* of wearing it.

Mesmerized, he stepped back from the case. He raised his arms, palms outward, saluting the Buffalo Bill portrait over the mantel, and in the silvery curves of the Hartsig Trophy the bright feathers came alive. He felt giddy with excitement, the sense of sudden power mixed with the unnerving realization that what he was doing was taboo. How wonderful, how strange . . . It was as if in putting on the bonnet he had actually become the Moonbow Warrior, and he drew his chin down, moving closer to the silver, still watching his reflection. He could feel the sweat running from under the headdress, down his brow and trickling alongside his nose. He shivered, his skin prickled with gooseflesh, and the hairs rose along his arms.

The feeling passed. Whatever it was, it melted away; he was just a two-bit camper—and what he was doing was terribly wrong; if he were to be caught the consequences would be dire. He must return the bonnet immediately—

As he turned from the fireplace he stopped short, sounding a gasp of alarm. Pa Starbuck stood in the open doorway, an expression of shocked indignation on his face.

"What can you be thinking of?" he demanded, advancing on Leo like some aroused Old Testament patriarch, his eyes flashing beneath his beetling brows.

The hapless Leo stared back, groping for an answer. "Nothing. I mean I was only—"

Pa raised his hand in a hieratic gesture. "Surely you must be aware that no one is allowed to don this headdress without being duly elected Moonbow Warrior, Chief of the Senecas. How do you come to be wearing it?"

Leo was at a loss to explain. "I just wanted to see how I looked. I—" It had all seemed so simple, really; but as he stammered this excuse he could hear how lame it must sound. He flinched as the bonnet was lifted from his head. Reverently Pa replaced it in the case, then again turned his watery blue gaze on the culprit.

"You were making fun of the Warrior," he said. "But the Warrior is not a figure for sport. He has a profound meaning for every single boy at camp. I am sorry you yourself do not feel his power." Again he raised his hand as Leo sought to protest. "My boy, my boy," he went on, "haven't you been here long enough to realize that this"—he rested a hand on the glass case—"this is a sacred trust? Never to be violated, never handled or touched by the uninitiated? You leave me to wonder just what sort of camper it is, what sort of careless, unthinking boy, who would deliberately flout the rules and the most sacred tenets of Camp Friend-Indeed." He clicked his tongue in dismay. "What, I wonder, will the Senecas think when they learn of this impious act? What measures will they be forced to take against such a sacrilege?"

Leo felt a cold blade slice through his heart. "Do you have to? Tell, I mean?"

"Must *I* tell?" Pa was wounded. "No, no, my boy, *I* shall not speak, it is not *I* who shall tell. But the spirit of Buffalo Bill, the Great Plainsman, it shall speak. As the very rafters of this room shall also tell their tale of a boy who is so unthinking. Come away now," he said, leading Leo toward the door. "We must allow the disturbed spirits to settle themselves, let them find renewed tranquillity."

He turned and with upraised hands paid obeisance to the portrait over the mantel, then strode from the room, shaking his head and rolling his eyes to heaven, as if to consult with his Maker over this renegade who had dared to put a feathered bonnet on his head.

To deal with the matter of the war bonnet, at powwow time that afternoon a special meeting of the Sachems' Council was convened at the lodge. The meeting took some time, and when, finally, they all came out again, the dinner bell was ringing. Leo wished he didn't have to go, but there was no way out. He hiked slowly up to the dining hall, entered, and headed for Jeremiah's table, blushing furiously as, feeling every eye upon him, he took his customary seat and bowed his head for grace.

What was the verdict? he wondered. Whatever it was, he wasn't likely to learn about it from Reece, who was acting as if nothing had happened at all. "Pass the potatoes, Wally," he said, and "May I have the milk," as his eye kept flicking to the staff table, where Pa Starbuck sat, benign and jovial and, like Reece, giving no sign that Leo could observe that anything was amiss, nodding and beaming at his fellow diners, now buttering a roll and crunching it between his store-bought teeth. The meal continued to unfold as usual, except that this evening there was an unusual amount of whispering, of looks exchanged, and neither Tiger nor the Bomber had much to say to anyone. Leo couldn't eat, his stomach was fluttering so, and he made only token passes at his plate. Finally, when the chinking of the kitchen "silver" on chinaware had died away and only the dull hubbub of many voices could be heard, he knew the moment had come. The large hall grew quiet.

"Friends and campers," Pa began, rising and speaking in a warm, natural tone, "it pleases me greatly to gaze upon your happy faces this evening, and I trust we all have spent a profitable day in our sundry pursuits. I myself had the pleasure of viewing one of our feathered friends, a scarlet tanager, perched on a fencepost along the roadside. It has a nest with two fledglings, and for those among you who would care to investigate this rarity, I am tomorrow at your disposal. . . ."

Leo drew a breath of relief: it was going to be all right; Pa wouldn't be going on about his feathered friends if he were planning to drop the ax on Leo's head. But he was wrong; no sooner had Pa closed his mouth than he opened it again. He coughed and cleared his throat, then, mopping his brow, went on. "Eee-*heh* . . . I regret . . . yes, I regret to say that there has come about a certain matter which deeply saddens me. And since this matter deals with the rights and privileges of the sworn members of the Seneca Lodge,

I must of necessity turn these proceedings over to the Chief of the Senecas." He looked across the hall to the Jeremiah table.

As occupant of this exalted post, Reece swung his legs over the bench and walked to the center of the room, where, folding his arms across his chest, he began speaking of his deep affection for the Seneca Lodge, and of the honor of having for the fifth year in a row been elected its leader, the Moonbow Warrior. He spoke of the feelings of amity and friendship among the members of the tribe, then, easing into the matter at hand, described how Pa Starbuck had happened by the Nature Lodge, where he had come upon a certain camper who, having broached the display case, had removed from it the Buffalo Bill headdress, which he had then presumed to place on his head.

At this announcement, a wave of indignation and disapproval rippled through the hall. Reece's eyes traveled around the room, coming at last to rest on the guilty party, whose face had turned blood-red. "I now call upon the misguided camper who ran so roughshod over our Friend-Indeed traditions and dared to imagine that he was the Moonbow Warrior—"

"Get up, stupid," Phil hissed. Dump nudged Leo with an elbow.

Leo gulped; as he made a move to stand, campers began pounding with their water tumblers and spoons, and a lively chant broke out.

"Wack-oh! Wack-oh! Wack-oh!"

"Get *up!*" Phil gave Leo's thigh a painful pinch.

Leo jerked to his feet, but, once standing, gazing around at the sea of cold, scornful faces, he felt his knees go weak. He darted a look to Tiger, who answered it with a helpless one; clearly Leo was on his own.

"I'm sorry," he managed at last. "I didn't m-mean—I only wanted to see how it felt—I didn't mean to insult the S-Sen-Senecas. I won't d-do it again."

"Darn tootin' you won't," a deep voice rang out. "You won't be *able* to!" Moriarity began to laugh, and the others joined in, till it seemed everyone was laughing.

Those were (almost) the last words any camper or staffer addressed to Leo on that day and for several days thereafter. For at the meeting of the Sachems it had been determined that, found guilty of flouting the camp's most honored traditions, the culprit was to suffer an undisclosed period of silence. Leo was dispatched to Scarsdale, where he would remain until the required steps to recall him were undertaken. No camper or staffer would be permitted to address so much as a word to him: he was banished to Siberia, the outer reaches of Mongolia, the craters of the moon.

3

even o'clock that evening saw the lodge filling up for the scheduled ghost-story telling, a venerable Moonbow institution that
always drew an enthusiastic crowd. Tonight the boys seemed in
uncommonly boisterous spirits, chanting, clapping, and stamping their feet, and otherwise demonstrating their impatience, as Hank Ives,
wearing a windbreaker with a green Sinclair Oil dinosaur embroidered on
the back, oversaw the traditional dimming of the lights: the chandelier was
lowered, the rope uncleated at the post and run through the seaman's block
and tackle that served as a pulley—with Bud Talbot and Blackjack Ratner
weighing on the rope (the contraption was so heavy)—and one by one the
lamps were extinguished.

As the chandelier was again hoisted aloft and tied off, the last of the
campers filed in, among them Leo Joaquim. Looking neither right nor left,
he took a seat at the end of a bench—he knew he was not welcome among
the Jeremians, seated several rows ahead of him; he was in Scarsdale now,
and not even Tiger and the Bomber could make a public display of friendliness, though they had covertly shown him a tacit sympathy.

Ankles crossed, leaning forward, Leo kept his head well down, trying
to ignore the whispers and jibes and fingers pointing at him, to act as if he
didn't care. When Fritz came in with Wanda, they sat as close to the
miscreant as they could, and Fritz gave him his usual friendly nod, Wanda
a little wave, as if to say *they* weren't going to cut him off simply because
he'd put an old Indian bonnet on his head for a minute or two. Close behind

them, however, came Reece, to take his place among the Jeremians. Desolately Leo watched as the counselor struck his lighter and applied the flame horizontally to his pipe bowl, his lips emitting puffs of blue smoke that hung about his head. The lighter remaining lit, the flame illuminated his face, and his eyes, dark and piercing, seemed fixed on Leo. It was only a fleeting impression—in another second Reece's index finger flipped the hinged cover over the flame, extinguishing it, and leaving only a vague, sinister impression to linger in the red glow of his pipe bowl—but Leo shivered as the wind, unexpectedly brisk and chilly for that time of year, gusted down the chimney, coughing from its throat spurs of fiery ashes that blew across the stone hearth. Now the leaping flames threw grotesquely painted shadows upward along the walls, which in the firelight gave off a shuddery russet glow, and even though scores of humans occupied the room it seemed that as a body they had no protection whatever against the Unseen, that by the potency of the spoken word alone some malevolence or misadventure could befall them, some dreadful, alien presence might appear among them uninvited, laying waste to their ranks, leaving them powerless to act.

As the boys' clamor died down, and an almost eerie silence fell in the room, Pete Melrose, who had charge of the evening, came before the hearth and, sitting on a canvas camp stool, kicked off the program. His tale was one familiar to many campers, but not to Leo, about the old lighthouse keeper to whom late one night there appeared the vengeful spirit of the woman he had betrayed as a young man, a grisly, beckoning phantom luring him from his warm bed to dash himself on the rocks below. Pete was followed by Jay St. John, and then Charlie Penny, each holding forth with a tale more lurid than the one that had come before, until the campers jumped with every snapping of a log, giving themselves up willingly to the spell.

Finally the way was prepared for Henry Ives, who unfolded his lanky frame and shuffled to the front of the room, dug out the dottle from his pipe, refilled it, and began to talk. *Ahhh,* the boys murmured, the story of the Haunted House, *their* Haunted House—the strange and tragic tale that had thrilled generations of Friend-Indeed campers.

Old Man Steelyard, a notorious miser, had once been a prominent Windham County banker. Bilked by his partners of a large number of treasury notes, he had renounced his former society and, removing his wife and daughter to Moonbow Lake, had put up the house on the Old Lake Road. There the family lived in sparely furnished rooms, and the old man's

160

wife died of influenza when he refused to put sufficient coal in the grate, though it was rumored that, having cashed in his remaining notes for gold and now distrustful of all banks, he had squirreled away a treasure somewhere among the foundations of the house. To guard his miser's hoard he bought a fierce dog, which, though a trial to peddlers and inquisitive neighbor boys—here Hank paused—became the pet of Mary, the old man's daughter. They called it Lobo, because the dog was like a wolf. And it was good that Mary had a pet, for she was not permitted to mix with the local children or even to attend school with them; Steelyard saw to the girl's education himself. Time passed, the girl grew to womanhood. Then one spring the well went dry.

Hank puffed thoughtfully for a few moments so that in the firelight his long, dour features were wreathed in blue smoke; he went on:

"Ol' Man Steelyard, he drove into town to find himself a likely feller with divining know-how, an' this feller come out to give the job a go. He must've ben good at his trade, for the folks hereabouts called him Digger. He went to pacin' the property with his divinin' rod an', sure enough, the stick drew, they dug down, an' they come to water. So the job was seen to, an', bein' a mean ol' skinflint, Steelyard was anxious to get rid of Digger, but Digger said someone was needed to shovel out the new well, an' since he was johnny-on-the-spot he got to stick around. An' while he stuck around, Mary, she took a fancy to him, an' Digger, he was makin' sheep's eyes right back at her. Then, when Digger got to layin' in the new plumbin' pipes to replace the old ones, his spade struck somethin' along the cellar wall—he wasn't called Digger for nothin', heh-heh. He'd dug up Ol' Man Steelyard's box o' gold. He didn't let on he'd found it, but, keepin' mum, he persuaded Mary to run off with him, proposed right in the ol' man's parlor, an' together they planned to elope."

Leo pictured the scene, Digger sitting close to Mary, whispering his plans into her ear, as Hank's voice rose and fell, and outside the wind moaned among the trees and rattled the windowpanes like a skeleton's bones. He missed having Tiger beside him, the Bomber, too, Tiger nudging him in the ribs before the good parts.

Now Hank had come to the night of the elopement, when Digger made an excuse to work late down in the cellar. "An' that," Hank went on, "was Digger's mistake. Fer the ol' man caught the thief red-handed an' slammed him hard with his own spade an' afterwards he hauled the body up the cellar steps an' dumped it in the well. Not the new one, the old one that has that big ol' slab of cee-ment over it. Digger wasn't dead yet, he was still breathin', but that didn't matter. Steelyard was a generous fellow, he give him all the time he'd need to suffocate, nice an' slow, the way a Chinee likes to do. An' no sooner had he sealed over the well than he dragged poor Mary up to that corner room, where he locked her up, sayin' she could sit there by her window and look out on the well where Digger lay a-dyin'.

"After that somethin' crept over the place, somethin' like a spell, so come evenin' drivers would hurry their buggies past, a man afoot would hurry his step. An' up there, in the window, there she'd be, Mary, a-starin' out. She never spoke to the ol' man again fer havin' kilt her man in such a cruel, inhuman way, an' the ol' man, he hated Mary fer her betrayal. So, though the two lived side by side, the house, it was silent as the tomb where Digger lay. Mary had only the dog, Lobo, fer comp'ny, an' at night when that critter went out, he set up such a deal of noise over there in Injun Woods, why, 'twas like a wolf's howl, a fittin' sound in a place where murder's ben done. That winter was bitter cold, an' Mary sittin' there by her window, till one day she was dead, too. Some said she died of grief, that or froze, an' when she went the ol' man drove Lobo off the property an' lived alone, until, on a gusty night, a night like this one, when he was tucked abed, he waked to the sound of a wolf howlin' outside his window. He jumped up an' run to look out. There he seen the big dog, come back again and a-howlin', and with the dog he seen his dead girl, Mary, sobbin' by the wellhead. Not long after, the ol' man up an' disappeared. Folks suspected foul play, so the constable, he come out fer a look. He poked about all over that place an' not a sign until, down in the cellar, he found that ol' miser hangin' from a beam. An' after that the house, it stayed empty, nobody but a fool"—here Hank paused again—" 'ud go in the place. 'Cept for one—the shade of poor Mary Steelyard. An' if you was to pass by on some dark an' windy night like this, who knows, you might see her up there in her winder . . . watchin' . . ."

Hank's words died away among the rafters. In the lodge the silence was utter and complete; it was the storyteller's supreme moment—that potent hush that signals the reluctance of any listener to articulate a syllable that might break the spell so skillfully woven. The fire burned low; outside, a tree branch scratched against the glass. The boys began to stir lethargically, as if awakening from a dark dream. Their feet scraped the floorboards as they got up and stretched.

Then, out of the sleepy silence, a moment that froze the blood. From beyond the windows, far off among the trees, came the deep, winding howl of a beast. A wolf! Yes—there it came again! No one moved, while the bloodcurdling sound rose and fell. No, not a wolf, they whispered, but Lobo, Mary's companion. And then—a shriek! A woman's cry, a sound of such horror that all who heard it became as stone. Lobo and—Mary! Leo hugged his ribs, his body trembling. The two, woman and beast, cried out together now; then, at their peak, the shrieks and howls broke, turning into a Tarzan yodel, and the room burst into relieved laughter.

That was a good one, ha ha. They laughed harder when Reece Hartsig walked through the doorway in the company of Gus Klaus, the two having sneaked off into the woods during Hank's tale. It was just the kind of gag Heartless would pull, adding a bit of spice to the story and winning everybody to his side; even Leo could appreciate that.

But, wolf or no wolf, the spell still lay heavily upon Leo as he left the lodge, hanging back until his cabinmates had gone on ahead—he didn't want to embarrass Tiger or the Bomber in front of the others. Then, rather than heading straight for the linepath, he wandered alone by a circuitous route that brought him out near the mailboxes, where he stopped and gauged the hour: there was probably a full thirty minutes before Wiggy Pugh would blow taps. He began to move again, turning left along the Old Lake Road. As he walked, a ghostly shadow rose up from out of the trees and went sailing off, a dark patch against the darker sky: Icarus, hunting for his supper.

Leo inhaled the night air; it had a deep, bronzy tang to it, like the ring of an old bell. With his chilled gut sucked up under his bony ribs, he pressed on, still only half-aware of the intention guiding his steps. The gravel along the shoulder crunched noisily under his rubber soles and he tried to walk more quietly. Suddenly he had the feeling he was being followed—by man or beast he could not tell—and he pictured Mary's yellow-eyed dog scenting his traces. There—what was that? The crack of a twig gave him a start. Yes—*there!* Again he heard it, a careless foot had snapped another branch. He was sure—well, maybe not, maybe he was just imagining it.

At Pissing Rock he stopped for the ritual leak, performing the act with anxious ceremony. Then—another sound. Now he felt sure: something was moving behind him, tracking him. He buttoned up hastily and went on. He walked quickly; not much time before taps. Now he knew exactly where his long strides were taking him.

Soon he was passing the beginnings of the picket fence whose crooked

163

posts stood like sentinels in the dark. With half an eye and only half-aware, he counted them: one two three four five . . . six seven eight nine . . . He rounded the bend and came to a halt. Peering ahead into the inky blackness, he could see it, standing there, silent and alone, expecting him. When he came to the crazy-paved walk, he planted his feet squarely on the stones and stared at the building, his fists clenched, as if he were facing some enemy he was determined to vanquish, then glanced over to the well. Were they really down there, the remains of Digger?

Feeling a chill, he shifted his eyes toward the house again, that dark, bleak—and somehow sinister—silhouette that exerted such a strange power over him. Why did his heart begin to flutter when he no more than looked at it? Since coming upon it on the night of the Snipe Hunt, he had deliberately shunned it, but this evening, listening to Hank's tale of the tragedy of Mary Steelyard, something had spurred him to return—to the scene of the crime, was that it?

He shut his eyes, thinking hard. There was something—in there—in the dark. Yes—something he wanted desperately to know. But what? He squeezed his eyes shut, trying to recall it. If he concentrated hard enough, maybe—A thought struck him: did Emily's ghost haunt the Gallop Street house the way Mary Steelyard haunted this one? He had seen a figure in the window. Who had it been? Mary or Emily? Or a figment of his imagination?

He picked up some pebbles and pitched them at a vacant window, heard the hollow clatter as they hit the parlor floor and slid to the corners.

"Come out!" he called boldly. "Come out, I dare you!" He heard nothing but his own voice reverberating against the clapboards. He walked the three steps up to the porch, then stopped as his flashlight beam swung across the paint-peeled door with its panels of shattered glass, the broken-out lamps on either side. He put his hand to the door handle and depressed the latch. There was no click, for the latch was broken; he pushed and the door gave edgily with a tiny explosion of air as the seal was broken. He pushed the door wider and stepped inside. He paused in the narrow hallway whose length his flashlight tried and failed to penetrate. Tatters of a brown print wallpaper curled away from the wall in torn shards, with rusty splotches of water-stained lath-and-plaster showing beneath. A broken light fixture hung from the ceiling, bulbless and festooned with pale cobwebbing. The yellow beam flitted along the floor, foot by foot along the oak strips, from the gouged and battered baseboard to the chipped and battered newel post,

164

where it lingered amid the rat castings scattered at the stair foot, then traveled slowly upward, riser by riser, to pierce the gloom of the stairwell.

He set a foot to the bottom step, then jumped as he felt it give with a noisy squeak. Incredible, but even here, *inside,* the house reminded him of the one on Gallop Street. This vestibule area, the hallway, the doors on the right (into the dining room?), on the left (into the stairway to the shop?), the radiator by the door and—there—on the floor—he shined the light on a dark blotch staining the boards.

He forced himself to go on. A second step, a third; doggedly he moved, his fear revealed in the trembling motion of the light beam whose scant illumination was all he could depend on. Odd smells assailed his nostrils, the odor of dust and mold and a sharp smell, like ammonia. He could feel his heart throbbing against the hollow cavity of his rib cage, and his stomach heaved. He gulped and went on, up and up, step by step, until at last he moved from the staircase onto the flat plane of the upper floor. There he paused, clutching for support the round wooden ball that topped the newel post. He caught his breath, then set his flash beam to probing the shadowy corners, painting the hall with a bright orange ribbon that flitted and skittered about like some demented creature. Up, down, ceiling, floor, along the cracked walls, where the paper had buckled and oblong patches in a paler shade revealed that pictures had once hung there, in the light he examined with care each of the closed doors, the empty wall spaces between the doors.

He moved forward again, consciously locking his knees and trudging along, his feet crunching in the gritty dust that covered the floor, so that no matter how soft his tread, it was amplified and easily heard. He reached the first door and tried the knob. The door opened inward to profound darkness, which the flashlight beam instantly probed. Here the stench, moldy and dry, stung his nostrils. Pinching his nose, he backed out and shut the door, then moved slowly down the hallway, finding one deserted, derelict room after the other. At the end of the passage, opening the final door, he found himself in the corner room—Mary Steelyard's room, with its rounded shape and pointed ceiling, its tiny fireplace and grate, its gently curving window where, according to Henry's tale, the unhappy maiden had stood gazing down at the well that was her lover's tomb.

With measured steps Leo crossed the room to the window—so like Emily's window—and shone his beam down onto the dark lawn and the overgrown wellhead, with its heavy slab of cement supposedly sealing in the bleached bones of the man who had conspired to rob Old Man Steelyard. The light crisscrossed the lawn before he pulled it back into the room. He gave the place a last glance. Yes, he thought, this room might have belonged, not to Mary, but to Emily.

He left the door ajar and returned the way he had come, the steady beam of his flashlight illuminating the stairs one by one as he descended. Then, halfway down, he drew a swift breath, freezing in place as he leaned against the stair railing. Something besides himself was in the house!

He stood poised for flight, all his senses honed to their sharpest edge. Though he held his breath, his heart was beating furiously, sounding to him like a drum announcing his presence. He waited several moments longer, then ventured onto the next step, and the next. He stopped again and waited, listening hard, his beam probing the dark. Nothing but empty corners did he see, and the floor of the lower hall. Nevertheless a chill ran through his flesh. He was inside the Haunted House, why should he not expect to see the ghost that went with it?

He reached the bottom and stood in the lower hallway before the front entrance. Then, before he realized what was happening, the parlor door was thrown back, slamming hard against the wall with a great noise, and through the opening there rushed a dark menacing form, which threw itself upon him. The swift, hard impact knocked the breath out of Leo, muffling the cry that sprang to his lips as he felt himself being lifted bodily from the ground and carried from the newel post back along the passageway. Suddenly he found himself staring down into an open hole. The trapdoor had been thrown back. He was about to be pitched twelve feet down into the cellar!

He flailed about and kicked his legs, struggling to free himself. At last a foot connected with his assailant, a hard blow that did its work; he was dropped to the floor, while, with a pained oath, his attacker fell back against the wall.

Leo scrambled up and, dodging past the hole in the floor, ran out the door. Down the walk he fled, away from the dark house, stumbling, then sprawling; the cinders bit painfully into the flesh of his palms and his bare knees. Oblivious to the angry sting, he picked himself up again and without looking back headed down the road, racing along it as fast as his steps could carry him, while the dark trees overhead seemed to enfold him, and no moon shone to dispel the ghosts that threaded the deep and somnolent night.

4

nce returned to Jeremiah, stretched out in his bunk—the jinxed bunk of Cabin 7—Leo tossed and turned against the canvas, threading dark waking dreams of what he had seen and what had happened in those dusty rooms of the Haunted House, willing himself not to sleep so that he would not dream for real and cry out. Over and over he asked himself what it was that had driven him to the house in the first place, and found no answer. But of one thing he was sure. Staring at Reece's empty cot, then feigning sleep as the counselor came in some-time between midnight and dawn and stood for a heart-stopping few min-utes beside Leo's bunk before settling into his own, he was sure who his silent attacker had been, the monster in the hallway. And, indeed, the next morning told the tale, for Reece rolled out of bed with a badly swollen eye, a circumstance concerning which he brooked no discussion in any quarter but one that provoked deepest surmise not only among the Jeremians but throughout the entire camp. Leo alone knew the truth, and he kept his own counsel, which wasn't hard, given that no one was permitted to speak to him and he was unable to communicate with any other party.

His trip to Scarsdale lasted for three days. This form of punishment was not unknown to him: at the Institute a boy might easily be sent to "Siberia" when he had incurred the resentment of the powers that be. But he had never experienced it himself, never seen boys deliberately turn their backs and snub him, not exchanging any word of greeting day or night. Now he did see it, and he might as well have been a Martian, so remote did he feel from his fellow campers.

Of his friends at Friend-Indeed, only Wanda and Fritz, who had made no secret of their contempt for the whole business (Fritz had even entreated Pa that reason and fair play should prevail, but Pa had replied that the matter was beyond his province to mitigate and that the camp's honored traditions must be upheld); Ma, who would have cut off her arm before turning her back on any camper, no matter what his crime; and Willa-Sue spoke to him, the latter oblivious to Leo's status, and going out of her way to engage him in a babble of fractured conversation at every opportunity— usually in front of others and making him appear more foolish than before. As for Tiger, he was too old and devoted a Friend-Indeeder to go against the rules, though he told Leo by diverse silent signals that he sympathized with his plight and was still in his corner.

One bright note: after discussion with Ma, who had given him the okay, Fritz invited Leo to help out with the completion of the Austrian village, and the next day Leo was mustering his talents to work on turning out Lilliputian trees from sponge rubber and matchsticks, carving balsa-wood houses, and creating a bell tower for the burgomaster's hall. But while he was grateful to Fritz for this special show of support, Leo was aware that in taking him on as his assistant Fritz was making enemies of his own.

In the end it was Tiger who saw Leo rescued from his ignominy. He appealed personally to the Sachems' Council, petitioning them to restore the wrongdoer to the camper community (Wasn't their motto "A Friend in Need Is a Friend Indeed"? Wasn't that what everyone here at Moonbow believed in?), and when the vote was taken the majority found in Leo's favor. That evening the edict was formally rescinded and the Bomber proclaimed Leo's new status by loudly saying, "Hey, Wacko, pass the bread and butter, willya?"

Now, several days after his return to general favor, as the normal roster of Moonbow handicrafters pursued their usual projects during morning crafts session, Leo, seated across the worktable from Fritz, was hard at work on a miniature paddle wheeler for the model. Already, on a platform temporarily attached to a work stand in the Swoboda Wood-Carving Shop, the model's substructure was on view: a tiny corner of the Danube Valley in miniature, with the river sculpted from plaster of Paris, and a mountain (crumpled chicken-wire mesh overlaid with papier-mâché made from cut newspaper strips soaked in flour-and-water paste). On the peak of the mountain would be sited the castle that was to be the crowning feature of the village.

The paddle wheeler was by far the most complicated construction Leo had ever attempted, and he found the work both engaging and enormously satisfying; more satisfying even than collecting spiders, he decided, and for the moment he was content. When the sections of the tiny vessel lay pinned to a template, he straightened, kneading a fist in the small of his back. The muffled ringing of the bell startled him and he glanced out the barn door. Across the compound, at the west corner of the porch, Hank Ives was perched on a ladder, buffing up the bell's bright chrome and keeping a watchful eye on Willa-Sue, who was sitting in the glider playing with her doll. Through the office window Leo could make out Ma's green eyeshade as she sat in her swivel chair at her rolltop desk, cashing allowance chits for some of the campers and putting the cash into their envelopes. Just inside the door Honey Oliphant was speaking on the wall telephone, and he observed her through the rusty screen—she had on the white sharkskin shorts she liked to wear, and a pink halter—as she hung up, paid Ma for the use of the telephone, then came out onto the stoop to pet Harpo, sprawled on the warm brownstone.

After a moment she crossed the compound and came to stand in the barn doorway. Leo's mouth went dry and his hand began to tremble.

"Gosh, haven't you been busy?" she said, stepping to Fritz's side. "May I look?"

"Look your fill, by all means," said Fritz, showing off the meticulously executed details added to the model in the past few days: a riverside hotel with tiny flower-planted window boxes, a church with a gleaming gold ball atop the steeple; the weathervane (made from a common pin and bits of gilded paper) on the tiny cupola of the burgomaster's hall; the sign on the outdoor café by the river, which you could actually read—*Die zwei schwartzer Schvannen,* The Two Black Swans—and Leo's unfinished paddleboat.

"What's the boat called," Honey asked Leo.

Blushing furiously, he couldn't answer.

"It's called the *Guldenbraut,*" Fritz said, filling the awkward gap. "It means 'Golden Bride.' "

Still Leo remained tongue-tied, and Fritz went on, describing how the summit of the mountain would be the site of the famous castle where the wicked Austrian Duke Philip had held Richard the Lionheart for ransom on his way back to England from the Crusades.

"I want Leo to tell me about the castle," Honey said, dimpling with enthusiasm. "Please?"

She was teasing him, but he liked it, and somehow his shyness vanished. Hitching up his stool, he recounted the old tale, complete with "once upon a time": how Richard waited in vain to be rescued by his treacherous brother, Prince John, who wanted the English throne for himself.

"And then?" Honey asked, playing the game.

"Richard had a faithful servant, a troubadour called Blondel, and he went in quest of the king, his master. And everywhere he went, to let the king know he was looking for him, he played a song he'd written, a favorite of Richard's."

"Did Richard hear it?"

Leo nodded soberly. "And he called down from his prison room, 'Blondel, Blondel, here am I, your king imprisoned. Come free me.' So Blondel helped the king escape his chains, and together they returned to England, where Richard was greeted lovingly by all his faithful subjects and—"

"And lived happily ever after!" Honey's gay laugh rang out and she clapped her hands like a child.

Leo smiled. "I guess maybe he did."

She laughed her bubbly laugh again, but Leo now was staring down at the barn floor, where the sun had suddenly cast a long shadow. Reece Hartsig sauntered into the Swoboda corner. "What are you doing around here?" he said, eyeing Honey.

"I stopped by to see how the work was going. See the pretty steamboat Leo is making? And the flags?"

Reece tossed a glance at the table but made no comment.

"You never did tell us what happened to your eye," she said teasingly.

He put his hand up to the fading bruise. "It's nothing. I walked into a door," he growled, staring hard at Leo, then abruptly ducked his head and disappeared up the steps, his heavy tread shaking the whole loft as he joined the radio-builders around the transmitter.

"Honestly," said the exasperated Honey, "he can be such a spoilsport sometimes. If you ask me, he's jealous." Her laugh lingered behind as she left the barn and took her bike from the rack near the office door. Leo watched her pedal away, then sat down on his stool again.

"Come on, don't look like that," Fritz said, noting Leo's downcast expression. "He's just acting that way to make you feel bad. Honey's right, he's jealous, I'm sure of it." He washed his brush in his jelly jar—he'd been adding some highlights to the foliage—then took the crosscut saw from the tool rack and went over to the dining hall to even-up the legs of Pa Starbuck's chair.

Preoccupied with fitting the paddle wheel to the boat hull, Leo was only vaguely aware of the sound of idle humming outside the barn until, glancing through the window, he noticed Willa-Sue sitting in the front seat of the Green Hornet. She was playing around with Reece's radio.

"Willa-Sue," he said, keeping his voice down. "You better scram out of there." But she just stood up on the seat and stuck her tongue out at him. He shook his head. "Naughty, naughty," he chided her, and pointed up to where Reece was working. Reluctantly she obeyed him. The next time he looked she was happily ensconced in the glider again, blowing up a balloon. Leo watched as it grew larger and larger, a white balloon of an elongate shape. He hoped it wouldn't pop in her face and set her to hollering. When she was done, she tied it and it sailed into the breeze—not strong enough to carry it aloft—and as it bobbed its way across the compound, she started blowing up another.

Suddenly it dawned on him what the "balloons" really were, and, jumping up, he dashed for the door. As he raced across the compound, scooping up the inflated prophylactic, he heard Ma calling for Pa ("Oh Lord, just see what the child's up to now!"), and by the time Leo reached Willa-Sue, the Reverend was also on the scene. But it was too late to stop the launch of the second balloon; as Willa-Sue squealed with delight, the thing spurted into the air in a gust of wind to catch on the utility wires strung from barn to house, where it hung in full view of the loft window, now crowded with the faces of boys—and, for a moment, that of Reece Hartsig.

"Where did she get these nasty things?" Pa demanded of Leo. "Did you give them to her?" Leo flushed and stammered a denial. But how could he explain that the "balloons" had come from the glove compartment of the Green Hornet? "Well, get the dadblamed thing down!" Pa sputtered. Shaking his head, he retreated to the office, washing his hands of the whole business, as Reece stormed out of the barn and advanced across the compound toward Willa-Sue, still seated on the glider with his personal property lying with her dolly in her lap.

171

"Give me that!" he snarled, snatching the wallet; the red packets she had taken from it fell on the ground, and he bent and scrabbled them up and stuffed them into a pocket.

"Balloons," Willa-Sue said, burring her lips and rolling her eyes.

"You tell him, Baby Snooks." Looking down from the loft window the boys couldn't help laughing, which didn't help matters.

As Reece scowled up at them, then down at Willa-Sue, her features began to contort; a loud scream was on the way. Reece, the color drained from his face, seized her and began to shake her. But the effect, though hardly surprising, was the opposite of what he intended. Willa-Sue began to screech as if she were being murdered. In an attempt to silence her squalling, Reece shook her harder.

"Don't do that!" Leo raced across the turf, and tried to grab Reece's arms to restrain him. From every barn window campers hung their heads out, shouting that Big Chief was being jumped by Wacko Wackeem, and Pa reappeared on the porch, now with Ma in tow, calling for Willa-Sue to come inside.

In the midst of this bedlam Dagmar Kronborg's Pierce-Arrow pulled into the drive. The car door opened and she hurried toward the porch to see what the trouble was. By the time she reached Reece, he had yanked Willa-Sue's doll from her hand. He raised it overhead, then brought it savagely down against the mouth of the pump, smashing the china head into fragments. Screaming louder than ever, Willa-Sue ran to hide her tear-stained face in her mother's skirts, and while Ma tried vainly to comfort her, Dagmar retrieved the headless doll from Reece.

"What can you be thinking of!" she demanded, outraged. "A grown man picking on a child like that!"

"She was in my car, the little nitwit!" Reece thundered. "In my glove compartment! She embarrassed me."

Dagmar made a sour face. "Oh, that is too bad," she said tartly. "You know what she is as well as I do. Allowances must be made. Grown men don't do this sort of thing, only spoiled little boys. Look at what you have done to this poor doll." She shook the broken toy in his face.

Humiliated in front of the campers ogling the scene from the barn, Reece turned away; his gaze fell on Leo.

"It's all his fault," he said. "He was supposed to be watching her."

"No, he wasn't," declared Hank, who had by now climbed down from his ladder and walked over. "I was supposed to watch 'er. Guess I got carried away with my polishin'. But don't blame Leo, 'twasn't his fault."

"Henry is right," said Dagmar to Reece. "And it will do you no good looking for a scapegoat. Why should Leo be made responsible for the child?"

"He's always playing with her, isn't he, encouraging her to act nutty?"

"Don't be asinine. You know you are talking utter nonsense."

Reece glowered at her; his frown deepened as he saw Augie taking a drink at the pump.

"What's he doing drinking from our cup?" he muttered.

"He is thirsty, I expect," Dagmar snapped. "Would you have him drink from the spigot?"

But Reece was no longer listening. He had stormed away to the Green Hornet, where he vaulted neatly over the side and sped off in a cloud of dust.

As he disappeared around the corner, Dagmar stared sadly at the broken doll. "What a shame. I wonder if it can be repaired."

Leo, down on his hands and knees picking the pieces from the dirt, looked up at her. "It's a little like Humpty Dumpty, but I'll try."

"Good!" she said, giving him an approving nod. Then she went into the office with Ma while Leo, having retrieved all the pieces he could find, retreated to the barn to see what could be done about making the doll whole again.

❩

A quarter of an hour later, order had been restored around the compound. The craftworkers had, for the most part, returned to their beaded belts and hammered ashtrays. Tears dried, Willa-Sue now swung in the rubber tire under the catalpa tree, while Leo, back in the Swoboda corner, tried to fit the fragments of the doll's head together.

When Dagmar reappeared, instead of driving away she came across the compound to lean in at the barn window. "But that's wonderful!" she exclaimed of his work. "You're meticulous," she added. "I like that."

Leo blushed; he thought he was making a botch of it. The pieces of the doll's head were chipped and made uneven joins, giving the face the look of a Frankenstein's monster.

"It will be better when the eyes are in," Dagmar said.

Leo shook his head. Though he'd scoured the area, he had found only one eye.

"Well, in the kingdom of the blind the one-eyed doll is king," Dagmar said, laughing, and Leo was forced to laugh too, though it embarrassed him to have her there while he worked.

She waited until he set the doll down; then, when he looked up, she nodded approvingly. "I like your boat, too," she said. "You are making strides."

"It's really Fritz's work," Leo said. "I'm just helping him out."

"Don't be so modest," she retorted. "According to Ma, Fritz says you are very clever."

Again he blushed. But because she seemed genuinely interested, he soon forgot his shyness and opened up a bit. They talked some more about the model village, and about Fritz, whom she liked; Leo could tell.

"And your counselor? What does Reece think about this village of yours?"

Leo was embarrassed again. "He calls us Santa's helpers." Dagmar covered her smile with her hand. "Reece doesn't like Fritz much. Or me," he added glumly.

"Is that so?" she asked sharply.

Leo nodded. "He doesn't think I fit in. I'm too different."

Dagmar became indignant. "Well, I should hope you *are* different! The only reason the world turns is because some people dare to be different. Most people are like so many sheep. You just go right on being as different as you like. As for His Majesty, don't pay him any mind. He doesn't own the whole world, you know, nor his father either. Just the whole of Tolland County." They laughed together; then, crooking her finger, Dagmar motioned him from the barn. Leo left his stool and covered his work, saying he had to quit anyway, it was time for swim.

"Come along with us," Dagmar said. "It's on our way. We can drop you off, and you can tell your friends you had a ride in my auto."

Leo was speechless. He knew it was against the rules for any vehicle except Hank's jitney to "ride" the campers. Dagmar, however, obviously paid no attention to such strictures, and led him to her automobile, where she introduced him to Augie. He smelled of shaving lotion, and his smile made Leo like him right away.

"Tack," Dagmar said, as Augie held the door and helped her in, Leo after her.

"What's tock?" he asked.

"Swedish. Means 'thanks,' " she said, pushing her short, sturdy legs out in front of her and propping her small feet on the footrest.

He liked that; *tack* had an interesting sound. He settled himself comfortably in the handsomely appointed interior, impressed by the folding footrests, the little chrome ash-receiver, cleverly set into the armrest, the tasseled handles, the shades of amber silk that drew up and down on slender, braided cords, the tops of magazines revealing their names in the puckered side pockets. The motor purred like a leopard, and the upholstered seat felt soft and bouncy, as if he were riding on a feather bed.

They went over a bump and Leo's head touched the upholstered ceiling above his head. "Whoopee—bump!" exclaimed Dagmar and they laughed again together. Then suddenly she turned to him and said, "I was surprised when Ma mentioned that you'd stopped playing your violin. Is it true, you're not practicing these days?"

Leo shrugged but offered no comment.

"But you must practice. It's very important, if you're going to have a career in music. You do plan to take it up, don't you?"

"I—I d-don't know," Leo stammered.

"Don't *know?*" she exclaimed. "Of course you do—gracious, don't talk nonsense." She sucked in her cheeks and ran her tongue around her teeth. "See here. I don't know what silliness came over you at Major Bowes. But these things happen at times. A string breaks, you hit a clinker, you forget where you are in a piece." She eyed him intently. "Look at me, please, when I am talking to you. Don't you *want* to be a musician? Don't you *want* to be an artist?" she demanded.

"Yes, I want to play on the radio with Toscanini," he blurted. Dagmar clapped her hands.

"Well, then—to be a fine musician requires not only diligence and practice but the *will* to *be.* No matter who tries to get in your way. All great artists have a sense of destiny, you know," she went on, "that is what helps them become great. And they are strong, like steel, hard, because they cannot let anything or anyone stand in the way of their talent. They make the most of the moment when it comes. *Carpe diem!* You know what that means, don't you? Seize the day! And fly on wings of song!"

On wings of song! Leo stared at her wonderingly.

She smiled her crusty, wrinkled smile. "Your mother would like that, wouldn't she?"

"Yes." Leo looked at her. How did she know about Emily?

Dagmar nodded with satisfaction. "I thought so. You loved your mother very much, didn't you?"

"Yes."

She used the hand-strap to redistribute her weight into her corner of the seat. "You haven't told me how you lost her."

"It was an accident. A train accident."

"Oh?" She drew down the upholstered arm and leaned toward him. "That is a tragedy, indeed."

She straightened and lit one of her Camels. "See here," she said, picking a fleck of tobacco from the tip of her tongue, "suppose I invited you to the Castle—you and your friends. Would you like that?"

Would he! He had thought to leave camp without ever clapping an eye on the famous shrunken head, and here was Dagmar suggesting a visit. And what a feather in his cap if he could walk into Jeremiah and make the announcement that they were going to the Castle.

"Oh yes! Very much," he said.

"Well, you shall come, then, and see the shrunken head." She paused, eyeing him. "And afterward, if you happened to bring along your violin, we might have a spot of music. Would you like that?"

"Perhaps. Who would listen?"

"I would, for one. And our friend, Fritz. I know you like Fritz. And, why, the boys of Harmony. You must invite them all, every one. Do you have any music?"

"Just some old pieces."

"Sometimes the old pieces are the best ones. Do you know 'Träumerei'?"

Yes. Leo knew the piece.

"Paganini's Caprice in A Minor?"

Yes, he knew the Paganini, too.

"Suppose you just brush up a bit, then," Dagmar said. "I shall have the piano tuned for the occasion. We shall play duets in the music room."

Leo stared; if he played with her—surely he could do it then, could— how had she put it?—fly on wings of song! And see the Castle! He could hardly wait to get back and tell the guys!

"We'll leave you here, then," Dagmar said as Augie pulled over at the mailboxes. "Goodbye. Don't forget—practice. It won't make perfect but it helps."

176

She waved and he waved back, cupping his hands and shouting: *"Tack; tack, tack."* Then he made tracks for Jeremiah to tell Tiger and the others all about it. The moment he walked into the cabin, however, he met trouble. Not unnaturally, it originated in Garbage Gulch, which was what, in his journal, he'd dubbed Phil and Wally's bunk rack. Tiger wasn't around; Leo had forgotten, there was a meeting of the Sachems, who'd asked Tiger to attend. But Phil was there.

"We saw you," he said, "getting out of Dagmar's car. Doesn't she know it's against the rules, giving campers rides?" He draped his swim towel around his neck.

"Gosh, I don't know," Leo said, feigning innocence as he kicked off his sneakers. "Maybe you can remind her on Saturday—at the Castle."

They didn't get it. "What are you talking about?" Monkey asked. "Everybody knows we're not allowed to go to the Castle anymore."

"That's where you're wrong," Leo retorted, flipping his hole card, an ace. "Because we're invited to visit Dagmar there—next Saturday."

Phil chose not to believe it. "Who're you kidding?" he scoffed.

"I'm not kidding. I fixed it with her. For lunch and everything."

Phil was astonished. *"You* fixed it?"

Dump snorted. "Aw, c'mon, Wacko, what d'you mean, *fixed* it? How?"

"It wasn't hard. I just talked her into it, that's all. I said it would be nice; a lot of the guys haven't seen it."

"Including you, I suppose."

"Why not? There'll be music, too," he added, tugging on his trunks. "Dagmar and I are going to play duets."

"Hope it's better playing than at Major Bowes . . ." Wally muttered as Leo hopped outside to pull his towel from the line.

"Don't worry, Wally," the Bomber said, saluting the news with a stupefying chain of farts. "You can always stop your ears."

Phil and Wally's expressions said there was something fishy in it all, but Monkey and Dump and, on the opposite side of the cabin, Eddie Fiske signaled approval, and in a few minutes the news was being spread among the assembled swimmers at the dock that the Friend-Indeeders had been invited back to the Castle—and, according to the way he told it, all thanks to Wacko Wackeem.

5

In the age of the electric Frigidaire, Kelsoe's icehouse was less a building than a relic of an earlier time, less a fact of life than a sentimentalized tradition. For years Moonbow campers had been hearing from Pa and Henry Ives tales of the "good old days," when the Friends of Joshua would come out from Putnam in wintertime, sleighing and jingle-belling over the backcountry roads, bringing their saws to cut the ice and their baling hooks to haul the blocks up the tin-sheathed ramp from the shore to be stored, covered with sawdust and battened down under tarpaulins, against the coming hot summer months.

Decidedly smaller than a barn, the icehouse nonetheless had the atmosphere of one, with its lofty, shadowy spaces, its thick rooftree and timbers set with trunnels, mortised and tenoned; there was hardly a nail in the whole place. High in the rafters, gray papery wasp nests the shape of footballs swung in the breeze among mud-dauber dwellings so firmly chinked into the corners that they blended with the architecture. Half-rotted surfaces were overgrown with dark-green mosses and blue lichens, with patches of chemical-orange toadstools that thrived in the loamy soil. Here and there along the well-adzed rooftree, families of birds nested—barn swallows in little half-cups of mud and, in one corner, the straw-and-twig sack of an oriole. The cool interior smelled of mold, a pungent, mushroomy kind of odor, and over the years the room had become the habitat of whole colonies of grubs and termites, and spiders of a sort completely different from those that inhabited the meadow.

Leo had already found the place a good one for spiders; now he had decided it would be a perfect spot to practice in as well, a hideaway where he could fiddle to his heart's content, where the walls would not only provide sounding boards for his music but prevent the sound from carrying to unwelcome ears. He shed his cap, the one Reece had objected to—these days the felt crown sported even more bottle caps, and buttons with views of Ausable Chasm and Niagara Falls that he'd traded for around camp; even a Coast Guard anchor he'd swapped for his Mel Ott bubble-gum card—and, having come across a beat-up peach basket to sit upon and an all-but-backless chair for a music stand, he made himself at home just within the side entrance. He opened his knapsack and brought out some sheet music, then unsnapped the catches of his violin case. He began softly, a do-re-mi scale, up and down, up and down, checking to see if he had gone rusty.

He practiced diligently for a while, performing the intricate finger exercises the way he'd been taught, endlessly repeating scales and arpeggios, coaxing the notes from his instrument, whose rich wood warmed against his throat. Then, when this became tedious, he had a go at "Träumerei." It felt sweet, the happy return to something both natural and deeply satisfying, the thing that signified to him he was someone, not just Wacko Wackeem, but Leo Joaquim, who played the violin. The melody grew, amplified by the empty spaces of the icehouse, and he could feel the pulse of the violin on the flesh of his cheek.

After that, he played a couple of other favorites—the "Meditation" from *Thaïs,* the Bach Solfeggio—then attempted the Paganini Caprice. Finally he lifted the bow; the vibration ceased, the notes faded into silence, and he took stock of his performance. He told himself it had gone well—and why not, when there was nobody around to make him nervous? For a time all was quiet.

Outside a light breeze caused the tree leaves to tremble and riffled the water in the cove, and the golden sunlight, sifting down through the branches, dappled the ground. Leaving his place, he went outside the icehouse and settled himself against the wall beside the door, where, contentedly devouring a Mr. Goodbar square by square, he reflected on his unexpected visit with Dagmar. It had been just the thing he'd needed to get him practicing again. Was it her own love of music that had caused her to interest herself in him? Had Ma said something to her? If so, what? Was it possible that he might have a career—that Emily's dream would one day come true? Happy as that prospect might make him, it hardly seemed likely; his destiny lay among the pimpled orphans at Pitt.

Somewhere hidden from sight a woodpecker rapped out its hollow tattoo, and cicadas sang their summer passions, their buzzing electrifying the torpid air. Now and then a small fish splashed in the water, a bright pip, a series of rings, and calm again. This was paradise, he thought, the Garden before the Fall, when Adam was banished and took Eve to live east of Eden in the Land of Nod. The high, bright, sultry heat of midsummer had come on, the gorgeous cloud-fleeced days, each one more perfect than the last, and reason enough for Leo to forget the trials he had endured. He lay back on his elbows and gazed up at the trembling blue sky and, drawing his deepest breath, held it. Then, shutting his eyes, he began to count—one two three four—out loud. He told himself that if he could count up to one hundred on the same breath he would never have to leave this place, he could stay here forever. No—forever and a day. (He liked the phrase: "forever and a day." That was as long as anyone could think of, forever *and* one more day. The extra day made all the difference.) He would never have to leave, never never, this place where the sky was ocean-blue, a huge bowl in which butterflies swam like the fishes in the deep blue sea—so many golden fishes waiting to be caught, trophies of his Moonbow summer.

He rolled over and pulled Fritz's book from his knapsack. Between its dark, worn covers he had discovered a glorious world of words and rhymes and images. There was a poem by Macaulay that he particularly liked, "Horatius at the Bridge," retelling the old Roman legend of three brave warriors defending the city of Rome against the Etruscan hordes. It had to do with something very much on Leo's mind these days: friendship.

" 'East and west and south and north,' " he read,

> The Messengers ride fast,
> And tower and town and cottage
>   Have heard the trumpet's blast.
> Shame on the false Etruscan
>   Who lingers in his home,
> When Porsena of Clusium
>   Is on the march for Rome.

180

He broke off as a warm, moist tongue licked the back of his neck. "Harpo!"

He rolled around with the dog, then sat up to see Tiger come charging across the meadow. He threw himself down beside Leo and looked at him with excited eyes and a big smile, while Harpo panted between them both.

"Is it true?" he said. "You fixed it with Dagmar for the Castle?"

"You heard?"

"Sure. Everybody's talking—you're the hero of the hour. Dagmar usually means what she says; you really must have fast-talked her."

Afraid to meet his friend's eye, Leo looked out across the pond. "Yeah. Sort of."

"Come on, what do you mean 'sort of'? Did you or didn't you?"

"Sure. I did. It's fixed."

"That's swell. Only don't look so unhappy about it."

Leo felt trapped in his lie—*he* hadn't fixed it, it had been all Dagmar's doing—and he didn't like being untruthful with Tiger. Still, he *could* say the invitation had been issued because of him.

Just then, from the far distance came the throb of Doc Oliphant's *Moonbow Maid.* Leo recognized Reece's trademark yachting cap, and the flutter of his Hawaiian shirt—and next to him a golden head that could only belong to Honey.

The two boys watched as the speedboat sped past the mouth of the China Garden and cut a wide arc north, heading for Turtle Bay.

"I guess you heard about the crazy stunt Reece pulled this morning," Leo remarked. Tiger, having finished up the Indian belt he had been making for his father, had been getting in some extra batting practice during crafts.

"Yeah, I heard about it."

Leo could see Tiger was embarrassed by the incident, but it was obvious he would see any real criticism of the counselor as disloyal. He did concede that Reece's display of temper had not been the most glowing demonstration of the behavior expected of the camp's Moonbow Warrior. "Reece's got a temper," he explained. "He gets it from Big Rolfe."

Leo was indignant. "But he's a grown-up, not a kid."

"Grown-ups don't always act grown-up. Besides, all Germans have tempers—look at Hitler." He rolled over and looked at Leo. "Were you able to mend the doll?"

181

Leo described the patchwork job he'd managed. "The left eye got lost, though. I looked everywhere."

Tiger said he'd help in the search; a one-eyed doll wasn't going to please Willa-Sue much.

"How was your meeting?" Leo asked.

"Fine." Leo waited; Tiger fiddled with a new Krazy Kat puzzle he'd bought, trying to roll the eyes into their sockets. "If you were wondering about the red feather Saturday night, don't."

"Was I blackballed again?"

Tiger's expression indicated the answer was yes. For Leo this was bad news. There wouldn't be too many more chances for him to be taken into the Senecas. He shook his head in woeful frustration. "All because of putting on the bonnet. What a dumb thing. With Pa right there."

Tiger put up a hand. "Forget it. I know you didn't mean any disrespect."

Leo reflected for some moments, then:

"What about Fritz? Was he blackballed again too?"

Tiger nodded. It was a matter of general camp knowledge that, though there was a party among the Senecas in favor of Fritz's nomination to the honor society, an opposing faction, headed, it was whispered, by Reece himself, violently opposed awarding Fritz the red feather. And why?

Because no Jew had ever been a Seneca, seemed to be the answer, just as no Jew had ever been allowed inside the Tunxis Country Club, where Rolfe Hartsig headed the steering committee.

Leo was disappointed for Fritz. It wasn't fair. He hadn't done anything to deserve the snub. And if camp was all about friends and friendships, well, it was just wrong, that was all.

Out on the water the Chris-Craft made another slow, curving pass. Leo watched glumly; the sight of Honey boating with Heartless depressed him.

Tiger began again. "I want to ask you . . . I have a question to put, okay?"

"Shoot."

"Are you afraid of something?"

"Afraid? Of what?"

"You tell me. I mean, is something troubling you? Something I don't know about?"

"What makes you think that?"

"I hear you sometimes. At night. You talk in your sleep."

Leo was instantly on the alert. "When? When did I?"

"Well, one time was the other night after the ghost stories. You went—where did you go to anyway?"

Leo rolled over and looked at the Steelyard house. "Over there."

"Are you kidding? What made you do that?"

Leo shrugged. "I guess it was Hank's story about Mary and—and the m-murder. I just wanted to look the place over again."

"Jeez. I don't get it."

"I guess it sounds crazy, but—remember I told you about the butcher shop and us living over it? Well, the Steelyard place keeps reminding me of that house. I got this screwy idea—I don't know, I can't figure it out—but there's something about it—it's spooky. Even the inside was like our house."

"Cripes! You mean you went inside?"

"Yup. It was really weird, the layout was practically the same. There was this dark spot on the floor—in the front hall—it looked like blood."

"Come on, kiddo. You're jazzing me."

"No, I'm not. Then I went upstairs."

"In the dark? By yourself? You're either fearless or you're nuts. Oh wow, sorry, I didn't mean—"

"It's okay, forget it. The doc'd probably say nuts; I say fearless."

They smiled at each other, then Tiger asked, "Did . . . did anything . . . happen?"

"Yes . . ."

"You're kidding!" Tiger was on his knees, his eyes flashing his eagerness.

"I went into Mary Steelyard's room. The corner room. It was like my mother's room."

"Oh, jeez, you're not going to tell me you saw the ghost."

"Worse. As I was coming down the stairs, I knew there was something there, something was hiding, I couldn't *hear* it but I could *feel* it. When I reached the bottom step the door flew open and this thing rushed in—"

"Thing? What thing?"

"It was just a thing. A big dark *thing*. I couldn't see what it was, but it grabbed me and it picked me up. I was hollering. I knew I was going to die. It was going to throw me into the cellar, but I kicked myself free."

"You *kicked?*"

"That's right. I kicked him . . . in the *eye*. Get it?"

"Oh my gosh! In the—Oh cripes, you mean to say—" Tiger's eyes grew wider; Leo was nodding to beat the band.

"So *that's* how he got the shiner." Tiger hooted, then launched himself at Leo, and they rolled over together in the grass, laughing as hard as they could; Harpo, who was drowsing in the shade, leaped up, tail a-wag, and joined in the fun. After a few moments they subsided, then, brushing themselves off, they lay back on the turf and were quiet for a while.

"What kind of things do I talk about?" Leo asked when Harpo had settled himself again.

"Well," Tiger began, gazing up at the sky, "once I remember you said 'Don't do it.' Right out loud. Then you said 'Put it down.'"

"Did anyone else hear?"

"No one, as far as I can tell. At least nobody's said." Tiger stopped and chewed his lip. "Is there anything . . . I mean, you're not exactly a blabbermouth, I know, but if you wanted to talk ever . . ."

Leo wanted, wanted so badly to get it all out, but he couldn't. The words wouldn't come.

"That's okay," he managed. "I mean, it's nothing, honest. It's just . . . well, nothing. But thanks, anyway." He moved a little way away and squinted at the pond.

Tiger sat up, his eye on the back of Leo's neck. "Come on, kiddo, don't go clamming up on me again."

"I wasn't. I was just thinking about something."

"What?"

"I was wondering what's going to happen when camp's over."

"Same old thing, I guess. It'll be back to school for me, and for you—"

"It's back to the Institute and the grease pits, I guess." Come September Leo would be apprenticed as a mechanic in the Pitt garage, a prospect he detested. "But we'll see each other, won't we? This winter?"

"Heck yes." Tiger was firm. "My mom's going to invite you and Bomber to come stay overnight. Up in the attic. I've got a swell room. Double-decker bunks just like at camp, and the electric train."

"Yeah," Leo said, "I can't wait to see that."

"Just remember, until then, try and keep your nose clean."

"Can't I even pick it?"

"That's not for me to say. And you need a haircut." In a final burst of laughter Tiger was on his feet, Harpo too, and away they sped like a pair of jackrabbits.

Leo watched them go, then, relieving a foot that was going to sleep, he craned his neck, checking the sky for the time. By now the sun had shifted several degrees; he felt a bright beam shining into his eyes, and angled his head into its warmth. Behind his lids lights danced green and red and yellow, pinwheels of color, a vivid burst of patterns and shapes like Fourth of July fireworks exploding on his retina. He reminded himself that he should practice some more, but it was hard to concentrate when his thoughts flitted about as errantly as the dragonflies that hovered above the surface of the water, or—he glanced upward, his eye attracted by a flashing motion in the air. Overhead, limned sharply against the opalescent blue, two pale-yellow butterflies whirled in a frantic spiral of passionate activity. There was evidence of desperate persistence in their wild gyrations as one pursued the other, driven to mate, now joining her, now parting, now joining again. Leo observed the ritual with a certain cynicism. Why wouldn't, couldn't she simply give in and accept his advances? What need to lead him such a mad chase when ultimately there would come the gossamer embrace, and death? Poor butterfly. Maybe that was the real meaning of the song . . .

> Poor Butterfly!
> 'Neath the blossoms waiting
> Poor Butterfly!
> For she loved him so.

He went back inside the icehouse, where he took up his violin again and resumed his practice. And as he played, he imagined her, Emily, seated in her chair, listening to the melody that was her favorite, brushing out her hair as she nodded and smiled approval. He could see the old woman who lived in the back room at Mrs. Kranze's, sitting in the iron bedstead in the corner, her bony fingers clasped under her chin, her eyes bright as she listened; and John Burroughs, the day they went to the park, when the merry-go-round played the song and he sat astride the painted horse with John standing at his side so he wouldn't fall off; and the night of the big storm, when John—suddenly the light seemed to dim around him. The bridge—the bridge was going to be washed out, it would fall into the river, carrying with it anyone unlucky enough to be on it. He had known it was going to happen, hadn't he? Somehow he'd imagined it every time he crossed the bridge. Why hadn't he warned them? Was he to blame? The questions pinwheeled in his head as he looked and turned away and looked

185

again, saw the bridge falling into the river, saw the truck engulfed and—

Mother!

Mother!

MOTHER!

He stopped playing. His hand was shaking. It was true. Here, beside the lake, in the shade and the summer sun, he was shaking. Why should that be so? Here, beside Moonbow Lake, he still felt afraid.

The sun had moved on. He didn't need a watch to tell him it was already three, and that he should get back to camp. No more practice today. He replaced his violin carefully in its case, gathered up his music, then turned to retrieve his knapsack. As he did so, in a shaft of light at the back of the icehouse, he spotted a spider, a big fat black-and-yellow one. He fished out his notebook and made one of his customary notes on the creature's web and habitat, then flipped it into a box. He was just sliding the lid home when the deep-throated roar of the Chris-Craft engine shattered his sanctuary, and, glancing out the door, he recoiled in alarm. The *Moonbow Maid* was speeding across the water, heading in a beeline for the China Garden—was only a hundred yards away. Even now, Reece, with Honey beside him, was cutting the motor, and Leo could make out their features clearly, including details like the radium-dial watch on Reece's wrist, the barrette in Honey's hair. What were they doing here? Had she come to pick the water lilies?

He felt the clutch of panic, as if he were about to be caught redhanded in some criminal act, and, keeping well out of sight, he tried to think. He knew he couldn't escape without being seen, but if Reece did see him, what would he say? And Honey . . . And even as he agonized he knew he'd waited too long. He dashed to the door and retrieved his violin and music, then retreated again into the shadows, while the brass-trimmed prow of glossy mahogany carved its way lightly, quietly now, through the bed of lily pads— in which Honey showed no seeming interest—and into the icehouse inlet, where there was a bit of beach. Reece was handing Honey out of the boat. He passed her a grocery sack, and, bringing along a blanket and Honey's portable phonograph, he joined her ashore. In a few minutes they had made their way to a spot where, tucked away amid a lush brake of ferns nestled under the drooping fronds of a weeping willow, they set down their things and spread out the blanket. Reece put a record on the phonograph and they made themselves comfortable.

What was Leo to do? If he showed himself to them now, he would stand accused of being a Peeping Tom—which was not far from the truth, as from his hiding place he continued to watch, knowing it was wrong, unable to stop himself. His gaze lingered on Honey as she took a brush from her bag and began brushing her hair. Reece turned on one hip, then leaned across her to pull a couple of bottles from the sack, a beer and a Coca-Cola.

"Toss us the church key," he said.

Honey obliged with the bottle opener, then lay back, watching him uncap the soda pop and drink thirstily, and Leo saw how her polka-dot blouse drew snugly across the curve of her breasts, how they rose and fell with her breathing—a trifle fast, he thought, as if she was excited. One at a time Reece raised his outstretched legs, exercised their muscles, and set them down again while Honey lay back, and the soft sound of her voice floated across the distance between her and the icehouse.

She laughed at something Reece said; he laughed too. He was making an effort to be entertaining and amusing for her benefit: Heartless hard at work. It was easy to see why people found him as charming and winning as they did; he certainly was plenty charming with Honey. He didn't touch her, but just talked in that bantering way of his. He lay back, one leg cocked over the other knee, hands clasped behind his head, looking up at the clouds.

Honey was laughing now, about a school friend summering on Cape Cod who'd been so badly sunburned she couldn't go on the beach where all the cute guys hung out. While she talked on enthusiastically about Sally, Reece turned the record over. It was Guy Lombardo, and Reece pinched his nostrils and sang through his nose like Guy's vocalist brother, Carmen:

> I saw you last night
> and got that old feeling.
> When you came in sight
> I got that old feeling

The music ended, and Reece took the record off; they talked some more, and suddenly Leo was shocked to hear his name mentioned. They were talking about him!

"I think he's very clever," he heard Honey saying, "getting the boys invited back to the Castle, when you couldn't talk Dagmar into it. I think he has a lot of moxie."

Leo couldn't believe it! They were talking about him, and Honey—Honey was sticking up for him!

Not Reece, though. "A lot of nerve, you mean," he said with a nasty chuckle.

"No, be serious, can't you? He's not like the other boys. He's different."

"Weird, you mean. One of these days he's going to pull one dumb stunt too many and it'll be goodbye Wacko Wackeem."

"I don't like to hear you talk like that. I feel sorry for him. He has no family, no one to look after him—living in that awful place—"

"How do you know it's awful?"

"It's an orphanage, isn't it? All orphanages are awful. He has such sad eyes sometimes. But he's so cheerful. He doesn't feel sorry for himself. He's really quite comical—"

"I don't think he's so funny," Reece growled.

"Oh, you—you're such a stick-in-the-mud." She drank from her Coke, then went on. "You have to admit, he plays the violin beautifully."

"You've gotta be kidding. Didn't you hear him at Major Bowes? Talk about chalk on the blackboard."

"So he made a mistake. That can happen to anyone—"

"Look, let's change the subject, huh?" He leaned toward her, and what happened next, Leo didn't care for at all.

Reece reached a long arm into the grass and plucked a flower—a buttercup. Then, tilting Honey's head back and bringing his head closer, he rotated the blossom under her chin to see if she liked butter.

"Do you?" she asked.

"Sure do." He came closer still.

"Oh, you," she said, laughing. His lips were right next to her ear; in a quick move, he kissed her. Leo felt his blood begin to rush. This was the last thing he wanted to see, Reece necking with Honey Oliphant, but what could he do?

"Don't," said Honey, shivering and ducking her head between her shoulders, "that tickles." She giggled, then, and lay back, and Reece took the cold beer bottle and laid it against her chest. She made tiny squeaking sounds of protest and pushed his hand away.

"Please don't do that!"

"Why not? Don't you like it?"

"*No.* It's cold!"

"I can fix that," Reece said, chuckling again. "Here's something warmer," and he set the bottle down and laid his cheek where the cold glass had touched her, between her breasts. Unable to look away, Leo swallowed and licked his lips, adjusted his position slightly, froze as Honey sat up again.

"What was that?" she said, peering toward the icehouse. "I think someone's there."

"It's a wolf," Reece said with a mock leer, "and he's coming to eat you all up, gobble-gobble-gulp."

"If you ask me, *you're* the one who's the wolf. What if somebody should come along and find us?"

"So what? We're not doing anything illegal, are we? Besides"—looking at his watch with the phosphorescent face—"it's swim time. Relax."

"I'm sure I heard something. Go and see," Honey urged. "Over there, in the icehouse—"

"Okay, let's have a quick look." Reece got up, vaulted the stream, and cut across the plot of grass in the direction of the icehouse. Frantically Leo looked around for someplace to hide. There was none that he could see. He crouched down, not really out of sight, praying that among the shadows he wouldn't be discovered. He held his breath, listening to the sound of Reece's footsteps, eyes shut tight, as if that alone might ward off discovery. For a moment or two everything was quiet; then he heard the sound of water. Opening his eyes and raising his head a little, he saw Reece standing just inside the doorway, peeing against the wall, now glancing back over his shoulder at a large fly buzzing around him. Leo ducked. When he took another look Reece was buttoning his shorts, glancing up at the rafters, where the swallows were flying about. Then, apparently satisfied, he left the building and trotted back to Honey.

Leo quickly resumed his lookout, but now he had difficulty seeing. Honey and Reece were no longer sitting up, they were lying side by side on the blanket. Reece was stripping off his shirt, tossing it aside as he slid an arm around Honey's waist, drawing her to him. Though Leo had seen them together before, though he'd seen them dancing close together, their bodies touching as they bent and swayed to the music, that distressing sight had been nothing compared with this; this was horizontal stuff! His heart began to pound. He tried improving his angle of sight but it was no good: Honey was mostly hidden by Reece, who was stretched alongside her on the blanket. Unable to make out what was happening, Leo listened with greater urgency, cocking his head, cupping his ear, frowning in studied concentration as he tried to catch some intelligible fragment of speech. No dice; it was all mumbles.

Risking discovery, he ventured from the icehouse, creeping around the doorframe and wriggling through the grass to get closer. Reece was sitting up now, and he had Honey lying on her back across his thighs; his fingers were unfastening the buttons of her blouse. As she murmured protestingly, one by one he undid them and then slipped the blouse down, baring her tanned shoulders, drawing it away little by little until her pink brassiere was exposed.

"No, don't, we mustn't," Leo heard her murmur.

"Why not?"

"Because."

"Because why?"

"Because my mother wants me to be a good girl." She tried to do up the buttons.

He fussed with her hands. "You *are* a good girl," he said huskily. "But listen, what did we come here for?"

"We came to have a nice time. You said you wanted to talk."

"I do, dreamgirl, I really do. Only you got me so darned excited. You really send me."

"Then suppose you just come back from wherever I sent you. I think we should be going, honest. We can't sit here all day, can we?"

"I don't know why not."

She started to get up and he reached out and pulled her down again, clasping her to him. He cupped his palms behind her head, gripping it while he kissed her hard on the mouth, kissed her until she began to struggle, until, as if she were drowning, her arms began to flail about, her fists to beat helplessly at him. At last their lips parted and, pulling back, she stared at him in shocked surprise, then tried to break away from him, but his hands gripped her shoulders. With his mouth buried in her neck he forced her back onto the blanket, and, in a quick move, rolled on top of her, tearing at her blouse. Now he had his fingers entangled in her hair, his face buried between her breasts. Her features were half-hidden by locks of hair plastered across them, and she moaned and called out as she thrashed about under the weight of his torso sprawled across her.

"Oh, no, *don't!*" she cried in a frightened voice. "Please don't! You're hurting me!" She began sobbing so hard that he released her. Then, when she had got to her knees and was struggling with her torn clothing he took her by surprise and dragged her down again.

"Hey, not so fast," he drawled, "Daddy's still got something coming to him."

He pinned her down as before, working at her with his whole body while she struggled to free herself.

"Help! *Help!*" she called out. Leo caught a glimpse of her face, pale and and terrified. Saw Reece's face too; he was panting like an animal. And then, suddenly, Leo was watching him smash the doll, seeing the broken pieces on the ground. Was this what he planned for Honey, to smash her, too?

"Damn you, Reece Hartsig!" Suddenly Leo was on his feet, running across the grass, hollering at the top of his lungs. Without stopping, he flung himself onto Reece's back, pummeling him until he rolled off of Honey, carrying his assailant with him.

"Jesus! What the hell!"

Twisting around, Reece got a look at his attacker—Wacko Wackeem— then he peered dazedly about for the rest of the ten-man powerhouse that must have struck him as Leo continued the assault, striking out blindly wherever he could land a blow. Finally, one wild punch connected with Reece's nose. He howled in pain, and there was a sudden burst of bright red as he began to bleed. Leo stepped back; groping in his pocket, Reece pulled out his bandanna and clapped it over his face, his eyes tearing from pain—effectively prevented from making any counterattack on his assailant.

As Reece threw his head back to help reduce the flow of blood, Leo turned to Honey, who was on her feet now, sobbing and covering her exposed breasts with her crossed arms. Her hair hung over her eyes, and her shorts were stained. Then, still sobbing, she grabbed her blouse and fled toward the beach, where she clambered into the speedboat, started the motor, and sped away, while Leo turned to face the wrathful, blood-spattered Reece. Standing now, his feet planted well apart for balance, he stared furiously at Leo.

"What the hell is this all about?" he growled. "Where did you come from?"

Leo pointed at his hiding place. "I was in there! I was watching. I saw it all. I saw what you were doing to her!"

"What are you talking about? I wasn't doing anything."

"You hurt her!"

Reece's look was scornful. "Why, you lousy little shit, I ought to brain you! You don't know what you're talking about. We were just having some fun." He patted his nose with the bloodied handkerchief. "You keep it up, Wacko, just keep it up. One of these days you're going to get it good."

He turned on his heel and stalked back to the blanket.

"What am I supposed to do with this crap, anyway?" He looked at Leo. "Okay, camper, let's have a little clean-up detail here. Pack up this gear and tote it back to camp. On the double."

"Clean it up yourself."

"What did you say?"

"I said clean it up yourself. You tote it, it's your stuff."

And while Reece, arms akimbo, watched him with sullen fury, Leo turned on his heel and headed for the icehouse to get his paraphernalia. When he reappeared—the counselor was nowhere to be seen. The lakeshore was empty, the waters of the China Garden quiet once more, and for a moment Leo thought he must have imagined the violent scene. But he could still hear Honey's cries in his ears, and suddenly, again recalling the broken doll, he felt afraid.

6

uring the warm forenoon of the following Saturday, Leo stood in the blinding July sunlight, gazing out from the parapet of the tall stone tower at the Castle. The view was dazzling. Six miles off, across the billowing treetops, he could just glimpse a wedge of glittering water that was a reach of Moonbow Lake, and intermittent sections of the Old Lake Road winding through the countryside. Above his head the Stars and Stripes snapped at the white-painted flag mast, casting its shadow across the worn slates beneath his feet, and the tower itself, girdled by its crenellated fortifications, seemed to him like the forecastle of a medieval galleon plying a dark-green sea.

Nothing he had yet heard from Fritz or Tiger about the Castle had prepared him for all that he had discovered here. Designed by an architect known for his advanced ideas, built of local materials—oak and pine, field-stone and quarried slate—the house had been constructed in tiers against the mountain, out of whose side it seemed to grow. The tower where Leo stood had been built almost single-handedly by Dagmar's husband, Knute, the thousands upon thousands of stones making up its walls, staircase, and crenellations gathered from fields all around the countryside or dug out of the earth of Mount Zion itself, to lend a touch of the European past to a country that had never known it.

Leo, who had climbed to the summit with a group led by Fritz Auerbach, reveled in the feeling of airy spaciousness, in the astonishing sense of freedom and glorious release. Only if he stared straight down at the gallery and terrace, where numbers of Harmonyites sprawled about on the redwood furniture, luxuriating in the sunshine while under the vocal supervision of Bullnuts Moriarity the collapsible lunch tables were being carried from the camp truck and the food pans readied, did he become prey to the sensation of vertigo. He blinked, shut his eyes, to get himself under control; today was no time for that sort of nonsense. Today was high adventure, the fulfillment of his hopes of getting a look at Dagmar's treasures, the impossible somehow come true. Nothing must spoil it—not even Reece Hartsig, who mercifully had not yet put in an appearance on the scene.

Leo had replayed in his mind the scene at Kelsoe's icehouse a thousand times in the days since it had occurred, and always it had a different, uglier, more tragic end, for in his thoughts he never got to Reece in time, never did save Honey. Of course, he knew that wasn't what had happened at all, that Honey was safe: on the pretext of visiting her friend Sally down on Cape Cod, she had removed herself from Moonbow without a word to anyone except her family. Not even Peewee was able to predict when she would return, and her departure from Friend-Indeed had left an undeniable hole in the fabric of the summer. Perhaps, Leo thought, it was the fact that she was gone, while Reece remained and went on as before—thus far not a word appeared to have been circulated about what had happened—that made him replay the scene as he did. For nothing was changed, yet everything was changed for Leo where the counselor of Jeremiah was concerned. Reece might pretend—as he did so well, and craftily—that nothing was wrong; in front of others he was equable, even friendly, but from a steely look, a frown, an unspoken word, Leo knew that Reece was now his enemy and there would be no making up. Not that Leo much wanted to make up; for him the hero was fallen, and his once admiring view of his counselor had become one of scorn and disapproval. And fear. Of course, Leo now saw, the awe in which Reece was held at Friend-Indeed had always contained an element of fear—of what would happen when a camper lost Reece's favor, when the clouds of anger gathered about that Herculean brow. And the fact was, Leo, in defying him, had now stirred him to a rage that would be unrelenting. Though in front of others he smiled and played his Mr. Nice Guy game; though, between the two, not a word had been uttered about the icehouse, about Leo's bruises, about Honey's sudden departure, Leo knew, and Reece knew that he knew, and Leo knew . . . . It was like the girl in the Land O'Lakes carton, an infinity of possibilities.

Reece could not know, however, that, for Honey's sake, Leo was determined to say nothing, not even to Tiger or the Bomber. He had confided in Fritz, who said that the whole incident was best forgotten. Honey was out of trouble, no one the wiser, and better to let the ugliness fade away. Which was all well and good, Leo thought—except that the hostility remained. Brief, private looks from Reece, in the dining hall, the coop, the crafts barn, revealed his feelings of resentment, and only Leo (and Fritz) could see the wolf's teeth behind the smile.

At least the hike to this astonishing place on this glorious morning had been free of the counselor's presence—he had had an "appointment he couldn't break" in Putnam, and would be driving over "later" in the Green Hornet. Upon receipt of this news, Dagmar had commented in that acerbic way of hers that if she had his number right he'd turn up just about the time lunch was being served.

There had been one arrival of note, however; half an hour ago a car had driven up, and its passenger—a stranger to Leo—had received a cordial welcome from Dagmar. She and the man were now seated on the terrace talking together, and as Leo looked down from his eyrie he saw both heads turned upward. Were they talking about the tower, or perhaps the sky, which was showing signs of weather—or about Leo? Though why he should imagine such a thing, he couldn't say.

His thoughts were interrupted by Fritz's suggestion that they go down. The rest of the viewing party had already disappeared through the small doorway that led to the circular flight of steps. "Come, let me show you the trophy room," Fritz said, pocketing his little telescope and steering Leo down the descending spiral and along the gallery to this treasure house, the high-beamed room where Dagmar's collection of artifacts was housed, a trove of exotic impedimenta that took up every flat surface, every inch of wall space. Here was a wastebasket hollowed from an elephant's foot, a matched pair of narwhale tusks; a grass skirt from Waikiki, and a pair of teakwood-and-brass opium pipes from Canton; a half-dozen fierce-looking Fijian ceremonial masks and an array of primitive weaponry, including bamboo blowpipes that shot poison darts—and the famous shrunken head.

"Ain't it somethin'?" the Bomber boomed. "Did you ever see anything so fierce-lookin'?"

Leo hadn't. The head was the most grotesque object he had ever set eyes upon. About the size of a baseball, it had black skin as wrinkled and stiff as old leather. Hanks of coarse hair, black and still glossy, sprouted from the scalp. The hideous features were at once alarming and strangely complaisant: on the one hand the owner seemed to have expired in a moment of extreme agony—this Leo deduced from the painful grimace of the cracked and torn lips—while on the other the closed eyes—sewn shut with a series of neatly taken stitches—lent the face a peculiar air of peaceful slumber.

Noting the others' eyes on him as they waited for his reaction, he turned away with studied indifference to find himself standing before a vitrine shaped roughly like a clock case on whose half dozen glass shelves were exhibited a collection of glass paperweights.

"That's the one, Wacko," Eddie said.

"The one what?"

"In the middle." Eddie pressed his fingertip on the glass, leaving a smudge. "That's the one Stanley stole."

Leo could understand why someone might want to steal the paperweight: it was a real beauty, a dome-shaped mound imprisoning a bouquet of flowers. And while the others went outside again, he lingered behind, contemplating the brightly gleaming object, thinking about the culprit and remembering the story: Stanley had pocketed it, then smuggled it back to camp and hidden it in his suitcase, where it was sure to be found. He should have known that was the first place they'd look for it. Stanley couldn't have been very bright.

The doorway of the adjacent room (this was Dagmar's music room) stood next to the cabinet, and, before joining the others—from outside now Moriarity could be heard bellowing "Come and get it!" as he banged on an aluminum pan—Leo stopped to check out the space where later he was to perform. Suddenly his heart began to pound. All morning he had resolutely refused to consider the fact that this afternoon he was to give his first public performance since Major Bowes Night. Now he couldn't help remembering that his playing had been part of the bargain between him and Dagmar that had made the visit to the Castle possible, and he steeled himself for the ordeal, praying he wouldn't disgrace himself again. He liked the look of the room very much. It was long and low-ceilinged, with the ebony grand piano standing in the corner at the far end, away from the fireplace. On the fringed shawl that half-covered it, next to a Chinese vase filled with roses, stood a bust in dark bronze (Beethoven, the eyes glowering sternly from under a majestic brow), and beside that, where Augie had placed it earlier, Leo's own violin.

Again he heard Moriarity's bellow—"Last call, last call"—and turned to go, heading for the chow line upon which hungry campers were converging from all directions.

"Can I eat with you?" Leo asked Fritz.

"Why don't we go see what Dagmar has to say?" he replied. "Well, come along, it's all right." Together, he and Leo crossed the gallery, to meet with Dagmar, who was heading in their direction. Accompanying her was the stranger. He was wearing a wrinkled suit; his head was bald on top, with frizzy locks that drooped over his collar, and he had warm, friendly eyes.

"This is Professor Pinero," Dagmar said as they came up.

The man smiled kindly. "How do you do, Leo," he said. Leo liked him right away.

"The professor teaches music," their hostess explained.

Leo took care to keep his eyes lowered. Dagmar was up to something; he didn't know what, but suddenly he was afraid. He could see the toes of the man's shoes and the cuffs of his trousers.

Dagmar must have read his thoughts, for, reaching for his hand to guide him along the gallery, she said, "I invited the professor to come and visit with us today. We're going to take lunch together."

"Yes," the professor said. "And afterward, your friend Dagmar tells me, I'm to have the pleasure of hearing you play. I'm looking forward to that, I assure you."

Leo felt trapped. This was something he hadn't counted on at all. Had the professor come to audition him or—or what?

While Fritz and the professor chatted in a friendly fashion, Leo glanced nervously at Dagmar, whose eyes snapped with interest, her look saying she was waiting to hear what Leo had to say to her unexpected guest. Rescue came at the hands of Augie, who, wearing a shiny black jacket and no cap, and comfortable-looking slippers on his feet, stepped up to his mistress with word that lunch was ready.

Dagmar looked toward the end of the gallery, where, in a little pergola, a table had been set. "Leo will be joining us for lunch," she announced. "But first he might want to wash his hands, if you'll show him where."

Obeying, Leo started to follow Augie, only to bump headlong into Reece, who had come bounding up the steps.

"Easy there, Kemo Sabe," he said brusquely, looking him over. "Where are you off to in such a rush?"

"He's just going to the bathroom," Dagmar said. "That's all right, Augie, take him along."

"Don't get lost," Reece said with a friendly wave, as Leo hurried after Augie, while the counselor turned, still smiling, to Dagmar. "You have to watch some of these guys every minute," he said, jokingly. "Hello, Auntie, how's about a kiss."

Dagmar presented her cheek, but her tone was tart as she returned his greeting.

"Hello yourself, renegade. I said you'd probably put in an appearance as soon as food was in the offing. Here's Fritz; say hello to him."

Reece and Fritz exchanged strained greetings; then Dagmar introduced Reece to the professor. "Reece is Leo's counselor," she explained. "We're just about to sit down," she said to Reece. "It might be nice if you joined us."

"Sure, why not?"

"Leo and Fritz will be with us, too," she added.

"An interesting lad you have there," the professor said to Reece. "Very bright."

"Oh, sure," Reece returned easily. "We're expecting big things from Leo. Very big." He glanced at Fritz, then grinned at Dagmar. "If it's all the same to you, on second thought I think I'll just eat with the hoi polloi and leave Leo to astonish you and the professor on his own—"

Dagmar drew her chin down. "Very well, counselor; if that is your wish, do by all means. Go along, go along, try to keep the boys from throwing food; they seem quite boisterous today."

As Reece trotted down the steps, Dagmar escorted her guests into the pergola, where they seated themselves at the round glass-topped table.

"A handsome young man, very intelligent-looking. Tell me something about him," Professor Pinero said, unfolding his napkin and laying it across his lap. "Is there some difficulty between him and our young camper?"

Dagmar hesitated, turning the ring on her finger while considering, then, including Fritz in her remark, she said: "I don't think 'our young camper,' as you call him, is exactly Reece's notion of a proper Moonbow camper."

She glanced down to where Reece leaned against the parapet, talking to a group of boys. "He sometimes—*Qu'est-ce qu'on peut dire de ce jeune homme-là?*" she said to Fritz.

"Madame is finding it hard to be tactful," Fritz explained. "Though one of our camp mainstays, Reece is sometimes forceful and demanding in his expectations of people."

"But Leo is a good camper," Dagmar said firmly. "It's not easy for a boy of his background to fit in with a pack of savages like these." She laughed indulgently at the boisterous crowd.

Leo returned to the table with spotless hands, and no sooner had he settled into his chair than Augie arrived with a tray of tempting-looking lobster salads, which he set out on the table with tall glasses of iced tea. When he disappeared, Dagmar used the tines of her fork to poke among the leaves of Hartford Bronze lettuce, turning over bits and pieces of lobster and celery, checking the quality of their preparation. She ate with precision, chewing each mouthful carefully and patting her lips with her napkin at intervals.

While the adults made small talk, Leo endeavored to keep his eyes on his plate, employing his cutlery as best he knew how and listening to the conversation. He learned several interesting bits he had not been aware of before. One, Dagmar had not been a childless wife, as Leo had assumed, but had borne a son, who had died in the Great War, at Ypres.

"But having lost my own boy," she said, "I have found so many other boys to take his place, which is why I enjoy having them running about our castle. They make me merry, and I'm glad I've got them back."

Then Fritz disclosed that two Swiss Red Cross officials, who were expected to arrive in Washington, D.C., sometime next month, might have word about his family. He hoped to be able to talk with them.

From time to time the professor's friendly look would make sure to include Leo, as if to say, Isn't it nice that we can share this bit of time together? But what was he doing here? Obviously Dagmar had invited him for some reason; he hadn't just dropped in out of the blue.

Leo's hand made a sudden, almost involuntary movement toward his water goblet, and instead of taking it by the stem he knocked it over. The water spilled across the tabletop and dripped between the glass and the wrought-iron frame.

"It's all right, no harm done," said Dagmar, mopping up, while Fritz shifted his gaze to the sky, which had turned a darker, more ominous shade.

"I wonder if our fine day hasn't ended?" he murmured. The wind had freshened and the trees were showing the pale undersides of their leaves.

Dagmar, too, scanned the heavens for signs. "Rain, Augie?" she asked.

"Didn't I say?" Augie replied. "Barometer's droppin'."

"And not a word in the paper. Perhaps you'd better close a few windows. Now," she went on, briskly rubbing her palms together and looking first at Fritz, then at the professor, "I think perhaps it is time for us to have a little music, eh? What do you say, Leo, shall we go along and see if my Pleyel is in good tune?" She leaned toward him to scrutinize him more closely. "Leo, are you all right? You're not ill, are you?"

"No."

"Good. Shall we move, then, to the music room? Professor Pinero is eager to hear you play. I want everything to go exactly as I have planned it."

Leo slipped a sidelong glance at Fritz, and another over the parapet to Reece in the driveway. Catching the look, Reece smiled up amiably, that amazing little trick of his. Leo felt his hands getting clammy. It was no use, he couldn't play; stubbornly he shook his head, his eyes riveted on the monogrammed napkin on his lap. There was a long pause, during which he felt all eyes on him and he wished the earth might open and swallow him up.

"Very well, then," Dagmar said at last, and, flinging Fritz an exasperated look, she went to the railing and called down to the other campers, telling them to come along, it was time for "a spot of music." As they came trooping up the stairs, she shooed them in the direction of the music room. "Come in, boys, come in, don't be shy," she cried, leading the way as knots of them hung about in the various doorways, reluctant to intrude into so hallowed a place.

While Fritz waited, Leo dawdled on the terrace, concentrating on the view. Overhead a flock of crows winged past the tower, veering steeply to disappear among the trees down in the glen, while from far up the valley, north of Moonbow Lake, there came a solitary clap of thunder that rolled out of the gathering clouds like the distant peal of a bronze bell and died away into nothingness.

"Leo?" Fritz prompted. "You remember what we talked about? You have been given a valuable gift—you must make the most of it. You want to play, you know you do. I can see it in your face."

It was true. He was feeling little feverish flickers of excitement, and an undeniable pleasure, but at the same time his fingers felt hot and swollen, and his stomach was churning. If only Reece weren't here.

Fearing the worst, he left the parapet with Fritz, and joined the stragglers leaping over the threshold to the music room, shuffling to distribute themselves, some on the soft, plumpy furniture, Reece and the Jeremians scattered along the window seats, the rest on the Oriental rugs dotting the floor. The professor was ensconced in a tall-backed chair, and while Leo squeezed in between Tiger and the Bomber, Fritz, his cap tipped back on his head, perched himself atop the woodpile between two doors.

Finally, when the last camper had hunkered down in a corner, Dagmar, standing in the bow of her piano, welcomed the newest visitors to the Castle and remembered the old ones. Then, shedding her fingers of their rings, she seated herself on the bench, checked the pedals, and raised her hands over the keyboard to begin. Leo recognized the selection at once: Tchaikovsky's "Marche Slave," a sonorous piece that brought out the best that the Pleyel had to offer.

Despite the arthritis in her fingers, Dagmar played expertly, with grace and élan, and as she played she looked over the top of the music rack and smiled at Leo; in that smile he read a variety of things: wishing and disappointment, and the fleeting expression of a stout will that seemed to be telling him that any musician who could execute such lyric passages should never be thwarted, only encouraged to play, and that music—oh, such music—was the soul's balm; let no one stand in the way of its purest expression.

When she had brought the final passage to its close, she let her hands drop into her lap while the boys' applause echoed about the room. As a group they had settled down now and become serious music-appreciators; no one fidgeted, no one giggled, no one looked bored. Dagmar smiled at the professor, and at Fritz, and after a moment she began again, this time the *Moonlight* Sonata. Her strong, wrinkled face expressed a simplicity of effort, as if the creation of such perfection of sound were the easiest trick in the world to manage, and once or two times more Leo felt that her wandering eye was seeking him out.

Then, rather than following the sonata's first, slow movement with the second, faster one, she stopped playing, and before anyone could react, tiddled the notes of "Kitten on the Keys"—her little joke.

"More! More! Encore!" the boys called, laughing.

But instead she sat, neck straight, head erect, her eyes now resting on Leo. Well, they seemed to say, what about it, my young friend? Are you willing? Or will you still sit there on my pretty velvet settee, stubborn and afraid? This is your last chance. Will you let the moment pass?

Leo hesitated. He knew that everyone was waiting for Dagmar to say or do something, unaware that she was waiting for him. He slid his eyes to Reece, who leaned casually against the wall, his expression unreadable behind his dark glasses, then drew another breath, and in that breath, suddenly in his mind he stood apart from himself; it was as if he had become another person, a disinterested party, someone else altogether. He saw himself getting to his feet, nodding to the professor, who sat very straight, his look filled with anticipation, saw himself walking away from the settee toward the piano, toward those blue-gray eyes. He placed his fingertips lightly on the neck of his violin. His brows rose; a silent question was both asked and answered. Now Dagmar smiled. *How did she know?* But she did, she did. He heard a clock striking somewhere, in another room, as if in some other house, but its message was clear. The hour was his. Now was the moment. He *would* play; *must* play.

Since they had already agreed on a selection—the "Träumerei" he had worked on—there seemed nothing more to do but begin. Jutting out his chin, he nestled the instrument into the nook of his shoulder, took a deep breath, glanced at Dagmar. She gave him a tiny nod, then leaned forward slightly, bringing her body into play, and her fingers softly sounded the first piano chords.

He began, sliding his bow across the strings, making music—awful music. The notes were on key, but they were parched notes, without luster, passionless. He struggled for mastery, attempting to focus his gaze on a neutral line above the sight line of his audience—but found his eyes straying helplessly to Reece.

Please, help me, he silently prayed. Prayed for a bomb to be dropped on the roof and blow him up, violin and all. Surely he could not go on. Better to quit now. Crazy to think he could get away with it this time. Then he struck a wrong note full out; its wretched sound screeched in his ear. Mortified, he glanced impulsively at Dagmar, and as though on cue her eyes met his. He expected reproach, but saw none. Instead, in that moment he recalled the words she had tried to impress on him: words about reaching out, about being hard as steel, about letting no one stand in your way. Make the most of your moment when it comes—seize it, seize it, he heard her saying. *Carpe diem, carpe diem.*

He *must* go on, he must. As he repeated these words over and over in his mind, something began to happen: a warm, comforting wave washed over him and suddenly he felt safer, calmer, more relaxed. His breathing came more easily, then the musical tone itself began to alter, the notes vibrated differently, they stretched themselves out, richly, roundly, his bow glided more smoothly and effortlessly.

Again his eye swung to Dagmar, bent over the keys, her body "helping the music," playing effortlessly, with great delicacy, traces of a smile now on her lips. Yes, she seemed to be saying. This. This is what I hoped to hear, *these* notes, *this* music . . . this, my young friend. . . .

Beyond the doors and windows, the sky had darkened so that additional lights had to be switched on to illuminate the room, their beams throwing circles across the plastered ceiling. As Dagmar took a hand from the keyboard to switch on the little vellum-shaded lamp at her shoulder, Leo's glance flicked along the row of faces, moving from one camper to the next, from Tiger to the Bomber, to Emerson Bean and Junior Leffingwell, from Pete Melrose to Gus Klaus and Oggie Ogden, all listening to him.

The piece ended, too soon, he thought, and marveled that it had gone so quickly. "On wings of song," wasn't that what she'd said? To fly on wings?

He heard the applause, saw Fritz's nod of approval, and he glanced again at Dagmar, waiting awkwardly while she riffled through the stack of music at her elbow. Approving a selection, she beckoned him to her side. When he saw its title, he felt a pang of fear. It was the Paganini Caprice in A Minor. But before he could protest she was off. He must follow. He touched his bow lightly to the strings, jerked his chin up, and he was off too. There, you've got it, he told himself as the notes danced into the air, light and bright and intricate, like so many children at play. His bowing hand flew, and his spirit soared with the music. He glanced at Professor Pinero, who sat now with his head against the back of his chair, eyes almost closed, on his face what Leo judged to be a look of approval. Glancing sideways now, he kept his eye on the tip of his bow. It was moving with control and rhythm, the angle changing as it made itself felt upon the strings, the bony wrist and long, thin fingers drawing forth the music. And, ah, the music! The melody seemed to pour from the curved belly of the violin to float upward to the ceiling, then come flooding down and out, filling all ears. He was performing with an assurance that was undeniable, his body hunching, tilting, swaying as he drew the melody to its sharp, pizzicato ending.

There was a moment's silence. Dagmar took her fingers from the keys, eyes shining with pleasure, while Leo, stiffly dropping his arms and instrument to his sides, stared at the floor. Then the wave of applause washed over him. A deep peal of thunder sounded, rolling across the valley, ominous in the way of all thunderclaps heralding storms, yet, for Leo, somehow a sovereign sign of his victory. He glanced at Reece, who was applauding—perfunctorily?—with the others. Swallow that, Heartless, he thought, giddy with happiness. Chew on those glissandos awhile.

Not knowing what else to do, he bowed slightly, catching sight of the smiling professor, who called, "Encore, encore!," to which solicitation Dagmar added her own, beckoning him with a curled finger and asking what piece he would give his audience now.

"Poor Butterfly" was Leo's choice. He plucked a string, giving Dagmar the key, and the room quieted again, but before they could begin their attention became unfocused, as outside, with a swift inevitability, the rain began to fall, first in a spasmodic patter, big, fat drops playing a ploppy sort of drumbeat on the tree leaves, beating on the roof; then, after this prelude, as if making up its mind to spend its force in a single assault, in an overwhelming surge.

Inside the room, once more the musicians picked up their cue and began to play. Once again Leo felt his eye drawn to Reece—and he knew surprise, elation, jubilation. Whatever Reece was now or might yet become, when Leo played he was every bit as good, every bit as powerful, as rich, as glamorous. He turned his eyes back to Dagmar, whose eyes enlarged fractionally, telegraphing her message: Fine, keep it up. And he thought, What if I hadn't tried? What if she hadn't made me? Would I ever have known this feeling? See what we've accomplished, her smile seemed to be telling him. Isn't this rich? Isn't this fun?

And it seemed to him as he played that through the bars of music Emily had stolen in among them, to stand in the shadows with gleaming eyes, a hand at her breast, nodding, smiling, singing . . . yes, there, just there. She parts her lips, the words flow from her mouth.

Poor Butterfly!
'Neath the blossoms waiting

204

Poor Butterfly!
For she loved him so.

Beyond the windows the full fury of the storm was upon them. Flickering zigzags of lightning daggered down from the sky to blast the valley, exhilarating, blue-white electrical bolts betokening more mighty thunderclaps. He was remembering again now the night of the big storm at Saggetts Notch, *that* night, in the house on Gallop Street, when they were in the parlor behind the big doors. He'd been scared . . . he'd taken out his violin and played to calm himself but . . . Rudy . . . the footsteps on the stairs, the door flung open, the dark, enraged face in the doorway, the loud, bellowing voice—

"No rhapsodies in this house!"

Suddenly he faltered—a second only, but his playing suffered as a result—and just when things were going so well. His glance entreated Dagmar for help; she gave him another encouraging nod and went on, and so did he, but it was no good. At every instant he had to fight the overwhelming urge to bolt, to run from the room and hide somewhere. Yes, run—upstairs—around the newel post and up the steps that creaked, hearing the crashing outside, the rain rattling on the panes, to hide under the bed.

Only there was no "upstairs" here in this house, no newel post, no squeaky steps, no bed to hide under, no Rudy behind closed doors.

Why then?

Something . . .

God! What was it? He saw the thing, or thought he did. Nearer it swam, and nearer, that bright little fish, only to flash out of reach, mocking him as he failed to grasp it. He felt queasy, feverish. His hand shook badly. It was Major Bowes Night all over again. He was going to make a fool of himself. Oh no, not that—don't let that happen this time, he prayed. But the boys—the rows of faces were staring, wondering, smirking at him. He struggled frantically to stay with the music, but now every note he played, every beat and pause called to his mind— Suddenly it was upon him, suddenly Dagmar's music room was another room, in the house on Gallop Street, and the smell of it was strong in his nostrils, it was making him sick; he was going to vomit.

He felt himself gagging as he struggled to go on with the music while jagged flashes of lightning, dark, light, dark, silver and black, black and silver lit up the room, throwing everything, listeners, furniture, objects, Dagmar, the professor, into garish relief. And there were others too—yes, now, among the familiar faces of the boys, others had begun to materialize— Rudy Matuchek, he was there, and John, yes, John Burroughs, he was there too, and Emily—Emily! Where was she? She had been there too, but where was she now? Though he felt her presence, he could not see her. How could he when he was upstairs, in his room on Gallop Street, hiding under the bed while the thunder crashed around the rooftop and the lightning flashed and—

He heard the angry shouts from below, heard the scream, and he disobeyed, opened the door, rushed into the hall, looked over the railing into the vestibule, and at that moment saw—

God!

He threw his head back and through the oval of his mouth wafted a long, wavering scream, like a ragged scarf being flourished

he stared

saw

clutched in Rudy's upraised hand the bright flash of steel, poised to strike at John

no, not at John, whose bleeding body was already staining the floor, but

"No! Stop! Don't!"

The violin and bow hung limp at his sides as he stared at the scene being played before him, as he watched Rudy's knife blade complete its downward path to find its mark in Emily's breast and the blood pour forth like the water from a spring and she fall like a heap of rags upon the floor. He saw Rudy drop the knife, heard the knife clattering on the floor, saw Rudy dash through the open doorway, out into the rain and the wind.

Mother!

Mother!

MOTHER!

The sounds echo in his head, reverberating as through endless, empty caverns, and the icy rain sweeps in across the doorsill and into the front hall, soaking the rug, while Leo lies on the floor beside Emily, staring at her face, which even as he watches loses color, never moves, becomes a dead face. . . .

Another thunderous blast shook the music room. Leo cringed, staring at the ranks of questioning faces, hearing the strangled noises pouring from his mouth, unable to stop them. His violin and bow had both fallen from his hands. Panicking, he crabbed his fingers on the ebony piano top and his fingernails dug savagely into the silken threads of the Spanish shawl, his knuckles turned white as he gripped the fabric, the roses red as . . . as blood. Then, as Dagmar, still at the keyboard, came to her feet, he jerked backward in a quick, stumbling move, his fingers dragging the shawl from the piano top, carrying with it the bust of Beethoven, the Chinese vase, everything crashing to the floor and shattering. He saw Dagmar reaching out her hands toward him, but before she could prevent him he eluded her touch and rushed blindly from the room. Fritz, who had sprung to his feet, hurried after him, while behind Dagmar Professor Pinero barred the door to the others.

❯

"Where is he?" Fritz called to Augie, who pointed to the music cupboard. Fritz opened it and peered into the narrow space. In the corner, eyes large and staring, Leo cowered.

"Leo—what is it? What's the trouble?"

"He killed her!" he cried, staring.

"What? What's he saying?" asked Dagmar, coming in behind Fritz.

"He killed her!" Leo shouted again, his eyes filled with terror. "Mother! *Mother!"* He burst into an agony of sobs.

"Hush, hush, my dear," Dagmar said, and, kneeling next to Leo, she took his hands and tried to reassure him. "Come, child, you mustn't do this." She looked frantically at Fritz, as Leo scuttled toward the wall like a frightened animal. Hugging his knees, he sank into the corner and buried his head in his arms. His shoulders shook, his sobs mounted hysterically, and he cried out once more "he killed her," while beyond the hundred windowpanes in the library the thunder rolled down the darkened valley, like tenpins being toppled in a giant's game of skittles, a chain of echoes dying away one after another into silence, dull, unnatural, and forbidding.

PART FOUR

The Night
of the Moonbow

1

nd so it had begun, the most besetting calamity that can happen at
any summer camp, a solid week of rain; and just when the end
of the month saw a troop of fresh arrivals being registered by
Ma Starbuck and settled into the bunks reluctantly surrendered by departing campers. This was no way for new boys out to enjoy
themselves for the rest of the season to be introduced to camping among
the pines of Moonbow; from Virtue through Harmony to High Endeavor the
cabins were shut up like so many wooden boxes, each a dark, damp,
lantern-lit world of its own, inside which random campers, bored and rest-
less, idly resorted to games of Parcheesi and Monopoly, to gum-card-scaling
tournaments and hours-long bull sessions. Cornsilk consumption rose, and
there was a brisk trafficking in printed contraband like *Film Fun, The Police
Gazette,* and *Pic* and *Click.* Gus Klaus upped his status all along the linepath
by reading once again to all comers the smuttiest passages from *Studs
Lonigan,* while the most adventuresome campers, in quest of the bizarre,
the prurient, or anyway the novel, ducked into the mephitic atmosphere of
Malachi to take a gander at "Big Billy" Bosey exhibiting his boner from
under an Indian blanket.

At intervals dreary, sodden processions of rainwear-clad boys slogged
their way about, from lower to upper campus for meals and crafts sessions
(though the rain came in through holes in the barn roof), then back again,
and a seemingly endless stream of disgruntled campers flowed through

Wanda Koslowski's dispensary, exhibiting swollen thumbs pinched in falling cabin flaps, burns from the careless lighting of kerosene wicks, bruises and contusions from slides in the wet mud, even a sprained ankle (Emerson Bean, ever fortune's fool, slipped off the lodge porch on the second day of the deluge). And many was the camper obliged to force the hint of a smile in response to the hoary chestnut Pa Starbuck loved to pull on any unsuspecting passerby:

"I sure hope this rain keeps up."

"Why's that, Pa?"

" 'Cause if it keeps up it won't come down."

Ha ha. Joe Miller lived.

A primary victim of the camp's darkened mood was Leo, who, unable to comprehend fully the knowledge that had been thrust so blindingly upon him at the Castle, felt more keenly than the others the growing disquiet along the linepath. By the time he had been driven back to the Castle that afternoon in Dagmar's Pierce-Arrow, word of what had happened was all over camp, and there was no escape from the jokes about his "Major Bowes nuttiness." Maybe, they said, Wacko Wackeem should just quit "fiddling around."

Secretly, Leo was almost glad about the jokes; anything was better than the boys' finding out the truth: that his stepfather had murdered Leo's mother and her friend. Of this, no one must know, never a word. For the rest of his stay at Friend-Indeed he must confide in no one—not even Tiger, who, whatever questions he might have been itching to ask, like the true friend he was, by neither sign nor word indicated that he expected or even wanted to be let in on things. Loyally he took Leo's part, standing up for him and telling the others to shut up and mind their own business. But his defense only caused Leo pangs of guilt. For what did friendship mean without trust? Yet how could he level with Tiger when doing so would only brand Leo a liar? How could he confess what he now knew to be so: that Rudy the butcher was still doing time in the state pen for manslaughter, Rudy Matuchek, the notorious "Butcher of Saggetts Notch," whose picture had been in all the newspapers?

At the council fire that night, moved into the lodge because of the rain, he watched the traditional rites and ceremonies, but for him they had now lost their magic. He was nervous and jumpy, couldn't concentrate. He never even felt the usually warm clasp of hands in the Friendship Circle. He never heard the groans of his cabinmates when Hap announced that Malachi was still ahead in the competition for the Hartsig Trophy.

Then Reece made his customary entrance in a puff of smoke—in the doorway of the staff room, with his Indian two-step illuminated, not by the moon but by the great horn chandelier—and as he made his progress among the rows, dispensing the biweekly total of red feathers, Leo's eyes tracked the bobbing tips of the Warrior's headdress as closer he came, and closer, his eyes gleaming like red coals, turning at last into the row where the Jeremians sat, moving toward Leo—could he see into Leo's false heart?—then passing him by (no feather for Wacko, never any feather for him), and disappearing into the shadows of the back hallway. And then Pa had told the Moonbow Tale. . . .

And later, after taps had sounded from the lodge porch, where Wiggy Pugh blew his cornet into the sheeting rain, Leo's nightmare returned—not the same old dream, but close enough and even more disturbing: There she lay, the Moonbow Princess, atop the rock, the evil medicine man looming over her. The watching Leo yearned to save her, was compelled to make an attempt, yet he could not, his feet were fastened to the ground and would not obey him. Nothing could free him, nothing save her! He stared helplessly as the dark arm was raised, the blade flashed in the light, and descended. The knife was plunged into her heart. But see! The Indian princess was no longer a princess but Emily! And the executioner, Misswiss, had become Rudy in his straw hat and butcher's apron!

Such was his new dream, and as he had his first night in camp, he woke up screaming, while his cabinmates stirred—"Wacko Wacko—dreaming again"—and went back to sleep. He lay panting and mutely sobbing, racked with shame and fear. The next night he dreamed a similar dream, and another night after that, and each time he awoke with a cry, each time terrified that he might have said something in his sleep to give away the truth that must at all cost remain safe.

In the face of these renewed nocturnal disturbances, Reece took it upon himself to have Leo transferred to a bed in the infirmary "for observation." There, when he awoke screaming, Wanda came padding in with her flashlight to sit beside him in the chair and talk him back to sleep again. He wanted badly to tell her about it; if he did she'd be sure to understand—Wanda seemed to understand about so many things; Fritz, too. But, much as he exerted himself, Leo couldn't bring himself to say the words. A couple of times he made up his mind to do it and he would get right to the point of starting—then he would clam up, and that would be the end of that.

When the time came for him to take up his abode in Jeremiah again, his counselor attempted to block his return, and only the intervention of Ma Starbuck kept Leo from being dispatched to a recently vacated bunk in High Endeavor. How could she know that such a move, though mortifying, would have been a relief to him? For, since the excursion to the Castle, of his seven bunkmates five had been barely speaking to him, and when Tiger and the Bomber were elsewhere the air in the cabin fairly crackled with hostility and ill will. If it wasn't Phil razzing him, or Wally giving him sullen looks, or Dump criticizing him, or Monkey, once so easygoing and friendly, it was Reece himself, always *there*—even when he wasn't—watching, measuring, assaying, and judging, as if by piercing Leo's thoughts with that sharp look he could discover the terrible secret Leo strove so desperately to hide, and thereby make his own secret safe. Reece, who knew that Leo knew . . . who would never forgive him for "spying" that day at the icehouse, or for the bloody nose Leo had given him.

As the rain hammered its monotonous tattoo on the tarpaper roof, sounding hollowly in the interior of the cabin, Leo's heart would jump at the sound of that instantly recognizable footfall on the porch. Or if by chance they met alone in the Dewdrop Inn, as happened occasionally, Leo, at the trough, would freeze with embarrassment, and his water would dry up as if a spigot had been turned off, while Reece would stare straight ahead, whistling or humming and pretending Leo wasn't there. And in the night, as he lay in his bunk, eyes open to keep from dreaming, he would stare across at the counselor's cot, at that blond head resting on the pillow, and it seemed to him that even with closed eyes Reece was watching him, and he would screw his own eyes shut, trying to blot out the scene that no one must ever discover.

And yet, and yet, it remained, it was always there, waiting to catch him out. He couldn't get away from it, couldn't stop seeing it, dreaming it—

No!

Stop it, I don't want to hear!

"Not a whore!"

"What?"

Reece's eyes were open now. "What did you say?"

Then he tossed a look around at the awakened boys as if to say "Didn't I say so? Nuts . . ." Wacko really *was* wacko.

During the day he avoided Jeremiah when he could, spending a good deal of his time working on the Austrian village, now almost finished. Because of the leaky roof in the crafts barn, it had been transferred from the Swoboda corner to the warmth and dryness of the lodge, where it was to be permanently displayed on a base specially constructed by Hank Ives. (Several notables, including some aldermen and Dr. Dunbar, had been invited to a formal unveiling-and-dedication ceremony, and the local paper had promised to send a reporter and a photographer to cover the story.)

When he had covered up his work with a sheet and put his tools away, Leo would leave the lodge for Fritz's cottage, which, while the bad weather continued unabated, had become among a certain group of campers a refuge from the stultifying atmosphere of their cabins, a place where boys unused to being kept indoors, unused even to one another's company, older boys as well as Virtue small fry, found themselves mingling together, the members of an unofficial club—the "Katzenjammer Kids" was what Reece Hartsig dubbed them. There might be an impromptu musical program, when Fritz would play records on his Victrola: Enrico Caruso or Rosa Ponselle, or Madame Schumann-Heink singing "Ich liebe dich." (One recording, a rare treasure, favored over the rest, was a talking disc on which could be heard a conversation between Alexander Graham Bell and Johannes Brahms.) Several of the boys, especially Tiger and Dusty Rhoades, were enthusiastic stamp-collectors, and, deprived of the pleasures of baseball, they spent hours poring over Fritz's well-worn stamp album with a magnifying glass, exclaiming at its most notable entry, a 1918 U.S. Airmail stamp with the airplane at its center inverted, which had been a present to Fritz from his grandfather. Others—Leo and, unexpectedly, the Bomber—were good at chess, and often as not, while marshmallows hung from wire coat hangers toasted over Fritz's hotplate, a game would be in progress, with four or five kibitzers following every move of the antique ivory figures Fritz's father had brought from Hong Kong.

It was perhaps inevitable that what had in fair weather been the welcome "cultural hub" of camp, in bad weather became the object of envy and rancor; that what had seemed only natural, ordinary behavior—for a few boys to drop by occasionally, during "free periods," for a bit of music, a picture book to page through—now struck chords of jealousy among those campers who were allotted no share in these activities (though they would have derived little pleasure from them in any case); inevitable that these malcontents and mischief-makers would begin holding meetings of their own, in places where one might least expect to discover them: up in the loft in the Marconi Radio Shop, for example, or at odd moments in the Dewdrop Inn, or hidden in Amos or Malachi or Hosea with the flaps closed. . . .

Oh, it ain't gonna rain no more no more,
It ain't gonna rain no more,
So how in the heck can I wash my neck
When it ain't gonna rain no more?

sang the boys, though this ditty was far from reality. Yet, upon occasion, the torrent would let up, and even show signs of clearing, and it was at such a time that Leo, crossing the sodden playing field, noticed a lively crowd of Harmonyites stripped down to their underwear, sliding on a strip of hard-glazed mud. Their satisfyingly wet, dirty sport looked like fun. He would gladly have shucked off his duds and joined them, but he knew they wouldn't want him. Their very hilarity and high spirits seemed to exclude him from their ranks.

The song had come from Hosea, and as Leo approached he saw one of the side flaps open and a small figure pop out and trot off toward the cadet unit.

"Hey, Peewee, wait up," Leo called. The boy slowed reluctantly, ducking his eyes as Leo joined him.

"What's doin', Peewit?" he asked.

Peewee frowned. "Nuthin'. And don't call me Peewit."

"Have you heard anything from your sister? Is she having a good time?"

"What do you care?" came the cold reply.

"I was only asking."

Peewee's scowl was fierce. "She ain't never comin' home, not ever."

Though Leo felt a pang, he knew better than to believe Peewee's exaggerations. When the boy started away, Leo reached for him. "Hold on, Elephant, I want to talk to you."

"I can't. I ain't s'posed t' hang around with you no more."

"Who says?"

"The guys. You know."

"Why not?"

"Because you hang around with Fritz. And you play dollies with Willa-Sue."

"I do not. And what's wrong with hanging around with Fritz?"

"He's a Jew."

"So what?"

"The Jews crucified Jesus Christ our Lord. Fritz shouldn't be here, this is a Christian camp. Let him go to his own camp if he wants."

Leo stared. Who had been putting these words in the boy's mouth? He glanced toward the cabin Peewee had just left. "What's going on in there?" he asked.

"Nuthin'."

"Are they having some kind of powwow?"

Peewee scraped a toe in the mud. "Well-l . . . sort of," he said, and squirmed free and ran away into the wet.

A day later, having gone over to the lodge in search of Oats's copy of the world atlas, Leo glimpsed Wally Pfeiffer's back as it disappeared down the cellar stairs. Sneaking down after him, Leo found him in the lower passageway, crouched on hands and knees, peeking through a space in the wall. Leo tiptoed up behind him and listened too. From the other side muffled voices could be heard, fragments of talk and laughter. As Leo leaned close to Wally's ear, Wally started in alarm, then retreated as if Leo were carrying the plague. When some more sounds were heard from the other side of the partition, Wally fled up the stairs. What was wrong with him? Leo put his ear to the wall, trying to make out what was being said on the other side, then knelt in Wally's place and put his eye to the crack.

Commonly used by Henry Ives as his work- and storage-room, the space contained an assortment of carpentry tools neatly arranged above a workbench under a low ceiling. Today, candles stuck in bottles gave off a meager light and the air that blew through the crack smelled not only of paint and turpentine, a bit moldy and fetid, but of cigarette tobacco too. Through the aperture Leo could make out the silhouetted backs of several heads, and in the candle shine he identified the faces of Moriarity, Bosey, and Ratner, along with Phil Dodge and Dump Dillworth; he also identified the voices of others he could not see: Tallon and Klaus—and Monkey Twitchell. What bits of conversation he could grasp through the partition seemed commonplace enough, and yet—had someone mentioned his name? Were they talking about him in there? Pressing now an eye, now an ear to the crack, he strained to see, to catch a word, some hint of what was happening inside, but all he got were tantalizing fragments.

217

Then he heard the scrape of footsteps and some louder talk. The meeting was breaking up. Leo scuttled along the passage and hid behind some barrels tucked away under the stairs, holding his breath as the store-room door opened and a dozen campers filed out, went down the passage, and climbed the steps directly above his hiding place.

When the coast was clear, he stood up, took a few steps, then jumped back as an arm shot out at him. Fingers grabbed the front of his shirt and jerked him forward so he was staring into the scowling face of Phil Dodge. Behind him stood Bosey, Moriarity, and Monkey.

"Well, well, look who's here," said Bosey with a burlesque leer; "Wacko the quacko."

"What are you doing down here?" demanded Phil.

Leo stared, unable to think of an excuse for his presence in the cellar. Finally he pointed to the door to Hank's storage room.

"P-paint," he managed. "I was looking for some paint. For Fritz's model."

"Screw the paint. And screw you, Wacko," said Bosey. "You better scram out of here if you know what's good for you."

"I bet he's been listening at keyholes," Moriarity said, shouldering his way in and jutting out his jaw. "You're always sticking your nose where it don't belong. That big potato nose of yours. That big, long, Pinocchio schnozz of yours."

He took Leo's nose between his knuckles and twisted it. "Big nose, huh?"

Leo's face heated up and his eyes stung as he tried to pull away.

Moriarity laughed and nudged Bosey, standing next to him. " 'Smatter, can'tcha take it? Big Jimmy Durante schnozzola." He gave the nose another painful twist, making Leo cry out.

"That hurts!"

"Aw, poor baby, he says it hurts. You know something, Wackoff, if I had that nose full of nickels I'd be so rich I wouldn't ever have to work again. Right, Phil?"

Phil was quick to agree; he turned to the others. "Come on, let's leave this spud and get out of here."

Abandoning Leo, the four ran noisily up the stairs and disappeared. Leo waited until he was sure it was safe to leave, then crept away, feeling lucky he hadn't got a fat lip for his snooping.

That evening, after he'd gone through the candy line (the store had been moved inside the barn because of the weather), he waited for Peewee to make his purchase, then grabbed him and walked him down to the lower camp, using the occasion—and Peewee's inability to keep quiet even in the company of one he had been told to avoid—to ferret out everything he could concerning the unexplained goings-on. The gatherings in Hosea and in the cellar had been meetings of a new secret club calling itself the "Mingoes," after the sinister Algonquin tribe described by James Fenimore Cooper in *The Last of the Mohicans.* Originators and self-appointed "chiefs" of the organization were Phil Dodge and Billy Bosey. Other founding members included—as might have been expected—Claude Moriarity and the other erstwhile Rinkydinks, who had been deprived by the rain of their usual meeting place at the Steelyard house. Gus Klaus, Bud Talbot, Blackjack Ratner, and Zipper Tallon had soon joined, then Dump Dillworth and Monkey Twitchell. Initiation into the club required a sacred oath, sworn in blood, to divulge nothing about the club or its meetings, never even to acknowledge its existence, never to squeal on a fellow member, and never to break the code of silence that had been ordained.

Having gleaned these wisps of information, Leo mulled them over privately, unsettled by the thought that whatever was going on had something to do with him. It was almost as if the club had sprung into existence for the sole purpose of excluding Wacko Wackeem from its membership, and intimidating him into the bargain. And now, everywhere he went around camp, it seemed, he caught "looks," observed silent but meaningful exchanges, heard stealthy whispers, glimpsed tight little granny knots of conspirators in conference, knots that quickly untied themselves at his approach. But when he expressed his concern to Tiger and the Bomber, he was reassured. "They don't mean anything," Tiger declared scornfully. "The Mingoes are just the Rinkydinks in full dress. It'll all blow over when the rain stops, you'll see. Besides, if Dr. Dunbar gets wind of it, *he'll* put a stop to it quick enough."

But Leo had his doubts. The way things were right now, no one could say when the rain would stop. And what if news of the Mingoes never reached Dr. Dunbar's ears?

🐻

And so the rain continued—after nearly a week, the trails were sluices of mud, the playing field a pond. Blessedly, Leo was alone this afternoon— Reece had taken a toothache to the dentist in Junction City, and the other

Harmonyites were all at the lodge, where Oats Gurley was giving a demonstration of taxidermy—and for half an hour or so, huddled like a mummy in his blankets, while outside the wind moaned among the wet fir boughs, and up among the roof beams moths swooned in a blind delirium around the amber lantern glow, he made entries in his journal, interrupted only by Hank Ives delivering the mail, late as usual because of the mud, which slowed his jitney.

Lying back, Leo closed his notebook and stared up at the handtinted snapshot of the delectable Nancy Driver in Reece's mirror. He turned his flashlight beam on it, reading the inscription at the bottom:

> Virginia Beach
> Summer 1937
> "Wish You Were Here"
> XXX
> Nan

He allowed his eye to trace caressingly the lines of her curvaceous figure and the way it filled her gleaming bathing suit, appreciating the way in which her wavy hair hung shoulder-length, the laughing smile on her lips. He enjoyed imagining he knew some girl like that, one he could go dancing with or take for a ride in his convertible coupe. Fat chance, he thought. Nancy was years older than Honey, and he'd been tongue-tied around Honey; maybe, though, he could say some things in writing, maybe that would make it easier. He liked the notion of having a pretty girl to correspond with. He'd never had a pen pal. Except, perhaps . . . now that he thought about it, perhaps he did: Leo's quota of mail had consisted of a single letter, from Miss Meekum ("don't forget to wear rubbers in the rain"; at Friend-Indeed nobody *ever* wore rubbers), and—more importantly—a postcard whose arrival had surprised him considerably. The card was from Honey Oliphant, from Cape Cod, and it depicted a lighthouse by the seashore. In her delicate, careful script, she had penned:

> Hello from sunny Cape Cod. The water here is so *cold*—brrrrr! Having a wonderful time, wish you were here. I think of you often and the brave thing you did. See you some time. Love,
>
> H.O.

Love, H.O.

He felt his heart beat faster at the mere idea that, some hundred miles distant, she had given him the slightest thought, let alone written to him. Maybe if he could talk Peewee into giving him his sister's address he could write her back.

He capped his pen and slipped his journal and the postcard under his pillow as footsteps sounded on the porch. The door opened and Phil marched in with Dump, Monkey, and Eddie, followed by Moriarity, Moon Mullens, and some others of the Rinkydink gang. Leo wondered where Tiger and the Bomber were—and Wally. For once Phil's ever-present shadow wasn't running behind him. Phil kicked the door shut and stood with his back to it, regarding Leo suspiciously, while the others stripped off their wet gear and, spreading themselves among the available bunks, made themselves at home.

"Hey, Wacko, whatcha doin' in here all by yerself?" demanded Moriarity. "Poundin' your pud, I bet." Leo turned scarlet but didn't dignify the crudity by making a reply. The room was so crammed with faces he feared and disliked that he didn't know which to look at. He glanced at Eddie for a cue, but Eddie, who was fiddling with his belt buckle, failed to make eye contact.

"You know something, Wacko?" This was Phil. "We've been thinking about you, all of us."

Leo looked around the circle of faces. "No kidding. Did you decide anything—you and your braintrust?"

"Don't get wise with me, Wacko. What we decided was that, if you were really smart, you'd get on that bus you came here on and head back to where you came from. This really isn't your kind of place." He put his hand in his pocket. "You haven't got the hang of things around here," he went on, "so we've all chipped in the four bucks it'll take to get you home." He held out a handful of quarters. Leo stared at them, then turned away.

"Skip it," he said. "Who needs your money?"

"Hey, you guys," crowed Phil, "listen to Daddy Warbucks."

"That ain't Daddy Warbucks, that's Little Orphan Annie."

This from Moriarity, who had been watching closely. "I can tell you one thing, if Little Orphan Annie don't scrammay-voo out of here while the scrammin's good, he'll be asking for trouble. A guy like him needs to be taught a lesson, right, Phil?"

Phil nodded grimly. "I think Wacko already knows we have ways of getting rid of people we don't like."

Leo returned Phil's glare. "Like Stanley Wagner, is that what you mean?"

Phil's brow furrowed. "You better shut up about Stanley Wagner before you—" He broke off without finishing as the door opened again and Pfeiffer slipped in, dripping.

"Well, here you are," Wally said, shaking out his poncho and staring around at the group. "You didn't tell me you were leaving."

"Jeez, Pfeiffer," said Moon Mullens, "does Phil have to draw you a map every time he wants to do something? He's not your mother, you know."

"Shut the damn door," growled Zipper. "My ass is freezing."

Wally slammed the door shut; he hung his slicker over Phil's, then began sneezing. "I'm catching a cold, I can feel it." He slid his red, bulbous eyes around the room. His long pale lashes were wet, as though he'd been crying. "I know you had another meeting," he said, failing to heed Phil's frowning look. "I'm sure of it."

"Shut up about that," said Moriarity; all eyes had gone to Leo.

"No, I won't shut up," Wally retorted. "Phil promised I could join."

"I never."

"You did! You said you'd take me, then you played ditch on me."

Phil's look grew menacing. "I said shut up about that."

Ignoring Leo, Wally stared rigidly at the others. "Well, am I going to be a Mingo or not? You promised. You said I could take the oath. You said—"

Phil raised a heavy fist. "You better shut up about what I said."

"I don't care. I'll tell. I know what's going on. You're not so smart. I'll tell Pa, he'll—*ooof!*" Wally crumpled as Phil's knuckles caught him in the midriff. When he'd got his breath back he lifted a face white as flour paste, and fell back toward his bunk.

Phil smiled. "Some guys just have to learn," he said. "On the other hand"—taking in Leo—"*some* guys *never* learn." He leaned over and, grabbing Leo's pillow, gave it a spin in the air.

"Albert, huh?" he went on. "First time I ever heard of a camper snuggling up to someone named Albert at night, right, you guys?"

As Leo reached to grab the pillow, Phil sent it across the room to Zipper. Leo rushed after it, but Zipper tossed it to Moon, and so it went, all around the room. As Leo made a last, desperate attempt to recapture his property, Moriarity siezed it with both hands and yanked it apart; the seams gave way and the pillow spilled feathers into the air like the snowflakes in a blizzard.

"Aw, gee, look what I done," wailed Moriarity. "I ruint poor Wacko's pillow. Now what's the baby going to sleep on, no more Albert."

The feathers floated to the floor; some of them cascaded onto Reece's bunk.

"Boy, Wacko," Phil said with a smirk, "you better get that stuff cleaned up before Big Chief sees it."

"Me? I didn't do it. He did. He—"

He had turned and was staring at Moriarity, who, having rid himself of the torn pillow, had discovered Leo's journal, and was now thumbing through its pages. Leo tried to snatch the notebook away, but Moriarity straight-armed him. "Screw you, Wacko, don't interrupt me—" While he read, the rest waited and watched with anticipation.

" 'Moriarity, the big bad Brobdingnagian boob—?' What's that supposed to mean? Where do you come off callin' me names, you little twerp?"

It was useless to explain about Jonathan Swift to the likes of Bullnuts Moriarity; useless to explain anything to anyone. Meanwhile, Phil and the other Jeremians were getting a big kick out of Moriarity being the butt of Wacko's joke.

"Don't laugh, you guys," Moriarity said. "Wait'll you read what he says about you and Reece. He calls him a cigar-store Indian, and then—listen to this—Reece is Snow White, and you guys are the Seven Dwarfs."

Abruptly the laughter stopped. Phil walked over to Leo. "I guess we know what you think of us now, don't we, guys?" he sneered. As Leo started to reply Phil put up a deprecating hand. "Don't bother to explain; we don't care what you think of us, Wacko. Go ahead, write anything you want to, we don't care."

"It was just a joke—"

"Yeah, sure, we know." He winked elaborately at the others. "*But—* we *do* care about what you wrote about Reece. He's not going to like being called 'Snow White,' is he?"

Again the door opened and the group increased by three: Tiger, the Bomber, and Fritz, who asked what was up.

"They have my journal and won't give it back," Leo said.

Fritz saw the notebook in Moriarity's fist. "I think you'd better give Leo back his property, Claude," he said in his softspoken way. "Gentlemen don't go around reading other people's private papers."

"I do when it's about *me,* damn it. He called me a Brob-Brobdy-something boob!"

Fritz's lips twitched with incipient laughter. "Never mind, Claude, forget it." He put a hand out. "Just let me have the book."

"Nuts," Moriarity said, sneering. "I betcha there's a lotta guys 'ud be real interested in reading some of what Wacko's got to say here. 'Specially about a certain trip to the Wolf's Cave."

The Wolf's Cave? What was Wacko doing at the cave when he wasn't a Seneca?

As Bullnuts brandished the offending pages in Leo's face, Fritz made a move toward him, but Bullnuts, surprisingly quick on his feet, sidestepped him, holding the booklet out of reach.

"Outta my way, Jewboy. Who wants you buttin' in around here anyways?"

"I must insist. Please let me have the book!"

"Go ahead, *make* me."

Fritz eyed him up and down. "Claude, if you think I'm going to expend any physical effort on you, you're wrong."

"Yeah. Know what you are, Katzenjammer? A coward, that's what."

Before Fritz could say or do anything, the door again opened, this time admitting Reece. He was togged out in his sporty military trench coat, with its nattily cinched waist and folded shoulder tabs, wearing his garrison cap, whose black patent visor dripped with water. He unbelted his coat, hung the cap and coat on the back of the door, then turned and coolly surveyed the scene.

"Maybe someone can tell me what's been going on in here," he said.

"It's Wacko's feathers." Moriarity laughed. "Wacko-quacko's feathers."

"Moriarity's got Leo's journal," Fritz said.

Reece gave him a deadly look. "What are you doing in here? And what do you mean, Moriarity's got Wacko's journal?"

"It seems plain enough. I am describing the situation as it exists; I am sure you will treat the matter as is called for. In the meanwhile, I must get back to my cottage. Like the lodge, it too has a leak in the roof."

He put on his rain hat and left abruptly. When he had gone, Reece addressed himself to Moriarity.

"Well, have you this stuff of Wackeem's?"

"Sure, we got it."

"Then give it back," he ordered.

"Yeah, but listen—"

Reece cut off the protest. "It's not yours, you've no business reading it."

"Yeah, but you don't know what he done. He was in the Wolf's Cave. He was messin' around with Seneca stuff. Read it yourself if you don't believe me." Moriarity held out the journal. Reece took it and began thumbing its pages.

"See? Right there—" Bullnuts used a dirty thumb to point with. "Read how he was pissing on the sacred fire ring! Read that!"

Reece looked up, his eye fixed on Leo. "What were you doing at the Wolf's Cave? Don't you know better than to go there? It's off limits."

Stammering, Leo tried to explain how he'd stumbled on the place the night of the Snipe Hunt. "I got lost. I only found it by accident," he said weakly. "Please make them give me back my book." His appeal went unheeded, however; Reece scrutinized page after page, the crease between his brows deepening as he read. Finally he closed the cover and slowly rolled the notebook up, scroll-like, in his hands.

"You know what I think?" he said quietly, looking around at the group. "I think our great author here should be made to eat his words."

Aah, they all thought, here it came, one of Heartless's big numbers.

"Yes, that's it," Reece reiterated. "I think our Ernie Hemingway should be made to eat every one of these pages he wrote."

Ahh, that *was* clever, the boys' looks said. Leave it to Heartless to come up with a way of making the punishment fit the crime.

"We'll just find out how they taste." Unrolling the notebook, Reece opened it and randomly tore out a page, which he proffered to Leo with exaggerated ceremony. "*Eat it,*" he said softly.

Leo blinked. "I c-can't."

"Go *on, eat* it." The words cut through the air.

"No."

"Eat it!" Again Reece's eyes blazed.

With a hopeless shrug Leo obeyed. Slowly he tore the page into quarters, crumpled the pieces, and took them one by one between his lips, munching slowly and methodically. He chewed for a long time, and when he finally swallowed, with an audible gulp, someone giggled—Gus Klaus. Instantly Reece's stern gaze fell upon the miscreant. This was no joking matter. He tore a second page from the spiral and held it out.

Leo backed off a step. "I can't. It's ma-making me sick."

"I promise you'll be a lot sicker if you don't," Reece growled. Leo took the page and munched it. A third followed, then a fourth.

The boys looked at each other. How many pages would Reece make him eat, they wondered—all of them? Finally Tiger was moved to protest. "C'mon, he *is* liable to get sick."

"That's too bad," Reece retorted. "From now on maybe he'll be more careful what he writes down for other people to read." He held up the notebook clenched in his hand. "See, Tige? This is what comes of indulging a spud, making excuses for him every chance you get." He addressed Leo again. "One of these days you're going to find yourself in deep trouble—you know that, Wackeem? And you know where you're going to wind up? Right back where you came from, at the Institute." He smacked the offending journal into his palm, clamped his fingers around it, and stepped back to the door, which he threw open. "Okay, you guys, hop it, all of you."

"Where to?" asked the Bomber. "It's powwow time. And it's rainin' out."

"I said scram. Wackeem and I are going to have a little powwow of our own."

When the cabin was cleared, Leo stood in the corner, waiting for whatever further punishment was scheduled to be meted out. Instead of the anticipated tirade, however, Reece tried a new, "confidential" tack, and when he spoke it was quietly, without rancor.

"So what do you think, Wacko?" he asked softly.

"About what?"

"Oh . . . about you—and camp. I don't think we could say that it's been the greatest success, could we?"

"I don't know."

"Is that all you can ever say? 'I don't know.' I hear tell you're brighter than that, a lot brighter." He jerked his head toward the door through which the boys had retreated. "Don't you care if they think you're a sissy and a coward?"

Leo's look was defiant. "I'm not a coward."

"You give a darn good imitation of it." He shook his head with mock despair, then sat down on his footlocker. He kicked off his wet moccasins, dried his feet, and put on a pair of dry socks from the tray inside the locker. Then, shutting the lid, he dragged his boots out from under the cot and went about the elaborate ritual of polishing them. The industry with which he conducted this chore meant that the silence was prolonged. In the stillness the moths resumed their mad romance with the lantern, until one, dusting past Reece's cheek, caused him to jerk his head back and softly curse. Leo watched as it whirled and made another pass, attracted by the flickering light. This time it brushed against Reece's head. His hand flashed out and he imprisoned it within the hollow of his fist. Instead of crushing it as another might have done, he plucked it out with care, thumb and forefinger holding it fastidiously by one wing. Then with his other thumb he depressed the lamp lever, raising the glass chimney and freeing the flame. There was a soft hiss, a crackle, and the moth was no more. Reece took his hand away, wiped it on his leg, and lowered the chimney again.

"There's 'Poor Butterfly' for you, kiddo. Go play that on your squawk box," he said, and resumed wiping oil on the toe of the boot, keeping his eyes on Leo to get his reaction.

Leo said nothing. They looked to him, those cold blue eyes, like eyes seen through a painted mask. *Cave cane,* they seemed to say: Beware the dog. And then, as his own gaze fell, Reece's lit upon the postcard lying on the bed, where Moriarity's destruction of the pillow had exposed it.

"What's that?" Reece demanded. He bent and picked it up, held it close to the lantern.

"Well, well," he murmured, "sounds like you two have got real chummy."

"She was just saying hello. To let me know she was okay. After . . ."

"Well? After what?"

"You know. You hurt her."

Reece glowered. "What're you talking about?" he snarled, his voice suddenly hoarse.

With a quick, savage movement his arm shot out and his fingers closed around Leo's throat. Leo felt the breath being choked out of him; he'd never seen Reece so angry. His face was a chalky color, his voice was a hoarse rasp; he yanked Leo up by the hair and shoved his face close. "Who the hell do you think you are? Where do you come off giving me all this crap, anyhow? You ought to learn to keep your trap shut." His hand squeezed tighter, making Leo wince with pain. "And I'm warning you," Reece growled between clenched teeth, "if you ever say one thing about that business, if anything ever goes around, you'll regret it, you hear me? You'll get it good. Understand?"

Yes. Leo understood: like Stanley Wagner got it good.

Reece neatened his clothing and tucked his shirt in carefully. He put on his freshly oiled boots, caught up his coat and tipped his cap onto the back of his head. A hint of a smile hid in the corners of his lips as he gave Leo a last look, then strode out. In the doorway he whirled for a parting word: "I don't want to see one single feather in here when I come back," he said. "Not if it takes you the whole dinner hour."

2

y dinnertime news of Leo's transgression had spread through the campground, and as he shuffled to his accustomed place in the dining hall, there was a palpable undercurrent of mischief in the air, a suppressed hint of something about to happen, but when he looked to the Bomber for a clue, all he got back was a blank, studied glance, not a sly wink, not a sign. As for Tiger, though he said nothing, his very silence was a reproach.

During the meal Leo couldn't eat a morsel and made only token passes at his food. The corned beef was rubbery, just the smell of the boiled cabbage made his gorge rise, and as he picked away at his plate he didn't have to look up to feel the battery of hostile eyes drilling him from every side; whatever talk there was, he was sure it had to do with Wacko Wackeem, who'd been forced to eat crow in the guise of a blue-lined spiral notebook. Dessert time came, rice pudding, and after Monkey, half of this week's waiter team, handed around the dishes, everyone seemed suddenly interested as Leo took his spoon and dug into his portion (no matter what, he couldn't resist pudding—with raisins yet).

The moment Oats's tin cricket sounded dismissal, the boys sprang up like jack-in-the-boxes, and the table waiters started hustling their trays, eager to get their tables cleared, while the balance of the campers went trooping outside, heading for the lodge and the scheduled early-evening "rainy-day" activity—a sing-along and a movie. Before Leo could get away, however, he was accosted by Bullnuts, also waiting on table that week. "Hey, Wacko, I see you ate all your puddin'," he said. His look was foxy as he hoisted his tray to his shoulder. "Hope you don't get the collywobbles from it," he added, before making his way back into the aluminum pandemonium of the kitchen.

Not that Leo really cared much what Bullnuts said. It was the rift that had erupted between him and Tiger: This morning they had been friends, this evening Tiger was making no bones of the fact that he was fed up.

"If you ask me, you're pretty dumb sometimes, you know that?" Tiger said now, as they walked down to the lower campus after dinner.

"But those things were private. How was I to know they'd read them?"

"You should have thought, that's all. Now you'll never get in the Senecas."

Leo was stung. For Tiger to take this tack was grossly unfair. "Who cares?" he said with a shrug.

"You cared bad enough two weeks ago." Tiger sighed. "I guess you were right. Maybe you shouldn't have come to Moonbow. Maybe Reece was right."

"What's that supposed to mean?"

"Maybe you're just not good camper fodder after all."

Leo saw red. "I think you're all a bunch of shits," he said.

"It goes both ways, kiddo."

"Okay yourself, *kiddo.*" Leo lengthened his stride and marched away. Turning in the roadway, he tossed Tiger a smirk. "Okay for you, *Brewster-r-r,*" he said.

Reece, who had been walking behind them, and had overheard the quarrel, caught up for a private word with Tiger. "Ya done good, camper," Leo heard him say. "Now you're being the guy we all know. You just got off track, that's all." And when they got to the lower playing field, Reece tossed an arm around Tiger's shoulders, led him over to the Green Hornet, and the pair sped away, radio blaring.

By the time Leo reached the cabin, he wasn't feeling very well; swallowing all that paper was making his stomach act up. He hiked it over to the infirmary, where Wanda got out the bottle of rhubarb-and-soda, her universal panacea for stomach woes, administered Leo a healthy dose, and sent him on his way, but when he got back to Jeremiah he felt sicker than before, and he fell into his bunk, where he lay, hot and panting and nauseated. From the lodge he could hear them singing "Down by the Station." He wanted to go pee, then brush his teeth and go to sleep. He did none of those things. Instead, he kicked off his sneakers, took his flashlight, and began to read.

But he didn't feel like reading either, and he shut his book and stared out at the deserted playing field. His stomach was making angry rumbles, and the rhubarb-and-soda made him burp.

He could hear the faint pitterpat of water dripping from tree leaves onto the roof; it had a nice cozy sound, reminding him of rainy afternoons with Emily in the house on Gallop Street. He must have dozed, because before he knew it he heard the sounds of the Jeremians trooping up the cabin steps. He doused his lighted flashlight quickly and feigned sleep as they came trooping in, talking and laughing as if he weren't there, then out again to the wash rack and Old Faithful to brush their teeth, and back in, to settle into their bunks with the usual last-minute quota of gags and giggles.

He hated lying there in bed, awake but unable to read, and in desperation began to recite "Hiawatha" to himself; he had reached the stanza that began

As unto the bow the cord is,
So unto the man is woman . . .

when the first spasm hit him, causing his body to contort as if it had been lashed. Then a second cramp seized him. When it passed, finally, he lay there in his bunk, trying to catch his breath. Sweat poured off him; his pajamas were soaked. Something more must be wrong than a few pieces of paper. When the next cramp came it made him sit bolt upright, clutching his belly. Stifling a moan, he felt an interior gurgling under his palms as his stomach lifted and heaved. He knew he had to get to the Dewdrop, but couldn't make a move. Squeezing his eyes shut and gritting his teeth, he forced himself to hold on tight until the pain passed; then he grabbed his flashlight and slipped from his bunk, dropping out the rear of the cabin onto the wet ground. The earth was drenched, each step sucked at his foot as, stepping over puddles, half bent over and clutching his midsection, he headed off in the direction of the latrine.

When he got there he pulled up short, pushed open the door and hurried in, loosening the string of his pajama bottoms as he grabbed the first hole. Blessed relief flooded through him as he relaxed and voided, and the gnawing seizure that had tied his innards in knots slackened its grip. Then,

231

through the window, he heard the call of a bird—what kind of bird he could not tell, but obviously one of the nocturnal sort. To this sound was quickly joined a second, as if in formal reply to the first—its mate, perhaps? The duet was joined by yet a third call, nearer, Leo thought, lower-pitched, its tone eerie and off-putting—an ominous note, followed by a protracted silence. He became suddenly alert, frowning as he forced his ears to pick out small, meaningful sounds, but for a time all remained quiet. No, no—wait—there! Something was moving outside, a telltale twig had cracked. Then, in one mind-shattering moment, a heavy object flew through the window and struck the kerosene lamp, sending it crashing to the floor, where, extinguished, it rolled away into the dark. Leo froze, waiting for more to follow, but nothing was forthcoming; he groped for his flashlight and snapped it on. A large stone lay in the corner. He shut off the light again and listened. Through the dark oblong of the window he picked out the faintest of sounds, as though several creatures, human or otherwise, had convened out there in the surrounding darkness. The next thing he knew, the walls of the building were being subjected to a series of violent blows, seemingly on all sides simultaneously, a hammering so thunderous that to protect his ears he pressed his palms over them.

When it stopped, he got to his feet, groping for his pajama bottoms and yanking them up to his waist; but before his fingers could locate the ends of the cord, the floor tilted and the building began to sway. Back and forth it pitched, its abrupt, rocking movement catching him off guard and propelling him from the buckets to the opposite wall, where he smacked his forehead against a two-by-four. With the sickening upheaval the noisy tattoo along the building's outer surfaces resumed, accompanied by voices—gleeful laughter. The rocking intensified. The building was being torn loose from its moorings! Defenseless, Leo felt his body tumbling head over heels as the Dewdrop Inn toppled on its back. He came to rest sprawled across the holes and, looking up, saw the door drop open above him. It missed his head by inches, swinging crazily on its hinges.

For a moment he lay where he'd been flung, dizzily trying to get his breath, his ear catching the fragments of laughter as they fitfully exploded and were suppressed in the darkness outside. Silence fell again. He could taste blood where his lips had been cut; more was running into his eye from a gash in his scalp. Beyond the oblong shape created by the open door, he glimpsed bits of tree foliage silhouetted against the sky. He got up and slowly, painfully made a futile attempt to reach the open doorway; then, getting another idea, he made his way to the window, which, because of the overturning, now lay close to the ground, and crawled free. Outside, he stumbled to his feet and looked around him. The Dewdrop lay on its back like some gross, wounded beast, its underpinnings naked to view; in the dark pit he could see patches of white where the usual ration of quicklime had been applied. The stench made him feel nearly as sick as he'd been before, and he covered his mouth to keep from vomiting.

Suddenly a figure in a slicker and sou'wester hat lurched into the pathway; it was Bullnuts Moriarity. He held up a lantern; in its light two shadows appeared behind him, advancing toward Leo, who now drew back: Bullnuts he could probably elude; a gang would make things truly difficult. He was filled with relief as he recognized the voices of Fritz and Wanda, who were coming along the path.

"What is going on here?" Fritz demanded sternly, shining a flashlight around. He frowned as he spotted Moriarity. "Claude, what are you up to? What was all that racket?" Finally he saw Leo, then the overturned latrine. "Leo, are you all right?" he asked, stepping toward him. "What's been going on around here?" He shone his light into the pit.

"Aw, gee, willya lookit that!" Moriarity pretended to have only just noticed the overturned latrine. "My golly—whoever do you think done that? Turned over the Dewdrop Inn."

The wet sputter of giggles issued from the bushes on either side of the path.

"All right, you fellows," Fritz called at the sound. "Whoever you are, you can come out now, the fun's over."

A sudden flurry of activity erupted among the shrubbery as dark forms broke from their hiding places and scuttled to safety in the encompassing dark.

Fritz now shone his light on Leo. "I think we'd better get you over to the infirmary and let Wanda have a look at that head. As for you, Claude," he went on, turning to Moriarity, "you may consider yourself on report."

"For what?" Claude bellowed. "I didn't do it all on my own. Those guys were in on it too."

"Rinkydinks, I suppose? Kindly give me their names and I'll see they're all properly dealt with."

"You got to be kiddin'."

"Try me and see, Claude. Now I suggest everybody get to bed. Leo, that means you, too."

As Fritz turned to go, Moriarity made a sudden movement forward. But Leo was swift enough to dodge him, leaving a space for Bullnuts to plunge headlong through, his momentum carrying him over the edge of the latrine pit. No one was more surprised than Claude to find himself hurtling through space, lantern and all, to hit the bottom with a wet, splishing sound.

3

The boys who had gone to bed during a final deluge of rain awoke to a bright world again, and although the entire camp was so waterlogged that it would take days for the place to dry out (from the red-painted designations on his dock pilings Doc Oliphant was able to demonstrate that the lake had risen two and a half inches in the six days of rain), with the return of good weather everyone at Moonbow cheered and roused himself and felt renewed, as if before the season's end Friend-Indeed had been granted a second lease on life. Like schoolboys too long cooped up in the classroom, the campers burst forth into the sunshine, giving full vent to their natural ebullience, spreading themselves across the breast of the lake in flotillas of watercraft, carousing north and south along the linepath, shinnying up the trees in Shinny Park, and catching snakes and firing slingshots at anything that moved. Every clothesline from Virtue to Endeavor sagged with damp shorts and polo shirts, and moldy bathing towels and bedding were spread out for airing on every available cabin roof and shutter.

To all outward appearances the world at Moonbow Lake was green and gold again. But not for Wacko Wackeem, whose stock at Friend-Indeed had plummeted since the exposure of the contents of his private journal. With his incriminating comments set down in Parker's blue-black Quink, how could he afterward deny what he had written? Or explain that his comments were just private jokes, not to be taken seriously—that Reece Hartsig didn't really look like a cigar-store Indian in his Moonbow Warrior's garb, that Claude Moriarity didn't really bear a resemblance in certain particulars to Farmer Kelsoe's prize bull, or that Pa Starbuck wasn't the Bible-thumping Billy Sunday of Moonbow Lake.

And the boys had had their private revenge. Knocking latrines off their beam ends was old-timers' sport at Moonbow—mischievous campers had been pulling such stunts since the days when Rolfe Hartsig was an adolescent bunkee and Jeremiah was only a tent—but it was not exactly customary for such barrelhousing to occur when a person happened to be inside the Dewdrop. Nonetheless, Pa had chalked the business up as another prank— and if it was more than that, well, Leo *had* trespassed, hadn't he?—and let it go at that. As for Moriarity's tumble into the pit, even Pa smiled at the reports, while Bullnuts went around camp loudly demanding reprisals. Thus far, however, he had done nothing along those lines, and for the time being the joke remained on him.

If only, Leo thought, that could have been the end of it. But now, from every quarter, starting in Cabin 7 and extending up and down the linepath to the outer reaches of High Endeavor and Virtue, he felt the resentment of his fellow campers. There was a general feeling that he had "got away with it," that peeing on the Seneca campfire was a violation on a par with dancing around in the Buffalo Bill War Bonnet, and fully deserving of punishment. But the Sachems' Council, convening to adjudicate the matter, stood divided on the issue, with a few, after an impassioned argument by Fritz Auerbach, maintaining that the real "crime" had been reading Leo's diary. Since the Sachems' decisions were required to be unanimous, no action was taken, as a result of which, two things happened: one, after an acrimonious row, Reece Hartsig resigned from the council, and, two, the Mingoes, whose clandestine meetings had been removed to the Rinkydinks' former bailiwick in the cellar of the Steelyard house, let it be known that they themselves would see to the matter.

When formal notice of the council's decision (or lack thereof) had been posted on the bulletin board outside the lodge for all to see, the paper was torn down in the dead of night, and in its stead a crudely lettered poster appeared:

WANTED
WACKO WACKEEM

236

Dead or Alive
(Preferably dead)
For Crimes Against the Camp
Also wanted
Fritzy Katzenjammer
alias
THE NOSE

Quickly removed, the placard was (as usual) ascribed to camper hijinks, with Pa listening to Fritz's objections with half an ear, then dragging out his "Boys will be boys" wheeze and declaring he was sure the whole thing was only meant as a joke. During his pre-dinner remarks after grace, he reminded the boys that this was Camp "Friend-Indeed," and that "Actions speak louder than words."

And that was that. Except that at night, when the sun had gone and a gibbous moon gored the dark sky with its horns, mischief was afoot. After lights out, campers would find excuses to visit the Dewdrop Inn. As they came and went they stopped in dark clusters for a few words, mirthful sputters and giggles, and then the mocking warning would be sounded among the trees: "Wacko, Wacko . . . someone's gonna getcha!" And along the needled paths the spores of poisonous toadstools—*Amanita muscaria*—blossomed in the potent dark.

Far worse than all this for Leo, however, was his fall from grace where Tiger was concerned. The two boys were constantly thrown together in the normal course of events, but since their quarrel no words more intimate than "pass the potatoes" had been spoken between them, no look had been exchanged. Though Leo was resentful of what he judged to be Tiger's failure to understand the situation—how could Tiger blame him when Leo's privacy had been invaded?—he regretted his flagrant use of the despised epithet and would gladly have called it back. But to do so required an apology he couldn't find it in himself to offer, and so they remained apart, each playing "Invisible Man" to the other.

Leo felt the schism keenly as the day approached when, with the completion of the village, he hoped once again to redeem himself for all that had gone before. The model would repose on its stand in its glass display case, the formal unveiling would be held, photographs would be taken for the paper, and the two creators of the village would be honored. By Tuesday morning everything was set, and he sat on his stool in the work corner of the lodge, surveying the fruits of his labors. Was it all right, he wondered? He had just given the castle one last coat of banana oil, the fortress was fitted securely into its mountain site, the banner with its Hapsburg device was flying over the portcullis. If only, Leo thought, Tiger would come by to make it up, everything would be just fine.

It was not Tiger who arrived, however, but Pa Starbuck, accompanied by two young men who were announced as the newspaper reporter and his sidekick photographer. While the photographer checked his camera equipment, the reporter asked Leo some questions ("What's your name, son, and where do you come from? Are your folks members of the Society of Joshua? What do they call you? Play baseball? What's your batting average? Ha ha"). Leo was relieved of further interrogation by the arrival of Fritz, who greeted the reporter with aplomb and provided him with some background on the real Durenstein. Pa kept looking at his watch, growing more impatient every minute until the Hartsigs, including Reece, finally arrived, twenty minutes late, Rolfe giving as an excuse for their tardiness the fact that he'd had to stop at the film exchange in Putnam to pick up the movie for tonight's program.

While Reece shook hands with the reporter, an old high-school chum he greeted as "Andy," Joy Hartsig walked straight to the model to look it over, her eyes shining with pleasure. As often happened when she was around, she quickly became the focus of the gathering, her gold and ivory bracelets jangling as she gestured, patting her coiffure or bringing her cigarette to her red lips.

"Goodness," she cooed, "haven't you two done a lot of work! I'm simply astonished." She smiled warmly at Fritz, her diamond rings catching the light as she crushed her fingers under her chin. "I just love the way you're making everything a little skewed, a bit crooked," she added. "It gives a nice fairy-tale effect. At least I imagine that's what you were after. Wouldn't it be fun to visit the real thing sometime?"

"I don't imagine you'd care to visit it just now, Mrs. Hartsig," Fritz said with a touch of irony. Joy's bright smile left her lips as she laid a hand on his arm.

"I know how much it means to you," she said. "Is that how it looked when you were a boy?"

"More or less. It's not easy making things look exactly the way you recall them. But it's close, I think."

"What do you think, Dutch?" Joy asked her husband.

"Looks pretty authentic to me," Rolfe replied. He was especially taken with the steamboat Leo had crafted, its wheel beating the waves of the blue plaster Danube.

Then the photographer, who had been trying a series of angles, asked that the model be moved out of its corner to a position where everyone could be grouped around it for the shot he wanted. Fritz and Leo, with the newspapermen, performed the job, carrying the worktable out into the middle of the room, after which several pictures were taken of the model with Pa and the Hartsigs (excepting Reece, who declined), and finally with Leo and Fritz, who was asked to make a further statement about his creation.

Fritz's expression grew serious and he groped for suitable words. "This is my gift to the campers of Friend-Indeed," he said at last, "and to Dr. Dunbar and the Friends of Joshua, who have invited me to spend my summer here and who have behaved kindly and generously toward an exile from his own land."

He paused, and the reporter's glance fell on Reece, who had been leaning nonchalantly against the wall and who now sauntered over.

"What's your opinion, Reece?" the reporter asked. "Got something to say about this project?"

"It's fine . . ." Reece said with a pleasant smile, ". . . if you like Tinkertoys," he added, and there was a moment's silence while the reporter tried to decide whether he was sincere or joking.

"Oh, but I do!" said Fritz, relieving the others of potential embarrassment. "Everyone enjoys toys, doesn't he? We're all children at heart, aren't we? And see here—"

They watched as he reached behind the model to move a tiny brass lever built into the foundation. In a moment a ticking sound could be heard, then tinkling music began: the familiar strains of the "Blue Danube" waltz.

"What a wonderful touch! Whose idea was that?" Joy asked. "Yours, Fritz?"

"No, ma'am." Fritz gallantly declined the intended compliment. The idea had been Leo's. The works had come from a dime-store music box.

"Clever lad," said Joy. "I'm sure he deserves a lot of praise." She beamed her brightest at Leo, who flushed with pleasure but modestly pointed out that the idea for the village as a whole had been Fritz's, that he, Leo, had merely "helped out."

"Let's get a shot of the whole group, shall we?" the photographer suggested, re-forming the gathering with Fritz and Leo in the center. "Come on, Reece, you get in on this too."

"Thanks. I'll skip it."

"Just one?"

"Didn't you hear me?"

"Okay, okay, sorry."

The photographer directed a puzzled look at his colleague, who shrugged, as if to say, "Consider the source," and went on questioning Fritz, jotting down statistics on the population of Durenstein and the Austrian wine industry. From these considerations he moved on to a general sizing-up of the political situation in Austria, and Fritz spoke heatedly about Hitler, saying that with the way things were going there was bound to be a war in Europe pretty soon.

Rolfe rubbed his palms together. "You've got it all wrong, Fritz; Hitler doesn't really want war, he only wants what's coming to him, what belongs to Germany by right, to guarantee her natural borders. Take it from me," he went on, "Stalin's the guy we really have to watch. If we're not careful, we'll have a bunch of Bolsheviks running the good old U.S.A. It's the Commies that are making all the trouble, on both sides of the Atlantic."

Fritz leaned forward, his look intense. "May I ask, sir, have you heard of *Mein Kampf*?"

"Sure. What about it?"

"If you were to read that book you would learn exactly what Hitler plans to do. And make no mistake—he *means* to do it! Already he is rounding up all who oppose him. He has taken my family, he has robbed us of our property, they are in prison. I may never see them again."

"Come on, pal, we mustn't dramatize these things. I'm sure your family is okay." Rolfe turned to the others. "Besides, Hitler's only after the big-money boys—"

Fritz's face had gone red with anger, and Pa, seeing it, stepped forward in an attempt to temporize. "Now, now, Fritz, let's exercise a little control, shall we? What's happening over there has nothing to do with us over here."

"You're wrong," Fritz said. "You don't know what you're saying."

Now Reece stepped into the argument. "Watch it, Katzenjammer!"

Fritz rounded on him. "I have asked you not to call me that."

Reece gave him his blandest smile. "It's just a joke, Fritzy."

"I do not find it amusing." Fritz glowered, and Joy began chattering to cover the awkwardness. Andy, who had been scribbling in his notebook, asked Rolfe, "Can I print all that, what you said about the big-money boys?"

"Sure, why not?" Rolfe replied. "It's the truth, isn't it?" Then he gave Andy a friendly clap between the shoulders and sent him off with his partner to write up his story.

Movie night always drew an enthusiastic crowd, and that night the boys seemed in uncommonly boisterous spirits, as shortly before eight they came trooping into the lodge and took their places. The movie projector rested on a card table in front of the model, which had been left in the center of the room to be ready for the dedication ceremony, but the older boys ranged their seats around it without much difficulty, so that no one's view was obscured. Big Rolfe's friend at the film exchange had selected *The Phantom of the Opera,* the Lon Chaney silent hit, and as the last stragglers appeared the audience began to chant, clap, and stamp their feet and otherwise demonstrate their eagerness to be scared out of ten years' growth by an actor whose fame rested on precisely that, a singular ability to terrify audiences in movie houses across the country, where fainting and horror-stricken females had to be carried on stretchers into the lobby and revived with ammoniac ampules and carted off in waiting ambulances.

There was a hitch in the proceedings—no one knew why, until Oats Gurley, whose duty it was to operate the movie projector, said they couldn't start until Reece put in an appearance with the film cans. A mixture of cheers and jeers sounded in the room. Then the boys began to chant: "We want Heartless, we want Heartless. . . ."

At last the courier arrived—at which the room erupted into louder huzzahs. After he had exhibited the cans of film and made mock bows to all sides, he slipped in among "his boys," and the reels began to turn.

Alas, anticipation soon turned to disappointment. Lon Chaney had gone to the Great Movie Show in the Sky, had in fact died eight years before, and his silent movie had a decidedly creaky look. In fact, the term "the flickers" had been coined to describe films such as this one; old and scratched, the reels had undoubtedly run through the sprockets of untold projectors over the years, and the titles leaped and danced about on the screen. Catcalls and whistles, groans and jokes greeted the coloratura singing her heart out on the stage of the Paris Opera House and the corny notes written by the "Phantom" threatening the end of her career, nay, her life, if she presumed to appear onstage instead of his beloved Christine. There followed a higher-scoring scene in which, while the heroine dares her fate, the giant crystal chandelier at the top of the opera-house ceiling is made by some sinister hand (Yikes! The Phantom!) to come crashing down into the orchestra, crushing to death those spectators unlucky enough to be sitting beneath the fixture. And then, finally, the electrifying moment when "Erik," the Phantom, first appears, his features hidden by a mask. With his long, slender, and enticing hand he lures Christine down, down, many floors below, under the opera house, where there exists a sullen black lagoon and, anchored at a stone mooring step, a slender, coffin-like vessel. Upon this slender vessel the lady is persuaded to embark for the Phantom's subterranean apartments, where she is safely, and presumably contentedly, installed, seemingly only a little intimidated by her bizarre surroundings and the Phantom's eternally masked presence. Later, unable to control her curiosity, as he plays the organ she slips up behind the unsuspecting Phantom and tears away his mask. *Oh, horror!* His features bared, he turns upon her and shows her that nightmare face, skull-like and awful to look upon, with grinning teeth and two holes where a nose ought to have been.

Ha ha!

The Phantom scornfully mocks Christine and her irrepressible curiosity, then moves menacingly toward her. Unable to tear his eyes from the screen, Leo watches with mounting horror. For him the movie is too real; it scares him. Heedless of where he is, he leaps to his feet with a shout, which rings out and reverberates against the ceiling.

No sooner had the sound burst from him than a wave of mocking laughter shook the room, and "Wacko, Wacko, Wacko," the epithet ran along the rows. "Scaredy-cat, scaredy-cat." Flashlights were switched on, their probing beams sought him out, illuminating his dazed features. Ducking his head, he stumbled up the aisle and rushed outside; the door clattered loudly at his back, producing another volley of laughter. Hot with shame and embarrassment, he rushed down the steps and made his way blindly along the first path he came to. It was dark and he had trouble finding his way. To his left he could hear the lake water lapping the shore, and he pushed on until he came out at Three Corner Cove. No lights were on at the infirmary, nor at the Oliphants' cottage, yet he judged someone to be home, because the car was pulled up on the grass. He trudged to the end of the dock and sat down, dangling his legs and listening to the sound of the water against the pilings. What a fool he was to act that way. When would he ever learn?

"Leo?"

He turned around to find Fritz and Wanda, who had stolen up behind him.

"Mind if we join you?" Fritz asked. No reply; but Leo was glad all the same for the company.

"You all right?" Wanda asked.

"Yes."

"It's nice here," she said, "but I'll bet it'd be nicer inside. I think if we looked in the icebox we'd find some ice cream. How does that sound?"

Leo was appreciative; neither had asked about his exhibition in the lodge; now here was Wanda inviting him in for ice cream, a thing camp rules strictly forbade her to do.

She gave Leo a hand up and they left the dock for the infirmary, where Wanda turned on lights and went inside. Leo and Fritz waited on the porch until she reappeared with a tray of ice cream and cookies. Then Fritz got up to tune in Wayne King and the Lady Esther Orchestra, and soon they had a little party going and, despite his embarrassment, Leo was enjoying himself.

His enjoyment was short-lived, however; another flashlight beam broke the surrounding dark, and Reece appeared. Leo tensed as the counselor marched up the steps and surveyed the scene.

"Well, this is chummy. Somebody's birthday?"

"We were just having a taste of ice cream," Wanda said lightly. "Sorry, there's none left."

Reece scowled at Leo. "I figured this is where I'd find you. What's the idea, running out like a crazy man?" Without waiting for an answer, he leaned over to take Leo's dish.

"Oh, let him finish," Wanda protested. "Stop picking on him all the time."

Reece swung on her angrily. "When are you two going to stop coddling this spud?"

Wanda tipped the ash from her cigarette into the nasturtiums below the railing. "Nobody's coddling him," she returned evenly. "Leo really doesn't deserve the kind of treatment he's been getting around here."

"Look, like I told you once before, he's not your camper, he's my camper," Reece retorted. "I'm the counselor of Jeremiah, and as long as he sleeps in my cabin he belongs to me. I'll decide what to do with him, not you."

"I'm only trying to help. He's got to have someone he can turn to in this place."

"And that someone is you, hm? The way you spoil him, he'll never get anywhere. You're like a mother hen."

"Then I'm glad—since he hasn't got a mother."

Reece's voice sharpened. "Lots of people don't have mothers and they get along just fine. So take my advice and steer clear of him"

Fritz snorted. "And you are going to make me, I suppose, with your Mingoes and your foolish posters."

Reece lounged negligently on the railing, his expression lightly mocking, as if he found Fritz a figure of amusement. "You just don't get the picture, do you, Fritzy."

"I expect you'd be happy to show it to me, though."

"Anytime you like, bud." Making fists, Reece assumed an offensive stance. "Come on, I dare you."

Wanda put out a restraining hand. "Don't, please, there's no point to it."

Reece crossed his arms and smirked. "Better listen to your girlfriend, Fritzy. And you better shut up about the Germans, too. I'm German and proud of it."

Fritz shook his head sadly. "Sometimes I think I shall never understand people like you."

"That's okay, Fritzy," Reece returned softly, "sometimes I don't think I'll ever understand people like you either. So why don't you just trot along and play with your toy village? Or, better yet, go back and join your family in that pretty little camp they're no doubt in."

"Reece!" Wanda sprang to her feet in protest and took Fritz's arm, only to have him shake her off. Suddenly the two men were grappling together, furiously pummeling each other. The muffled sounds of blows punctuated the dark while Wanda cried out for them to stop, trying to get herself between them but unable to separate them.

Reece's tall, muscular form towered over the smaller, wirier Fritz, who seemed to be catching the worst of it, until the sounds of the struggle produced results: lights came on at Three Corner Cove, and Doc Oliphant appeared on his porch. "What's going on over there?" he demanded, peering across the water.

"There, then—will you two please stop now?" hissed Wanda. "It's all right," she called back, "just a little kidding around."

"Wanda, dear, try and control your hot-blooded beau, won't you?" came the doctor's admonition as he went back inside and turned off the porch light.

Panting from their exertions, the two combatants faced each other with dull, sullen looks.

"You're bleeding," Wanda said to Reece, whose lip had been opened by a lucky punch from Fritz's hard knuckles. "Let me get something for it."

"Skip it." Reece spat over the railing, then turned to Leo.

"All right, camper, skip off to where you belong," he said, and, his lip red with blood in the lamplight, he swung away down the steps. With a prompting nod from Fritz, Leo followed. At the head of the path Reece split off without a word or sign to disappear in the direction of Bachelors' Haven and the game of poker in progress, while Leo limped back to Jeremiah, where, as taps blew, he fell onto his bunk with his clothes on.

The crescent moon hangs high above the lake. Nothing stirs, except, in Hosea, Gus Klaus snores fitfully, making liquid flutters under his nose. Presently, from among the cabins of the Harmony unit, a solitary figure emerges, creeping stealthily along the linepath, crouching low as if fearful of discovery. With purpose and intent he moves onto the lodge path.

High in the Methuselah Tree the owl Icarus spies him soft-walking along the path, stealing up to the lodge. Inside, like a wandering moth, a pale light flits across the wide-board floor to the upright joist where the rope supporting the great horn chandelier is figure-eighted over the cleat. The dark phantom bends closer; in his hand a knife. Its sharp blade presses hard against the twisted fibers of the rope, then begins its calculated work, making a ragged cut. It is not difficult: the rope is old. One after another the strands give way, until only a handful remain intact to carry the weight of the fixture. Satisfied with his handiwork, the phantom sheathes the knife and melts into the darkness.

All is quiet again in the lodge. But in the darkness the implacable force of gravity works upon the weakened rope, exerting its power, causing the remaining strands to relinquish their hold, one after another parting. Icarus cocks his head. Soon now . . . any moment . . . yes—now!

The ponderous mass of iron and animal horn breaks free of its beam, the severed rope speeds through the tackle, the wheels turn noisily, as the chandelier comes crashing to the floor. The pine grove is rocked by the deafening sound, the lodge walls tremble from the impact, the panes in the windows rattle. In the cabins along the linepath campers and staff spring to sudden wakefulness. What is it, they ask? What has happened? Shouts and calls break out, fifty pinpoints of light are seen flickering along the pathways, converging on the lodge. And inside:

"Ah, too bad," they mutter. "What a thing." For the old worn rope, frayed after many years of use, has, it seems, given way, dropping the horn wonder to the floor. Beneath the clutter the village of Durenstein lies ground to dust.

4

uietly, with great determination, the small spider tried to spin her web across a wide crack in the weir at Kelsoe's Pond, where Leo had taken refuge. Poor thing, he thought, I know just how you feel. He had bestowed a name on the spider—Elsie—and hoped she would prosper in the way of her kind. Under more promising circumstances he would have collected her for his arachnid exhibit, but where was the point? Tonight he might return to the lodge to find that the shelves of his display case had suffered a fate similar to that of Durenstein.

Again he was swept by a hot wave of resentment and frustration. It had been Fritz who had noticed the ends of rope that when put together butted neatly; but when Fritz produced the evidence for Pa and voiced his suspicions—that Reece Hartsig, who had been seen leaving Jeremiah after midnight, was the guilty party—Pa had turned a deaf ear, bemoaning the loss of the model but saying there were no grounds to suspect the counselor, who had no doubt been answering a call of nature at the Dewdrop. And in the end what did it matter, really? It was the spirit of a gift that counted, wasn't it? As for the work that had gone into it—Jeremiah would get the points Leo had earned for it, *eee*-heh.

And that was pretty much that. Before the end of the day the formal dedication had been canceled, the newspaper story and pictures were yanked, and the platform for the model had vanished without a trace.

Leo wanted to stop thinking about it all, to blot everything from his mind; there was no one he cared to be with—not even Fritz, while Tiger, it seemed, was a lost cause. So here he was, back at Kelsoe's Pond, alone except for little, hardworking Elsie; good enough company, he decided, if it came to that. The spider's unflinching persistence put him in mind of the tale Emily had read to him about the Scottish hero Robert the Bruce, who "seven times had flung himself into the fray against the English" (Emily read) and who "at nightfall still had not won the day. Knowing all was lost and that on the morrow he must yield or die," he had taken refuge in a crofter's cottage, where he had watched a spider—just such a spider as Elsie, Leo imagined—trying desperately to throw a filament from which to hang her web. Each time the line fell short, yet each time she would climb back up and bravely attempt the toss again, until—until at last—success! The line held, and the spider suspended her web from it. And having watched this little drama enacted, "Robert had slept soundly, then, awakening refreshed, strode forth to marshal his troops one more time and finally to carry the day."

The moral, Emily said—all the tales in the book had morals at the end—was "If at first you don't succeed, try, try again." Whatever it was, you did it, and you did it over and over until it came right—until you won. It was like Tiger's motto: "Never say die." Leo guessed that was easy if you weren't the butt of every prankster in camp, if every bully wasn't looking for a chance to knock you down, if nearly everyone wasn't lying in wait for you, to call you a liar, to destroy all your handiwork. He wasn't Robert the Bruce, after all, he was only Wacko Wackeem, and this spider wasn't going to bridge the gap in the stone in a hundred hundred years.

His thoughts were interrupted by the sound of an auto motor, and he recognized the expensive purr of Dagmar's Pierce-Arrow. He straightened up and, looking across the turf, saw the car tooling toward him, Augie behind the wheel, Dagmar peering out the window. In a moment it pulled up; Augie helped Dagmar out, and, giving Leo a wave, she made her way toward him.

"There you are," she called agreeably. "Ma said we'd find you here. May I join you?"

Without waiting for his response, she seated herself on the grass. "What a pretty spot. I haven't been here for years. Knute used to fish in this pond, I remember. Do you come here often?"

"Sometimes."

"I was very sorry to hear of what has happened to the model village. A terrible thing, I have been talking with Ma and Fritz about it. That young man must be taught a lesson! He can't go around behaving like some thug simply because he's big and strong or because he's Rolfe Hartsig's son." She had a good deal more to say on the subject of Reece's recent behavior, none of it flattering. "I say he had better change his ways and quickly," she concluded. "When he flies from the nest next year he won't find the world half so well-feathered as it is at home."

She paused expectantly, but when Leo said nothing, went on. "Fritz also told me about these Mingoes, or whatever they please to call themselves—"

"They're out to get me, I know they are," Leo cried, unable to stop himself.

"Don't be a blubberer," said Dagmar starchily. "I'm sure Pa will put a stop to them."

"He won't. He never does. Fritz *told* him!"

"Then someone will have to talk to Dr. Dunbar. Perhaps I'll ring him myself."

She jerked her chin firmly for emphasis. "But Leo," she went on, "in any case, you must not think it was wrong, your coming here. I am not a superstitious woman, but somehow I know, I am certain, that you were meant to come here to Moonbow, that it would—*will*—lead to very important things. Things that will change your whole life." She regarded him long and a trifle wistfully. "Leo, you are young and do not see it; but if you did . . ."

"See what?"

"See that you are standing upon the golden threshold. You are waiting just outside the door, nearly ready to step through. Into a world so glorious not even you can imagine it. But if you could see, you would realize it is there, for you to grasp and make the most of. If only you will do it. If only you will make the most of your talent. Yes! You cannot appreciate this—not yet—what it means to be an artist, how hard you must work and struggle for it, how hard you must fight against those who cannot understand. And you must make up your mind to it, that as an artist you will always be apart, always different. *That* is what helps *make* you an artist, that difference."

Her eyes held an urgency as she spoke, talked on, trying to reach him with her words. Leo listened, knowing they were meaningful things she was trying to express, but he felt uncomfortable nevertheless. Even while they sat beside the water the dusk was gathering around them, and as she talked her face grew pale in the purple light, the wrinkles in her skin more pronounced.

She changed her position to bring herself closer to him, forcing him to attend more closely to her words. "What I am trying to say is that you have displayed your talents to me on two different occasions. Both times things were amiss and the performance was interrupted, but that fact takes nothing away from your God-given abilities. Professor Pinero agrees. Yours is a rare gift, a gift that requires nourishment. It seems to us that if you were given the opportunity to pursue your studies as your mother wanted you to, you could go farther than even she dreamed."

This mention of Emily caused him to drop his head. Using her thumb, Dagmar raised it again. "Leo?"

"Yes?"

"Why did you tell me your mother and father had died in a train accident?"

"Did I?"

"Yes. Don't you remember?"

He shook his head. "It's true," he said. "They did! It's true!" But even as he spoke he knew she had found out the truth.

"Leo, my dear, listen to me, please," she went on. "You needn't be ashamed. I have spoken with Ma. She told me. You mustn't think I am being a nosy Parker, but I believed you would wish me to know. Isn't that so? Aren't these things we should speak of, you and I, if we are to be friends?"

"I suppose so." He feigned a profound interest in the spider. "But what if someone else finds out?"

"Who? The campers, do you mean? Or Reece? They won't, never fear."

But Leo was remembering the village. Suddenly he looked up at her. "Can we talk at the Castle?"

"Why there, please?"

"Because I want to come."

"And you shall," she replied. "We'll have a nice visit before you leave."

"No. Not a visit. To stay."

"To stay?"

"Yes. Then you can ask me anything you want. And I'll play for you. But you must promise to keep me. Forever and ever."

"Oh, my dear, how can I do that?"

"Tell Mr. Poe and Miss Meekum you want me," he said eagerly. "Say I'm to come and stay with you."

"That's a very nice idea. Perhaps you can come for Christmas vacation. But I'm afraid a longer visit would be out of the question."

"Why?"

"Leo, I am an old woman, I cannot have the responsibility of a boy to look after. What would happen if I became ill—?"

"Augie! Augie will take care of me."

"Nonsense! That's ridiculous. Augie is older than I. He's not well. I wouldn't think of burdening him."

She consulted her watch, then stubbed out her cigarette and dropped her Camels into her bag. "My stomach's rumbling," she said. "I must get home for supper." She stood and brushed off her seat, then put out a hand and wiggled her fingers coaxingly. "Come. Augie will drive you back to camp."

She reached for his arm but he pulled away abruptly.

"I don't want to."

"I thought you liked riding in my automobile."

"No, I don't want to," he said again.

She laughed her robust laugh. "What *do* you want, then?"

"I told you. I want to come with you and live in your castle."

"But I have explained that is not possible. You must go back, of course." She smiled encouragement. "Before the summer's over we'll play duets again, how will that be?"

He stiffened and spoke coldly. "That's okay. You don't have to be polite."

"But I am not being polite. I mean what I say. I *want* you to come. I hope you will visit me many times in future."

He turned a little away. "I'm liable to be pretty busy."

A faint line of dissatisfaction drew itself between her brows. "Come now, please don't scowl so. I may be an old woman, but I know what I'm talking about." She smiled and touched a finger to the back of his hand. "Be a good boy, Leo, won't you? Aren't we friends, you and I? I hoped we were . . ." She tried to force his chin up, but he ducked his head and stubbornly refused to look at her.

She sighed. "I had not thought to find you so ill-mannered. I fear I have mistaken myself in you." She sighed. "Very well, then, let us part, not as I hoped we would, but as we must. Good-bye."

He only half-watched her as she marched away, her back stiffened with affront, bits of leaf and straw attached to her skirt. He wanted to run after her and say he was sorry, but his feet wouldn't obey his brain. He pretended not to notice as Augie helped her into the car, shut the doors, turned the car around, and drove away down the lane. She never even looked around once. Leo felt tears sting his eyes.

"Okay for you," he said aloud, tossing a pebble into the water, and returned his attention to Elsie, who had labored on without letup. In the end he felt compelled to take her; she was probably the last spider he would add to his exhibit before leaving camp. More happy points for Jeremiah: what a joke that was. He fished out a codfish box from his knapsack, pulled back the lid, and, using his pen, flicked the creature inside and slid the top home.

It was not until the following morning, after cabin clean-up, while they waited for inspection, that he remembered "Elsie." The Robert the Bruce spider had passed a supperless night, and it was with some trepidation that Leo now removed her box from the knapsack to have a look. Elsie lay on her back, her eight legs bent and shriveled up. But when Leo gave the inert form a shake, she miraculously revived; her legs straightened, she flopped onto her belly, and began to scramble frantically around her prison.

"Yikes! It's alive!" cried Peewee (having "dropped by" as usual), as the spider crawled up the side of the box. Leo tried to contain her by reinserting the panel into its grooves, but he wasn't fast enough and she escaped, describing an arc through the air to land near Reece's footlocker, where Tiger sat sewing on the button that had popped off his polo shirt during the last ball game.

"Look out—look out!" shouted Peewee, dancing up and down like a dervish. "It's on you! It's on your leg!"

Tiger was frozen in place, staring at the spider clinging to his thigh.

"Don't worry," Leo said. "It's not going to hurt anybody." Slowly he put out his hand to seize the towel hanging at the end of Eddie's bunk, and with a quick pass brushed the spider from Tiger's leg into the box.

"You ought to keep those dumb things out of here," Phil said darkly as Leo slid the top shut.

"Yeah," said Dump. "What if he'd got bit? We've got a game tomorrow, you know."

"It wouldn't matter if he did," Leo said. "The spiders around here aren't poisonous."

"How do you know?" demanded Phil.

"Because there are only two venomous spiders in the whole United States, and neither is indigenous to Connecticut."

"Aw, screw you and your fifty-cent words, Wacko," Phil sneered. "You think you know everything."

"I know which spiders are dangerous and which aren't, and that's a lot more than you seem to know."

"Spiders can bite, even if they're not poisonous," Monkey argued.

"I think it did," Tiger said, with a sheepish laugh. As the others crowded around, he indicated a small red mark visible on the inside of his thigh. Leo got down on his knees and inspected the bite.

"It's nothing to worry about," he said finally. "But just to be on the safe side, maybe you should go let Wanda take a look at it."

"Naw, forget it," Tiger said, without looking at Leo. "I'll just put some stuff on it." He found a half-dollar-size tin of Campho-Phenique and dabbed some on the mark, and let it go at that.

By the next morning, however, the mark had enlarged and turned purple. "*Now* I go see Wanda," Tiger announced, and after breakfast off he went to the infirmary, while the other Jeremians waited at the cabin. A scowling Phil let Leo know just where the boys—and their counselor—stood on matters.

"I hope you're satisfied," Phil said grimly, while Dump and Monkey muttered about "Wacko's spider," making Leo feel worse than he already did. Fortunately, when Tiger came back, the bite washed and dressed with a square gauze pad fastened by adhesive tape, he reported that Wanda's diagnosis was that there was nothing to worry about: he was still good for today's game.

Later, just before powwow Leo came in from the cottage, where he'd been listening to records with Fritz, to find Tiger sitting in his bunk discussing with Phil the results of the game (Red Sox 9, Cards 2; Abernathy slammed three homers, putting Jeremiah in the lead for the Trophy at last). Leo looked at the bandage on Tiger's leg, wanting to say something, but unable to find the right words. In the adjoining bunk the Bomber was thumbing through a dog-eared copy of *National Geographic,* studying a bevy of bare-breasted maidens. Suddenly he sat up.

"Hey, watch it, guys, here comes Heartless," he said, and, stuffing the

253

magazine under his pillow, he hopped out the side of the cabin to hang his wet towel and trunks on the line, while inside Jeremiah, Reece greeted his boys, then sat down on his footlocker and shucked off his tennis shoes. Removing his sweaty socks, he folded them neatly before dropping them into his laundry case. One foot crossed over a knee, he dusted his toes with foot powder before donning fresh socks.

"How's the bite?" he asked Tiger offhandedly.

"Okay," came the reply.

"Let's have a look anyway."

"No, really, it's okay."

"So let me see," Reece insisted.

"It's bandaged," Tiger demurred. "Wanda said not to take it off."

Reece scowled. "Look, Kemo Sabe, I want to check it, okay? So hop down here toot sweet and let's have a look at it."

Knowing better than to argue when Reece's mind was set, Tiger jumped down from his bunk, hitting the floor hard. "It's okay, I'm telling you," he said.

"Good," Reece declared. "But I still want to make sure. Jeremiah may be ahead on points, but we've got to stay that way if we're going to cop that Trophy." He drew Tiger to him and, using his fingernails, he lifted away the adhesive strips so the gauze pad hung down like a miniature trapdoor. Leaning closer, he whistled softly.

"Whoa, now, fellah, this doesn't look so good." What had been a small red mark had now developed an angry-looking whitehead of pus at its center.

"Jeez, I thought you said it was clearing up," Phil said.

"It doesn't hurt," Tiger returned stolidly.

Reece got up and rummaged around in his footlocker. "If it's come to a head, that just means it needs lancing, to get the pus out."

"That's okay, I'd rather have Wanda do it," Tiger protested, trying to tape the pad back in position.

"Sure, sure, I know; but she's not here." It was true: Fritz and Wanda had driven into Putnam to see a movie show. Reece brought out his canvas sewing kit and unrolled it, slipped a needle from among several others, then meticulously rerolled the kit. He took the needle, produced a matchbook and, using his last match, passed the tip through the flame. He laid aside the burnt match and empty book, blew on the needle to cool it, then began to probe the head of the pustule.

Tiger squirmed. "Ouch, that hurts."

"Come on, hold still, can't you? Stop fidgeting."

"I just wish you'd quit," Tiger said.

"It's got to be done, camper, if you'd just—goldarn it!" he exclaimed, as the needle escaped his fingers. He retrieved it quickly and, steadying his hand, broke the skin of the pustule, releasing the fluid. "There—see, all done!" He pulled a tissue from the Kleenex packet on his shelf and blotted up the leakage, then deftly restored Wanda's gauze pad with its adhesive strips as the other Jeremians burst into the cabin.

By all rights this impromptu job of surgery should have done the trick; unfortunately, it did not. Next day, when Tiger reported to the infirmary to have the dressing changed, there was a degree of increased inflammation that caused Wanda to wonder, but she washed the infection thoroughly, dressed it, and applied a fresh bandage.

"Better lay off the swimming for a day or two," she advised. "And check back with me this afternoon."

Though Tiger did his share of grousing, he heeded Wanda's advice and stayed out of the water, morning and afternoon. But by the following morning he was limping, and, he announced, his leg had begun to throb. The boys watched as he peeled down the tapes and dropped the gauze pad. Overnight the inflamed area had enlarged to the size of a quarter, and there were scarlet lines extending above and below the infected area. Again Tiger headed for the infirmary.

"What does it mean?" he asked Wanda, who put on her glasses for a closer examination.

"It means I think we'll consult the doc." Unfortunately, this did not mean Doc Oliphant, who night before last had turned the dispensary keys over to Wanda and driven to Hartford, thence to New York, for a medical conference. In the event of an emergency, she was instructed to seek out old Dr. Malcolm over at Woking Corners, and this she now proceeded to do, using the office telephone. The doctor obligingly drove over and examined Tiger's leg, pronouncing him a fine fellow but allowing as how they might do well to keep him in the infirmary a day or so, until the "local low-grade infection" was cleared up. To "take the strain off," a Rube Goldberg harness was rigged up with ropes and pulleys and a window-sash weight that kept the patient's leg hoisted into the air, and a prescription was written for the new sulfanilamide drug.

All afternoon Wanda's latest charge garnered numbers of visitors who sat jawing with him and joking about his "torture-chamber rig." Not only did the Jeremians come trooping into the room with Reece at their head, but other campers from up and down the linepath paid duty visits, including Peewee, whose rambunctiousness became so annoying that Wanda banished him from indoors and he had to resort to standing on a box with his head inside the sickroom window. Even Pa took time out from his birding to pass by for an encouraging word, while Hank Ives delivered Ma and Willa-Sue by jitney for a get-together. (Ma had baked brownies for general consumption, which she brought packed in a candy box.)

Only Leo stayed away, watching the procession to and from the infirmary with a heavy heart. Already he was being blamed for Tiger's predicament, and though he was sure the spider's bite had not been poisonous, there was no doubt that it was Leo who had put Friend-Indeed's star camper in a position to be bitten in the first place. His anguish over this fact was compounded by his quarrel with Tiger. With each day that had passed since their foolish argument Leo had looked for a way to make it up with his friend, to have things as they had been before, had tried and had failed. But now . . . now he must get in to see Tiger and explain, apologize, he *must.* Around and around his thoughts went and still there was no resolution. Then, during powwow that evening, as the conversation turned to the upcoming glee-club concert, the answer came to him, and after supper he took his violin and crept up to the sickroom window, where he settled himself against the wall and began playing, listening for some reaction from inside. It came almost on cue, the mirthful sputter that said Tiger was getting it. Leo beamed. Nurse Koslowski, however, didn't find it so amusing. Leo had just reached the release when her reproachful features appeared in the window.

"Okay, wise-apple, what's the big idea?" she demanded, poking her head out at him. "You think this is an amusement park or something?"

Leo grinned and shrugged. "I was just playing."

"What kind of song is that, anyway?"

" 'The Music Goes 'Round and Around.' Tiger likes it."

"If he does, he's the only one. Now suppose you just put that harp away for a while and get your baganza inside here."

"How's he doing?" asked Leo as he came around the porch and up the steps.

"He'll live. Go ahead in, he'll be glad to see you."

Behind the screen that helped close off the doorway to the sickroom, Tiger lay in his white hospital bed, his leg hiked as if from a skiing accident.

"Hi," Leo said.

"Hi yourself."

"How're you doing?"

"Okay. How about you?"

"Me? I'm fine."

"Well, don't just stand there, come on in."

Leo sat in the chair, maintaining a discreet distance.

"What brings you down this way?" Tiger asked.

"I was—that is—I wanted to see how you were coming along. If it weren't for my spider you wouldn't be here."

"Don't give it a thought. It's not your fault. I'm glad to see you."

"You are?"

"Yup. Real glad. We're some pair, you and me. Acting like two dumb-bells."

Leo dropped his gaze. "You were right. I've been acting like a jerk. And I'm sorry I called you that name."

"I don't think I'll die because of it. Let's just forget it ever happened." Tiger held out his hand. "Shake?"

Leo held out his. "Shake."

"Your playing was really neat," Tiger went on.

"Glad you liked it."

"How's Harpo? I miss him."

"He's okay—he misses you, too. He's really been dogging it since you haven't been around."

Tiger laughed at Leo's pun. "Listen," he said, lowering his voice. "I was wondering. Do you think you could bring him down here so I could see him?"

Leo lowered his voice too. "Would Wanda let you have a dog in here? He's liable to have germs and stuff."

"Maybe you could fix it for when she's not around."

"I heard that, Tiger Abernathy!"

A stern-faced Nurse Koslowski stood in the doorway. " 'When she's not around,' what? What plots are you two brigands hatching?"

"He wants to see Harpo," Leo explained.

"Oh no you don't, not that flea-bitten hound; not in *my* infirmary. Is that completely understood?"

"Yes, m'am," replied Leo.

"Aw, Wanda—"

"Never mind the 'Aw, Wanda's,' Abernathy. Just remember. And for your information, Leo, visiting hours are just about *fini*'d, so suppose you trot on out of here while our boy gets some sleep."

Leo adjusted his position, then glanced up at her. "I was wondering— could we read a little?"

"Reading, huh? Okay, go ahead. I'll sneak a smoke on the porch. But keep it down in here, or I'll have to toss you out on your baganza." Her uniform rattled as she turned down the radio, then left the room, her rubber soles squeaking on the painted floor.

Leo pulled his chair closer to the bed and took out several books from his knapsack. Tiger's choice was "Horatius at the Bridge," and so Leo began with the tale of "The Captain of the Gate," set with two stalwart companions to defend the bridge to Rome until the span could be destroyed and the city made safe. He read the hero's credo:

"To every man upon this earth
Death cometh soon or late.
And how can man die better
Than facing fearful odds,
For the ashes of his fathers,
And the temples of his Gods . . ."

And he read how, in those days,

. . . none was for a party;
Then all were for the state;
Then the great man helped the poor,
And the poor man loved the great:
Then lands were fairly portioned;
Then spoils were fairly sold:
The Romans were like brothers
In the brave days of old.

He read until a figure in white appeared in the doorway. Finger to her lips, Wanda signaled Leo to leave.

"Don't stop," Tiger murmured. "I'm not asleep."

"If you're not, you're giving a darned good imitation of it," the nurse replied. "Doctor wants you to rest."

"But I want to hear the end."

"Next time. Pretend it's a cliffhanger. Like Pearl White and that stuff."

"Tomorrow?" Tiger asked.

Wanda blew out her cheeks. "I suppose—only no dogs, got it?"

"In the infirmary, right?"

"In the infirmary, right."

"Okay, kiddo."

Leo went away whistling "The Monkey Wrapped His Tail Around the Flagpole."

Next day, when Leo looked in at the infirmary window, he found the patient entertaining a pair of visitors whose presence both surprised and pleased him. Seated on chairs brought in from the other rooms were Honey Oliphant, returned at last to Moonbow late the night before, and her Cape Cod friend, Sally Berwick. Also attending the invalid were the Bomber and Emerson Bean, along with Dusty Rhoades and Junior Leffingwell. The Bomber had just got off one of his corny jokes and everyone groaned when an alert-looking, hairy head appeared in the open window.

"Harpo!" Tiger exclaimed with pleasure, stretching out welcoming arms.

"Good evening, Mr. Abernathy," said Harpo, wagging his shaggy head. He spoke in a deep, solemn voice, and sported a bow tie along with the famous Eddie Foy derby. "I don't believe I've met the dark-haired young lady," Harpo declared, his pink tongue hanging out moistly from under his whiskers. "Is she a new girl in town?" Sally, as dark as Honey was fair, giggled.

"Please be so kind as to introduce us," Harpo went on, and managed cleverly to doff his headgear.

Getting into the spirit of the thing, Tiger performed the social amenities from his bed. "Sally, this is Harpo the Talking Dog. He can perform twenty

259

tricks in twenty minutes, or ten tricks in ten, take your pick. Harpo, shake hands with Sally."

"Hullo, Sal," said the dog and shook hands in a friendly way. "How's tricks? Say, is she in the movies?" he asked Tiger.

"No, she is *not* in the movies," Honey replied.

"Would she like to be? I know a guy in Hollywood."

The girls giggled.

"And I see the Belle of Moonbow Lake has returned to grace our shores once again," the dog went on suavely. "I would like to say on behalf of all the other dogs in the neighborhood that we are very pleased to see her again. We've been leading a dog's life since she's been gone."

Honey laughed outright. "Why, *thank* you, Harpo. You're *so* complimentary. Especially for a dog."

"Oh, we dogs know our onions, girls," Harpo returned, and laughed. "Being nearer to the ground, we can spot a well-turned ankle with the best of them."

"Oh, Harpo, you're making her blush!" exclaimed Sally as Honey clapped a palm to each cheek.

"If so, it is the blush the sun provides the peach," replied the dog majestically. Then, so intriguing did the hairy visitor find the gathering inside that he clambered over the sill and bounded into the room. In two more bounds he was up on the bed, keening with pleasure and joyfully licking Tiger's face.

"Harpo, you get right down from there this minute!" Honey jumped up and clapped her hands; in another moment Leo followed Harpo in over the sill, hurried to the bed, seized the dog around its middle, and hauled it bodily from the covers. With the animal's jumbo-sized head blocking his view, its four paws sticking straight out, its animated tail swinging like a clock pendulum, Leo energetically wrestled it toward the doorway—where something impeded further progress.

"I thought we said no dogs in here!" came Wanda's stern voice as, pushing him backward, she marched into the room and confronted the gathering. "Isn't that what we said, boys and girls?"

"Yes—only—" Blindly Leo engineered an awkward circle, trying to get his bearings.

"Only nothing!" Wanda retorted with mock fierceness. "*Out!* O-u-t, *out!* All dogs, all boys with dogs. Now. This minute. This very instant, Leo Joaquim, or you'll rue the day, I promise."

So the hairy object of Tiger's affection was banished from the premises—not far, however: Harpo took up a position outside the window, tongue still hanging a-pant, earnestly cocking his head, the model of canine rectitude. Meanwhile, Wanda cleared out her place of work, dispatching Tiger's visitors to their respective cabins, Honey and her friend Sally back to Three Corner Cove.

The two girls were on the path when Honey, having spotted Leo on the point, waited for him to catch up, while Sally went on ahead to the cottage.

"Well, Leo," Honey began as he came up to her, "how are things?"

"Okay."

"Just 'okay'?"

"Well, sort of—only—"

"Only what?"

Leo blushed, stumbling for words.

Pretending not to notice, Honey put her hand in her pocket. "Would you like to see some of my snapshots from the Cape?" Without waiting for a reply she took them out and one by one handed them over: the bridge at the Cape Cod Canal (Honey arm-in-arm with Sally Berwick); several shots of the beach (Honey in her yellow bathing suit building a sand castle; Honey with a lifeguard); the lighthouse at Nauset Heights (Honey on her bicycle) . . .

The exhibition got no farther. Suddenly the screen door at the cottage flew open and Peewee came racing across the porch and down the steps, an orange Popsicle melting in his fist.

"Peewee—here's Leo," his sister called. "Come say hello."

The boy shot Leo a fierce scowl. "I can't talk to him, he's a spud," he said, and ran on toward camp.

"Gosh, what's been going on around here while I've been gone?" Honey asked. "Why are you and Peewee on the outs? You used to be such good pals."

Leo ran his tongue around inside his mouth. "It's nothing. Peewee's just—" He shrugged.

Honey laughed. "Young; I know. Master Harrison has a lot of growing up to do, I'm afraid."

"Is that Peewee's name? 'Harrison'?"

"Yes. Isn't it ridiculous?" Her expression sobered. "I was real sorry to hear about what happened to your model village. After all your hard work.

261

I know how disappointed you must be. However could such a thing have happened?"

Leo didn't see any point in hashing the matter over again, so he let it go at the "frayed-rope" story, though he wasn't sure Honey bought it, any more than he did.

"Honestly, I don't know what this place is coming to," Honey said. "Everyone always has such a good time, really. But this summer—well, it's almost over. Doesn't seem possible, does it? Labor Day'll be here before we know it."

Sally's round, jolly face appeared at the sink window, where she was pumping water (she was making lemonade). Honey drew Leo aside for a more personal word.

"I've been telling Sal about your music," Honey confided. "I said you were just about the best violin player I'd ever heard."

"You did?"

"I certainly did. I can't wait till you're famous and I can tell my children I knew you when."

"I've been wanting to thank you," Leo said shyly.

"For what?"

"For the postal card."

"Oh, that. I wondered if you ever got it. I love sending postcards. I send them to all my friends. Some collect them."

Leo was deflated by this news. *Others* got cards, too.

"Will you keep yours?" she asked. He nodded, eyes cast down to his toes.

"Good. And sometime, when *you* go somewhere, I want you to be sure and send *me* one. For *my* collection. Okay?"

"Okay," he murmured.

The quietness was suddenly rent by a shrill blast on a whistle. "Oh, gee, I think you're being paged—"

Leo looked up to see Reece standing on the infirmary porch with his whistle.

"All right, camper, let's hop it," he called through cupped hands.

Honey gave Leo's hand a brief, encouraging squeeze. "You'd better go." She ducked inside; Leo had no choice but to return the way he'd come.

Reece was waiting at the head of the path, a disapproving frown on his face. "What were you doing over there?"

262

"Talking."

"About what?"

"Just—talking, that's all."

"About me, I bet. Weren't you?"

"No. We weren't. It was something else."

Using the palm of his hand, Reece propelled Leo along the path in front of him.

"Where've you been all afternoon?"

"I was with Tiger."

"You keep away from the infirmary. I don't want you going there. Tiger's not feeling well, he doesn't need spuds like you bothering him."

"I wasn't bothering him. He said he was glad I came."

"He's just being nice. That's the way Tiger is."

"We're friends. I'm going to visit his house this fall. He's going to have me stay overnight."

Reece gave him a look of disgust. "You're nuts if you believe that. The only reason he bothered with you was that Ma told him to. If she hadn't—"

"We wouldn't be friends, you mean?"

"I mean you're not up to his standard. It takes a special kind of guy to be friends with Tiger Abernathy."

They had reached a fork in the path; Leo started off toward the infirmary, only to have Reece hold him back.

"I told you, Wackeem, I want you to keep away from there."

Reece wheeled and went loping along the path to the Oliphant cottage, where the girls were sunning themselves on the dock.

5

riday morning the talk was all over camp: Tiger Abernathy was being sent home. For once, Hank Ives wasn't first with the bulletin: Leo had already heard it from Ma. She was waiting for him as he passed her office on his way to breakfast. Wanda had telephoned Lake Winnipesaukee and spoken directly with Pat Abernathy. He and Tiger's mother were cutting short their stay and driving down as soon as they could pack up and get started.

Leo had listened to the news with two minds. He realized that whatever it took to make Tiger well again must be done, but even though, thanks to Reece's edict, he hadn't seen his friend for two days, the prospect of his leaving camp for good was a daunting one. With Tiger gone Leo would have only the Bomber (who had taken his cue from Tiger where Leo was concerned) to depend on.

When the Bomber came up from the lake after swim, the two boys wandered off to the woods for a private confab.

"I have to see him," Leo declared. "I have to tell him something. Something important."

"Whyn'tcha tell me and I kin relay the message to him," the Bomber suggested.

"No!" he blurted. The Bomber's offer was well meant, but not one Leo could accept. What he had to say was for Tiger's ears alone.

The Bomber sensibly suggested Leo wait until after dinner that evening to get to the infirmary. Tonight was Counselors' Night at the lodge; Hap

Holliday was putting on a locker-room skit, featuring Reece in the role of the "Little Bambino," Babe Ruth. With the counselor thus occupied, Leo would have his chance.

It was getting dark when Leo, on KP, finished drying and putting away the last stack of chinaware, and once dismissed he ran all the way down to camp. Skirting the lodge, where the evening's program was already in progress, he made his way into the sickroom by vaulting in over the sill. Tiger was listening to the radio. A fine sheen of perspiration gleamed on his brow, and his cheeks looked unnaturally flushed.

"Hi," Leo said.

"Hi. Come on in. Where've you been?"

"Reece told me to keep away. He doesn't like it that we made it up between us."

"Tough stuff, I'd say. He'll just have to get over it."

Leo was grateful for the vote of confidence. He tiptoed to the bedside and sat in the chair.

"How're you feeling?"

"I feel okay, I guess. Sort of. I've been having weird dreams, though."

"What kind of weird?"

"Well, just—you know—weird. Sort of like nightmares. Everything's screwy. You know what that's like."

Did he ever.

"Have you heard?" Tiger went on. "I'm leaving."

"Ma told me."

"I don't want to," Tiger said glumly. He adjusted his position and his eyes swerved about the room as if reluctant to light anywhere.

"Will we still see each other?" Leo asked. "Like we said?"

"You mean when camp's over? Sure we will," Tiger said expansively. "Leave it to me."

"Reece said—"

"Said what?"

"That you were just pretending. About inviting me to visit. He said you didn't mean it."

"Sure, I meant it, otherwise I wouldn't have asked you."

"He said you've been acting friendly just because Ma said to."

"It's true, Ma did ask me to show you the ropes, me and the Bomber. But she never *made* me. I had you pegged right from the start."

"Pegged as what?"

265

"Well, as—as different, see? But good different. Something we didn't have too many of around here. Remember 'Icarus'?"

"I guess you thought that was nervy of me, naming your owl."

"Not my owl. He was yours, right from the start. I told Bomber later, I said you were going to be a very interesting member of Jeremiah, very unusual. And you were. Are. So don't pay any attention to what Reece—or anybody else—says. We're friends now and we'll go on being friends. When you come to our house, I'll have my mom bake you her special lemon pie—"

"Great."

"And my dad has a friend who's a barnstormer. Maybe dad'll get him to take us up for a spin. Is it a deal?"

"A deal."

Solemnly they shook hands. Tiger lay back, fatigued. "Something else on your mind?" he asked, as Leo started to speak, then stopped.

"I was thinking . . ." Leo began again.

"What?"

"There's something—you ought to know before you leave. I wanted to tell you before now, only . . . only . . ." He groped for words that wouldn't come.

Tiger roused himself sufficiently to be attentive. "That's okay. Whatever it is, just spit it out. That's the best way."

Now that he'd initiated the conversation, Leo was having serious doubts about going through with it. "You'll probably get mad at me," he muttered.

"Try me."

Leo leaned close to Tiger's pillow and lowered his voice; he couldn't take a chance on anyone's overhearing. "I've been keeping something from you. And if we're going to go on being friends, it's something you should know about. Only, after I've told you, maybe you won't want to be friends anymore. It has to do with something that happened a long time ago, except—well, it's still going on, in a way. I mean it's still—"

He broke off.

Tiger studied him. "Does it have something to do with when you were in the asylum?" he asked.

Leo shot him a grateful look. "You remember that time at Dagmar's? When I—when I—well, ran out of the room? During the storm?"

Tiger nodded.

"That's when I remembered." Leo stopped, then went on, confessing the truth of what had happened that stormy night in the house on Gallop Street, getting it all out at last. Tiger listened with the thoughtful, earnest expression Leo had come to know so well.

"And Rudy's still alive, isn't he?" Tiger ventured.

Leo was taken aback. "How did you know?"

"I just figured. He's doing time in the pen, isn't he?"

Leo confessed that this was so.

"And that's why you get those bad dreams," Tiger went on. "Cripes, that's enough to give anybody nightmares. I'd be screwy myself." He produced a wan smile. " 'Ya done good in spite of it, camper,' " he said.

This affirmation made Leo feel better; his spirits were further cheered when he was instructed to open the table drawer: in it lay Tiger's Bowie knife in its leather sheath.

"I want you to have it. To remember me when you go back to Pitt."

"I can't do that. It's yours, you won it."

"I'm leaving, remember? I won't need it. But you might."

Leo shrugged. "I don't think I'll stay, after you're gone."

"Why not? Listen, I know the guys've pulled some lousy tricks on you, but you don't want to let that stuff get you. Don't give in to them."

Leo shook his head stubbornly. "I don't want to stay without you."

"That's crazy! It's just what they want you to do—quit. You don't want them thinking they licked you, do you? That you're another Stanley?"

"Do you think I am?"

" 'Course not. And you're no quitter, either. 'Never Say Die'—remember the Count?"

Leo was in no mood for talk about the count. "They're saying it's my fault you're sick. The Mingoes—"

Tiger was scornful. "Forget the Mingoes, they're all full of you-know-what." He gestured toward the knife. "Now take it, will you? I want you to."

Following the command, Leo took the knife, undid his belt, and slid it through the slits in the sheath. He thought about what Kretch would say when he showed it off; how Measles and all his loudmouth bunch would carry on. Tiger's gift was a token of friendship and esteem, honor, even, things guys like Measles didn't know—or care—anything about.

They fell silent for a time. Leo's eye wandered to the night table, where Tiger's medicine bag lay, beaded and feathered, guarding its tantalizing secret. He still yearned to know what it contained, what made those provocative little bumps in the bag. From the Oliphants' dock came the strains of music from Honey's Victrola. Then, "Finish the poem, why don't you?" Tiger said, opening his eyes. "I don't want to go to sleep this time without knowing how it ends."

Leo was agreeable. Opening Fritz's book, he picked up where he'd left off three days before, with the Etruscan forces making a bid to cross the Tiber bridge.

> Four hundred trumpets sounded
>   A peal of warlike glee,
> As that great host, with measured tread,
> And spears advanced, and ensigns spread,
> Rolled slowly towards the bridge's head,
>   Where stood the dauntless Three.

"The dauntless Three." Leo glanced over to the bed to see if Tiger had heard, but his eyes were on the ceiling. Leo went on:

> Alone stood brave Horatius,
>   But constant still in mind;
> Thrice thirty thousand foes before,
>   And the broad flood behind.
> "Down with him!" cried false Sextus,
>   With a smile on his pale face.
> "Now yield thee," cried Lars Porsena,
>   "Now yield thee to our grace."

But the stubborn Horatius would never yield; he fought on until the bridge went down, and Rome was saved. For his valor he was awarded public lands to till, and a bronze statue was erected in his honor.

> It stands in the Comitium,
>   Plain for all folk to see;
> Horatius in his harness,
>   Halting upon one knee:
> And underneath is written,

268

In letters all of gold,
How valiantly he kept the bridge
In the brave days of old.

When Leo looked up he saw that Tiger's eyes were shut, his cheek lay upon the pillow. Leo watched him a moment longer, then reached over to switch off the bedside lamp. Unwilled, his fingers went instead to the Seneca bag, lying in a pool of light. He picked it up and held it by its string. The chamois sack twisted slowly in the lamplight, not heavy, but somehow weighted by the mystery of its contents.

He hefted it, then let it drop into his cupped palm. What power did it contain? Just touching the bag made his hand tremble. Gingerly he kneaded its contents between his fingertips. What was it? Something small, hard, round. He inserted two digits into the neck of the bag, loosened it, and felt inside. Three small objects, round, sort of, about the size of raisins. Nuts? Beans? Checking to make sure Tiger's eyes remained shut, he spilled the objects into his palm: three pebbles, that was all, just three ordinary pebbles, one black, one white, one red. It didn't make sense. Why were three common pebbles of such significance? He was about to return them to the bag when one of them slipped through his fingers and bounced on the floor. He bent quickly and picked it up. When he straightened, Tiger's eyes were on him. Leo turned scarlet with guilt.

"I—I—"

Tiger reached over and took the pebble, dropped it into the bag and closed the neck. "It's okay, don't worry," he said.

"I only wanted to—to—"

"To know. It's natural, I guess." Tiger opened the bag again and spilled out the pebbles, then picked up the black stone and held it to the light.

"This stone is for the earth, who is the mother of us all, who births us and feeds us and protects us all our lives. And this"—holding up the red one—"is the blood of the Senecas, who are blood brothers, bound together in friendship and loyalty through all our lives. And this"—the white stone—"is for purity of soul. The shining spirit of the Great Manitou who awaits his sons in the Happy Hunting Grounds."

He closed his fist around the pebbles and clenched them tightly so his knuckles turned white. Then he spilled them back into their bag, pulled the drawstring, and set the bag back on the night table.

"Thanks for the poem," he said, leaning back on the pillow. "It's a good one. 'Specially the ending."

Through the trees came the light notes of Wiggy Pugh's cornet as he blew retreat. Leo knew he should be getting back to camp; he'd have a tough enough job explaining to Reece why he'd missed Counselors' Night; there'd be docked desserts to pay for that crime. And for the hundredth time a vision of Stanley Wagner crept into his mind, that shadow that had a habit of reappearing at the moment Leo least expected it.

Such thoughts failed to force him from the sickroom, however. Tiger had shut his eyes again; there were drops of perspiration on his brow; it felt hot to Leo's touch. Then he stirred in the bed and spoke a few words, which Leo failed to catch.

"What?" he asked.

Tiger mumbled again, but again the sense was lost.

From across the way at Three Corner Cove came the soft strains of dance music:

> You go to my head
> With a smile that makes my temp'rature rise,
> Like a summer with a thousand Julys,
> You intoxicate my soul with your eyes.

There was a curious thing about music heard across water, an indefinable something that altered the tonal qualities of the notes, not subtracting but adding to their sum, rounding and hollowing them, making them both remote and somehow more intimate, like the warming gleam of a familiar but faraway star. And in years to come, whenever he might hear that song, no matter where he was or what he was doing, for Leo Joaquim it would always be the summer of '38, his Moonbow summer.

☾

Beyond the partition, Wanda lay on the day bed, listening to the soft burr of the boys' voices. She glanced at her alarm clock. Eleven. It was late. She tried to picture the Abernathys in their car, rushing through the night to their son's bedside. No need, of course, no *real* need, she told herself. But as well they were coming, just in case. She must go in and shoo Leo out. Hearing a sound, she sat up: a dark shape slipped through the open doorway. Wanda smiled to herself as she listened to the nails clicking on the floorboards. Well, who cared, really? A dog wasn't going to hurt anything. She could hear the music from over at the Oliphants'. She lay thinking in the dark, then felt her eyelids drooping. . . .

She hadn't slept. She was certain of it. Yet, when she looked at the clock again, its phosphorescent hands told her it was ten minutes past midnight. She got up quickly and tiptoed from the room. In the adjoining one Tiger lay on the bed with his eyes shut, his free leg angled and sticking out from beneath the sheet. In the chair Leo slumped, head canted to one side, his mouth partly open, hands loosely folded in his lap. Between the chair and the bed lay Harpo, who raised a sleepy head to regard her with inquisitive eyes, then dropped his muzzle to the floor again.

Wanda felt Tiger's forehead; it was moist and warm—too warm. Still, if he was resting she didn't want to disturb him; there was no telling if he'd get back to sleep again. She checked her watch. She estimated the Abernathys would arrive some time after breakfast, certainly not before. A hundred and fifty miles was a good distance to travel.

She went back into the other room, lit a cigarette, and sat smoking as she looked out into the darkness.

Hours later, in the sickroom, Leo came awake in his chair. It was Harpo who'd roused him. The dog was sitting close to the bed, rubbing the crown of his head against the bedrails, whimpering, and Leo got up and went to calm him. Absently he stroked the animal and stared down at Tiger's head on the pillow. His cheeks had lost their bright color, and when Leo touched his friend's forehead it felt cool. He got his chair and sat close to the bed, wishing Tiger would open his eyes so they could talk some more. After a while Harpo sat up, then clambered awkwardly into Leo's lap, where he sat licking his face, looking from him to Tiger in the bed. The animal felt hot and heavy and Leo wanted to put him down; but he didn't. Under his thick curly coat the dog was trembling. Probably he should be put out; Wanda would be annoyed if she awoke and found she'd been disobeyed.

Through the window he could see familiar shapes as the dawn began to break. The lake surface was already glinting in the early-morning light. A fine mist curled along the edges of Three Corner Cove. On the washline three sets of female bathing attire hung: Maryann's, Honey's, and Sally Berwick's. Doc's Chris-Craft rode at easy anchor, calm and motionless.

Leo tensed as from the bed came the sound of Tiger's voice.

271

"Ha . . . al . . . yee hepp . . . ridge," Leo heard. Was it fever talk? Tiger's eyes were open and he stared up at Leo but didn't seem to recognize him.

"What? What did you say?" Leo asked.

Tiger turned his head restlessly on the pillow.

"How al—keh . . . uh . . ."

Leo frowned slightly. Then it came to him. "How valiantly he kept the bridge," he said. Tiger moved his hand on the coverlet, smiled, and shut his eyes again. He looked peaceful. Leo felt exhausted but not sleepy. Harpo had become too heavy. Leo put him down, then got up and stretched a couple of times.

"Come on, Harp," Leo whispered, but the dog, now lying near the foot of the bed, made no move. Leo paused a moment longer, then backed away and left the room. Through the dispensary doorway he could see Wanda stretched out on the cot. She moved, then sat up, rubbing her eyes.

"Is he going to be okay?" Leo asked.

Swinging her feet to the floor and kneading her back, Wanda drilled him with a look. "Of course he's going to be okay." She took her thermometer, shook it down, and went in to look at the patient, while Leo wandered out onto the porch. His backside ached. The camp was already stirring. Over at the Oliphants', Maryann appeared on the porch. She was wearing an Indian-pattern bathrobe, carrying a coffee mug and a lighted cigarette. Leo returned her wave, wondering why nobody ever saw her in curlers like other women.

Just then Harpo forged his way through the open doorway, bursting from the place like the hound of hell itself, bounding down the porch steps and racing off along the path, past Three Corner Cove to disappear into the woods. A moment later an unearthly howl arose that raised the hair on the nape of Leo's neck.

"Gosh, what's wrong with that poor creature?" Maryann called over. No one answered. On the infirmary porch Leo was backed against the railing so hard a spur hurt his leg. Heedless of the discomfort, he was staring at Wanda, who stood motionless in the doorway. Her brimming eyes sparkled in the morning light. But people like Wanda didn't cry, they helped others dry their tears. In a husky voice she told him she was going over to use the Oliphants' telephone. Gripping the porch post, Leo followed her with his eyes as she went down the steps and along the path; then he walked back inside.

In the sickroom the shades were pulled down to the sill. The bedsheet was drawn up over the pillow. He could make out the general shape of Tiger's head underneath. He did not go inside the room. His knees seemed about to fold on him, and he sat down suddenly in Wanda's chair. He tried to think, but his thoughts floated out of reach like ghostly things, as if what was happening wasn't *really* happening, was just part of a dream, another bad dream he'd had. Yes, that was it, he was still asleep, he hadn't woken at all, and he was still dreaming. In a moment he would wake up and everything would be okay—it would, wouldn't it? If only—

He heard the sound of an auto engine. Through the opposite window he saw a car pull into view. It came to a stop on the grassy spot beside the infirmary and the Abernathys got out. They came up the steps and into the room. "Hello, Leo," they said. "How is our boy?"

Leo didn't know what to say. He ducked his head and didn't look up again until they'd gone into the other room. He went onto the porch again. Over at Three Corner Cove, Wanda came out of the cottage with Maryann. Honey was with them. She had a handkerchief to her eyes. When she looked over and saw Leo she turned away, her shoulders shaking. Leo wanted to go and comfort her but didn't know how to do that. Maryann and Wanda embraced; then Wanda came back along the path. Leo began to tremble. His eyes were blurring. As Wanda came up the steps, he turned and clambered over the railing to sprawl in the nasturtiums growing along the foundations. He scrambled up and without looking back raced along the path, passing the Oliphants' cottage head down, to disappear into the same woods where Harpo was still howling.

Later Leo asked himself: how had the dog known when he himself had not?

6

Rock of ages,
Cleft for meeeeee,
Let me hide
Myself in thee-eeeee . . .

hey were in the grove, all of them singing out the rousing old
Protestant hymn whose words affirmed the help that cometh
when a man's faith abides in the Lord God of Hosts. Leo, however, could not take heart. Sitting in his rowboat, lost in thought,
he doggedly kept his back to the somber gathering in the council ring, where
every seat was filled and where the Reverend G. Garland Starbuck had for
a half hour past been haranguing the assembled in his best William Jennings
Bryan style. In truth, Leo had not wanted to admit to the fact of what lay
atop Tabernacle Rock: the black box, covered with flowers; had not wanted
to hear about "the young sapling alas too young cut down," about "that
peaceful lamb taken unto the Holy Shepherd's loving flock," who now "slept
in the soft sweet bosom of Eternity and a Life Everlasting."

The mere idea made Leo want to laugh. Far better to give Tiger a
Viking's funeral, the way Michael and his brothers had done in *Beau Geste:*
set the coffin on fire and launch it out to sea in flames. Tiger would have
loved a send-off like that! A burning vessel, the dead surrounded by battle
shields and horned helmets, and a dead dog lying at his feet.

From where he sat Leo could make out certain figures in the congregation: the Abernathys were seated down front, along with Dr. Dunbar and a number of the Society of Joshua elders. Wanda Koslowski was there too, and beside her Fritz, and a clutch of females he recognized as Ma Starbuck and Willa-Sue, Dagmar Kronborg, and Honey with her mother and Sally Berwick; on the log where the Jeremians were gathered could be seen the crop of blond curly hair belonging to Reece Hartsig.

At last the singing ended. Quickly, before the service could be brought to its pious conclusion, Leo took his violin from its case and began to play. Slowly, lugubriously, the notes rose from his strings and bow to float across the water to the council ring, where Pa and his congregation, recognizing the burlesque, were stunned to silence. Indignant heads craned toward the water to view the solitary and defiant camper out in the middle of the lake, and as the tune's title was whispered among the subdued rows of campers they asked themselves who but Wacko Wackeem would have chosen to play a dumb ditty like "The Music Goes 'Round and Around" at such a time.

Pa was already enjoining his boys to raise their voices in an impromptu rendition of "Washed in the Blood of the Lamb," which resulted in a sort of musical duel, with all contestants—the multitude in the grove and the party of one in the rowboat—doing their utmost to be heard. Then, as the onshore chorus swelled mightily, Leo switched tunes and tossed "Pop! Goes the Weasel" back in their teeth. The louder they sang, the louder he played, as though his solo rendition could drown out the choir of voices mounted against him. Louder grew the clamor, more jarring the contrapuntal notes, the jazzy, syncopated beat vibrating against the stolid, declarative phrases of the hymn. There would be the usual reprimands for his mischief-making, of course—that was to be expected—but Leo didn't care. This was what Tiger would have wanted. Tiger would have understood; Tiger, who lay in the box on top of Tabernacle Rock.

If only Leo could share his grief with someone, as Harpo did. Ever since Tiger's death the dog had roamed the camp road up and down, baying his sorrow. This morning he had been locked in the old cold cellar under the crafts barn (where Ma stored her jams and preserves in an ancient icebox of yellow oak lined in zinc) so as to keep him from creating a disturbance during the service. But he must have escaped, for now he had taken up a picket post somewhere in the woods and was howling his fool head off. Leo had a pretty good idea of how lonely Harpo must feel.

He looked down at the knife: the Bowie knife Tiger had insisted be his. Since Tiger's death he had kept the knife hidden from sight; he wasn't going to let anyone rob him of Tiger's parting gift. But today, he had decided, he had to wear it no matter what. Just as he'd had to play Tiger's favorite song. . . .

Finally the singing stopped and the last bars of Leo's music hung in the torpid air, then melted into silence, leaving only their mocking memory. By now the gathering was breaking up, the council ring emptying, and Leo, laying away his instrument, noticed someone standing on the canoe dock; the thick, burly figure of the Bomber stood waving him in. He must go in, mustn't he? Go in and face what awaited him? For with Tiger's death he had become more than ever the camp pariah. Though no official decree of Scarsdale had been issued regarding him, hardly anyone was speaking to him. Every look, every pointing finger and whispered word said it was his fault, that he, Leo, was to blame. If it had not been for Wacko there would have been no service, no coffin, no dead friend. As for Reece, having forbidden Leo to visit the infirmary, and then learning that he'd been at Tiger's bedside when he died, he was more vindictive than ever, determined to extract the last ounce of punishment.

Feeling imperiled on every side, Leo was wishing he had never come to camp. How was it possible for him to feel like this, when only a few short weeks ago he'd been so happy, when everything had seemed so fine? It was as though he'd been drinking water from a well, good, sweet, clear water, and now that water had been muddied and riled, it tasted bitter, as if the well had been poisoned.

He packed up his violin and headed for shore, paddling with neat, controlled strokes, the way Tiger had taught him. Off in the distance Harpo's howling had ceased. As he neared the dock, the Bomber gave him a look.

"What the heck was that you was playin'?"

"Beethoven's Fifth. Like it?"

"Somebody's plenty burned about it," the Bomber said.

Leo had no difficulty guessing who "somebody" was. With Leo at the bow, while the Bomber bent his broad back to the stern, the two boys jerked the canoe from the water and racked it up. The Bomber went to the clipboard to sign it in, and Leo, straightening, looked around the council ring. Everywhere stood knots of campers, staffers, and visitors, mixed together, talking, but moving slowly, as though their feet were held down by heavy weights. When he came nearer, Leo glimpsed more faces he recognized: Big Rolfe and Joy Hartsig, Hap Holliday, Hank Ives, a baker's dozen church elders in black suits, doughty, gray-faced and official-looking; Honey Oliphant was now holding tight to her brother's hand, as if he were a baby she was afraid of losing. They all stood in silent clusters regarding the casket, which in another moment was being removed from its resting place on the rock. Because it was so small, the box required only two bearers, who carried it up the aisle to the hearse parked near the top of the ring. Burial was to be private; no campers would be there.

Then Harpo came straying toward them from among the trees, tail quivering but not wagging, a forlorn look in his eyes that made Leo want to fling his arms around the dog's neck and hug him; but that would only make Leo cry and he had promised himself not to do that. Consequently he ignored Harpo, who finally wheeled and trotted away, while Leo climbed the ring and headed for Jeremiah.

Midway up the aisle he paused at the sight of Wanda, standing beside Fritz near a tree. She always seemed so different out of uniform. Today she had on a street frock and a little hat with a veil and she was wearing gloves. Leo hadn't spoken with her since the morning Tiger died.

A group of Virtue cadets was standing nearby. "It's all Wacko's fault," one of them was saying, "him and his spider—"

"Don't say that, it's not so," Fritz said quickly. "You boys oughtn't to repeat untrue stories. Now, run along." Leo ducked his head as the group broke up and moved away. "It's all right," Fritz said, giving his shoulder an encouraging pat, "don't pay any attention to that kind of talk." The gesture, meant to be comforting, somehow only made Leo feel worse.

As he came onto the linepath, he saw the Abernathys talking with Pa Starbuck and the Hartsigs. Mrs. Abernathy was holding a sheaf of gladioli and staring at the black box, its foot protruding eloquently through the open doors of the hearse. Leo flushed with embarrassment as she turned her eyes on him, then quickly looked away again. He desperately wanted to say something to her, to explain about the music and why he hadn't been at the funeral, though something in her expression said she already understood, a little.

Instead, to his surprise, he found himself going up to her and holding out the sheathed Bowie knife. Misunderstanding his gesture, she shied and turned her face into her husband's shoulder.

"Isn't that Tiger's knife?" Pat Abernathy asked.

277

Leo nodded. "He gave it to me," he said. "I think you should have it."

Mrs. Abernathy's voice quavered. "I'm sure that if Tiger gave it to you, he wanted you to have it. Keep it and remember him always. I know he thought a lot of you."

Then, as Leo watched her from under his brows, she seemed to give out all of a sudden. The flowers slipped from her grasp and, with Rolfe's assistance, her husband led her toward their car, parked just behind the hearse.

Leo went on, holding the knife in one hand, his violin case in the other. Across the linepath a grim-faced Phil was waiting on the porch of Jeremiah. Leo veered off toward the Dewdrop Inn; he wasn't up to a confrontation right now. But Phil quickly intercepted him, hustling him into the cabin, where seven or eight boys were sitting around silently in the bunks.

"Okay, Wackeem, let's hear it," Phil began with an angry scowl. "Suppose you tell us what that dumb stunt was that you just pulled with your fiddle?"

Leo shrugged. "Nothing. Tiger liked that song, is all."

"Liked it? That dumb thing? You sure have a lousy sense of the fitness of things. You're holding every camper here up to ridicule. Isn't that right, fellows?"

Leo glanced about at the funeral-solemn, resentful faces: Dump, Monkey, Eddie, Ogden, and Klaus, faces that had shown no friendliness in some time, and others—Dusty, Emerson—who since Tiger's death had kept their distance. It fell to the Bomber to take Leo's part.

"Cripes, leave him alone, Phil, why don't you?" he protested. Phil whirled on him belligerently.

"Listen, toad-face, you better button up if you know what's good for you. And what are *you* looking so bug-eyed at?" he demanded of Wally, who had been standing by the door.

"Nothing," Wally murmured and climbed into his bunk.

Phil was staring at Leo's hand. "Cripes—look!" he exclaimed, pointing. "He's got Tiger's knife! Where'd you get it?"

"Tiger gave it to me. He wanted me to have it."

"Liar! You stole it!"

"The heck I did!"

"Why would Tiger give you his knife?" Phil stuck out his hand. "Give it to me," he demanded.

When Leo refused, a scuffle began as Phil tried to wrest the knife from him. Failing in his attempt, he called for assistance. Dump jumped up and pulled at Leo, who, turning quickly, got an elbow in the mouth. In another moment a figure had appeared behind them, an arm reached out, a hand seized Phil by the scruff and pulled him away.

"All right, boys," said Fritz Auerbach brusquely, "that's enough of these strong-arm tactics. We don't want any fighting today."

Phil struggled in Fritz's grip. "Let me go."

"I'll be happy to—after you return Leo's property to him."

"It's not his! It's Tiger's!"

Coming in behind Fritz at the doorway, Wanda spoke up. "It *was* Tiger's. Now it's Leo's. That's how Tiger wanted it."

"Who asked you?" Phil said, rudely. Fritz was about to take him to task when Reece came into view on the path. "All right, what's all the racket about?" he demanded, joining the group. "Don't you guys know we just had a funeral service around here?"

"Phil is bent on keeping Tiger's knife," Fritz explained. "But Tiger wanted Leo to have it."

Reece eyed him. "How do you know? Did Tiger say so?"

"No, but Leo told me—"

"Oh? So you'll take his word, then?"

"He's not a liar. I believe him."

"It's true!" Leo cried. "We talked about it the night before he—he said—since he was going home—he—he—"

"Be quiet," Reece ordered. "Phil, give him back the knife."

Phil drew back in outrage. "No, I won't! He can't have it."

Reece repeated the order in stronger terms. Cowed, Phil grudgingly handed over the knife, which Leo took and held behind him. Turning, Phil deliberately jabbed him in the ribs. "You really are a crummy little spud, you know that?"

"All right, you guys hop it over to the lodge and wait for me," Reece said. "I want to talk to you."

Obediently the boys trooped out of the cabin, all but the Bomber, who lingered in the doorway, waiting for a word with Leo.

"Hey, that means you, too, Jerome!" Phil snapped from outdoors. Reece fixed his eye on the Bomber, who nodded, then turned to Leo.

"I gotta go. I'll see you after, huh?"

He left the cabin, bringing up the rear as the others followed behind Phil and disappeared along the path to the lodge. Reece turned his attention to Fritz, who was examining Leo's bruised lip.

"They just won't stop, will they?" Fritz said.

"They would if they weren't given provocation. And while we're on the subject, what are you doing around here anyway? I thought I told you to keep out of my campers' business."

"They were ganging up on Leo again."

"Sure, I know, everyone's always ganging up on 'poor Leo.' "

"But they were," Wanda insisted. "Look what they did to him."

Reece waved an impatient hand. "Yes, take a good look at him. If it weren't for him and his damnable spider Tiger Abernathy wouldn't be being carried out of here in a box. He—he—"

He broke off, then turned and marched out. The others watched him go. Wanda turned to Leo. "You'd better come with me, while I put something on that lip of yours." She was halfway out the door when she encountered the Hartsigs. There was an awkward shuffling of positions as Wanda stepped aside for Joy, who stood in the doorway, her eyes sparkling with fresh tears.

"What is it? Why was Reece weeping? What did somebody say to him to upset him like that? Fritz, did *you* say something?"

"Nothing that mattered, Mrs. Hartsig. I was *thinking,* however."

"Thinking what?" She teetered on her high heels. "Exactly what do you mean?"

"I was thinking that Reece will soon be going into the air force."

"Yes? We know this."

"And I was thinking how fortunate Camp Friend-Indeed will be when he has gone. I myself will be very glad to see the last of your son."

"What? What are you saying?" She clutched fiercely at his sleeve. "How can you say such a thing? Especially after all his father has done for the camp? After all *Reece* has done?"

Fritz looked her in the eye. "What *has* he done, Mrs. Hartsig?" he asked quietly.

"How can you ask such a question? He's done *everything,* simply *everything!* He's set an example, for one thing, he's given the boys someone to look up to and emulate. Why, wherever they go from here they will take the memory of Reece Hartsig with them."

280

Fritz's shoulders lifted, then drooped. "Let me just say this, please: I consider it just as well for Camp Friend-Indeed that your son should not be back next year. This place does not need men like him among its counselors, no matter how long he has been coming here."

Joy stopped dabbing at her melting mascara and stared at him. "What nonsense are you talking now, Mr. Auerbach?"

"He's thoughtless, your Reece, he's careless of other people's feelings. No matter what some may find to admire in his character, flaws are also evident. I would not like to think of campers' emulating those as well."

"Everyone has flaws!" Joy retorted, her mouth pulled down in an angry bow, her pale cheeks bedizened with two flaming spots of color. "I'm sure you have your share, Mr. Fritz Auerbach! You should think of that before you go around saying nasty things behind people's backs!"

"I will be glad to say them to Reece's face if you wish me to," Fritz replied with icy formality. "I have said nothing but the truth."

"What truth?"

"The truth that it is wrong to blame Leo Joaquim for an act he had no part in."

"If you mean Tiger's death I suggest you remember that it was Leo's spider that inflicted the fatal bite."

"Pardon, dear madame, but that is also untrue."

"Say, wait a minute, Fritzy," demanded Rolfe, lunging into the group. "You calling my wife a liar?"

"I am merely trying to point out that Leo is in no way to be held responsible for the tragedy that has happened here. And to wrongfully blame him is not to be tolerated. I will be leaving tomorrow morning and—"

Rolfe hiked his chin. "Running away, are you?"

Fritz colored. "I assure you, sir, I am not running away at all. I am going to Washington to talk with some Red Cross people who may have knowledge concerning the fate of my family. But while I am gone from this place . . ."

"Yes? Go on."

"If upon my return I should learn that Leo has been mistreated or persecuted for any imagined sins, I would then be obliged to go to Dr. Dunbar and inform him of the facts."

"What facts would those be?" demanded Rolfe, his heavy arm cradling his wife's small form against his side.

281

"For one, the fact that if it weren't for an act of carelessness on the part of your son it is highly likely that Tiger Abernathy would be alive today."

Rolfe blinked; the muscles in his face began to work. "What the hell are you talking about? What act?"

"Leo knows. It happened here in this very cabin one afternoon. Reece insisted on inspecting the bite Tiger had from the spider."

"*Leo's* spider, let's remember," said Rolfe.

Fritz shot him a look. "That has nothing to do with it, since the spider was not venomous."

"Then why did the boy get sick?"

Wanda spoke up. "Because the bite became infected. Reece used a soiled needle to open up his wound."

"I don't believe it," Rolfe protested. "Reece would never do such a thing. He'd sterilize it. A good camper knows that."

Fritz shrugged. "He did sterilize it—"

"There!" Joy cried. "Didn't we say so?"

"But then he dropped it on the floor and forgot—he just—"

"Hey, where'd you get a story like that?"

Again Wanda spoke. "From Leo. He was there."

Rolfe snorted with contempt. "Who do you think is going to believe anything he says? You're all in cahoots."

"Is that what you think, sir?" Fritz said.

"No!" Joy's chin quivered and tears came to her eyes as she spoke. "Reece had nothing to *do* with Tiger Abernathy's dy—— Oh, I can't say the terrible word! It was an accident, that's all! Just an accident!"

Fritz spoke quietly but firmly. "Yes, Mrs. Hartsig, that is so. But now Leo is being blamed. And he is innocent. Do you think that is fair?"

Joy's eyes snapped with hostility. "What does that matter? What my husband says is true, you and this—this—!" Without warning she whirled like a demon and rushed at Leo. "Oh, you naughty, vindictive boy! This is all your doing! To tell a story like that! Reece is right, you never should have been brought here. They had no business sending you. You've caused nothing but trouble from the day you arrived in camp. You're the one who's responsible! *You* killed Tiger with your nasty spider! *You're* the killer if anybody is!"

She rushed out of the cabin onto the linepath, taking pittering little steps up and down, moaning and clawing at the air. Appalled, Rolfe went lumbering after her, making helpless, chastening gestures around her pathetic, birdlike, fluttering form. As the others watched in embarrassed silence, he managed to get her into the car and drove quickly away.

When the field had once more fallen quiet, Leo left the cabin and walked across the linepath into the pine grove, where the tall, silent trees rose beside the lake, and the light filtering down through the boughs was made visible in the dust stirred among the fallen needles by many pairs of feet. In his mind the place seemed just the same as it had been on the evening of his arrival: at a glance nothing had changed, yet now all was changed. He felt intensely the presence of his lost friend, as if Tiger Abernathy stood here beside him as he had on that first evening.

Mr. Ives's jitney leaves a lot to be desired. I suggested he call it Bellerophon.

What a show-off Leo had been, a real spud. It was a wonder Tiger had put up with him for a minute, let alone taken him in hand and been his friend. He leaned back on his palms and sighted up to the top of the Methuselah Tree, where the owl still kept its eyrie among the topmost branches. Icarus the flyer.

Icarus.

Icarus?

That might be a good name for the owl. What do you think?

Fingering the hilt of the Bowie knife, Leo thought of the promise Tiger had made him give, to never say die. No matter what, he must, would, stay at camp to the end. As he watched, the owl spread its wings and sailed from its perch. From somewhere over in Indian Woods the dog began to howl again.

That evening a memorial torchlight parade was held, vividly recalling to Leo his first evening in camp. Again the lines of boys bearing their flickering brands wound through the pine grove and along the tiers of the council fire, but tonight the trembling flames were in token of a fallen comrade, prayers for a lost friend. And as, holding their torches, the campers joined voices in the old songs, each was suffused with his own personal memories of their dead companion, each in his heart had the hope that somehow at any moment he might come trotting in from a ball game, whistling between his teeth.

The service lasted no more than a half hour, and afterward, Reece in the lead, the boys wended their way silently back to the linepath, to gather in front of Jeremiah for the benediction. A breeze had arisen, making the torches flicker. From the White House came intermittent gusts of music—Leo, unwelcome among the Jeremians, was there with Fritz and Wanda.

Afterward, people blamed what happened next on moon madness compounded by grief. But in truth there was no explanation for the hot dry wind of excitement that rushed lightly but noticeably among the campers, inciting them to movement and agitation, and more.

Through the window, Leo observed them as they held aloft their torches, the flames flickering in the darkness. Among them he was able to make out Reece and the Jeremians; Hap Holliday was there, too, and some of the bullies from High Endeavor. A dance began, an Indian toe-heel step, and they uttered savage Indian war cries behind their palms—*ooooh-woo-wooo, ooooh-wooo-woo*—bending low, leaping high, wilder and wilder they danced. Then, some six or eight of them broke free and went racing toward the cottage, where silhouetted in the open doorway stood Leo and Fritz, with Wanda at his side. The boys began yawing and japing at them, poking and lunging with their torches; Leo spotted Hap again, standing on the sidelines, entertained by the mischief.

Then, without warning, a torch was seen to pinwheel through the air and land on the roof, whose newly oiled shingles quickly took fire. A second torch flew up, and a third. The three standing in the doorway ran inside to rescue Fritz's possessions, but the heat quickly drove them out again, and a rushing, cracking, snapping sound was in the air. The enamel on the shutters popped in ugly blisters. The clapboards buckled with the heat, singing out their protests against the flames, while the little grove of white birch trees became so many torches, writhing in their turn, their foliage burning away until only black poles were left, like the bars of a prison.

By the time the firefighting equipment arrived from Woking Corners, nothing remained except a heap of blackened ruins. Everything was lost: the chess set from Hong Kong, the pewter-lidded stein from Neuschwanstein, the precious album of stamps, including the upside-down airmail special, the record collection, its shellac discs melting and flowing together to form a black viscous puddle of classical composers and that singular novelty Fritz had been so proud of, the voice of Johannes Brahms talking on the telephone with Alexander Graham Bell.

7

n those waning days of summer Ma Starbuck's Concord grapes had reached perfection, their gleaming purple jackets dusted with white, like frost or sugar-glaze. But this summer Ma hadn't put up her usual batch of grape jelly, and so the boys had been allowed to pick an occasional bunch, until the arbor had been largely denuded of its fruit. Now, early in the afternoon, on the last full day of camp, Ma sat with Dagmar Kronborg on the slatted bench beneath its dusty, fading leaves, snapping string beans into an enameled colander. The two women had been commiserating over the recent tragic events, Ma tearfully blaming herself for Tiger's death, as if she had somehow been remiss in not having looked after him more closely, and Dagmar, more pragmatically, saying that such things happened in life, no one could have prevented it. The terrible fire that had consumed the cottage, however, that was something else. What could they have been thinking of, those boys?

Dagmar's eyes flashed dangerously as she considered the unfortunate incidents that had led up to the disaster, and the fact that thus far Pa Starbuck had not found it necessary to bring any kind of critical pressure to bear as a result of the boys' wicked behavior. Moreover, while the police and fire officials had been interrogating both campers and staff, nothing had as yet come of their inquiries. Nor, thought Dagmar, did such seem likely. Even Wanda, when questioned, had been unable to identify any of the perpetrators, though Fritz, never one to take things lying down, had sworn that upon his return he would force the issue with both Pa and Dr. Dunbar.

"And Fritz—has he left camp yet?" Dagmar asked.

Ma dabbed at her eyes with a handkerchief. As planned, Fritz had departed on the morning bus for Hartford, where he would entrain to New York and Washington to meet with the Red Cross group. Ma described the farewell between him and Leo, who, after Hank's jitney had taken Fritz away, looked as if he'd lost his last friend.

"Maybe he has," Dagmar said. With both Tiger and Fritz gone, Leo was more vulnerable than ever, and she deeply regretted the coolness between them.

Ma's eyes welled with tears again as she confessed that she hardly knew what to make of it all anymore. How could things have gone so wrong? Camp Friend-Indeed wasn't a place where bad things happened, it was a place for boys to spend a pleasant summer and enjoy themselves. They'd never lost a camper, never had the least bit of trouble—except for Stanley Wagner, who was the exception that helped prove the rule. And now, and now—Tiger, best trouper in camp, dead and buried, and all of Fritz's things gone up in flames. A dark cloud seemed to hang over the camp, Ma said, and she feared that worse was to come.

Dagmar declared tartly that a man who walked around with his head in the clouds all the time couldn't expect to avert trouble. "Gar's either a child or a fool," she added, then looked up to see the man himself coming into the arbor.

"Welladay, welladay," Pa said as he lowered himself onto the bench where long ago he had lovingly carved a pair of initials (his and Ma's, intertwined). Pushing back his hat, he wiped his brow, wagging his head in disbelief, like a farmer at a two-headed cow. "Welladay," he repeated mournfully.

Dagmar's lips pinched at the corners; she knew what "welladay" meant—the trials of Job were nothing compared with those that were now to be retailed in her ear: What, Pa dolorously asked, had he done to deserve all that now beset him, whence came these tribulations? And why Tiger, of all boys, to be taken?

"Tiger Abernathy! Now, *there* was a man!" he exclaimed. "A boy, true, but in time a man. Regrettable loss. Indeed, no one mourns his death more than I. But we can't bring back the dead, can we? 'Do not mourn me when I have crossed the bar, for I am mortal clay'—that's what that boy'd be

286

telling us if he could." He passed a hand across his face. "Well, enough, enough. The world's a garden of roses if we can but forget the thorns." He sighed again and contemplated the middle distance. A frown creased his brow and he tugged ruminatively at his lip. "Never should have had that orphan kid at camp," he went on illogically. "Trouble's his middle name. *Spiders.*"

"Oh, don't talk such foolishness, Gar!" Dagmar exclaimed. "You ought to be a comfort to the boy, not blame him for what was not his fault."

Pa sighed and cast his eyes heavenward. *"Eee-*heh. We have tried, we have endeavored—"

Dagmar was clearly at the end of her patience. "Oh, bother endeavor!" she snapped. "If you'd just kept your eyes peeled, if you'd only paid a little attention, instead of always going in search of a new warbler or titmouse—"

Pa's smile was beatific. "Dagmar, I confess it, when I am with the birds, I am one with my Maker. As I tell my boys about our feathered friends—"

"Yes, your boys, your boys, but not the one boy," Ma put in. "Dagmar's right. I've got bad eyes, it's true, but it's not me who don't see, Garland Starbuck."

Pa stared at her, taken aback by this unexpected outburst. "Why, May-ree," he began with some consternation, only to be cut off.

"Never mind the talk. You know as well as I do Leo didn't cause Tiger's death."

"And if he didn't, he's still a mischief-maker. Look at what he wrote in that journal of his. And putting on the Buffalo Bill War Bonnet the way he did and prancing around in it. Why, it's like spitting on the flag."

Dagmar moved her torso around inside the jacket of her blue suit, too hot for the weather. "Oh, be quiet, Garland, for pity's sake. If I hear another word about your precious Buffalo Bill I shall lose my patience."

"Oh, never do that, my dear," Pa expostulated mildly. "The great man presented me with that headdress with his own two hands. It was the greatest day of my life, the very greatest. Why, I remember the look in that old Indian fighter's eye—"

"Oh, Pa . . ." Ma looked at him with a baffled expression. "Must you go on so?"

Pa hiked his chin. "Why not? I pride myself on possessing such a momento."

"Oh, stop it, can't you?" she said, at the end of her patience. "You may possess that bonnet, but it never came from Buffalo Bill. And don't look at me like that. You know perfectly well Buffalo Bill never gave you a nickel in change, let alone the time of day." She turned to Dagmar and explained. "It's just a story, just one more of his fanciful tales to tell to the boys, it's no more true than his moonbow tale."

Dagmar straightened in her seat. "You mean it was all made up? About the bonnet?"

Ma nodded sadly. "Yes. All made up."

Dagmar was shocked. "Are you saying that boy was sent to Scarsdale over a fake?" She glared at Pa. "What a fraud you are, Garland Starbuck!"

"*Eeee*-heh." He countered this accusation with his characteristic wheeze. Then, as though coming out of a reverie, he gazed at his wife with brimming, reproachful eyes. "It was a good story, May-ree. The boys always liked it."

"But it was a lie!" Dagmar exclaimed.

"I don't see where's the harm in a bit of exaggeration. Everything in life can't be true, can it? It can't all be real. Sometimes a little story eases things along. Truth's not the only thing makes a man happy." He furrowed his brow and gave Ma a small, wistful smile. "If I am wrong, I hope I may be forgiven."

He gazed entreatingly at both women, then heaved himself up, jerked his head round, and ambled off.

As he headed for the house, Leo emerged from the office, shading his eyes as he peered into the sun. Dagmar got up suddenly. "Well, I'll be off as well," she said crisply. She kissed Ma, and, tucking her bag under her arm, she marched away, meeting Leo halfway between the office and the arbor. His face was pale and pinched. "If you're looking for Ma, she's over there," she said. "Try not to upset her more than she is." She unsnapped her bag and took out a bill. "Here's a dollar for you. Come, take it and don't be foolish."

He shook his head.

"Stubborn boy." She snapped the money back in the bag. "I won't see you again once you're gone, I expect." She started away, then turned back. "Ask Ma to tell you about Pa's famous Buffalo Bill War Bonnet," she said; then, pulling in her chin, she marched away, while a mystified Leo went on to the arbor, where Ma set aside her colander and made room on the bench beside her.

Leo glanced at her. Her iron-gray hair had a side part today, and was rolled around her ears on a bit of ribbon.

"What did Dagmar have to say to you?" she began.

"Nothing."

"She must have said *something*. I saw her talking."

"She said to ask you about the war bonnet."

Ma shook her head ruefully. "It's of no matter now, honey. Your old Ma shamed her mate of thirty years in front of company, and she's mighty sorry. But how are you? Are you all right? You've lost your friend—"

"Fritz."

"Fritz, too—though I was thinking of Tiger." A tear appeared behind her glasses. When she took them off to wipe her eyes she seemed a stranger to Leo. Her pupils were clouded by a milky film, and she visored them with her crabbed hand, attempting for vanity's sake to hide her affliction. "It's not right to weep for the dead, I suppose," she said, fumbling for her handkerchief. "God don't want that, I know. Tiger's with his Maker in paradise now, and 'twon't do to mourn him overmuch."

Evidently her glasses didn't please her, because she took them off again and rubbed the lenses with her handkerchief. "You're a good boy, Leo Joaquim." She still pronounced it "Joakum." "Don't seem possible the summer's over." She sighed. "Seems like you all just got here and soon you'll be leaving." She beckoned him nearer. "See here, Leo, Dagmar's told me how bad you want to stay with her at the Castle. I'm sure she'd like to have you come visit, thinking a good deal of you the way she does. She's got plans for you—musical plans. You've got to get your schoolin', 'n' t' do that you've got to go someplace where there's folks to teach you proper, don'tcha see? Now, before you leave, I want you to phone her up and tell her you're sorry. Yes, she told me how you spoke. And *y'are* sorry— aren'tcha?" He nodded and dragged his toe in the dirt. "Of course y'are!

"And, dear," she went on, "I know you've been meanly treated by some of the boys. But, oh, honey, I don't think they meant to be bad. I'm sure they didn't. Our boys are good boys, Moonbow boys, only—I don't know, this summer something seemed to get into them. They were all mischief-bent. I don't know why, *this* summer. 'Twasn't like that before and I'm sure it won't be that way again. Besides, a body's got to go on. I've got to go on, you've got to go on, we've all got to go on. My mama said it, a man's got to find his own way home."

Leo nodded.

"Well, go along, then," she said. She sighed again and peered at the cat, lying on the slates. "Jezzy, suppertime, is it?" She heaved herself up and went to get Jezebel the tasty fishhead Henry Ives had saved for her.

When Leo crossed the compound he found Pa waiting for him.

"I wish a word with you," Pa said, beckoning. Leo approached hesitantly, not knowing of what he might be found guilty this time.

"Well, young man," Pa began, running the tip of his tongue around his store-bought teeth, "and how are we today?"

Leo offered a positive report on his current state of health and general well-being while Pa managed not to look directly at him.

"Eeee-heh," he said. His tone took on an unaccustomed intimacy. "See here, son, I want you to know I have been deeply distressed, *deeply* distressed, at some of the things that have happened around here this summer. Can't think what possessed our campers to behave like savages. A pack of miscreants, they were. But let us not be too harsh in our judgments, eh? Boys will be boys, I always say. Too quickly they all grow up, too soon they must face the cares and burdens of adulthood. 'Glad Men from Happy Boys,' eh? There's the spirit! The good old Friend-Indeed spirit." He smote his kneecap. "I say let the lads have their fun while they may, make hay while the sun shines, so to speak."

Before Leo could properly respond to this, Pa sighed again, then went on. "We must take these setbacks in stride, you know. After all, God gives us no heavier burden than He provides us with the strength to bear, isn't that so?" He took out his pocket square and pressed his lips. His eyes were moist as he looked at Leo, planning his next words. He started, stopped, began again, employing a confidential tone. "I find myself hoping that, should occasion arise when Dr. Dunbar and the Friends of Joshua come among us again, that you might withhold comment as to what has transpired here. It's all in the past now; why make more of it than necessary? Hm? So I am wondering if I could possibly prevail on you—we don't like to get Big Rolfe upset, do we? Not when he's in such a giving frame of mind. I think I can say we would be one of the first camps on the whole Eastern Seaboard to have chemical toilets—should Rolfe decide to afford us them. In the meantime, if it's all the same to you, we needn't say anything to anyone about these matters, need we? After all, accidents will happen. And Dr. Dunbar, fine gentleman that he is, is not required to know everything that goes on here at camp, now, is he—hem?"

He wove his fingers into a basket, allowed his eyes to meet Leo's, and quickly shifted them. "Well, well, go along, then," he said and sent Leo from him with a finger on his shoulder. The screen door slammed behind him and in a moment the radio came on: "Vic and Sade."

Leo did not linger but headed for the lower camp.

In the loft doorway, Reece Hartsig leaned against the lintel, his expression coolly thoughtful as, fingering his cedar heart, he watched Leo trot down the meadow path. He straightened; then, moving quickly down the stairs, he crossed the compound and crept up to the office door. He peered through the screen and, satisfied that the place was empty, opened the door quietly. Once inside, he went immediately to Ma's desk and slid his fingers under the ink-stained blotter. He used the key to open the pie safe, from which he removed the manila folder Ma had placed there. He shut the door, returned the key to its place, then slipped the folder and its contents inside his shirt. As he started to cross the room again, something caught his eye and he froze. Willa-Sue was watching him from the hallway.

He glared at her.

The girl started to shake. He thrust her roughly aside and headed for the door.

Not long after, Leo was standing in the Dewdrop Inn, where he'd made a stop, his pee creating a satisfyingly tinny sound against the trough. Suddenly the door opened and someone ducked quickly inside: Wally Pfeiffer. He halted, back to the door, staring at Leo, his large eyes blinking rapidly. Leo grimaced; he had paid hardly any attention to Wally since Tiger got sick.

"I've got something to tell you," Wally began, a worried expression on his face. "I know you don't like me but—"

"Cut it out," Leo said. "What is it?"

As Wally darted a furtive look out the window, the sound of cheering could be heard coming from the far edge of the playing field, where the final round of the last archery tournament was in progress. Obviously someone had just hit a bullseye. Sliding a sidelong glance at Leo, Wally said, "You better get out of here. You're in trouble."

Leo couldn't resist a snicker. "Tell me something I don't know."

"It's true. The Mingoes. They're going to get you." Wally lowered his voice further. "Remember Stanley? Stanley Wagner?"

"What about him?"

"Do you know what happened to him?"

"Sure—he stole a paperweight from the Castle and got caught."

"*He* didn't steal it. *I* did."

"You did?"

"The whole thing was Reece's idea. He wanted Stanley out of camp and he would have done anything to get him out. Right from the start."

"You mean he didn't want him in Jeremiah, isn't that it? Because he was afraid Jeremiah'd lose the trophy?"

Wally nodded.

"Then Stanley was framed."

Wally nodded again. "I sneaked the paperweight out of the cabinet and slipped it to Phil. He hid it in Stanley's suitcase. Then Reece held an inspection and made believe he accidentally found it."

"Why didn't Stanley deny it?"

"He did. But the Sachems put him in Scarsdale anyway. Reece thought that would get rid of him, but Stanley fooled him. He stuck it. Reece was really mad. When Scarsdale didn't work, they locked him up in the Haunted House—in the cellar—and scared the heck out of him. Stanley was a mess. He called his folks and they came and took him."

"Why didn't they do something?"

"Maybe they didn't believe him. He was a big storyteller, Stanley."

"Then why didn't *you* do something? You knew the truth."

"I—I couldn't. Phil threatened me. He said if I told, he'd fix me. And he would. He likes hurting people. You remember after the Snipe Hunt— when he was mad at you—he was the one who put the guys up to making you climb the ladder. He said you'd never jump, so you were bound to get paddled."

Leo buttoned up, then stepped away from the trough, looking Wally up and down. "So why are you telling me now? You never liked me."

"No, I never. Only—" A fierce scowl knit his brows and his voice was a hoarse rasp as he again looked out the window, checking for eavesdroppers. "It's because of Tiger," he said earnestly.

"What do you mean?"

"He was the best guy in camp, Tiger," Wally said. "And he didn't have to die. It was Reece."

"How do you know?"

"I was *there*," he declared forcefully. "I was just coming in when Reece dropped the needle. I saw it too."

Leo shook his head in disbelief. "You *saw* it? And you didn't say anything? Everybody blames me."

Wally spoke urgently. "I know. That's why you've got to get out." He looked around before going on. "They don't want you leaving camp without getting back at you. If you're smart, you'll scram while you still can get away."

Leo squinted hard at him, trying to see the truth. Wally was about to say more when the dinner bell rang. There was no more time; Wally would leave first, then Leo.

"Be careful," Wally cautioned as he started out. "They're watching you."

He slipped through the doorway; in a moment Leo followed him.

The camp seemed eerily quiet. A light breeze drifted from among the trees on his right, carrying with it the faintly recognizable calls of baseball players on the upper playing field, their voices distorted by distance. The gradually fading light produced a milky iridescence, uncommon greens tinged with blue, blue with violet, purple shadows flecked with gold, and over all an opalescent glaze, like the mother-of-pearl in seashells. As Leo headed away from the Dewdrop, strains of music reached his ears. Someone was playing a violin—badly. He broke into a run. When he reached Jeremiah he was confronted by the sight of Billy Bosey, perched on Reece's footlocker, Leo's instrument clamped under his chin as he sawed away on the strings. The Bomber, sitting crosslegged in Eddie's bunk, was grinning hugely, while Peewee Oliphant peered down from Tiger's empty bunk.

"What do you think you're doing?" Leo cried, outraged. "You don't know how to play that!"

"Hell I don't. Give a listen, kiddo."

He sawed some more, while Leo stood by, not knowing what to do. If there was a scuffle, the violin might get damaged.

Bosey grinned. "Some hot stuff, huh?"

Leo tried to seize the instrument, but Bosey held it out of reach. "Hold your water, Wacko, I'm not finished," he said, then passed the violin behind him to Dump. Leo ran around the cot and tried to take it from Dump, only to see it handed to Monkey, who handed it down to Eddie, who slipped it back to Bosey. Each time Leo tried to grab it, he ended up empty-handed.

Furious, he stormed at Bosey again, who this time handed it up to Peewee, who in turn slipped it to Blackjack, who began strumming it like a ukulele, singing "Sweet Leilani" through his nose.

Then the Bomber let out one of his blasts, causing further ribaldry and the usual chorus of "Bomber did it! Bomber did it!" The Bomber heaved himself up and began fanning his rear end.

"Pee-you!" Peewee shouted, holding his nose.

Just as the Bomber went to reseat himself in the bunk, Ratner inserted the violin under his rear end. The Bomber fell heavily into the bunk, and there was an ugly sound of splintering wood.

A silence fell. He reached under himself, and sheepishly extracted the mutilated instrument, which he gripped by its neck and held up.

"Jeez, it broke!" he exclaimed with mock surprise. There was a chorus of *ooh*s and Leo felt the sting of tears as he took the pieces, several of which dangled from the strings.

"Cripes," said Bosey, "look at him, willya, he's going to cry. A lousy violin and he's going to cry over it."

"I am not."

"Sure you are—look at you, you got tears in your eyes already. Go ahead and cry. You're nothing but a sissy anyway. Cry all you want."

Leo squeezed his eyes shut; when he opened them again he was staring accusingly at the Bomber.

"Don't look at me like that, Wacko," he said. "You seen it was an accident."

"You're a liar! You did it on purpose, you know you did." He glared around at the others. "All of you, you planned it!"

"Aw, you're crazy. Why would we do a thing like that, Wacko?"

"B-because—because you're—you're all a bunch of shits."

Bosey got up and squared off at Leo. "Hey, wait a sec, Wacko, who you calling names?"

"You! The whole bunch of you—"

He had more to say, but he was silenced by the sound of cheers, coming from the playing field. A few minutes later Phil jumped onto the porch, clutching something in his upraised hand.

"Look at what Reece knocked off," he declared proudly. Hanging by its feet, like a Christmas goose, head down, eyes glazed, was the owl, an arrow still piercing its breast. Blood dripped on the warped floorboards.

Leo turned and bolted. Outside the sun had slipped behind the clouds. And it seemed to him to have taken with it all the warmth of the world, all the sweetness and goodness of it, leaving behind only a dusky bleakness and changing ordinary objects—the archery butts, the Dewdrop Inn, the cottage ruins, the Green Hornet—into ribbony shadows, as if the edge of the playing field were the edge of the world and beyond that lay terra incognita.

8

vening saw the farewell banquet in the dining hall, with the tables decorated with ferns and flowers in token of the camp's last big night of the summer. Ma and Willa-Sue were in evidence at the staff table, along with Doc Oliphant and Maryann, Honey, too, everyone eager to learn who the winners of the Hartsig Memorial Trophy were going to be.

When the meal ended Leo watched as Pa rose to offer some choice parting words—the usual Friend-Indeed talk, which Leo only half heeded; he was still thinking about Icarus, felled by Reece's arrow, never to fly again. And the violin. What, if he had lived, would Tiger have thought of the destruction of Emily's violin, the treasure that to Leo had been such a potent talisman, not only of the past but of the future that Dagmar had spoken of?

A stir among the campers marked the end of Pa's speech, as he turned to the presentation of the initial awards: Bibles and felt badges for various camp competitions. He was followed by Hap, making the athletic awards, then Rex, who handled the aquatic awards in a like fashion, and Oats, who bestowed certificates of merit for nature studies and, in Fritz's absence, for crafts. As each camper received his prize there were cheers and applause, until Leo's name was announced—to be greeted with silence, not a jeer or a knock, only a titter or two from the back of the room. Leo cursed the spider collection that made it necessary now for him to exhibit himself before the camp and, blushing furiously, he all but snatched the paper from Oats and regained his seat.

Finally it was time for the awarding of the Trophy. The winning cabin's name did not come immediately to Pa's lips, however, for some fulsome words of general commendation were required to lay the carpet, so to speak, before the grand announcement could be made. During these remarks Hap stood by, exhibiting the silver cup for all to see. And, finally, the winner was—Jeremiah! Reece strode to where Pa stood, to accept the cup "in the name of all Jeremians, past, present, and future," with special thanks to Tiger Abernathy, who had contributed so much toward winning it.

So, the Jeremians, as expected, had taken the Trophy. That any other cabin should have won seemed unthinkable, yet as he left the dining hall Leo harbored a curious sense of "so what?," as if, with Tiger gone, the whole thing had never mattered much after all.

☽

At eight o'clock that evening, as he'd done all summer before the start of each council fire, Pa made his customary appearance at the head of the linepath, bearing aloft the Great Torch, its sacred flame a beacon for all to see, there to be met by the trio of honorary runners, who lighted their torches from his, then separated to carry the flames to all three units.

Was it possible, thought Leo, watching the ceremony from Old Faithful, where he'd been waiting alone, that this was the final campfire of the season, the last time the Senecas would meet, the last telling of the moonbow tale? Could it really be that eight whole weeks had elapsed since he had come to camp? Possible that Tiger Abernathy was actually dead, that Leo would never see him again, that on this last evening they wouldn't be sitting side by side at the council fire sharing in the fun? Half an hour earlier, as he prepared for the evening's activity, he had felt the prick of goose pimples along his legs. He still wanted to leave, to get out, but he had promised Tiger he wouldn't run away, and he wouldn't, despite all that had happened—"Never Say Die." As a result of Wally's warning, however, he had slipped Tiger's compass into his pocket, and had buckled the knife onto his belt. The funny thing was, Wally himself hadn't shown up since dinner, which didn't necessarily mean anything, since, for the past several days, he'd been giving both the cabin and Phil a wide berth. Still, the torchlight parade had started and it wasn't like Wally to miss formation.

By now the runners had passed along the line with the fire, and, the torches having been lighted, the procession began, as it had begun on Leo's first night at camp. Then he had thrilled at that bobbing, flickering necklace of flames, and at its promise of friendliness and good fellowship; now it seemed silly, almost meaningless. As he fell in line behind the others he was glad he'd put on his sweater. The evening air suddenly felt moist and clammy, and presently a fine, silvery mist, too light to be a fog, began to fall, refracting the smattering of pallid moonlight and giving the night an uncommonly eerie look, pale and silvery.

Entering the council ring behind the rest of the Jeremians, Leo noted that Pa had already assumed his customary place in the twig chair, his back to Tabernacle Rock, watching the boys as they filed into the rows, nodding at this one and that, his cheeks red as pippins, his blue eyes twinkling in the firelight. As always, the air in the grove was scented with the pungent odor of pine, but the damp chill this evening caused Leo to shiver and, taking his seat among the Jeremians, he hunched forward, hugging his bare knees.

When everyone was seated, Pa rose and, extending his arms, began weaving the traditional Friendship Chain that joined one camper to his fellow, all around the ring, arm over arm, hand clasped in hand, the boys of all three units linked according to tradition. And Leo, too, joined hands, with Eddie on the left and Monkey on the right, yet their touch was cold, not as it had been on that first night.

> Camping in the pines of Moonbow
> Down by the lake . . .

they sang, and when the anthem ended Pa began his introductory remarks, commenting on the unusual change in weather, then lapsing into one of his long-winded circumlocutions concerning "the true meaning" of Camp Friend-Indeed, including the inevitable sentimental reminiscences that earned the usual ripples of approval and indulgent laughter among his auditors. Yet this evening they seemed less content than usual to devote full attention to his words, and as he glanced about him Leo noted the absence of certain parties: Tugwell and Ogden, Bosey and Mullens and Klaus. All ought to have been present, but all were missing. And Wally—he, too, was still absent. What had become of him?

But there was no time to ponder minor mysteries. The time had come for the final selection of new members for the Seneca Lodge. As usual, Pa settled back in his chair, and out of the magical puff of smoke the familiar figure of the Moonbow Warrior appeared, in one hand the medicine bags, in the other the bouquet of red feathers. His body painted, his face daubed with color, his brow crowned by the war bonnet, the Indian Chief stood in the firelight, showing off his nearly naked form, until the tom-tom beat was heard, and as the dance began the usual awed silence fell along the rows. Who among the campers would be picked tonight? With muttered congratulations, three of the last four-weekers received their feathers and medicine bags, and so it went, until the Warrior reached the row in front of the row where the Jeremians sat, and Willard, of Obadiah, received the feather. Leo could hardly look at the dancing figure of the Moonbow Warrior; he felt a rush of emotion—anger, resentment, even fear, as Reece, in his war paint, moved into Leo's row. As the Warrior loomed larger, Leo suddenly realized it wasn't Reece at all, but Jay St. John, who was impersonating the Warrior. Others among the watchers were also aware of the unscheduled substitution, and furtive whispers ran among the rows. Leo heard his name muttered and he had a sudden feeling of apprehension; something was afoot, something to do with him.

Closer came the Warrior, then, as Leo stared unbelieving, the dark arm extended and the hand offered the Seneca red feather and the medicine bag—to him!

Reflexively he reached for them, and held them before him, and the muttering grew louder, louder still. Campers were talking openly, but not about him, not him now, but something else entirely. Something was happening, something strange, even wonderful, and for that moment Leo forgot all about the red feather. *Look,* they were saying, *look at it! See? What is it?* And all around the council ring boys were turning their gaze skyward. There was a sudden break in the overcast, like a ragged tear in a curtain, and through the tear the moonlight brilliantly streamed downward, setting into silvery vibration the accumulated molecules of mist, millions upon millions of them, each globule spinning and floating in the livid atmosphere. Was it—? Could it be—? Hardly daring to breathe, they watched as, above the mist-shrouded waters, the particles of moisture began to gather themselves together, resolving themselves into a thin veil, a curtain of shimmering light, and the broad bow took form, shaping itself into a luminous arc that spanned the lake, from the hills behind them to the tall tip of the Methuselah Tree.

As if pulled by some magnetic force, one by one campers and counselors alike rose to their feet, some abandoning their places to make a concerted movement toward the waterfront, where the view was unobscured. *Aaah,* they breathed, it is the moonbow! The moonbow they'd been hearing about for so long—the moonbow of Pa's story suddenly made real, a light like no other in the world.

To Leo, standing with the rest by the lakeshore, it suddenly seemed that the magical arc bathing them in its silvery glow was a sign. A sign that the bitter events of the summer should be forgotten, that from now on everything would be all right, that they were all true Friend-Indeeders here together, boys of Moonbow who, having passed through a long, dark way, had again emerged into the light. As he gazed up at the sky it was as if all the mean tricks that had been played on him had not been played, the angry words not spoken. *This,* this was the thing he would take with him when he left, the moonbow. If only Tiger were here to see it.

The phenomenon lasted for three minutes, no longer. Then a breeze rose up from the east to tear at the gauzy mist, and before their eyes the arc dissolved, ending as it had begun, in darkness. Leo sat down again, shivering and hugging his ribs. Clutched in his hand was the red feather, from his neck hung the empty medicine bag, soon to be filled with magic. The sight of them brought him back to reality. Yes—he remembered—the Moonbow Warrior had presented it to him. Within the hour he would be made a Seneca brave. Already someone was tapping his shoulder. "Get going," came the whisper, and Leo saw the other Seneca designates leaving their places to go to the Wolf's Cave.

Like an automaton, Leo jerked to his feet and switched on his flashlight; as he joined the rest of the honor party his mind again strayed to Tiger, and his fingers caressed the empty medicine bag on its string around his neck. Suddenly, another, more sobering thought crossed his mind: There was something fishy in all this.

Again he recalled Wally's warning and his heart beat fast. Yes—he was certain—this was just another Mingo trick and he'd fallen for it! What a sap! He wasn't to be made a Seneca; they were planning to get him off in the woods and do a Stanley Wagner on him! Holding his breath, he glanced discreetly to both sides, ahead and behind. No one seemed to be paying him much attention as they trudged along the path toward Indian Woods. He made up his mind. He must make his run for it—right now, or it would be too late. Scarcely breaking stride, he turned down the nearest crosspath and sprinted forward. No sooner had he begun his move than a shout erupted behind him and they were on to him. He ran as if from the devil himself, dashing blindly along the path, panting, his breath coming in heavy, exploding bursts, hearing nothing but the sound of his own feet hitting the needled ground, legs frantically pinwheeling as he spurred himself on. The light grew dimmer and he was forced to slow his gait; the ground was boggy; pale scarves of mist threaded among the trees, and with every headlong step the way grew more treacherous. Though the sounds of pursuit had died away, still he did not feel safe, only alone. He had started off with such a violent rush, and now he wasn't sure where he was. It was the Snipe Hunt all over again, only tonight the games were over, the games, the jokes, the fun. No anagrams this time.

He picked up his pace, stumbled, then stopped dead, staring ahead. Before him in the shadows a quartet of menacing silhouettes barred his way. He blinked once, twice, thinking he must be imagining them, but the four, mute and motionless, remained, staring back at him. Their faces were smudged with burnt cork, their eyes shone white. Who they were he did not know; but what matter? They were there and they wanted him. No sense in running anymore. They had him.

Then "Come with us," he heard one say in an ominous, oddly manipulated voice, a bit of playacting.

"What do you want?" he said, trying to pump some sound of courage into his words.

The order was repeated. The air was very still.

Suddenly Leo felt his body go flaccid, like old rubber with no spring in it, and he knew he was licked. It would be Stanley-time at the Wolf's Cave. A robot, he proceeded as directed by his summoners.

9

ingle file, like Indians, they broke away from camp property onto the Old Lake Road, heading, surprisingly, not into Indian Woods, as Leo had figured, but farther east, toward Pissing Rock. Trudging along the shoulder, he could hear the open-throated drag of his captors' breathing as they marched doggedly on, the two backs ahead of him sturdy and somehow brutal-looking, while, from behind him, his every flagging step earned him a helpful prod in the small of his back, forcing him to keep pace. There was no other sound except the rhythmic crunch of their shoe soles; no cars passed, no dogs barked, nothing. Done with its brilliant show, the moon had hid its face. The night was dark, and Leo fearful of what lay ahead.

They came around the bend and then he saw it: there, beyond the treetops, rose the slanted roofs and chimneys of the Steelyard place. It was to the Haunted House that they were taking him, then, not to Indian Woods, not to the grove, not the cave. Tonight Leo Joaquim would witness no gathering of the Senecas, nor would he be made a member of that honorable lodge.

Larger and more sinister the roof peaks and gables loomed as they drew near. He wanted to look away but could not. He dragged his step, only to suffer another prod that made him jerk, forcing him on. Now they were hustling him up the crazy paving, past the beds of cinders and weeds. At the front steps he balked. Nothing could make him enter that house another time. They would have to kill him first.

"Go up, or we'll drag you by your hair," ordered one of them, his face disguised, voice too.

"Be a man," advised his partner. "Go forward."

Yes, thought Leo, be a man. Above all, he must be a man. Glad Man from Happy Boy. Ha ha . . .

The first pair marched onto the porch. Leo must follow. Making up his mind to it, he placed his foot on the bottom step and began his ascent behind the two rigid backs, the other two close behind him. The floorboards creaked, and the structure protested under their combined weight. As the party approached the doorway, the leaders held up their lanterns, then stepped inside. Leo stared at the dark portal.

"Go on in," growled a warning voice.

"No. I won't." But his stubbornness was to no avail. A shove from behind propelled him across the threshold. He grew dizzy as the familiar shadows rose about him, and the odors assailed his nose. He clenched his fists, trying to control his trembling, fighting against the wave of sickness and fright that was raising the flesh on his bare legs.

"Well, bring him along then," commanded another voice, one he hadn't heard before, and he was given another shove. Despite his protests they manhandled him along the hallway to its end, where the heavy trapdoor stood open, with the two masked leaders waiting beside it, holding up their lanterns.

Leo was forced to stop at the edge of the hole in the floor, aware by now that they were conducting him to the Rinkydink cellar.

"We're here," called a voice from behind him.

"Come down."

"Go down," Leo was told. He stiffened.

"No, I won't."

"He says he won't come down."

"Who cares what he says? Make him. And quick, we haven't got all night."

Leo cried out as he felt the push from behind and he fell through the trapdoor. He was falling—falling—but instead of hitting the earth he felt his fall broken by pairs of arms, which caught and set him on his feet.

Dazed, he blinked, staring around him. The cellar seemed to be alive with light. Torches flamed everywhere. He could make out some twenty or thirty huddled forms arranged along the walls of the room, a band of grotesque, fearsome-looking figures, their faces besmirched with blacking and garishly painted. Others were wearing animal masks, furred and horned, and were clad in weird wild-man and Indian outfits. In addition to the torches, their hands clutched makeshift weapons—sticks and staves, tomahawks, axes and shields taken from the exhibition wall at the lodge, Leo realized.

But this ragtag-and-bobtail lot was no brotherhood of Senecas come together in a ceremony of honor and friendship. Tonight, the night of the last campfire—night of the moonbow—there would be held not Seneca ceremonies, but Mingo revels. In the flickering torchlight, one by one he examined the evil-looking bunch, seeking hints as to who was who. Yet so successful were their disguises that they were to all intents and purposes impenetrable—except—yes—maybe the one got up as a fox, who now took up a position of importance before Leo, eyes glinting behind his furry muzzle. In one "paw" he displayed an Indian rattle, which when shaken gave off a menacing sound, like the tail of a rattlesnake. It must be Phil, Leo decided. He'd been clever enough to remove his ring, but there was a telltale white band around his finger that the burnt cork had missed.

"Go ahead, look about you," the fox suggested with a spurious show of affability. "See what is to be seen. Think where you are, and to what purpose."

He gestured beyond the intervening heads, past the furnace and the coal bin, toward the shadows at the far end of the cellar. There a line of Indian blankets was hung with wooden clothes pins on a wire stretching fully across the room, effectively shutting off the farther view, while in the corner was something else Leo hadn't noticed before. He stood tiptoe, trying to make out what—no, *who*—it was.

"Go on, take a *good* look," urged the fox smoothly. "It's a friend of yours. Maybe he'll give you an idea of what's going to happen—just in case you were wondering."

Oh no! Leo stared in alarm and astonishment as he recognized Wally Pfeiffer. His arms had been pulled back over his head and secured, his ankles and legs bound as well. On his bare chest a crude swastika had been drawn; his lips were swollen.

"What have you done to him?" Leo demanded in consternation.

"See for yourself," said the fox. "That's what we do to traitors. And that spud's a traitor if ever there was one, isn't he, men?"

"Yeah, traitor!" they shouted. "Lousy traitor." And, "Liar!" they called, and "Lousy, dirty creep!"

The fox resumed. "We've been teaching him a lesson, we have. We've been reminding him whose side he's supposed to be on, and not to go warning *other* traitors. Present company *not* excepted."

"But he's hurt—"

"He needed a lesson," someone muttered.

"It's true," said the fox. "He needed to be taught. Like certain others need it, too." He paused for effect, allowing his words to sink in, then he spoke again. "Let's see how well the lousy spud's learned his lesson." He gave Wally a jab with his staff. "All right, traitor, hop to it. Come on, say it—"

Wally's eyes rolled in their sockets and his lips moved, but no sounds came out. The fox seized him by the hair, and yanked his head back.

"You heard me, speak! Do as you've been told."

"I—I—"

He tried to speak but couldn't manage it. Again the fox's hand snapped out, catching him a crack across the lips.

"Say it!"

Wally turned a pitiful face toward Leo. "Y-you—d-dirty—murdering—bas-bas-tard."

And he spat.

Leo recoiled as Wally's spittle flew into his face.

"Make him say the rest," prompted another voice, deep and resonant. It came from the lips of a "wolf." Leo could see the flash of eyes behind the mask. Eyes and voice, he knew both: they belonged to the Brown Bomber. His friend, who had smashed his violin.

"Well, speak up," urged the wolf. Wally only stared in fright.

"Leave him alone, Bomber," Leo said in a low voice. "He didn't do anything to you—"

"Silence!" came the fox's crisp command. "There is no Bomber here. We are the brotherhood of Mingoes." That much, ironically, was true: no Bomber here, not really. The third of the Three Musketeers had betrayed not only Leo but Tiger Abernathy as well.

As if reading Leo's thoughts, the wolf turned away and prompted Wally again.

"Go on, now—say it."

"I forget . . ."

"Tell him what *you* are," he commanded.

Wally's head lolled. "I'm nothing b-but a dirty—traitor. I d-deserve—t-to—d-die."

"All right, that's enough of that crap," came an impatient voice. "Let's get on with it and stop all this screwin' around."

As hands reached for Leo, he broke free and, ducking under their outstretched arms, headed for the hatchway steps. Before he could reach them he felt a heavy blow across the back of his neck; he crumpled to the floor. Amid shouts, they grabbed him and dragged him back into the light, securing him with rawhide thongs to a post in the same way Wally was tied. Bodies huddled closer now; faces, hot and sweaty, were streaked with soot.

"Let the trial begin," the fox intoned.

"Yeah," they all muttered, nodding, "the trial . . ."

Still dizzy from the blow to his neck, Leo peered around at their faces, at their eyes agleam, anticipatory, hungry for action. So he was to be tried, then. But on what charges? What was his crime?

"A man should be told what he's being tried for," he said, trying to keep his voice even.

The fox stared back at him. "I'm the judge here. You must say 'Your Honor' to me, like in a real court."

Leo put on a show of bravado. "This isn't a court, it's just some stupid game. You're all nuts!"

The forthright declaration provoked a volley of laughter: *they* were nuts? No, pal, Wacko was the one who was nuts. After all, Wacko had been to the asylum. The fox's fist flew up and caught him across the mouth. The blow hurt. Tears stung his eyes and he was helpless to wipe them away. Now he was certain the fox was Phil. "He likes to hurt people," Wally had said. Leo could taste blood, feel his lip swelling.

"Hey, come on, you guys," someone called out wearily. "Let's get on with it." His companions muttered agreement. They wanted the whole show. The group parted as another figure, this one featuring a bear's physiognomy, made his appearance.

"Who is it that now comes before the tribunal of the Mingo Lodge, and to what end?" intoned the fox.

"It is I," said the bear, "Nananda the All-knowing Spirit of the Mingo tribe, and I have come to accuse. Am I permitted to continue?"

"Who do you accuse?" came the query.

A grubby finger was raised, pointed.

"I accuse the prisoner." From the voice Leo thought perhaps the bruin was Bosey; the thick-set "crocodile" at his shoulder was Bullnuts.

The fox nodded gravely. "Very well, you may continue, Mr. Prosecutor. Call your first witness."

The bear turned and surveyed the group on both sides of him. "I call the frog," he said. "Let him come forward and testify. Listen carefully, all of you, to what he has to say."

The group gave way and yet another figure, smaller than the others and costumed as a frog, was pushed forward.

"Say, then. Give evidence," instructed the fox eagerly. The bear prompted the frog. When the frog spoke it was in the accents of Peewee Oliphant.

The whole idea of Peewee's being in on this monstrous show turned Leo's stomach.

"Why have you dragged him here?" he demanded. "He's only a kid, he should be in bed."

Haw haw! A wave of scornful laughter filled the room.

The fox held up a restraining hand. "We know of no 'Peewee' here," he said sternly. "We know only the frog. Speak, frog. Tell the warriors of the sacred Mingo tribe all you know."

The frog talked fast, as if by rote. The prisoner, he said, had tried to do nasty things with the frog's sister.

"What things?" demanded the fox.

The accusation was made: He had shown her dirty pictures at Three Corner Cove! He had corrupted an innocent girl.

Leo was speechless. They had put the words in Peewee's mouth and got him to repeat them.

"Well, what have you to say for yourself?" Nananda the bear growled impatiently, stepping up to Leo. "Do you deny it?"

"I deny everything!"

"We knew you would. All right, the witness is excused. *Now* you can go to bed, froggy."

Further mirth greeted this sally. The fox quickly squelched it.

There was still one who was missing from the stage as far as Leo could tell, an important player at that: Reece. Where was Heartless? Taller and more formidable than all the rest, he should be a stand-out among the boys, yet he was nowhere discernible, not to Leo, not yet, anyway. As for the other Jeremians, though he could not pick them out in their disguises, he knew they must be there, all of them, come to have their revenge on Wacko Wackeem.

"You all have heard the first witness," the fox went on, raising his voice for everyone to hear. "There are others. And evidence."

Ahh, they said, *evidence.* What kind of evidence?

"It grows late. Let us proceed," declared the fox. "You see before you the lowest type of criminal, brought here to our meeting place for trial and judgment. He had thought to be inducted into the Seneca Lodge this night— not knowing the Senecas would never have his kind. For we will prove how unworthy a brave this prisoner is. We will show him to be a liar and a cheat—"

"I am not!" shouted Leo, straining at his bonds, wishing he could free his hands. Tiger's knife still sat on his hip; they hadn't noticed it. If he could reach far enough, catch the hilt with his fingers, maybe . . . He worked the cords to stretch and loosen them.

"Aw, someone shut him up!" called one.

"Yeah, quit grousin'."

"Snuff it, Wacko, or we'll do it for you."

The fox shook his rattle vigorously, commanding attention. "The prisoner has not been given leave to speak! He is therefore instructed to remain silent until the court advises him otherwise." He addressed the prosecutor again. "Tell the court, what lies has the prisoner told?"

The bear was inclined toward obsequiousness. "If it please the court, not just one lie, but many. Many lies. And many are those who have heard him speak such lies."

"Make your accusations."

The bear nodded gravely. The others shifted among their ranks; audible whispers of anticipation ran around the circle; the bear went on. "To begin with, he has made it known to everyone at camp that his father is dead."

"And is this a misrepresentation of the facts?"

"Yes, Your Honor. His father's as alive as anyone in this room." At this disclosure exclamations of surprise erupted; heads bobbed and jockeyed for a better look at the accused. The blood had drained from Leo's face and he could feel his body trembling.

In the "prosecutor's" hand was a manila folder with a white tab. "It is the prisoner's private file," the bear went on, "loaned to us for these proceedings by Ma Starbuck."

Leo strained forward against the thongs. "I don't believe you—Ma never would have! Somebody stole it!"

"Silence!"

With grimy paws the bear opened the file. "Your Honor, I wish at this point to introduce as evidence the following documents." He shuffled through and extracted certain items, which he identified in the same solemn tone:

"First, the standard registration forms of Camp Friend-Indeed. Second, copies of the records of the Pitt Institute for Boys, stating the truth beyond any shadow of a doubt. Third, a handwritten letter from one Miss—Miss"— he riffled his way to the end of the letter for the name—"Miss Elsie Meekum, a member of the orphanage staff. Will the court please allow these documents to be noted and entered as 'Exhibits A, B, and C for the prosecution'?"

The fox looked the documents over with burlesque judiciousness. Leo watched mutely. He knew Ma: she would never have willingly surrendered her file, to anyone. But what did that matter? Now everyone in camp would know the truth about the butcher's boy.

"Where *is* his father, then?"

The prosecutor turned to the prisoner for an answer. "Where is your father," he demanded. "Speak!"

"He's dead," he said.

The prosecutor snorted and raised a scornful voice so all could hear. "Do you hear, men? He lies even to this court."

Leo lifted his own voice to be heard over the other's. "He *is* dead. He's talking about my stepfather."

"Listen, all of you," came the bear's voice, projecting so the sound carried among the trees. "He's not dead, this father. His name is Rudy Matuchek, and he has drawn the sentence of twenty years imprisonment."

At this news the band of watchers put their heads together and again jabbered among themselves.

Once more the judge raised a hand for silence and addressed the prosecutor.

"We are interested in your words. For what crime is this man in prison?"

"For the crime of murder!"

Murder! The word swept through the ranks. "It is a fact," the prosecutor continued. "Here is the proof, in my hand." Again he waved the documents. "Now ask me, for *whose* murder?"

"Yes, whose?" they demanded in unison, jostling one another in their eagerness to see and hear. Again the "judge" was forced to call for order.

"For the murder of his wife!" came the reply. "And his wife's boyfriend." Another eruption greeted this sensational revelation. The bear eagerly pressed his point. "Hear me, men. It's all here in the file, every word." He held up the folder.

The alligator had a further word to add. "His mother was a slut. She was having an affair with this other guy—" He would have gone on, but was silenced by the bear, who with obvious relish provided the details.

"The father was a butcher and he took his butcher knife and stabbed them both to death. He was convicted and sent to prison. That's why the prisoner was sent to the orphanage. And before that he was in the nuthouse—the loony bin. It's all here, anyone can read it!" He brandished the papers over his head while the commotion grew louder. Leo strained harder to free himself, his eyes wildly staring at his accuser, who just shook his head at him. "You see how it is—you think you can go around telling these lies—"

"They're not lies!" Leo shouted defiantly. "They're not!"

"Are they the truth, then?"

"Not exactly, but—"

"Well, there you are! You're a liar; and furthermore . . ." the bear went on, ignoring Leo's denial and taking up a position close to the fox. "Furthermore . . . I stand here before this tribunal to accuse the prisoner of being responsible for the death of Tiger Abernathy." He raised his voice so it echoed off the cellar walls. "Like father, like son!"

Angry mutters ran about the circle. Leo stared at the bear-head. "That's not true!"

"Silence!" the judge roared. "On what do you base this accusation?" he asked the prosecutor.

"It's simple. The prisoner is a collector of spiders. One of these spiders was poisonous and it bit the deceased and gave him blood poisoning. If it weren't for that, Tiger wouldn't have died."

Leo again protested. "The spider wasn't poisonous and everybody knows it! Ten spiders like that one could have bit someone and they'd never have died. The bite became infected because—"

"Silence in the court! The prisoner has not been given leave to speak. Mr. Prosecutor, you may continue."

"Thank you, Your Honor," returned the prosecutor, bowing. He came closer to Leo. "So, prisoner, you will call others liar, will you? When it is you yourself who is the liar!"

"Everything I've said is true."

"I don't think so. In fact"—turning to the courtroom again—"I think we have already proved beyond doubt that if there is any lying being done here, the prisoner is the one doing it. And his hands are stained with the blood of Tiger Abernathy, who except for him would be standing here at this very moment."

"He *wouldn't!* He'd *never* be here! Let me go!" Again Leo strained against his bonds. This was more than a game, this was diabolical. He thought of Stanley Wagner. "You have no right!"

"Shut up!"

"Silence him."

"Give him a poke to shut his mouth."

"Silence! Silence, I said!" shouted the judge. "Enough of this. If there are any more outbursts I'll order the prisoner gagged. We won't waste any more time. We'll have the verdict. And the sentence—!"

" 'Ray! 'Ray!" the boys shouted. "Time for sentencing."

"Jury! What is your verdict?" came the call. As one they spat the word out in his face.

Guilty.

Guilty!

GUILTY!

The cellar rang with shouts and cries, while Leo stared in disbelief and mounting alarm. No use for him to struggle more. But the end—where was that? And when it came, what would it be?

The fox again stepped forward and raised his arms for silence. In the sudden hush he spoke to the prisoner:

"You have been found guilty of the worst kind of crime—the crime of breaking faith. Everybody knows it was your spider that killed Tiger. It won't do you any good to go on lying about it. A liar is what you are and you will be punished accordingly."

He paused, turning to speak *sotto voce* with the bear and several others who crowded around him to hear what he had to say. Leo watched, hating them all. The fox turned back, cleared his throat. "The penalty you will pay for your lies and treachery is as follows—watch—watch, all, see what has been arranged for the guilty."

Leo watches. The fox reaches up and pulls a cord. Bright lights flash on as the curtain of blankets is pulled back, revealing a makeshift stage upon which a tableau is being enacted, a grisly tableau whose essence swiftly communicates itself to Leo. He shouts out in horror. He would look away, but cannot. There, in full view, stands the menacing figure of Rudy, the butcher of Saggetts Notch, in his shirtsleeves and his bloodied apron, his straw hat perched on his head, his drooping mustache, his ever-present cigar, and, clutched in one upraised hand, his butcher knife, its blade besmirched. His other hand is closed around the throat of Emily, her breast covered with blood. She is dead; he has killed her!

"Mother!"

The anguished cry echoes in the room. In terror and surprise, Leo springs forward, free at last of his bonds, his fingers scrabbling at his hip. As his body knocks heavily against the exposed flank of the murderer, his fingers close around his own knife, freeing it from its sheath. Its steel blade flashes in the light.

"No—stop!" comes a cry from among the crowd—a futile cry, for Leo's avenging knife thrusts home. As the blade strikes there is an explosive sound of shocked surprise from Rudy, who gasps, groans, crumples, then falls backward. Frantic hands snatch at Leo, yanking him away from the stage. He stares dazedly at the gory sight of the murdered Emily, who in some unaccountable yet miraculous transformation has been restored to life, her blood-spattered features now changing into those of Gus Klaus, a look of bug-eyed horror on his face as he peers down at the lifeless body of Reece Hartsig, who lies bleeding on the floor, an expression of surprise frozen forever in his eyes, Tiger Abernathy's parting gift to Wacko Wackeem buried to the hilt under his ribs.

Epilogue

either lofty nor inspiring, Mount Zion was never what you could call a real mountain, merely one of a range of low hills, the site chosen by Knute and Dagmar Kronborg as their home in America. On a bright, sunny morning toward the middle of November 1938, a thin plume of smoke curled from the hen's-egg chimney, and high atop the observation tower the Stars and Stripes marked a brisk wind from the east. With the coming of autumn, even the sky had changed: no longer the soft, limpid cerulean blue of summer, it was a harder, more enameled blue, the blue of a Delft plate, and host to wavering wedges of geese flying south from Canada. There was a good nip in the air, too; all through the valley the leaves had turned, and in the farmers' fields the pumpkins ripened their way toward Thanksgiving pies. Except for a black-winged hawk knifing earthward, the valley seemed to drowse in a sort of fairy-tale slumber.

On the topmost gallery off the music room, Augie Moss was leaning over the parapet, spilling to the wind the contents of two ashtrays. Through the open doors behind him came the sound of music, a lively glissando of notes that lay melodiously on the ear. Augie slid a look up to the cruising hawk, then stepped back into the music room, where Leo Joaquim stood behind the Pleyel piano, some sheets of music open on the rack (Mendelssohn's Violin Concerto).

Augie watched from under knitted brows. The boy had changed some.

He looked older, not as thin and gangly—Augie's cooking had helped to accomplish that—and with an indefinable something more grown-up in the line of the jaw that rested on the curve of the violin.

Returning the ashtrays to their decreed places—the jade one on the big table, the crystal beside the piano keyboard—Augie slippered his way from the room, while Leo continued his practice undisturbed. If he paused for longer than the time it took to run to the bathroom, he would hear from "upstairs" the signal for him to resume pronto or catch it. At the Castle one had certain obligations: in the matter of musical practice, diligence was called for; Dagmar was no easy taskmaster.

As he bowed away, Leo's eye traveled to the framed photograph on the piano, a pair of suntanned campers clad in khaki shorts, grinning into Dagmar's box Brownie, two summer pals, arms across each other's shoulders, two friends now parted—one dead, one alive. One buried under the earth, the other here, playing Mendelssohn; Felix Mendelssohn for Tiger Abernathy.

Victim of whimsical impulse, Leo broke off his concerto and switched to another, possibly more popular but far less classic, rendition. He tossed it off with polish and verve, even for so humble a ditty, and before long he heard Augie's sandpapery voice singing the words as he came back along the passageway:

> I push the first valve down.
> The music goes down and around,
> Whoa-ho-ho-ho-ho-ho,
> And it comes up here.

In he came with his turkey duster, lightly feathering his way around the room, "rearranging the dust," as Dagmar called it. When he reached the piano he clapped a hand to Leo's shoulder and they sang the next verse together.

> I push the middle valve down.
> The music goes down around below, below,
> Dee-dle-dee ho-ho-ho,
> Listen to the ja-azz come out.

314

They had swung into the last verse when a clarion voice rang out from overhead.

"No one had better push that other valve down or there'll be hash for dinner. August, more coffee! Leo, more Mendelssohn!"

Augie slipped Leo a conspiratorial wink, then trucked his way across the tiles to disappear around the corner while the boy had recourse once more to his music. Not long after, the old man again passed the doorway as he carried her morning coffee tray to Dagmar. He found her at the desk in her bedroom, writing letters.

"Was it you who encouraged him to play that dreadful stuff?" she asked, adding sugar lumps to the cup (she liked her coffee black but sweet).

"No, ma'am," Augie replied in his soft, dusty voice. "That was his own inspiration. Ask me, I think it's hot."

"Hot!" Dagmar was indignant. "The notes of that composition are as nails on a blackboard," she declared. "And the words are pure jabberwocky."

Augie chuckled, then picked up the objectionable refrain as he left the room, "Oh you push the third valve down. . . ."

Hiding her mirth behind the rim of her cup, Dagmar looked over the front page, which detailed how Nazi thugs all over Germany had gone on a rampage, smashing their way into the shops and homes of Jews, setting fire to synagogues, brutalizing the Jewish population. Dagmar shook her head at the thought of such violence and wondered where it all would lead. She thought of Fritz, who had learned his family's fate at last. Trying to escape Austria, they had been betrayed, and had disappeared behind the walls of a concentration camp called Mauthausen.

When she had glanced through the rest of the newspaper she returned to her letter. Her lines were addressed to Elsie Meekum at Pitt Institute, whom Dagmar had promised to keep apprised of Leo's progress. In the weeks since the coroner's inquest in Putnam, when she and Elsie had frequently found themselves together, they had struck up a correspondence, having discovered that they shared an interest not only in Leo Joaquim but in other matters as well, including mulberry ware and the paintings of Renoir, and it had been between the two women, widow and spinster, that the plot had been hatched to bring an end to Leo's stay at the orphanage. Now Dagmar enjoyed receiving Elsie's correspondence from

Pitt, and responded with news concerning their "protégé," which was how Leo had come to be regarded.

Looking back to that July day when the boy had first come to the Castle, it hardly seemed possible that so much had happened in so short a space of time: so much bad—and how much good?

There had been a great hubbub during the weeks following the tragedy. The town of Putnam, the Windham County seat, had filled up with reporters who had been drawn to the scene of the tragedy like flies to rotting fruit, and who, despite the best efforts of all concerned, from Dr. Dunbar of the Joshua Society to Dagmar Kronborg, would not be denied. Even the services for the slain young man had provided grist for their mill: It had been held under the sponsorship of the German-American Bund, whose rank and file had appeared in numbers, many wearing swastika armbands in token of respect to their "fallen comrade"—Rolfe's doing, of course. During the last rites the mother of the deceased became hysterical and had to be forcibly restrained, and one persevering photographer managed to get a dramatic shot of Joy being helped into a waiting car.

None of this had Leo Joaquim witnessed, for within hours of his arrest he had been returned to the same hospital where he had been a patient as a child. In a state of shock, he lacked all comprehension of what had taken place at the old Steelyard place, or the fact that he had been the instrument of someone's death. At the hospital he was once more placed in the care of Dr. Epstein, and there, while he waited for the inquest to begin, the same Miss Holmes sat again in the corner of his old room (or one exactly like it), smiling and nodding.

Due to his youth, the coroner's proceedings were conducted behind closed doors, and no photographers were allowed. However, the enterprising young man who had been on hand to photograph Joy Hartsig, hysterical with grief, was also the one who had photographed the ill-fated model of the Austrian village, and (hardly believing his luck) he had gone through his negatives, culling those in which Leo appeared. His future was assured when these shots were subsequently run in a series of double-truck spreads under headings that read:

CAMPER FROLIC TURNS TO HAVOC
Friend-Indeeder Runs Amok with Hunting Knife
BUTCHER'S BOY APES LIFER-PA
Medicos Wonder—Is It Inherited?

316

The denouement proved an anticlimax. When the various parties involved—Doc and Maryann Oliphant, Peewee and Honey, Fritz Auerbach and Wanda Koslowski, the Abernathys, the Starbucks (Willa-Sue reliably described the moment in the office when Reece had stolen the folder from Ma's drawer), Dr. Dunbar, Supervisor Poe and Miss Meekum, some of the campers who had been present, Wally Pfeiffer in particular—had given their testimony, and Dr. Epstein had taken the witness chair, no charges were filed. (The ruling cited "provocation" and "abnormal mental strain.") Those most nearly concerned, the parents of the deceased, were not present at any time during the hearing—they were in fact not even in residence, Rolfe Hartsig having taken his wife away to a sanitarium in West Virginia.

The presiding official at the inquest had interviewed Leo in his private chambers, entreating him to put the events of that unlucky night out of his mind and not to dwell on such morbid matters. With little to look forward to other than being returned to the orphanage (with a heavy mark against him for having killed someone), Leo found it hard to oblige, for who could not think of such things? But then Dagmar and Miss Meekum had put their heads together, and before he could be returned to the Institute he had been spirited away in Dagmar's car to the Castle. It was a likely solution to a problem that had been troubling Dagmar for many weeks. Of course, the simplest solutions were often the best. And when she was gone—she would be sixty-seven in January; she had some few years yet—but when she did pass on, all that was hers would be Leo's. He would be King of the Mountain; she liked the notion of happy endings.

After the killing the camp had been shut down in short order, and no one knew if it would open again next summer. The elders of the Society of Joshua were as yet undecided as to what the future of Friend-Indeed would be. One thing seemed clear: whatever its ultimate fate, the camp would not again see Pa Starbuck as its director. The elders having made their own private inquiry into the tragedy, he had received a stinging rebuke from his superiors and been summarily relieved of tenure. This fact had, however, been successfully concealed from the press, lest the unsavory nature of the affair rub off on the Society itself.

Indeed, before taking his final leave, Pa had been honored by a testimonial dinner at which he was presented with a gold-dipped pocket watch engraved with his initials and the date, after which he held an "impromptu" news conference. Modestly beaming, he reiterated "matters of health" as the reason for his retirement, and stated his intention of removing to Miami, where Ma, his spouse of thirty-six years, could live year-round in bathing suits and drink coconut juice—ha ha—that was a good one.

Now the Teddy Roosevelt Memorial Nature Lodge stood boarded up, the diving raft had been dragged ashore against the winter frosts, the official camper files had been sent to the Society's main office at Hartford, and in the dining hall mice feasted on uneaten foodstuffs, forgotten at the back of cupboards. Cobwebs were being spun nightly in the tool crib and the Swoboda corner and upstairs, in the Marconi Radio Shop. The Buffalo Bill War Bonnet had been removed from its display case, to end up in Pa's duffel (eventually to find its way to a similar exhibit case in Miami, where Pa would eagerly repeat the same old story to anyone who would lend an ear). As for the Hartsig Memorial Cup, its fate remained in doubt. The plaque at its base was never inscribed with the names of the Jeremians who had won it, those boys of Lucky Cabin 7, whose parents had descended on the camp en masse and hustled their sons away as fast as they could. Indeed, after the night of the last council fire the cup was not seen again at camp. (Rumor suggested that Hap Holliday had absconded with it, though nothing was ever proved.)

Fritz was living in Hartford, working for a printing company and looking forward to advancement and a raise. Of his family, no news since he had been told of their incarceration, and little hope; yet, being Fritz, he did hope. He and Wanda were seeing each other on a regular basis, she having accepted a position on the staff of a prominent specialist at Saint Francis Hospital. Meanwhile, beginning in the new year, Fritz would be looking out for Leo, who would be staying with him while studying music under Professor Pinero. Dagmar would miss having the boy at the Castle, but the bus trip was only seventy minutes; he'd be home often enough. She addressed her envelope to Elsie, inserted her pages, and licked the flap. Now for a stamp: Augie would know where they were. . . .

In the music room the Mendelssohn continued as Leo fiddled away. Set out in a mulberry bowl on the Chinese shawl, a cluster of winter cherries bobbed on their stems, marking the change in the seasons. Also marking, Leo hoped, the change in his fortunes. And he wondered how he had ever made the difficult passage from Gallop Hill in Saggetts Notch, from the stone-cold rooms of Pitt Institute, to Dagmar Kronborg's Castle.

His present state of near-equilibrium had not been easily won. Murder—that was what he'd done: committed murder, though all he remembered, really, was the figure of Rudy looming above that of Emily, knife poised over her heart. But it hadn't been Rudy—only Reece, dressed up like Rudy, play-acting; a little joke meant to drive Wacko nuts, a gag that had backfired and ended up with Reece dead and Leo having killed him. He didn't like to think about Reece being dead, but it was hard not to when your mind made up pictures, your brain ticked with memories, and your fears were like so many vultures, with hard hooked beaks; or maybe crows, a flock of them with black wings beating around your head. But in time . . . in time . . .

From the corner of his eye he glimpsed someone watching him from the hallway: Dagmar. How long had she been there? Did she approve of what she'd been hearing? How did it sound?

"That last needs work," she said, marching briskly up to the piano. "You're letting your tempo lag. Why don't we try it together?"

She adjusted the metronome weight from allegro to allegretto, then, smoothing the folds of her skirt along her backside, she slid onto the bench, toes seeking the pedals. "Keep your mind on your notes, Leo," she remarked wryly, for she knew that on such days as this it was hard for a boy to attend to his work, when the whole outdoors beckoned with its red-and-gold glory and the pungent smell of autumn smoke in the air. There were woods to tramp, creatures to hunt, caves to explore. But not if a boy wanted to be a great violinist, not if he wanted to play on the radio with Maestro Toscanini.

With a quick, decisive gesture, she shed her rings and dropped them into the ashtray, then poised her fingers above the keyboard. "Play for me as you would if the professor were here," she commanded. "Now, all together, one, two, three . . ."

Her joke. Leo knew.

She smiled and nodded as, together, they began to play, picking up the downbeat and setting off to a lively start, the notes and chords tumbling over one another in their eagerness to be expressed and heard. From time to time as she played, Dagmar tucked her chin under and worked her brows, her eyes sparkling with that keen, alert pleasure that is given to those who make music and make it well.

A boy could let himself sink back into the darkness, there to be seen no more, or he could make his way up into the golden blaze of noon, into the night's starred firmament, where the air was nimble and buoyant as the salty sea and carried you along, a feather in the wind. As the notes swelled, Leo felt a welcome lightening of spirits. He imagined himself being carried away in a kind of rapturous flight, up, up on white feathered wings, unfettered and unleashed. High above the treetops a lone bird idled in its vast blue domain, climbing higher and higher, growing smaller and smaller, until it was only a daytime star, winking there, and disappearing into the empyrean.

Icarus.

A NOTE ON THE TYPE

The text of this book was set in Century Old Style, a type designed in 1894 by Linn Boyd Benton (1844–1932). Benton cut Century Old Style in response to a request by Theodore L. DeVinne for an attractive, easy-to-read typeface to fit the narrow columns of his *Century Magazine*. Early in the 1900s Benton's son, Morris Fuller Benton, updated and improved Century in several versions for his father's American Type Founders Company. Century is the only American typeface cut before 1910 that is still widely used today.

Composed by ComCom, a division of The Haddon Craftsmen, Inc., Allentown, Pennsylvania. Printed and bound by R. R. Donnelley & Sons, Harrisonburg, Virginia.

Designed by Virginia Tan

Map, illustrations, and ornamentation by the author